Book 3:

Stories from the Sea

1st Edition

ISBN: 978-0-6451986-9-0

Copyright © 2024 N.J. Ewing

Cover Design by Brand Artisans Australia
www.brandartisans.com.au

— Acknowledgments —

A big, huge thanks to everyone who contributed to making this whole project happen.

Anita and Jeremy Walker, Amanda Bentley, Karyn Tulloch, Ben and Tracey Kreplins, Kate and Tim Brand, and Karen Weaver for donating to the editing process.

To the rest of my family and friends who have helped and supported me in immeasurable ways, this book wouldn't have been possible without any of you.

And to the people who came into my life to teach me some challenging lessons, thank you for making me stronger.

Nikki x

- *Dedications* -

This is for all my late-diagnosed neurosparkly tribe
out there who have struggled in silence for their
whole lives.

For everyone who has ever been told they're 'less
than', 'too much', 'not enough' or generally broken in
some way.

Just know that you are whole, and you are amazing.
Be proud of what you've achieved.
You've survived in a world that wasn't made for you
and you endured despite all the barriers.

Keep being you.

Don't hide your shiny.

The world is full of 'normal' people, but it's the 'weird'
ones that make life better. We bring the colour, and
the light. We bring the fun, the abstract thinking and
the creative ideas, so don't wish that power away.

Don't ever try to be 'normal'.

Be the unicorn in a field of horses.

♡ Nikki x

Contact N.J. Ewing

Website: www.brandartisans.com.au/njewing
Facebook: www.facebook.com/N.J.Ewing
Instagram: www.instagram.com/n.j.ewing/

Sales and Distribution enquiries to Brand Artisans Australia
Email: info@brandartisans.com.au

STORIES *from the* Sea

N.J. EWING

brandartisans.com.au

"I don't know. Maybe," I said with a dismayed shrug.

"This isn't a joke, Nathan. I'm worried about you. I'm sorry I've been hard on you lately, but it's just because I care about you."

"I'm fine Gaz, I've just had a lot to deal with."

"Exactly. These last few months have been a lot and I… I don't want to lose you."

"Lose me?"

"Nath," he said urgently, grabbing my shoulders again, "promise me that if you ever get to a point where things feel too much, you'll tell me."

"O-ookaay." I glanced over at Ryan for moral support, but he merely shrugged with a wry smile and fled from the unexpectedly emotional reunion.

"You and your Mum are the only family I've got, and I don't know what I'd do if lost you. Or how I'd tell your mother."
I stared at him in stunned silence as I gathered my thoughts, opening and closing my mouth like a fish out of water.

"I'm fine Gaz," I said eventually, patting his shoulders as best I could from beneath his firm grip. "I've had a lot going on but I'm fine. You won't lose me. At least not to my own devices." A wave of guilt swept through me as I realised how much I'd cut him out of my life over the last six months. We'd gone from chatting at least twice daily, to barely twice a week. "I'm sorry I haven't been keeping you in the loop."

"Sorry to interrupt folks, but they're ready to get started," announced the Director.

"We'll chat later," said Gaz quickly, as the big guy started issuing directions.

"Ritchie, Mrs Vaughn, could you please come with me to get seated. Pallbearers, Mike will take you through to the casket room," he explained, gesturing towards a young guy standing un-obtrusively in the corner of the room. I hadn't even noticed he was there until that moment.

"Thanks Simon," said Gareth, releasing his grasp on me to shake the funeral guy's hand. I stared at Gaz again, still wondering why he was in here with us and not out there with the rest of the gathering. "Shall we do this?" he asked, patting my back encouragingly.

"I'm confused," I admitted, "how come you're in here and not out there? Are you dating Mrs Vaughn?"
Gaz laughed and clapped me on the back.

"I'm a pallbearer you plonker. Veronica asked me to help. And no, we're not dating. I reached out to her to offer my condolences after you told me what happened, and she needed an ear." He dropped his voice and leaned in closer, "she got a letter in the mail from Amy yesterday so she's not doing so great."

"Oh," I said, still not fully comprehending the situation. "Did you pay for the funeral?"

"No," he said with a quizzical look. "I offered to contribute but Veronica said it was all covered. Why do you ask?"

"Nothing, just-"

"Oi," hissed Ryza, standing amidst the group of pallbearers, "we're on, fellas."

"Right," I nodded. Gareth and I joined the rest of the group. My heart pounded as Mike directed us to our positions. This was it. I was about to bury my friend. There was no coming back now. No returning from the dead like Ash had. Amy was really, truly gone.

"The casket is on a trolley so there's no need to lift it," Mike explained, "just hold the handle in front of you and wheel it forward. When you get to the front, slide it into position and then take your seats." His voice faded into the distance as the thudding in my chest began to reverberate through my head. All I could hear was the rapid thumping from inside my body. I peered over at Ryan on the opposite side of the coffin. The look on his face mirrored my feelings. I gave him a stiff nod, and he returned in kind. It was all we could do to keep our shit together.

The doors swung open and I gripped the big brass handle so tightly my knuckles grew white. We all turned into position and, from behind me, Gaz gave my shoulder a firm squeeze of support. I felt the trolley inch forwards and thus we began our torturous decent down the aisle.

I spotted a lot of familiar faces as we slowly made our way down the long carpet. My soon-to-be in-laws were the first faces I saw. They stood quietly at the back of the chapel and Mary caught my eye almost immediately. I attempted a smile, but her compassionate look of encouragement nearly brought me undone. Geoff rested his arm around her shoulder and nodded stoically at me, as if attempting to lend me some of his strength. I nodded and returned my focus to the journey.

It looked like most of the Artemis staff were there, scattered amongst other faces that I didn't recognize. About halfway down the aisle, I saw a face that deserved nothing less than a swift punch. My body flared with rage as Jock's eyes locked with mine. What the fuck was he doing there? How dare he?

Every bone in my body wanted to leave the casket and pummel him, but my logical brain held tight to the reigns as I glared darkly at him. My feelings must have been visibly clear, because he shrunk backwards when I passed him. That bastard had practically handed my fiancé to her psycho ex on a silver platter, and yet he still had the gall to attend a funeral for someone he barely knew? If he showed up at the wake, there would be trouble. And if he tried to get anywhere near Ashley, I'd take him down without hesitation.

- ASHLEY GRANGER -

I watched the slow procession from behind a sheet of warm, salty tears. I'd been overly optimistic in applying a full face of make-up for the funeral, and I suspected I somewhat resembled The Joker, as it all ran down my cheeks. I did my best to focus my eyes, but I could barely see Nathan's face through the blur as he and the other boys wheeled Amy's coffin down the aisle. Between my pregnancy hormones and the raw emotion of losing a best friend, I didn't see much point in holding back the tears. It didn't feel like a day to waste energy on pretending not to be sad. I wiped my cheeks as best I could, but it was a pointless exercise.

The pallbearers deposited the casket gently at the front of the room and swiftly retreated to their seats. When Nathan got closer, I was able to make out the stern set of his square jaw. He was pissed about something. Others would assume he was trying to hold back tears, but I knew that jaw clench. That was his angry face. He slid quietly into the pew and draped his arm over my shoulder.

"You okay?" he whispered into my ear.

"Not really," I whispered back. "Are you?"

"Not really," he said simply, jaw still clenched tight. I studied his face a few times. It was obviously more than sadness he was fighting. I rested my hand on his thigh and gave it a comforting squeeze as I tried to focus on the service. Nathan leaned in closer and rested his head against mine. "Jock's here," he muttered softly.

"Kesha mentioned she'd invited him, but I didn't think he'd actually come," I said, realising that I was still in the dark as to what had transpired between he and Nath after Dom's attack. So much had gone on that we'd never actually circled back to that particular conversation. In fact, I hadn't even had one thought of Jock since we'd returned to Artemis. "What happened with you guys?" I whispered quietly. "You owe me an explanation before the wake."

"He's not welcome at the wake," Nath hissed definitively. I paused our hushed discussion and eyed him again, trying to understand exactly what the fuck had gone on. Nathan noticed me staring at him and cast me an apologetic glance, before cuddling me closer. "I'm sorry babe," he said, watching the service.

"Sorry for what exactly?"

"I should have filled you in sooner."

"Yeah," I agreed, resting my head on his shoulder. I let the subject drop and we remained silent for the rest of the service. It was beautiful but heart-wrenching. The eulogy was perfect; the readings were well-chosen; and someone had put together a video with old photos and footage of Amy.

Ritchie was up the front with Amy's Mum, and he looked so forlorn that I wanted to run over and wrap my arms around him. Kat and Ryan were on the other end of our bench, taking turns to bounce Mia up and down the exit aisle. I knew Mum and Dad were up the back somewhere, but I couldn't see them. I didn't like that we were all separated. It felt foreboding and hit way too close to the truth of our near future. Ritchie would be going back to Australia alone; Kat and Ryan would be distracted with family life; My parents would be around but not close; and Nathan and I would be somewhere on the edge of it all, clutching to each other for support.

A sob escaped my throat at the realisation that nothing would ever be the same again. The sob was loud and unwelcome, but it hit me too fast to stop it. Nathan gripped me tight as I buried my face in his jacket. If there had been any makeup left on my face, it was now smeared all over Nathans expensive suit. He too had let go of the need to contain his tears and I felt the movement of his arm as he wiped his eyes. Despite everything that had happened over the past few months, losing Amy was by far the worst. How could she have done this to herself? Why hadn't she just talked to me?

When the service concluded, Nathan and I stayed where we were. Neither of us had the energy or inclination to move. We watched people filter out of the chapel, nodding to us as they passed, and offering their condolences to Ritchie and Mrs Vaughn at the door. But we just sat, holding onto each other like the world depended on it.

"We should get out there," Nathan said, rubbing my arms.

"Yep," I agreed with a sigh, "but maybe you should fill me in on Jock first."

"I'm not sure that's a good idea."

"Why?"

"Err…" he mumbled, "because you might make a scene."

"I might make a scene?" I answered indignantly, pulling away from him. "You're the one who had the murderous look on your face, but I might make a scene?

"I've had an hour to reign myself in," he said sheepishly, "but I'm barely keeping it at bay so if I tell you now and you storm over to punch him in the face, I won't have the restraint to stop you."

"What could he possibly have done that would make me cause a scene like that at my best friends' funeral?"
Nathan sighed and squirmed in his seat, visibly weighing up the pros and cons of telling me.

"Okay," he said eventually, as the last of the stragglers meandered towards the door, "but you have to promise that you won't confront him today."

"Fine," I breathed, clueless as to what I was agreeing to. Nathan wriggled around in the seat to face me, seemingly biding his time. "Spit it out Stone," I said sternly.

"Okay…" he paused dragging the moment out. "He's still a cop."

"What do you mean?"

"He was working undercover when you met him."

"Uh-huh, and why would that make me cause a scene? I totally get that he couldn't reveal that info."
Nathan grimaced and took my hand.

"Because he was assigned to you Ash. He was part of the ops team trying to track down Dom."
The air evacuated my lungs as I realised what Nathan was saying.

"Jock used me as bait," I said breathlessly.

"Yeah."

"I'm such an idiot."

"No, he's such an idiot."

"Nathan, I knew in my gut that something wasn't right, but I trusted him anyway. I assumed he was working with Dom, but this is so much worse." I said, feeling like a gullible fool. "He's an opportunistic arsehole, but I'm definitely the idiot."

"You're right about one thing. He is an arsehole," Nath agreed unforgivingly. We fell silent as I processed the gravity of Jocks betrayal. Was it really betrayal if we were never actually friends? Or was it just that I was a naïve sucker who let herself get used? "So… where are you at with this?" Nath asked hesitantly. "You're very calm."

"I'm thinking," I said quietly. "I don't really know what to make of it to be honest. I'm angrier at myself than him. I knew in my bones that something was suss about the whole thing. I mean, this guy who was friends with my bestie just happened to be working in the apple store near my house and had coincidentally worked as a cop in the cybercrime unit? It was way too convenient, but I ignored my intuition and believed his bullshit story."

"Nope," he huffed angrily, rising from our pew, "I'm not gonna let him get away with it."

"Nath," I beseeched, reaching out to him as he straightened his suit, looking like he was preparing for a fight, "now you're the one about to make a scene. Please leave it alone for today."

"He led Dom straight to you babe. It's his fault you got attacked."

"No… that was Dom's fault. No one else was to blame for that."

Nathan fumed. "Why aren't you angry about this?"

"I am," I said calmly.

"You're doing a good job of hiding it."

"Babe…" I said, grasping his hand, "I'm done fighting. I don't have anything left in me. Yes, I'm angry at Jock, I'm fucking furious in fact, but he's not worth the energy, especially not on a day like today. I'll confront him at some point, but right now, I don't want to look back. How about we let it go and move forwards with this beautiful life we're creating for ourselves.

Nath sank back down onto the bench and took my face in his hands. "I love you so much."

"And I love you so much," I said with a tired smile.

"So, you're honestly telling me you can go out there and play nice with him?"

"I played nice with Dom for ten years and he did way worse."

Nathan winced but nodded in agreement. "Okay, if you can do it, so can I."

"Of course you can," I said, running my hand across his freshly shaven cheek. He planted a firm kiss on my lips which was filled with so much passion it left me reeling.

Nathan sat back and my heart thumped at the look of devotion in his eyes.

"Our happy ending starts now," he said with such assurance it made my chest heave with emotion. I nodded silently, as Nath glanced over at Ritchie, who was standing at the entrance looking shell-shocked.

"Let's get out there huh?" Nath suggested, "Ritchie needs us."

"Yeah," I agreed, following his gaze as Kat materialised out of nowhere and gently took Ritchie's arm. Nath helped me up off the hard pew and we joined Ritchie and Kat as she guided him away from the entrance.

"You alright mate?" Nath asked him, planting a supportive hand on Ritchie's broad shoulder as he walked.

Ritchie stared at us with glazed eyes, looking empty and lifeless, as if his soul had retreated and left his body behind.

"Yeah," he said flatly.

Ryan strolled towards us, wheeling the pram with one hand while clutching Mia against his chest with the other. He'd been chatting to Kellie, who was now making her way towards the carpark. Her baby bump had started to show, yet she hadn't gained an ounce of fat anywhere else on her body. I was a few months behind her, and I'd already gained eleven pounds without any noticeable bump. How was that fair?

I let my eyes wander over the remaining crowd. It consisted primarily of our Artemis colleagues. They were all standing around talking solemnly and exchanging hugs. Gaz was over near the entrance, consoling Amy's Mum; and standing at the edge of the fray with my parents, were Jock and Kesha. My eyes locked with Jock's and my stomach dropped as anger bubbled in my belly. Jock held my gaze. It was clear from the look on his face that he knew Nathan had told me.

Jock's pale face filled with regret and sincerity as I stared coldly at him. My teeth were so tightly clenched that my jaw was starting to ache. We held a silent conversation across the courtyard, and when he lowered his head apologetically, I felt my anger ease a little. I nodded stiffly in response, but our interaction ended with the arrival of a huge black limousine. The ridiculously opulent car pulled up out the front of the chapel and all eyes turned as Sandrine Delfontaine stepped out.

"Well," said Nath wryly, "I guess we know who paid for the funeral."

***

- RITCHIE CARLTON -

I couldn't believe Sandrine had shown up at the funeral. I knew she was an indomitable woman but crossing continents to attend the funeral of your ex-fuck-buddy's, ex-fuck-buddy was a whole new level of determination that I hadn't expected. To Sandrine's credit though, she had handled the rejection better than I'd expected. I'd presumed she would crack it and throw a hissy-fit, but she'd just accepted my 'goodbye' and driven away.

It was a relief not to have the shadow of that bizarre relationship hanging over my head anymore. There were only so many times and so many ways you could break-up with one person, but it was finally done. No more Sandrine.

With that weight off my shoulders, I had managed to get through Amy's wake with relative ease, but after putting on my best face on for several hours, I was peopled-out. I couldn't face any more withering looks or sympathetic hugs, let alone more stilted conversations. I just needed to be alone with my thoughts so, before anyone could argue, I jumped in a cab and escaped home.

The McPhersons had been great letting me stay with them, but I needed a night to myself where I didn't have to pretend I was okay, or convince anyone that I wasn't in need of another cuppa.

My house was dark and cold after being empty for a week, but the stark silence was a relief to my senses. Not bothering to turn the lights on, I walked straight over to my comfy old couch and plonked down in the middle of it. I sat, unmoving in the lifeless room, enjoying the peace and quiet.

I hadn't been home long when my phone jiggled excitedly in my pocket. I assumed it was probably Kat or Ryan checking up on me, but when I pulled out the phone, the screen was lit up with my brother's name. I hit the green button to answer the call from the other side of the world.

"Sean?" I asked with surprise. I hadn't heard from him in months.

"Hey big bro," he said solemnly, "how you holding up?"

"I'm fine. How are the wedding plans going?"

"Mate, cut the bullshit," he said brusquely, "Mum and Dad told me about your girlfriend, and they said the funeral was today."

"Oh."

"I'm checking-in to make sure you're alright."

"Thanks mate. Mum and Dad weren't supposed to tell you."

"Yeah right Ritch, as if they weren't going to tell us something like that," he said with amused frustration, "in fact you should have told us in the first place. Why didn't you call? You know you can always talk to me, right?"

"Cheers Seany, but I didn't want it to overshadow the wedding excitement."

"Fuck off, cunt," he blurted, sounding more like the Sean I knew. "I don't give a fuck if I'm standing at the alter in the middle of my vows… this is the sort of shit you tell your brother."

"Noted."

"And your sister," he said pointedly. "Jaz is super pissed you didn't tell her."

"Well, she needs something to be pissed about."

"True," Sean said, his tone changing, "So… are you okay?"

"Honestly Sean, I don't really know, but I'm not going to slit my wrists if that's what you're worried about." There was silence at the other end, and I glanced down at my watch. It was almost 5pm in London, which meant it must have been around twelve in Perth. "It must be midnight over there? Shouldn't you be out partying?" I teased.

"Nah, I'm a domesticated man now. Isla has me on a short leash these days."

"Mate, I'd give anything to have that problem."

Silence again.

"I'm sorry you're over there on your own," he said earnestly, "it must be really hard."

"I appreciate that Seany, thanks," I said, wondering if I should tell him that I was moving home.

"It's good to hear your voice man," he sighed.

"Yeah, you too," I replied… the words were on the edge of my tongue.

"We all miss you bro. Why don't you come home? You've been away so long."

I paused, deliberating on my next move.

"Yeah, funny you should mention that," I said, deciding it was worth ruining mums surprise, "because I've booked a one-way flight to Perth."

"Whatdoyoumean?" he asked in a way that made it sound like a single word.

"I'm moving home."

"You are?"

"Yeah, I'll be back in time for your bucks' weekend."

"Mate, that's awesome," he said, sounding a little emotional, "I'll let Kane know you'll be there. He's my other groomsman. Actually… you should talk to him about a job. He owns an agency."

"Cool man, we can chat about that once I'm back."

"I'll ask him if he's got anything going."

"Sure," I agreed, as a tsunami of home-sickness crashed over me. Keen to get off the phone so I could curl up and cry again, I wound up the conversation. "I should let you get to bed mate."

"Oh, right," he said, at the abrupt end to our chat. "We'll chat soon though?"

"Absolutely."

"I'll give you a buzz to check-in again in a week or two."

"Sounds good. See ya Seany."

"Bye Ritch. Love you man."

"Love you too." I hung up the call seconds before tears exploded out of my eye sockets. I sighed in frustration at myself. "Fucking hell Carlton, get your shit together."

- *Introduction* -

The Land Down Under

- KANE THOMPSON: THE GOLDEN CHILD -

Yeah...The Golden Child... I guess that pretty much sums me up. A privileged white male who can do no wrong according to some, Perth's Most eligible bachelor according to others.

As a kid I was the dux of my primary school; at high school, Head Boy; Uni, Guild President, and now I'm the CEO of my own Marketing agency and the Director of several industry related boards. I'm 'The Guy'. The leader. The man about town. Yay for me.

I know I sound ungrateful, but I'm not. I love my life and I wouldn't trade it. It's just that, I've spent my entire existence being pushed to be the best at everything, and now that I'm forty, I'm struggling to see the point of it all. For twenty years, I've worked my arse off to get where I am. In fact, I've been working my arse off since I was five, always going above and beyond just to impress my stern father. I don't think anyone has the faintest idea exactly how hard I've had to graft and how many failures I've had along the way. They all seem to think that I've had my life handed to me on a silver platter. Yes, a percentage of my so-called success has been good luck and my private school connections, but I've sacrificed a lot to make it all happen.

The question is, 'why?'. Who have I been working so hard for? What have I been trying to prove? Why have I been obsessed with meeting other people's expectations rather than focusing on what I actually want? What's the point in having all of this, if I go home to an empty house at the end of the day?

When I stand back and take stock of my life, all I can see is a bunch of achievements that I've made for other people. Half my life has slipped by and none of my successes have been for myself. Sure, I've enjoyed and celebrated each achievement, but nothing I've done has filled the void. The problem is, the one thing I know I truly want, is the one thing I can't have. Sophie Harris. Well... technically she's Sophie Thompson now. She married my douchbag of a cousin ten years ago and became part of our family in a totally different way to how I'd envisaged when we were kids. As such, I found it difficult to embrace her name change. To me, she'd always be Sophie Harris. The only way I'd accept her as a Thompson would be if she married me. But it was too late for that. I'd missed my chance decades ago when Brenton had swooped in and made his move.

He'd known I was in love with her, but he had a compulsive need to compete with me and unfortunately on that occasion, he'd won. Sometimes I doubted that he even loved her. Part of me suspected that he'd gone for her out of spite and, if I hadn't been so worried about ruining our friendship, things might have worked out differently. But they didn't. Brenton got the girl and, astoundingly, they had stayed together. Not that he'd been faithful mind you. He played AFL for the West Coast Eagles, and he seemed to think his sports stardom gave him free reign to be a cheating arsehole. He'd go away for matches while Soph stayed home with their son Taj. Brenton humped anything that moved, while Soph continued to be the perfect housewife.

I couldn't tell whether she stayed with him for Taj, or if she genuinely didn't know about his cheating, but I didn't want to get involved. Their marriage was none of my business, but it did leave a gaping wound in my soul.

No matter how many years passed, I could never forget the day I met her. I was a gangly twelve-year-old kid, sporting a floppy white-blonde fringe and a Thundercats T.shirt that I thought was 'mintox'. It was mid-January, and the day was sweltering, as was standard for an Aussie summer. Mum had sent my younger sister and I, out to the front yard to eat our Zooper Doopers and, as usual, my little sister Frankie, who looked like a mini version of me, was complaining.

"Come on Kane, it's my turn," Frankie whined as I sat on the tyre swing licking my bright blue icy pole.

"I just got on," I told her, slurping up the melted liquid inside the plastic tube.

"Nah-ah, you've been on for ages," she argued, her mouth stained an odd shade of green from her Lime flavoured popsicle. I ignored her protests and continued happily swinging. As I reached the bottom of my icy pole, I spotted a moving van chugging down our little suburban street. I watched as it drew closer, and Frankie turned to see what had caught my attention. "Must be our new neighbours," she said, with a shrug.

"Looks like it," I agreed, as the truck pulled up outside the house next door. A white Holden Commadore, pulled into the carport and I stood to get a better view of the action.

Frankie quickly jumped onto the tyre swing. "Haa-ha," she jeered, green-mouthed, but I cared not. I'd caught site of a pretty, blonde-haired girl, staring out the back window of the station wagon. I couldn't tear my gaze away. Her bright green eyes were wide with fear and filled with sadness as she peered out at her new home, clutching a pink Care Bear against her chest. From that moment, I was completely smitten.

"Earth to Kane," said my best mate Sean Carlton, punching me hard in the bicep as I stared blankly at the girl who was attempting to chat me up. "You still with us man?"

"Huh?" I asked, bringing myself back to the present. It was mid-October and the glorious Spring season was paving the way for a record-breaking summer. The afternoon sun shone through the shade-sails above our heads, and the turquoise ocean glittered and lapped gently at the white sand, on the other side of the long glass wall.

"Lucy asked what your agency is called," Sean said, giving me a 'you're blowing it' look. The guy was about six foot five with broad shoulders and flame orange hair that swept across one side of his face. He was like a cooler, older version of Ron Weasley.

"Sorry Lucy," I apologised, glad Sean had mentioned her name, because I hadn't taken note of it back when the conversation had first begun. I'd been too busy watching Soph mingling with the other footy wives, looking hot as ever in a tight little summer dress that hugged all her curves in the right places. "I've got a lot on my plate at the moment, so my mind is a million miles away," I lied to the pretty brunette in front of me.

"No problem," Lucy said with a tinge of an American accent. "I know you're a busy man," she added with a flirty smile.

"Kane's been voted Perth's most eligible bachelor three years in a row," Sean told her, using his best wing-man material. "Right Kane?" he added, nudging me with his elbow.

"Yeah," I agreed, as I saw Brenton sidle up to his trophy wife and show her off as if she was the light of his life. My stomach churned at the performance. "Although I may have some competition now that Sean's brother is coming back to town," I joked, with my eyes still fastened on Sophie. "Apparently he's quite a catch."

"He'd have to be pretty special to outdo you Kane," Lucy said eying me up and down. I laughed politely and placed my hand gently on her shoulder. Sean was visibly pleased by my initiation of physical contact. I got the feeling he'd been living vicariously through me since he got engaged.

"Would you excuse me for a minute," I said to Lucy. It wasn't a question. "It was lovely to meet you," I added with my most charming smile, before slipping away through the crowd of beach-side party-goers.

I heard Sean apologise on my behalf and I knew it wouldn't be long before he caught up to give me a 'get back in the game', speech.

I wove my way through the well-dressed crowd, smiling and nodding to each person as I passed. All the fake tans, fake boobs, fake hair, and fake smiles. This was the sort of party where being yourself was frowned upon, and anyone earning less than six-figures would not make it onto the guest list. It was a veritable array of everyone who was anyone in our little city, with the egos to match. Big fish in a small pond, and they all took pleasure in eating the guppies for breakfast.

"What the fuck mate?" Sean hissed in my ear as he fell into step beside me. The smile was still plastered to his face so as not to alert the sharks that a death was imminent. "Lucy's a fucking supermodel and she's only in town for a few days before she goes back to New York."

"So?" I shrugged, matching his phony smile, as I nodded my acknowledgment to a couple posing languidly on a pristine white-cushioned daybed.

Sean grabbed my arm and stopped walking, failing miserably to hide the look of sheer horror on his face.

"Who are you, and what have you done with my best mate?" He asked appalled. I sighed and rolled my eyes before realising that we had amassed a small audience. Sean smiled and waved at our onlookers. "He thinks the Dockers could win the Derby next week," he joked jovially, provoking laughter amongst the immediate crowd, who included several West Coast players. Sean chortled mockingly along with them, although none of them would have realised it was fake, and then turned back to me with a serious expression hiding beneath his forced smile. "Seriously Thommo, what's going on with you man? In the ten years we've been mates, you've never once turned down a hot, no-strings-attached root."

"Maybe I'm bored of it," I said, heading towards the exit, as Sean stared after me in shock.

"Maybe you're…" he let his sentence trail off as he followed quickly behind me. "Are you kidding?"

"No, I'm not," I said, focused on making my escape.

"That's crazy," he hissed, bewildered. "Oi, where are you going?"

"Home."

"You can't go home; this is the hottest party of the season."

"So I've heard," I said dryly.

"Is this 'coz of Soph?"

"Look Sean," I said, turning to face him, "I can't stand here and watch her playing happy families with that arrogant prick."

"That arrogant prick is your cousin remember?"

"Unfortunately I haven't been able to forget that fact."

Sean sighed sympathetically and guided me inside, past the wine bar and through to the white marble foyer. The lavish area was deserted save a few people coming and going from the bathrooms. Sean looked around to make sure no one was in ear shot, and then let rip.

"Mate, I know you're in love with her, but she's married."

"To a cheating scumbag," I muttered childishly.

"Yeah, no shit. So that means either sack up," he said, back-handing my balls, "…and tell her how you feel, or get over it. There's no other option here." He paused and let his words sink in. "So, what'll it be? You going home like a pussy or you staying to have some fun? Jacko has some ripper blow and Isla's given me a free pass to get trashed this weekend, so I want to make the most of it."

"Like I said… I'm going home."

"Really? You're gonna leave me here by myself with a bunch of rich wankers?"

I arched my blonde brow. "I thought it was the party of the Season," I mocked.

"It is, but they are rich wankers and you make it bearable."

"Sorry mate, I can't do it."

"Kane?" I turned to see Sophie standing in the foyer entrance. "Are you leaving?" she asked, making her way toward me, her beautiful blonde hair cascading down her tanned shoulders.

"Uhh... hey Shorty," I mumbled, hoping like hell that she hadn't been standing there for long enough to hear the earlier part of our conversation. Sophie was anything but short. She'd been six foot tall since we'd hit puberty, and that was when her nickname had come about. Being an awkward fourteen-year-old, Soph had been super self-conscious about her height so, even though I'd only had a few inches on her at the time, I'd started calling her Shorty to make her feel better.

"Any chance I could get a lift home?" she asked, noticing my keys in my hand.

"Sure," I said, casting Sean a furtive glance, "but wouldn't you rather stay and have fun? Frankie loves hanging with Taj so there's no rush for you to get home."

"Yeah, I know," she said, rubbing her arm nervously, "it's just that Brenton is hitting the coke pretty hard, and I don't like being around him when he gets geared up."

"I should leave you guys to it," said Sean, making a hasty retreat, "I'll give you a buzz tomorrow brother."

"Sweet," I nodded.

"See ya Soph."

"See ya Seany." Soph waved to Sean and turned back to me. "Ready to go?"

"Don't you want to tell Brenno you're going?"

"I'd rather not," she said, peering down at her feet. Her hair tumbled around her face but not quickly enough to hide her awkward blush.

"Soph…" I said, stepping closer to tuck her silky hair behind her ear, "is everything okay?"

Soph peered up at me with fear and sorrow shimmering in her big green eyes. It was the exact same look she'd had on the day I'd seen her sitting in that old Holden.

"Things aren't good," she admitted quietly.

"Hope you're not trying to steal my wife Thommo," said Brenton loudly from the direction of the courtyard doors. Soph's shoulders rose so high they were almost against her ears. She kept her back to him for a moment as she took a breath and collected herself. "I come in for a slash and find you two inside alone."

"I've asked Kane to give me a lift home babe," Soph said, regaining her composure. "Frankie just rang to say that Taj isn't feeling well."
I was impressed by how quickly she'd come up with that line, given that she was normally an appalling liar. Which made me think she'd been rehearsing it for a while.

"Oh right," said Brenton, eyeing me suspiciously, "well, that'd be handy, 'coz I'm not ready to leave yet. The party's only just getting started."

"Yeah, that's exactly what Soph said," I jumped in, embracing her lie. "You stay and party and I'll get her home to look after your boy."

"Cheers," he said with a sceptical nod before turning back to his wife. "Don't wait up, I'll be out late."

"Okay honey," Soph said with her best fake smile, "I'll see you in the morning."

"Sure thing," Brenton agreed noncommittally, as he gave her a quick peck on the cheek. "Anyway… I'm busting for a piss. Catchya later Thommo." He said over his shoulder as he strutted off to the toilets. We stood silently and watched him vanish down the hallway. I looked sideways at Soph and raised my brows with amusement.

"Impressive lie Harris."
She looked up at me with cheeky smile.

"I learnt from the best, Jughead," she retorted, as her shoulders dropped back down to a normal height. I frowned, noticing the absence of her mole.

"Don't tell me you actually got it removed?" I asked, pointing at the spot on the front of her left shoulder where her mole should have been.

"Nope," she said wiping at her collar bone with an elegant finger. "It's make-up," she explained, showing me the beige smudge on her finger.

I shook my head and rolled my eyes. "I don't know why you're so weird about it. I like it."

"Yeah, but Brenton doesn't."

"Shall we get out of here?" I asked, offering her my arm.

"Yes please," Soph said with a nod as she linked her arm inside mine. She peered up at me through her long lashes. "How would I ever have survived without you, Kane Thompson?"

- SOPHIE THOMPSON: THE TROPHY WIFE -

"You would have figured it out," Kane said, as we wandered out to the carpark arm-in-arm. For most of my life, he had been my safe zone and my saviour. Through all my poor decision making and crazy teenage antics, no matter how out of control things had gotten, Kane had always been there to bail me out, fix me up or take me home.

"I don't know about that," I said, glancing at him sideways, "I suspect I'd either be in jail or tied up in the boot of that stalky cab driver's basement."

Kane laughed loudly, with his Sophie laugh. I loved the fact that I was the only person in the world who could make him laugh like that. He had many different laughs, but that one... that uninhibited belly laugh of his...that was reserved solely for me. Kane had no idea that he did it, but I knew.

"Imagine all the extra time I would have had if I hadn't been cleaning up after you and Spanks," he teased, unlocking his shiny white Ranger Rover.

"Yeah, you could have really made something of yourself," I retorted with a wink.

Kane chuckled and opened the drivers' side door. "Or maybe I would've found a girl and settled down," he said, shooting me a cheeky grin over the bonnet.

"And deprive Perth of its most eligible bachelor?" I mocked, as we both climbed into the luxury four-wheel drive. "Imagine all the women who would never have experienced the pleasure of Kane Thompson."

Kane blushed and pressed the 'start' button of his fancy ride. For a guy who was the epitome of an alpha male, he was one of the humblest men I'd ever known. It was no wonder he'd been dubbed 'Perth's Perfect Catch'. He was 6ft 7inches of pure muscle, with brains, charisma and an amazing sense of humour. He was tanned, toned and perfectly chiseled. Kane couldn't have been any more perfect if he'd tried.

"I'd trade it all to have one good woman by my side," Kane said, as an unfamiliar look flickered across his handsome face. My heart fluttered in response to his intense stare. If I hadn't known better, I would have sworn there was desire in his eyes. My breath stuck in my throat for a moment, until Kane looked away. "Right, let's get you home woman."

We drove in silence, a strange tension hanging in the air. I peered over at him a few times and he looked deep in thought. I pulled out my phone, texted Frankie to let her know we were on our way, and then shoved my phone back into my handbag.

Kane cleared his throat as we cruised down Curtin Ave. The sun was sparkling off the turquoise ocean and the beach carparks were overflowing with cars. Beachgoers were arriving and leaving with varying degrees of sunburn, and the ice-cream van looked like it was doing a roaring trade.

"So, what's going on with you and Brenton?" Kane asked, focusing on the slow-moving traffic. I sighed, unsure where to even start. Kane was Brenton's cousin, so it felt weird to talk to him about our relationship. "That bad huh?" he asked perceptively.

"I think he's cheating," I blurted so quickly that I had no time to stop myself.

"Hmm…" Kane said, paying excessive attention to the boot of the car in front of us. I studied his profile suspiciously. His square jaw was set hard, and he was actively avoiding looking at me.

"What does 'Hmm' mean?" I asked. I knew him well enough to know when he was keeping secrets.

"Nothing. Just… hmm."

"Not once in the 30 years I've known you has 'hmmm', ever just meant 'hmmm."

"Well, it does this time."

"Nah-uh. You know something," I accused, unwilling to take mercy on the big guy.

"Ugh, Soph, please don't put me in the middle of this," he pleaded, glancing quickly at me, before retuning his gaze to the road ahead.

"In the middle of what exactly?" I asked suspiciously. "If you know something, please tell me."

"This is a conversation you should be having with your husband," he said, guilt written all over his face. My heart sank. Kane didn't even need to say it, that look was all I needed to confirm my suspicion. Brenton was definitely cheating. I felt devastated, but strangely, the thing that hurt more than the actual infidelity itself, was the fact that Kane had been complicit in Brenton's philandering. I'd suspected my husband was unfaithful for longer than I cared to admit, but I never would have expected Kane to be an accomplice. I felt completely betrayed.

"You knew and didn't tell me?"

"No," he said, shaking his head adamantly. "Well... sort of," he paused. "I mean... I guess I thought maybe you guys had an arrangement."

"Seriously?" I said feeling tears stinging the back of my eyes. "You've known me pretty much my whole life and you thought I was the kind of woman who'd be okay with an open relationship?"

"No, not really," he admitted sheepishly.

"So you just decided to stick your head in the sand and let me stay with a guy who clearly has no respect for me?"

"I'm so sorry Shorty," he said, trying to dig himself out of the hole. "I didn't think it was any of my business and I guess I thought-

"No," I said sternly, interrupting whatever pathetic excuse he was about to feed me. I shook my head and rubbed my face, as if it would wipe away my hurt and rage. It was like a knife to my heart, and I could feel my insides starting to crumble.

"You okay?" Kane asked, looking over at me guiltily as I took a few deep breaths to fight back my tears.

"Yeah," I said through clenched teeth. "Fine." I couldn't say anything more and I couldn't bring myself to look at him. Kane peered at me a few times and then pulled into a side street, bringing the car to a halt in front of one of the extravagant Cottesloe homes. He unclipped his seatbelt and opened the door. "What are you doing," I asked, swallowing back my tears.

"This," he said, climbing out and closing the door behind him. I watched as he marched around the front of the car to my side and opened the door to wrap me up in a massive bear hug. His familiar embrace was so comforting that I collapsed against him and burst into tears. I was furious at him, but my need for reassurance trumped my anger at that moment. He squeezed me tightly and stroked my hair as I sobbed uncontrollably into his chest.

"I'm sorry," he whispered. "I should have told you. I hope you can forgive me."

I wanted to tell him it was okay, but I couldn't. All I could do was cry. I wasn't by nature, a crier but once the tears started, I couldn't stop them. Anger, betrayal, shame, and embarrassment all swirled together. What a sucker I was. Brenton had been my first boyfriend, and the only guy I'd ever had sex with, but meanwhile, he'd been out shagging other women. I felt so stupid. Why hadn't I seen it sooner? Especially as he'd completely lost interest in sex since Taj had come along. It seemed really bloody obvious now that I was thinking about it. What a naïve schmuck I'd been.

After a while, my tears began to subside, but Kane didn't let me go. He held on to me until I looked up at him with a sad smile.

"You alright Shorty?" he asked, wiping the tears off my cheeks.

"I will be," I said, forcing a smile to my face, "but how do I go home and at normal for Taj knowing I'm about to destroy his world by breaking up our family?"

"Taj is an amazing kid, Soph. He'll be fine," Kane said, squeezing my arm. "Besides, it's not you breaking up your family. Brenton did that when he cheated."

I nodded and wiped the remaining tears from my eyes.

"What am I going to do?" I asked as I was hit with the reality of what laid ahead of me. "I'll have to find a job and a house and a babysitter-"

"Soph," Kane said, halting my panicked babbling. "You have nothing to worry about, okay? Whatever you need, I'll sort, and you'll have me and Frankie here to help with Taj. Plus, there's no way Aunty Joan would let you and Taj struggle. You're not alone in this, kiddo. We've got you."

Meanwhile, in not-so-sunny London...

- RITCHIE CARLTON -

It was the early hours of a dreary Saturday morning when I was rudely awakened by my phone as it buzzed and chimed on my bedside table.

"Fuck off Sandrine," I muttered tiredly, putting the spare pillow over my head to block out the annoying sound. I was reaching the end of my tether with the determined businesswoman who was refusing to take 'no' for an answer. The woman had been relentless since Amy's funeral, which had made it impossible for me to grieve properly.

Eventually the ringing stopped, and I allowed myself to relax back into sleep. Unfortunately, my dreams weren't peaceful as she had somehow infiltrated my subconscious too. Memories of her desperate attempts to stop me from leaving as well as her disturbing admission that she'd once drugged me, floated through my dreams. With each conversation we had, the situation became a little more alarming.

"How do you know what my house looks like Sandrine?" I'd asked one day when she'd let slip some finer details about my flat during one of her many phone calls. "You've never even been here."

"Oh, but I have Mon Amour. Not long after you left Paris."

"What?" I asked, leaning forward in my chair as if that would help me hear better.

"I came over to visit you," she admitted with a hint of veiled pride, "and then we checked in to the Bulgari Hotel for the weekend."

"Sandrine, are you joking right now?" I asked, confused. "I'd remember if we spent an entire weekend together."

"No," she said simply. "You felt guilty and wanted to tell Amy, so I put something in your drink to make you forget."

"You did what?!" I was flabbergasted, as my dad would call it.

"It's fine," Sandrine purred, "it was nothing dangerous. Just enough to wipe the weekend away."

I felt like I was going to vomit. I couldn't believe she'd actually drugged me. What sort of person would do that? I didn't want to believe Sandrine, but there was a nagging voice somewhere in the back of my mind that told me she was telling the truth. My brain flicked back to a point in time when Amy had still been alive. I remembered us having a big argument which was followed by a very drunken and blurry weekend. When I'd woken up on the couch, I'd had a vague recollection of seeing Sandrine but thought I must have imagined it.

"Holy Shit," I swore in shock. "I can't believe you did that. Why would you do that?"

"I already told you," she answered casually. "You were going to tell Amy and she would have ruined everything."

My dream began to fade out as ringing infiltrated my sleep again. My brain pulled me back into consciousness and I reached out my hand to search for my phone without opening my eyes. As I fumbled around blindly, I knocked the damn thing onto the floor and was forced to haul my torso out of the bed to retrieve it. I located the offending technology and squinted to read the name on the screen, pleasantly surprised that it wasn't Sandrine.

"Oh, hey Seany," I croaked, heaving my aching body back onto the bed as I answered the call.

"Ritchieeeeee," he shouted drunkenly down the phone.

"You're trashed," I laughed. "What time is it there?"

"Umm…" he mumbled, the sound muffled as if he'd just rearranged to phone to check his watch, "3pm," he announced.

"You sound like you're out."

"That's 'coz I am," he said, before lowering his voice to a loud whisper, "I'm at a rich wanker party," he sniggered.

"Then why are you calling me?"

"I just wanted to tell you that I love you bro," he slurred. "and I'm really sorry your girlfriend killed herself."
He meant it sincerely, but his words felt like a knife in my heart.

"Uhh, thanks," I said, clearing my throat of the lump that had suddenly formed. I peered around my room at the half-filled boxes. I'd been packing all week, yet somehow the place looked worse than it had when I'd started.

"It's pretty fucked up huh?" he said, completely unfiltered thanks to the alcohol and, probably, class A's.

"Yeah, it's pretty fucked up," I agreed. "And speaking of pretty fucked up… I bet Isla is stoked you're off-chops," I teased, knowing that my soon-to-be sister-in-law was going to have his balls on a platter.

"She's away on a girl's trip so she gave me a free pass," he said with a conspiratorial giggle.

"Are you sure this is what she meant?" I asked, pretty convinced that Isla hadn't planned on this level of intoxication.

"Nah, I already rang her, and she was fine. She couldn't even tell I'm smashed."

I laughed and sat up against my headboard.

"I'm sure she's none-the-wiser," I agreed with amusement. "Seriously though, why are you calling while you're out at a party."

"Oh yeah," he said, as if he'd just remembered the reason for his call. "I spoke to Kane today, and he's looking for a Managing Director."

"An MD role? That's a little above my pay grade mate."

"Fuck off," he said, and I could visualise him waving his hand around in the air, "I already sent him your LinkedIn profile and he's keen to interview you."

"Seany, I've been a Program Director for a few months. Running an account is completely different to running an agency."

"Well Kane thinks otherwise."

"Only because he's doing you a favour."

"It's already a done deal mate," he slurred, "so you'll have to sack up and take the interview."

"Right," I said, rubbing my tired face. "Let's save this discussion for when you're sober."

"Not need for me to be sover – sober," he corrected himself with a hiccup. "There's nothing to discuss. It's a fucking interview for the job of a lifetime."

"I'll think about it."

"Kane's calling you this week to fill you in on the buck's night, so you can tell him you're too much of a pussy to have an interview."

"Cheers bro," I replied sarcastically.

"Anyway… I better go back to the party, or the rich wankers will wonder where I am."

"You don't wanna let down the rich wankers," I mocked.

"Oh mate… I can't wait for you to get home. We're gonna rip this town right up."

"But only on days when Isla lets you out of the house."

"Fuck you," he said with a smile in his voice. I could tell he was quite satisfied with his new domesticated life. "Just you wait," he added sagely, "I bet you'll find a nice bird and settle down the second you step off that plane."

"Highly unlikely." That situation was almost impossible to imagine in the wake of Amy's death.

"There's going to be heaps of single chicks at the wedding mate. You'll have your pick."

"Not sure I'm ready for another heart-break just yet," I said with an awkward laugh. It had only been a month since the funeral and last thing I felt like doing was dating. "You should go dude," I said, hearing the party kick up a notch in the background.

"Yeah," he agreed. "Love you brother."

"Love you too Seany. See you soon."

- NATHAN STONE -

We drove down the A5 in quiet contemplation, every mile taking us closer towards the horrible psychiatric hospital where my Mum was kept. The overcast sky reflected my dreary mood, grey clouds hovering overhead like a bad omen. I was too anxious to talk, so I focused on the road ahead, hoping the weather would hold out for a bit longer. Ash seemed to sense my nervousness. She rested her hand gently on my thigh and gave it a supportive squeeze.

"You feeling okay?" she asked, when we pulled into the empty hospital carpark.

"Yeah, I'm fine," I nodded, noticing that her face was unusually pale. "More importantly, are you feeling okay?"

"I'm fine babe. Why?"

"Because you look really pale," I said furrowing my brows with concern.

"I'm just a little tired," she said, patting my leg with a forced smile. "Making a human is tiring work."

"Maybe you should wait in the car."

"No, I'm not letting you do this on your own," she said adamantly. "We're in this together, remember?"

"Yeah, but I don't want you pushing yourself."

"I'll be fine." Ash smiled and kissed me gently. "Come on Mr Stone, let's go see your Mum."

I led Ashley into the creepy building and my stomach lurched in apprehension. I hated these visits, but at least this time I had my woman by my side. My steps slowed as we neared my mother's room, and I stopped out in the hallway to take a deep breath. I looked to Ash for reassurance.

"Do you want me to come in with you?" she asked, as I held her hand tightly.

"No, it's probably better if I go in first and see how she responds." There was no way I wanted Ash in there if mum was having a bad day, especially if it was anything like the last time I'd visited. I stared vacantly at Mum's door, as I recalled the last time I'd seen her...

"Oh, Jack you're home," Mum said to me as if I was my dad arriving home from work. "Nathan's been waiting up for you. He won the spelling bee at school and wants to show you his certificate."

I had no idea what to say. I never knew what to say. I sighed. It would have been easier to play along with her, but I couldn't do that to either of us.

"Mum, it's me Nathan," I told her calmly, knowing things could go either way. Some days she'd have a flicker of recognition, and some days she'd be fully lucid for a moment. But sometimes, like that day, she'd freak out.

"You're not my son!!!" she howled with panic. "My son is a child. Where is Nathan?! What have you done with my son?" She punched at me, and I held her still as the nurses rushed in to sedate her, but it was taking most of my strength not to cry.

Those were the days I really hated.

Back in the present, Ash squeezed my hand.

"I'll be right here if you need me," she said encouragingly.

"Thanks babe."

I took another deep breath and opened the door.

"Jack!," Mum greeted me, as I stepped into the tiny, cluttered room. Oh fuck, it was going to be one of those days. I'd hoped that Ash wouldn't have to witness Mum going schizoid. I glanced quickly back at her, perched uncomfortably on one of the visitor chairs in the hallway. Despite the fact that she was clearly not well, she nodded her head in support, so I forced a smile to my face.

"No mum, it's me, Nathan," I answered carefully, keeping my distance in case she flew off the handle again.

"Nathan?" she asked in confusion, "how could that be? You're so grown up." The fact that she was accepting my explanation was a good sign, so I edged closer to her.

"Yes mum I'm thirty-six."

"Nathan, you look just like your father. You're just as handsome as he was," she told me proudly, looking me over. "You got his height too."

"I did," I agreed with a sad smile, as I sat down next to her on the bed. "Are you okay?"

"Not really," Mum answered hopelessly, "nothing makes sense anymore Nathan."

"I know Mum," I said, giving her a hug. It killed me to see her like this, "you've been in here for a while now."

"Yes, I'm starting to remember that."
She sighed sadly.

"How are you feeling?" I asked, trying to take her mind off the hopelessness of her reality.

"Old and crazy," she joked, patting me on the knee with a smile, "So are you married? Do I have any grandkids?"

"No Mum, not yet." I laughed, pleased that she hadn't lost her sense of humour.

"Why not?" Mum asked, running her hand down my freshly shaven face.

"I guess I've been busy with work," I said with a shrug, wondering whether I should tell her about Ash and the baby.

"You don't want to turn out like Gareth love. He's a good man, but he'd be so lonely if it wasn't for his work." That much was true. Outside of Mum and I, Gareth had very few personal connections. He'd sunk so much of his life into Artemis that he'd never had time for a wife. I guess watching over the two of us had been enough commitment for him. Don't get me wrong, Gaz had always had plenty of women around him, but he'd never let anyone get close. Hmmm… that sounded familiar.

"I won't end up like Gaz, Mum," I agreed with a nod.

"Well, hurry up and get on with it then," Mum joked, "I don't want to die without meeting the next generation of Stones."

"Okay," I laughed, and glanced out the door. Ash was out of sight, but I knew she was there. "I promise that won't happen." I kissed Mum on her head again. It was nice to have her back, even if it was only for a few minutes. "So how have they been treating you?"

"I can't find my pearl earrings," she said randomly. And with that, she was gone again. My mum once again disappeared behind the confused eyes of a woman that looked a lot like her. I swallowed back my sorrow and turned to the nurse, who had suddenly materialised out of thin air.

"Do you know where her Pearl earrings are?" I asked the stern woman.

"I don't think she has any," the nurse answered brusquely, "I've never seen a pair of Pearl earrings in here."
I sighed heavily as Mum squeezed my hand. None of the nurses in that place ever seemed particularly willing to help.

"Okay," I nodded and turned back to Mum. "Are you sure you have Pearl earrings mum?"

"Yes, I'm sure. They were right there, in that cupboard. I had them yesterday."

"No, you didn't Hellen love," the nurse told her gently but firmly. Was it appropriate to say something like that to a mental patient?
"I did. They were right there," Mum defended herself, as the tension began to rise.
Come on nursey, help me out here.

"I know you think they were love, but that's just your mind playing tricks," the nurse said condescendingly. Errr… I wasn't an expert in psychology, but that didn't seem like the best way to deal with the situation.

"I did," Mum argued. "They were there Nathan, I promise," she said in a panic, desperate for me to believe her. I was trying to form a response, when Ashley stepped through the door and took control of the situation.

"Why don't we have a look and see if we can find them for you Hellen," Ash suggested calmly, walking over to pat Mum's arm reassuringly. "I'm sure they're here somewhere."

"Oh, thank you love," my Mum replied appreciatively, grasping Ashley's hand in gratitude.

"Thank you," I mouthed silently to Ash, who winked at me and then opened the cupboard to hunt for the imaginary pearl earrings.

"Are you new?" my mother asked Ash, "I haven't met you before, have I?"

"No, you haven't met me before, Hellen," Ash said, emerging from the cupboard momentarily to smile soothingly at mum, "my name is Ashley."

"Ashley. What a lovely name."

"Thanks Hellen."

"You're very pretty," my mother informed her, making Ash blush furiously before she quickly shoved her head back into the messy wardrobe.

"That's sweet of you to say," Ash said from the depths of the cupboard, while I enjoyed a perfect view of her bottom.

"…and you're nice and tall like my Nathan," Mum added, flashing a mischievous smile in my direction, "have you met him? He's 36 apparently. How old are you, Ashley? Are you married?"
Wow, my mother might have lost her memory, but she certainly wasn't lacking in her ability to meddle.

"Umm…" Ash mumbled.

"Mum, Ashley is-…" I began to say before Ash interrupted.

"Is this what you're looking for Hellen?" she asked abruptly, emerging from the cupboard with a little maroon box containing a pair of white pearl earrings.

"Oh, thank you love!" Mum replied, taking the earrings from Ash. "I'm so glad they've finally hired someone with some common sense," she added snidely, casting a sideways glance towards the actual nurse before turning back to Ash.

"Mum, Ashl-"

"Would you mind fetching me some water love?" Mum asked Ash, "these pills make me really thirsty."

"Mum Ashley isn't-" I attempted for a third time, but Ashley shook her head at me and patted Mum on the shoulder.

"Not a problem Hellen," she said, shooting me a reassuring smile as she walked past.

"Just a moment Mum," I said, moving to follow Ash towards the door.

"Take your time love," Mum said with a cheeky smile then whispered quietly, "she's perfect for you Nathan."

I chuckled and squeezed her shoulder lovingly, amused that even in the midst of a psychological crisis, my mum still had the ability to match-make. I had to admit though, she did have great taste in women.

When I reached the door, I glanced over my shoulder at my Mum, who was grinning smugly. She waved her hand, indicating for me to get out there and talk to Ashley. I nodded with a smile and joined Ash out in the hallway.

"You don't have to fetch water babe," I told her quietly, trying to look casual, as if I wasn't already shagging Mums 'hot new nurse'.

"I know, but I think it's best to leave it at that for now. Let's keep it simple," she said, peering in to see Mum pretending not to be watching us. Mum saw us looking and quickly concentrated all her attention on her pearl earrings. Ashley and I giggled quietly, sharing a moment of affection for my meddling mother. I guided her away from the open door so we could have some privacy. Once we were out of view, I planted a firm kiss on her lips.

"Thank you," I told her earnestly, resting my hands on her hips. "I couldn't have done this without you."

"Yes, you could have," she answered, raking her elegant fingers through the back of my hair, "but we're in this together now babe, so you don't have to."

"I love you," I said resting my forehead against hers.

Ashley grinned. "In that case, I'll leave my phone number with your Mum so we can line up a date," she joked, sinking to the seat behind her.

"Are you alright?" I asked dropping to my knees in front of her to make sure she wasn't going to fall off the chair.

"Honestly babe, please don't worry about me," she said, patting my cheek. "Being tired is perfectly normal."

"Yeah, but you looked like you were about to pass out," I said with concern. "I think we should book you in to see Dr Nolan."

"I'll give her a call on Monday," she agreed patiently. "Now get back in there and be with your mum while she knows who you are."

I studied her stubborn face and rose to my feet knowing that she wasn't going to give in. "We'll circle back to this."

"I don't doubt it."

I strode towards the door and then turned back to Ashley with a grateful smile. For the first time in my adult life, I actually felt like I wasn't alone. The hollowness in my chest, had finally vanished. Over the last six months, the empty space in my heart had been completely filled-in. Ash smiled encouragingly and I re-joined my mum.

"They look beautiful on you Mum," I told her, motioning to the earrings as I sat on the bed next to her.

"Your father gave me these on our wedding day," she replied with sorrow. It always hit harder on the days when she was lucid because she had to re-live the grieving process all over again. "I only ever wore these on special occasions, and he never understood why. He used to say that life was too short not to enjoy the best things while you could." She sighed sadly, "I guess he was right. I should have worn these everyday so he could have seen me enjoy them."

- ASHLEY GRANGER -

As I sat in the drafty corridor, I couldn't shake the feeling that there was something seriously wrong with the hospital, over and above the awful nurse. The place gave me the creeps. It had a sinister vibe that I couldn't explain, and I totally understood why Nathan hated going there.

The grumpy nurse stepped out into the hallway and scowled at me. The way that she had treated Hellen had been totally unacceptable, it was as if she'd been deliberately trying to confuse the poor woman. I couldn't hold my mouth.

"Do you think that was really the best way to handle the situation?" I asked her as politely as possible.

"I beg your pardon?"

"Telling Hellen that she didn't have any pearl earrings," I replied bluntly. Feeling as crap as I was, I couldn't muster the strength to be tactful. "I'm sure there could have been a gentler approach."
The nurse sniggered scornfully with a passive aggressive smile.

"Well, I suppose it's easy to judge when you don't deal with these people on a daily basis," she answered condescendingly. "It's lovely that you care, but perhaps it's best just to leave the nursing to those who are trained. Okay?"

"Okay," I agreed with an equally fake smile. I needed to play nice for Hellen's sake, but I wasn't going to let it go. The nurse began to walk away, when I stopped her with another question. "Can I ask what pills you're giving her?"

The nurse rolled her eyes and sighed impatiently, as I gave her the sweetest smile I could. I'd played the 'pretend friends' game with the master of manipulation for an entire decade, so I could continue all day if I had to. When the nurse realised, I wasn't going to back down, she sighed and answered my question with a huff.

"Thorazine, Citalopram and Inderal," she replied unhelpfully. I didn't have a clue what any of those tablets were, but it sounded like an awful lot of medication to be pumping into one person. I wasn't an expert by any means, but from my own experience, I knew that mixing different drugs, prescription or otherwise, was rarely a good thing.

"That sounds like a lot of medication," I said undiplomatically, causing the nurse to finally break.

"I need to fetch Hellen some water," she snapped snidely, "so if you'll excuse me..." She turned on her heel and marched down the echoey corridor. I watched her storm down the dimly lit hallway and once she'd vanished from sight, I pulled out my phone and began to Google the drugs she'd listed. What had she said? Enderol, Thorazone and cital-something? Shit. How was I going to search for them if I couldn't even spell them? After a bit of trial and error, I finally found each of the medications, and as I read through the list of side-effects my stomach churned.

"Oh my god," I mumbled quietly to myself when I eventually found the write-up for Citalopram. The more I researched, the more my suspicions were confirmed. I glanced into Hellen's room where

Nathan sat holding her hand, and my heart sank for him. How was I going to tell him about my disturbing discovery?

I heard footsteps echoing down the stark hallway, and quickly stashed my phone in my pocket, feeling like I was breaking some sort of law by investigating Hellen's medication intake. I leant casually against the chair as the narky nurse returned with a jug of water for Hellen, pushing past me to get in the door. Nathan stood up to get out of her way and peered out to check on me.

"You okay?" he mouthed. I nodded, stuck my thumb up, and smiled as reassuringly as I could, but Nathan wasn't fooled. He excused himself again and joined me out in the corridor.

"Hey, sorry. I won't be much longer," he whispered apologetically.

"Don't be silly Nathan, take you time. I'm fine here."

"You're lying. What's up?"

I sighed and glanced inside at Nurse Narky. "I'll tell you later," I told him, nodding in her direction.

"Okay," Nathan agreed with understanding.

"I think I'll take a look around. Why don't you meet me at the car whenever you're done?"

"Sure," he answered with a serious nod, sensing my unspoken concerns.

"No rush," I said, squeezing his hand quickly, before sneaking off like a ninja down the sterile corridor. As I wandered stealthily along the silent halls, I felt shivers up and down my spine. There was nothing noticeably problematic with the place, it seemed clean and looked like it was reasonably maintained, but there was something weird in the air.

I continued to explore the building, and it finally struck me what was strange about the place. It was unnaturally quiet. I hadn't seen one unoccupied room, yet there was barely a sound coming from any of them. When I was a teenager, I'd been to a dementia ward to visit my Grandad, and the one thing I remembered most about that experience was how noisy the hospital was. I had only been thirteen, but I recalled it vividly, because the confused shouts coming from the rooms had been utterly disturbing.

Admittedly Dementia was a slightly different kettle of fish to Schizophrenia and other mental health issues, but surely these patients would share that same sense of panic and confusion about their situations?

"Excuse me can I help you?" asked a stern voice from behind me. I jumped with a startle, and turned to face a big, gruff, male nurse, who did not look impressed to see me.

"Oh sorry, I was trying to find the bathroom," I lied, impressed by my own quick thinking.

"It's down that way to the left," he said, without a flicker of friendliness.

"Okay thanks," I replied with my well-perfected fake smile, heading back the way I had come. I'd seen all I needed to see. There was definitely something dodgy going on… I just had to figure out what it was. A small wave of nausea washed over me and stopped me in my tracks for a moment. I rested my hand on my stomach and the feeling eased a little, but my head still felt light. I needed some fresh air.

I wandered slowly out to the carpark, breathing in the cool air and dreaming up all sorts of conspiracy theories about the hospital. Money was the most viable explanation. After all, more patients meant more income, right? I leant against the bonnet of Nathans Tesla, studying the building suspiciously. Besides a few visitors, the building was completely void of any signs of life. It was more like a mortuary than a hospital.

"Wow, do you come free with the car?" Nathan joked, from somewhere in my peripherals. I glanced over at him and grinned as he strutted across the carpark towards me, looking even sexier than usual.

"No, I'm very expensive," I retorted, as he wrapped his arms around my waist.

"Thanks for being here," he sighed, nuzzling my hair with his chin. I could tell that he was concerned about his mum but was trying to hide it.

"I wouldn't be anywhere else," I said, snuggling into him. "How was she when you left?"

"She was okay," he said with another sigh, "but I'm really worried about her."

"Nath…" I began hesitantly, "tell me if I'm over-stepping here, but I think you might want to consider moving your mum elsewhere."

"I was beginning to think the same thing," he agreed, peeling himself off me. "I didn't like how that nurse spoke to her. I'm glad you stepped in because I'm not sure how I would have handled that otherwise."

"You would have figured it out," I said with a smile, running my hand through the back of his hair as he sank against the bonnet next to me. Nath sighed and closed his eyes, tilting his head towards my hand as my fingers trailed through his hair.

"So, what happened with her out in the hall?" he asked, opening his eyes. I stopped massaging his head and stood up to face him properly, making my head spin a little. His eyes studied my face with apprehension as if he was sensing what was about to come.

"I asked her what drugs they have your mum on," I paused, taking his hand as I tried to construct my sentence as delicately as possible, "Nath…those pills they're giving her…I think they might be making her worse."

"What makes you think that?" he asked curiously.

"I looked up each of them and the side effects are insane," I said, as I pulled my phone out of my handbag and leaned up against him so he could see the screen. "Thorazine helps control schizophrenia, but it causes anxiety, which is probably why they have her on Inderal… but one side effect of Inderal is depression, which is what Citalopram is designed to treat… but here's the clincher… Citalopram not only sedates the patient, but it's known to cause dizziness, insomnia… and hallucinations."

"Holy fuck," Nathan breathed, as the information sank in, "they're using the drugs to keep her crazy." I nodded solemnly, and the movement made me dizzy. I felt my eyes glaze over, so I grasped Nathans arm to stop myself from sliding off the car bonnet. "Whoa," said Nath, gripping me tightly. "You still with me?" he asked staring into my vacant eyes until I felt them return to normal.

"Yep," I breathed, still clinging to his arm.

"What happened there?"

"Just a dizzy spell," I said, straightening myself up. "I'm okay."

"No way," he said, shaking his head firmly, "that's what happened to Tails when she was pregnant, and they put her on bed rest. We're not taking any chances. I'm calling Dr Nolan right now."

"Can we at least wait until Monday?" I pleaded. "It's not an emergency so there's no point in bothering her on a Saturday morning."

"Fine, but you have to take it easy this weekend."

"Yes boss."

"And if it happens again, I'm calling her immediately."

"Okay," I agreed, to placate him. "Oh," I said, as a raindrop hit my nose. I looked up at the dark rainclouds as they began to slowly and teasingly unleash their contents.

"Let's get going," said Nath, herding me into the passenger seat. "I don't want you catching a cold."

"Stop fussing," I told him with a laugh, pushing him out of the door as he attempted to buckle my seatbelt for me. "I'm not an invalid."

"No, but you're my woman so it's my job to take care of you." He winked, and closed the door while I stared at him, speechless. It was possibly the most wonderful thing anyone had ever said to me. He jumped into the driver's seat and looked quizzical when he noticed me staring at him, open-mouthed. "You okay?" He asked, starting the engine.

"I'm better than okay," I answered with a smile.

"Good," he said, pulling out of the carpark. He tapped the steering wheel anxiously. I could tell he was blaming himself for his mum's situation.

"Let's see if we can find somewhere better for your Mum to stay."

"I can't believe I've left her in that place for so long and never once questioned them."

"Stop beating yourself up babe. We'll get it sorted."

While Nathan drove, I googled. I scoured through a long list of alternative psychiatric hospitals for Hellen, and finally found one that sounded perfect. "I think The Priory is the best place to start," I said, scrolling through their comprehensive website. "It's not cheap, but apparently the doctor there, Robert Blakely, is one of Europe's leading experts in psychosis."

"Sounds perfect," Nath agreed with a nod. "I don't care how much it costs, as long as she's out of the Hospital of Horrors."

"Okay, I'll give them a call." I rang the facility and lined up an appointment to meet Doctor Blakely, but the soonest appointment was a month away, then after that she'd still have to go on a waitlist, which could see us waiting for months before she'd even get an assessment, let alone moved. I'd hoped the call would have made Nathan feel better, but instead he was visibly deflated. "Somehow things always work out in the end," I told him confidently. "I promise she won't be in there much longer."

Nath peered over at me, with a smile.

"How are you still so positive after everything that's happened?"

"Because despite everything that's happened, things have always worked out in the end," I said with a shrug.

"Fuck I love you."

"I love you too."

- Chapter 1 -

One month later: November Rain

- RITCHIE CARLTON -

The rain pissed down outside, making me more certain than ever of my decision to leave this dreary city. Winter was already setting in and, very soon, the daylight hours would be few and far between. Heading home to a long, hot summer was all that was pushing me forward.

I had one week left of work, and three weeks before I left the country, but first I had to make sure that all of my shit was packed and in transit, which felt like an impossible task. I'd been packing for a month, and the house was looking worse than ever. As I walked around aimlessly, popping random items into half-filled boxes, my phone rang from somewhere amidst the box labyrinth.

"Shit," I muttered, as I scrambled to find my phone, hoping like hell that it wasn't Sandrine again. The more I refused that woman, the worse she got. In fact, she was teetering dangerously close to being a Glen Close level of Fatal Attraction.

I scaled the staircase and climbed over a pile of books to locate the device. Seeing that it wasn't Sandrine, I scooped up my phone before it rang out.

"Hello?" I said breathlessly.

"Hi, Mister Carlton?"

"Yep, speaking," I said, perching on the top of the stairs.

"Mister Carlton, it's Sandra from Australasian Logistics."

"Oh hi," I said, leaning back against the wall as I surveyed the chaos from my first-floor vantage point. "What can I do for you?"

"I'm just calling to confirm that your truck will be arriving at 9am tomorrow."

"Cool, thanks."

"The final cost will be calculated once the truck is loaded, and we'll send you the outstanding invoice before the shipment is transferred into the sea container. Once the payment is made, we'll confirm your shipping dates to Perth."

"Great. Cheers."

"Do you have any questions?"

"No, I'm good." I grunted, rising ungracefully from my awkward position on the stairs. After four solid weeks of packing and hauling boxes, my body was aching in places I never even knew I had.

"The moving team will call you when they're on the way."

"Great. Thanks. I'll see you guys tomorrow," I said, hanging up. Only another 24 hours before all my earthly possessions would be loaded into a truck to begin their journey to Australia.

"Fuck," I said, taking stock of the box-maze that used to be my apartment. I knew it had to be done, but I couldn't see how I'd have it all finished by tomorrow. "But first coffee," I told the empty room. I'd only just located my kettle when the doorbell rang.

"Shit," I muttered again, climbing back over the piles of boxes to get to the front door. "Coming," I called to my mystery visitor, as I tripped over a rogue ski pole. "Fuck," I swore as I plonked heavily onto the floor.

"Ritch?" called Ryan from the other side of the door. "Are you okay?"

"I'm good," I said crawling the last few yards. I reached up and flicked the lock so he could get in. The door swung open, and I greeted him from my knees. "Welcome to boxland," I announced, arms wide open. Ryan laughed and surveyed the cardboard landscape.

"Wow," he said, stepping inside.

"Yeah." I climbed to my feet and closed the door behind him.

"Thought you might need this," he said, handing me a large coffee, "but maybe I should have brought you bourbon instead," he joked, shrugging out of his winter coat and hanging it on the rack.

"Thanks," I said with a laugh, "I'll save that for when all this shit is gone." I glanced around at the fortress of boxes inside my flat.

"Right," Ryan said, snapping into work mode as he eyed the cardboard chaos, "you get started on this pile and I'll call in some reinforcements."

Despite the bad weather, the troops rallied and within the hour, we had a house full of helpers, which was lucky because Ryan and I had barely made a dent in the pile. Kat, or Tails as Nathan and I called her, was the first to arrive with a couple of the Artemis guys in tow.

"I've brought some muscles," she called into the house, ushering Cody and Christian out of the rain and into the box-cluttered hallway. They all stripped off their wet layers and rolled up their sleeves to get stuck in.

"Hi Tails," I called, peeking out from behind the stack of boxes I'd been packing.

"Hey big boy," teased Cody with a grin, as he climbed over a large pile of linen to get to me.

"Hey man," I said, embracing him in my manliest man-hug. "Good to see your face," I added, playfully patting his cheeks, before saluting Christian, who was stranded at the front door, unable to get past Tails and the tower of boxes at the entrance. "G'day champ, what did she bribe you with for this?"

"It was more of a threat than a bribe," joked Christian, shooting her a wink.

"A threat that is still very much on the table if you don't watch yourself," teased Tails, stepping over one of the many piles of stuff.

"Where's Mia?" I asked, as she made her way through the mess, with no sign of a pram or baby carrier.

"I dropped her with Kellie," she said, giving me a one-armed hug as she leaned across some boxes. Kellie was Ryan's ex-fuck-buddy who was now pregnant with his second child and, in true Artemis melodrama style, a child that Tails was going to adopt as her own. "Where's my husband?" Tails asked, peering around the box maze.

"Upstairs somewhere."

"I'll go find him. Come on Christian, we might as well start up there and work our way down."

"Sure thing boss," said Christian, following along behind her like an obedient puppy dog. Cody looked at me and grinned, nodding at Christian as he disappeared up the staircase.

"He's been acting all mature and responsible since he got the promotion."

"Had to happen sometime," I chuckled with a shrug.

"I think he's trying to be the new Ryan."

I laughed loudly. "Watch out world, Ryza mark-two is in town."

We hadn't been working long when a cold blast of wind shot through the house, accompanied by a familiar voice as it echoed from the doorway.

"Oi, oi," called Nathan, slamming the door behind him. "I heard you needed some muscles."

"So why are you here then Stoner?" I teased, as his face appeared from behind the box tower in the entry.

"He's the eye candy," joked Cody.

"I'm beauty and braun," laughed Nath, "I take it you're the brains?"

"Of course," said Codes. "Where's the better half?"

"She's at the gym, winding things up," he said with a grimace. "It's her last class today."

"Eek," said Cody, "how's she coping with that?"

"Surprisingly well," Nath said, throwing his coat over the banister.

"Amazing what a bit of red meat'll do for ya," I joked. Ashley had been diagnosed with anemia a month prior and had been given strict instructions by her doctor to put a hold on her vegan diet for the rest of her pregnancy. I'd taken the news as a personal victory for carnivores across the globe, but Ash had been less than pleased. Nathan snorted with amusement, but then put his serious face on.

"Time to give it a rest dude. You've been gloating about this for a whole month now."

"Nah, I can't do that," I said with a laugh, "It's a victory for meat-eaters all over the world."

"You're cruel Carlton," said Codes disapprovingly, yet the look on his face indicated that he was in agreement with me.

"Oh, come on," I jeered, "how many times did we have to listen to her 'red meat causes heart disease' bollocks? You'd better believe I'm milking this thing for all it's worth."

"Fine," said Nath, "but don't say I didn't warn you."

"Warning heeded," I retorted with a salute. "She might even stand a chance of beating me up now that she's eating like a proper human."

Nath chuckled and shook his head, popping a large brown paper bag on top of the nearest box, along with a tray of coffees. "I brought croissants and coffee," he said, pulling one of the large paper cups out of the tray.

"Noice," said Cody, reaching for the bag.

"Awesome," I agreed, swigging what was left of my existing coffee, "I'm going to need an extra caffeine hit to get me through this."

Nathan laughed and looked around the room, sipping his own coffee. "So, this is really happening huh?"

"Sure is," I said, swatting Cody's hand away from the pastry bag as he went for a second croissant. I scooped up the bag and peeled it open, inhaling the buttery scent. It wasn't quite the same fresh-baked aroma that wafted out of the French Patisseries, but the smell still made my mouth water.

"It's the end of an era," Nath sighed. "I can't believe you'll be gone in a few weeks."

"Yeah, then you and Ash next month," Cody said as he watched me fish around the croissant bag. "By next year, Artemis is going to be a very different place."

"How else would any of you guys get a chance to move up the

ladder," Nath teased. I pulled out one of the large crescent shaped pastries and took a big bite of it, savouring the crisp flakiness, before handing the rest over to Stoner. "How you feeling about it Ritch?" Nath asked, resting his coffee cup on the nearest box.

"Not quite as good as the French ones, but still pretty decent," I said, my mouth full of croissant.
Nathan and Cody both laughed hysterically.

"I wasn't talking about the croissant idiot; I was talking about moving home. How do you feel about it?"

"Oh, yeah, okay I guess," I said, half-heartedly. "Feels weird, but it's time for a fresh start."

"Yeah," Stoner agreed with a solemn nod, pulling a croissant out of the bag for himself, "but you know grief follows you wherever you go right?"

"I'll go help the others upstairs," said Cody clearing his throat awkwardly, as he quickly grabbed the entire croissant bag. Nath and I both eyed him questioningly. "They might need some sustenance," he said with a shrug and a cheeky grin, before prancing up the stairs.

The two of us then turned back to each other, shaking our heads. Stoner stared dubiously at me for a moment as I silently chewed on my croissant.

"Are you really okay man?" he asked, resting his elbow on the stair banister. "I'm worried about you."

"It's weird," I admitted with a sigh. "I've been in London for a decade Stoner, Perth won't be the same as it was when I left."

"Probably not," he agreed with a nod, "but like you said, it's a fresh start."

"True," I shrugged. At least there wouldn't be any reminders of Amy.

"Right," Nath said, as he took another bite of his croissant and looked around the room, "where shall I start?"

- KANE THOMPSON -

Another fucking Saturday wasted inside, working. I had monthly budgets and progress reports to go through when all I wanted to do was get out for a hike. I seriously needed to get this Managing Director position locked in. Sean's brother, Ritchie, sounded like he could be a good candidate, but it would still be another few weeks before he got back to Perth, and then another couple of weeks for him to settle in. At best, I'd still have to wait a month before he could start.

I looked over at his CV that I'd printed out and glanced over the references section. Gareth Hemsworth. That was the bloke who had started Artemis Advertising in London. He'd built it from the ground up with his business partner and turned it into a billion-dollar business. The man was a legend in my industry.

I cast a glance at my watch. 4:30pm our time, meant about 9:30am London time. That was somewhat acceptable. Would the legendary Gareth Hemsworth want to take a work call on a weekend? Meh, fuck it. It was worth a shot. I tapped in the long +44 number and hit dial. It rung for a while and then he answered.

"Hello, Gareth speaking," he said brusquely.

"Hi Gareth, my name is Kane Thompson, I'm the CEO of Black Box Marketing in Perth."

"Oh, hi," he said, perhaps with an inkling of what I was calling to discuss.

"Sorry to call you on a Saturday, but sadly I find myself working more than I'd like over the weekends these days."

Gareth chuckled. "I remember those days well," he said with a hint of nostalgia. "What can I do for you Kane?"

"I was hoping to get your thoughts on Ritchie Carlton. His CV has come across my desk in relation to a Managing Director position."

"Absolutely," he said cheerily. "What do you want to know? Besides the fact you'd be an idiot not to hire him."

"Well, that's a pretty glowing recommendation," I laughed, caught off-guard. "I take it you've been happy with his performance then?"

"Look, Kane, I'll be honest with you," said Gareth in a gravelly tone, "I was gutted when he told me he was leaving. Ritchie has worked for me for years and this last year, he's really hit his stride and has proved himself to be a very strong leader. I'd had my sights set on him to move up the ranks until he resigned."

"So you think he's got what it takes to be an MD in a smaller agency?"

"I think he's got what it takes to be an MD in any sized agency. The kid has talent, and he has a way about him that makes people rally. Not that being liked is essential for a top-level team, but it is a nice bonus, especially when it encourages staff to perform well."

"Yeah, of course."

"Ritchie single-handily saved the Delfontaine account from going under. I lost two of my key senior staff on the account and he stepped up to the plate and has led it impeccably since then. He won't tell you this, but Sandrine Delfontaine was so impressed with him that she tried to poach him from me."

"Really?" I asked, gobsmacked.

"She offered him a position as her COO."

"Gosh," I said, lost for words. "Well... thanks Gareth, I don't really think there's anything else I need to know," I paused for a minute. "Do you think he'll get bored in a slow town like Perth after living in London for so long? Would this role would be enough to keep his interest?"

"Oh, I expect so," Gareth said solemnly. "The boy has had enough excitement for one lifetime. As far as I can tell, he's looking to slow down and settle down now so it sounds like it could be a perfect fit for him."

"Great. Thanks Gareth, I appreciate your time."

"No problems Kane," he said warmly, "let me know how he goes."

"Will do. See you." I hung up the phone feeling elated that Ritchie Carlton might just be the answer to my staffing issue. How come Sean hadn't mentioned Sandrine Delfontaine? Ritchie must have really been something special if two major players like Gareth Hemsworth and Sandrine Delfontaine were both after him.

Not wanting to sit on it, I dialled Ritchie's number. I normally would have made him jump through hoops to join my team, especially in such a high-level position, but all signs were pointing to him being the right guy for the job. I'd figured from the outset, that if he was anything like Seany, he'd be a good workhorse, but given how highly Gareth had spoken of him, I'd all-but made my decision.

"Hello?" Ritchie said at the other end of the line.

"Hi Ritchie," I said, talking unnecessarily loudly, as if to make my voice travel across the globe, "it's Kane Thompson."

"Kane. Hi," he replied with a grunt.

"Sorry, have I caught you at a bad time?"

"Nah, just packing. I've got the moving truck coming tomorrow."

"Oh, shit sorry, I can call back during the week."

"Nah all good man, as long as you don't mind me packing while we chat."

"Not at all. You do what you have to do," I chuckled.

"So, to what do I owe the pleasure? Have we got a Bucks night issue?"

"No that's all under control," I said, leaning back in my chair and stretching out my aching legs. "This is work-related actually."

"Oh," he said with surprise.

"I know you didn't want to talk about it until you got home, but I was hoping you might have had a chance to look over the job description I sent over?"

"I have had a look over it."

"And what do you think? Would the role be of interest?"

"It's definitely of interest," he said, as I heard muffled voices talking in the background.

"Great!" I said with more excitement than I'd intended. "Because I just had a very enlightening conversation with Gareth Hemsworth, and I think you'd be a perfect fit here. Would you consider doing a video interview with myself and my CFO this week?"

"Ummm.."

"I know it's a full-on week for you, but I'm keen to get this locked away asap."

"I guess I could make that work."

"I don't want to add more pressure, but I genuinely think you're the person we've been looking for."

"Well, I can't say that isn't flattering," Ritchie chuckled. "Just shoot me a time and we'll lock it in."

"We'll nut-out a few time slots and I'll have my assistant email you."

"Looking forward to it."

"Me too. Good luck with the packing."

"Yeah, thanks mate. Chat soon."

"Chat soon." I hung up the phone and did a silent happy dance at the prospect of solving my MD problem. If Ritchie took the job, I'd no longer have to pick up the extra workload and therefore wouldn't need to work on weekends just to get it all done. I might finally have time to have a life. Maybe even find myself a girlfriend, or at the very least, start dating again.

Feeling elated about the situation, I got stuck into my work. I knocked most of the tasks off my to-do list and was deep in concentration reviewing the monthly budget when I was startled by a loud bang downstairs.

"Jughead?" I heard Frankie's voice echo from the foyer.

"Hey Spanks," I called, stretching back in my chair, to ease my aching muscles. Weekend work was fine when I'd been young and driven, but now I'd hit my forties it was beginning to take its toll. "Up in my office," I added as I heard her footsteps trotting up the stairs. Soon enough, her little blonde head appeared in my doorway.

"We have a Sophie issue," she said, without pre-amble, causing me to sit upright.

"What's wrong?" I asked, ready to spring into action.

"She's refusing to get out of bed."
I sighed and relaxed in my chair again.

"That's hardly an issue,' I said with annoyance, "she's got a weekend without her child, I think she's allowed to have a sleep in."

"It's 5pm Kane. On a Saturday night. She should be going out."

"Why?" I asked, unable to fathom why any of this was an issue.

"Because, besides school runs, she hasn't left the house in an entire month."

I sighed again and rubbed the back of my neck in contemplation. I knew Soph had been struggling with the split, but I'd been so snowed under at work, I hadn't kept tabs on her.

"Okay," I agreed, "what do you think we should do?"
Frankie pulled up a chair and wheeled herself closer.

"I don't know, but I think you're the only one who'll get through to her," she said, crossing her legs as if she was getting settled in for a lengthy discussion. I locked my computer screen and gave her my full attention. "When she's got Taj, she's fine. Well… not fine, but she just gets on with life. Then when he's at school or Brenton's, she just lies in bed in the dark. I'm not even sure if she's eating."

"So how exactly do you propose I fix that?"

"You do your Kane thing."

"What's my Kane thing?"

"You go in there, boss her around and torture her until she does whatever you want," Frankie said, as if she wasn't simultaneously insulting me.

"Thanks," I huffed indignantly.

"What?" She shrugged. "That's what you do."

- SOPHIE THOMPSON -

It had been over a month since Brenton had moved out, and life hadn't gotten any easier. In fact, I felt worse by the day. I was a chubby, middle-aged single mum with no job prospects and a shitload of emotional baggage. How had my life come to this? Brenton was living his best sports-star life and I was left with nothing. Well… not nothing, I was lucky enough to have a roof over my head and money in my bank account, but how long would any of that last if I didn't find a job?

Frankie had been bugging me daily to get up and get back into the world, but I didn't see the point. The few times that I'd ventured out of the house, I'd been photographed by the local media, who'd then splashed my photo all over the internet with captions like 'Eagle flees the nest', and 'West Coast wife left with egg on her face'. It was awful, and the fact that they'd all assumed Brenton was the one who'd ended it, was even more insulting.

How the hell would I ever get a job when my marital breakdown was being broadcast on every fucking device in Western Australia. Nope, leaving the house was no longer an option. My bed was my only solace, and I had no intention of leaving it unless absolutely necessary. While Taj was here, I had to put on a brave face and pretend like everything was okay, but when he wasn't, I was free to fall apart and be a mess. So that was exactly what I was doing.

Today had been one such day, and Frankie had already been in once to check on me. I had thought that meant I'd remain undisturbed for the rest of the day, however at some point in the late afternoon, Frankie waltzed into my bedroom and flung open the curtains.

"Ugh," I groaned, as sunlight streamed through my window, stinging my bloodshot eyes. "What are you doing?"

"I'm getting you out of bed."

"No, you're not. I'm staying right here until Taj comes back on Wednesday."

Frankie tutted and opened the window to let in some fresh air.

"Is this about missing Taj or missing Brenton?" she asked, hands on hips.

"Both," I said, burying my head back into my pillow.

"Babe…" Frankie said, softly perching at the edge of the bed that I'd once shared with my cheating husband. "I know it hurts, but you can't hide from the world forever."

"Why not?"

"Because life awaits you. There's so much going on out there, and its nearly summer. We've got parties to attend and hearts to break."

"I can't face anyone. Haven't you seen what they're saying?"

"Yes, I have, but isn't that more reason to get out there and slay?"

"Slay Brenton maybe," I muttered under my breath.

"Come on, let's do your hair and your nails and then you'll start feeling much better."

"I doubt it."

"You haven't done any self-care since Brenton left. Don't you think it's time to look after yourself?"

"This is self-care."

"No, this is self-pity. You're a fucking mess."

"Oi," I said peeling my face out of the pillow and scowling over my shoulder at her. "Why don't you just kick me while I'm down."

"Well, I think you need a swift kick up the butt right now," she said sternly. "I've given you a month to mope and now it's time you suck it up and get back out there."

"Nope," I answered, flopping my face back down into the pillow in the hope that she'd go away. I heard a sigh, a shuffle and then she climbed to her feet. My plan had worked.

"Then you leave me no choice," Frankly announced gravely.

"No choice for what?" I mumbled into the pillow.

"Kane!" she called out the door.

I sat bolt upright.

"You didn't?"

"I did," she confirmed, as I heard his footsteps down the hallway.

"Why would you do that?" I asked feeling betrayed.

"Because he's the only person who can ever talk any sense into you."

"I hate you."

"I love you too," she retorted with a sweet smile, as Kane's head appeared in the doorway.

"Shorty?" he said, hesitantly edging into the room.

"Ugh," I groaned again, pulling the covers over my head so he wouldn't see me in such an unruly state. "Go away Kane. I told Frankie I'm not coming out so you can both save yourself the trouble and leave now."

"You know I can't do that," he said, the bed sinking a little, as he sat down. I heard whispering between the two of them but couldn't make out what they were saying from underneath my blanket fort.

"I'm not coming out Kane. The whole of Perth thinks I'm pathetic."

"I can tell you for a fact that that's not true," he said with compassion in his voice.

"Yes, it is."

"No, it's not, because I don't think you're pathetic. I think you're amazing," he said, shuffling up the bed slightly, "and in case you haven't heard, I'm Perth's most eligible bachelor, so my opinion should count for more," he joked. I snorted with a cry/laugh, and sank further under the cover, as the unwelcome tears shed.

"You have to say that; you're family," I sniffed, sounding eerily like my child.

"Not really," he disagreed. "In fact, technically I should be defending my arsehole cousin, but I like you much more than him," he said factually. I laughed through my tears and felt him take hold of the doona. "Can you please come out?"

"No."

"Soph…" I heard him sigh and felt his grip on the blanket loosen. Silence abounded and then I felt the movement of the bed as he rose to his feet. I relaxed with the knowledge that I'd won, and waited to hear the sound of his footsteps exiting the room. There was one step, two steps, and then the world spun around as Kane scooped me up blanket and all. He lifted me off my bed and I let out an involuntarily squeal, unable to grip on to anything from inside my blanket cocoon.

"What are you doing?" I called in panic as I was carried across the room.

"Since you won't see sense, I'm taking the choice out of your hands."

"What do you mean?" I asked, desperately trying to wriggle out of my quilted prison. Rather than answering, Kane plopped me down on something hard and, before I even had a chance to escape from the blanket, I heard a rush of water.

"Oh my god!" I screeched, realising that he'd put me in the shower. The blanket began to soak through as I fumbled my way out of it. "Why?" I asked breathless with shock as I burst out into the fresh air like a butterfly emerging from a cocoon. I coughed as I was hit in the face with barrage of luke-warm water. "Why would you do that?" I asked, looking up at him with utter betrayal.

"You left me no choice," he shrugged, as if it was no big deal. "Now…" he said in his business-like tone, "…I'm going to run out to do some errands, and when I get back, I expect you to be dressed and ready to go."

"Ready to go where?"

"Out."

"Out where?"

"You're going to be my date to the charity ball."

"You're kidding me, right?"

"Absolutely not. I've left a dress downstairs for you and there's a hair and make-up lady on the way."

"Kane," I spluttered, dumbfounded.

"See you in an hour," he said, waltzing out of the bathroom. I sat, stunned and speechless, still wrapped in the sopping wet blanket as the water rained down on me. What the actual hell had just happened?

- ASHLEY GRANGER -

After receiving a very stern talking to from my Obstetrician about my iron intake, I'd been including red meat in my diet and, as much as I hated to admit it, I actually felt a lot better for it. The dizziness had stopped, my energy levels were at an all-time high and even my yoga seemed to be better, despite the fact that my baby bump was beginning to protrude a little.

As I finished my last Yoga class, a wave of sadness hit me. I couldn't believe I wouldn't ever stand on that little stage again. I accepted the hugs and well-wishes from my regulars, feeling like I was going through a break-up. Some of these people had seen me through some crazy times. Obviously, none of them knew the full story of my recent absences, but they had still been there, supporting me and cheering me on.

Kesha rolled up her mat and waited for the room to clear out, before joining me on the stage. "I should have come to one of your classes ages ago. I never realised how good you were."

"Gee thanks," I snorted, rolling my eyes, "you really know how to boost my confidence."

"I meant that as a compliment," she said with a cheeky wink, "no need to get hormonal and moody."

"Ooh, you're on thin ice lady," I said whacking her gently with my rolled-up yoga mat. We laughed and then fell silent.

"I'm going to miss you," she said, a sad look crossing her face.

"I'm going to miss you too babe."

"London won't be the same without you." She plopped her mat onto the floor and hugged me tightly. I wrapped my arms around her and swallowed back unwanted tears.

"You'll have to come down for a visit."

"I most definitely will," she said, pulling back and glancing over my shoulder briefly. "And maybe one day I could bring Jock with me?"

"Don't push it," I warned.

"Ash, it would mean a lot to me if you'd talk to him."

"I honestly wouldn't know what to say."

"What if I did all the talking?" came a deep Scottish accent from behind me. I jumped and turned to see Jock standing at the studio door.

My head shot in Kesha's direction. "Seriously? You parent-trapped me?"

"You two need to talk."

"Don't you think it should be up to me to decide that?"

"If I left it up to you, you'd just disappear off to Cornwall and never sort it out."

"And that would be my prerogative."

"Please don't get angry at Kesha," interjected Jock. "I pressured her into it."

"Nice try, but I know what she's like," I replied, still glaring at Kesh. She held my stare with pleading eyes.

"Come on Ash, let's all go grab some lunch."

"No way," I said, slinging my gym bag over my shoulder.

"Please Ashley," Jock begged.

"He's trying Ash," Kesha said desperately. "He really wants to make things right between you."

"He wants to, or you want him to?" I asked sceptically.

"Both."

I sighed, my eyes darting between the infuriating pair. Jock stared at me beseechingly, while Kesha's big brown eyes told me how important this was to her.

"Fine," I conceded grumpily, "I'll go with you, but coffee only. I'm not staying for lunch."

"Deal."

"Let me close up and I'll meet you out the front."

"Why?" she asked sceptically, "are you gonna make a run for it?"

"No. I need to call my fiancé and let him know I'll be later than expected."

"Okay. But I will hunt you down if you vanish," she added, heading towards Jock and the exit.

"Righto," I agreed, rifling through my bag to find my phone. I waited for the couple to vacate the area and then dialled Nath.

"Hey beautiful," he answered with a grunt.

"Hey babe," I said, curious as to what he was doing. "All okay?"

"Yeah, just at Ritchie's helping him pack."

"Oh right. I didn't realise that was the plan."

"It was't. He was way behind schedule, so Ryza called us all over. I'm going to order us all pizzas for lunch so you might as well come here."

"Okay," I said with a nervous sigh. "I'll probably be an hour or so."

"Why? What's going on?"

"Kesha brought Jock to my class."

"She what?"

"Yeah… and I agreed to have a coffee with them. They're waiting out the front now."

"Are you going to be okay? You want me to come down there? I don't want you getting stressed out."

"I'll be fine. Besides, it's probably best to clear the air before we leave anyway."

"Alright. As long as you're okay. Call me if you need me and I'll be there."

"Thanks babe. Love you."

"Love you too. Goodluck."

"Thanks. You too," I said, flicking all the studio lights off. "See you in an hour." I hung up the phone and looked around the dark room. It was the last time I'd be walking out of that room.

The memories replayed in my mind as I closed and locked the door behind me. Flashes of the good and the bad. My first day; meeting Kesha; the pink rabbit; Nathan joining my class; the welcome back party; and a million other seemingly insignificant moments that now felt incredibly precious.

That job had been the first thing I'd done for myself when I'd rebuilt my life in London. My parents had helped me secure the flat and get back on my feet after Bali, but this yoga class… that had been all me. It had been my marker of independence and now I was making the choice to walk away from it. I knew I was moving on in a positive way, but it was still hard to let it go. So much had happened since I'd started working there, but the gym had always remained my one constant and now it was time to say goodbye.

"Come on," called Kesha, jogging towards me from the reception area, "let's get out of here."

"Yeah," I said with a sad nod. I dropped the key at reception and followed Kesha out the door for the last time. The blustery wind whipped around us as I stepped out under the awning, taking one final glance back at the gym. I was so focused on what was behind me, that I walked straight into Jock.

"Oh, sorry," I said, trying to control the loose stands of hair that had escaped my ponytail and were flapping about my face.

"You okay?" he asked, with concern in his eyes, "I know this must be hard for you."

I felt myself immediately shut down. The sadness quickly dissipated with my need to keep the giant ginger man at arm's length.

"I'm fine," I said brusquely with a fake smile, "much better things in store for me now." Although we'd only told our closest friends and family, I figured Kesh had probably filled him in on the pregnancy situation.

"Absolutely," Kesha agreed, throwing her arm over my shoulder. "So where should we go?"

"South Bank?" I suggested, remembering back to the day Nathan had crashed my yoga class and taken me on a 'non-date'. "There's a great little place at the Oxo tower."

"Sure," Kesha shrugged. "But I don't fancy walking in this weather." We jumped on the next bus and arrived at the café much less cold and windswept than if we'd walked across London Bridge in near gale-force winds. Kesha spotted an empty booth and, as I followed her past the table that Nath and I had sat at, I couldn't help but smile at the memory. It had only been six months ago, but it felt like years.

"What are you grinning at?" Kesha asked, as we settled in.

"Nothing really," I said, not inclined to talk about it with Jock's piercing eyes locked on me.

"That's not nothing," Kesha teased, picking up the menu.

"Nathan and I came here that day he showed up at my class."

"Ahh," she said, knowingly, before focusing her attention on the menu. "So, what are we ordering?"

"I'm just getting a coffee," I said quickly.

"It's all vegan?" Asked Jock nervously.

"We'll get you a steak later babe," laughed Kesh, patting his giant thigh.

"Thanks." He flashed her a grateful smile and I saw genuine love and affection in his eyes. He wasn't using Kesha. It was clear from the look on his face that he had real feelings for her. Kesha caught my eye and abruptly dropped her menu.

"Wait… aren't you supposed to be eating meat young lady?"

"I'm not eating," I answered with a shrug, "and she never said anything about switching to cow's milk."

"Well why the fuck are we here then?" she asked with a laugh.

"Old habits I guess," I said apologetically.

"Right, coffees all round then," she said pushing her chair out. "I need to pee. Babe, could you please order me an almond matcha if they come around?"

"Aye," Jock nodded, helping her out of her seat. We watched Kesha walk away and the tension grew ten-fold. We looked at each other awkwardly and Jock cleared his throat, pushing his menu away.

"Soo…" I said, unable to sit in silence. "You and Kesha huh?"

"Aye," he replied with a nod.

"Are you in love with her?" I asked bluntly, determined to make this as painful as possible for him. "Or are you just using her to get to me again?"

"Ash, you've got to understand the situation I was in."

"Do I?" I asked snidely. "Because the way I see it, I don't owe you anything." I glared at him angrily, feeling all the emotions bubbling back up again. Jock sighed and sank lower in his chair.

"I'm sorry," he said, with what appeared to be sincere remorse. "This isn't how I'd envisaged this going."

"How exactly had you expected me to respond?" I seethed. "You fed me to the big bad wolf, Jock."

"I know," he agreed shamefully, catching me off-guard. "I'm not proud of the part I played Ash, but that's my job. Do I regret putting you in harm's way? Absolutely. I'll regret that every day for the rest of my life, but I can't let my personal feelings interfere with my assignments."

I sat stunned for a moment as my brain processed the ups and downs of his so-called apology.

"So, you're sorry, but not sorry?" I asked sarcastically. "Because I was just an assignment?"

"No, that's not what I'm saying," he said with frustration. "You weren't just an assignment and I'm nothing but sorry Ash.

"Were we even really friends?" I asked, with the bitter taste of betrayal in my mouth. "And what about you being in love with me? Was that all part of the cover too?"

"No, that was real," he said, reaching over the table to rest his hand on mine. I pulled it away instinctively. Jock sighed and leaned back again. "All I ever wanted was keep you safe. That's why I asked you to come away with me. I tried my best to tell you without compromising the operation. I was stuck in the middle Ash."

I sat back in my chair and silently held his gaze. He had asked me to flee the country with him, and he had come to my parents to try and tell me about Dom's escape. He'd also gone to the hospital to warn

Nathan, so I guess he had made some effort to keep us safe, but still… I thought back to that horrific night in my old flat, when Dom had been waiting for me. I felt my throat begin to tighten at the memory.

"He raped me Jock," I whispered, swallowing hard to try and dislodge the lump that had begun to form. Tears shone in Jock's eyes, and he looked down at his massive hands.

"I know," he muttered quietly, balling his fists tightly in his lap. "And I'll never forgive myself for that."

"Well, that makes two of us," I blurted before I was able to stop myself. Jock recoiled like he'd been slapped in the face. "Sorry, that was a bit harsh," I apologised, peering down at my own hands as my diamond engagement ring sparkled in the light.

"Will we ever be okay?" he asked with a sad sigh. I looked up at him and held his eyes with mine.

"Maybe one day… but not now," I said, rising from my chair. "All I want to know right now is that you'll take care of Kesha."

"Aye, of course I'll take care of her."

"Good. You keep our girl safe and happy, and maybe one day we'll be okay."

"Ash…"

"Bye Jock," I said definitively. "Tell Kesha I'll call her later," I added, then trotted quickly out of the cafe before Kesha could emerge to try and stop me. I'd had enough closure for one day.

- NATHAN STONE -

We'd made good headway on the packing and, by the time Ash arrived at Ritchie's place, there were only a few random bits and pieces left to box up.

"Oh wow," said Ash, looking over the box maze as she hung up her coat. "You guys have smashed through it."

"Many hands make light work," I said, planting a kiss on her cold cheek. "How was it?"

"It was okay," she nodded.

"Hmmm…" I said, as studied her sceptically. It was hard to believe, but she genuinely looked okay. "You know what? I actually believe you," I joked. "I don't have to provide you with an alibi, do I?"
Ash laughed and wrapped her arms around my waist.

"No, he's still alive."

"Does that mean you gave him a serving?"

"I said my piece," she said cryptically. My typically neurotic fiancé was strangely calm and in control. Certainly not how I'd expected her to be after an interaction with Jock the Ginger Cock.

"You seem way too chilled. Are you sure you didn't kill him?"

"You're the only murder plotter around here," Ash teased with a smile as she tugged on the collar of my polo shirt to pull me in for a kiss. She let her lips linger on mine for a moment and then peered up at me with her big green eyes. "All is well my love," she said, resting her icy hand on my cheek. "Jock is in our past, and we're only looking forwards from now on."

"Okay lady, who are you and what have you done with my fiancé?" I teased.

"I'm serious Nath," she said smacking me on the chest. "No more looking back."

"Ah, the boss has arrived," declared Cody as he came down the stairs carrying an open box. "How was your last yoga class?"

"A little emotional if I'm honest," Ash shrugged.

"I can imagine," he said, reaching the bottom of the stairs and plonking the box down to give Ash a hug. "But better things to come now," he said with a wink. "I hear congratulations are in order."

Ash darted me a sideways glance. I hadn't told her that I'd told Cody about the baby. Her brow arched questioningly, but thankfully the doorbell buzzed loudly and spared me a tongue lashing.

"That'll be the pizza," I announced loudly, striding over to the door as fast as I could.

"Literally saved by the bell," Ash said dryly. As the smell of the fresh pizza wafted through the house, the rest of the crew emerged from various rooms and congregated in the lounge. I plopped the pile of pizza boxes on the coffee table, and we all tucked in.

"Make sure Granger gets a piece of that Meat Lover's," teased Ritchie.

"I hardly think that processed rubbish counts as meat," Ash retorted.

"How's the new job Ryan?" asked Cody, changing the subject as he pulled a cheesy slice out of the box.

"Yeah, it's good being back in the fray," Ryza said, swallowing his mouthful, "but I don't think I'd be able to go back to a full-time job yet. I kinda got used to being a househusband, so part-time is perfect. Besides, someone will have to look after the kids now that my wife is a high-flying Client Partner."

"Whaaat?" Christian asked, with a mouth full of pizza.

"Oops," said Ryza, realising that we had an 'outsider' in our midst.

"Kat's the new Delfontaine Client Partner?" asked Christian, swallowing his food.

"Sure is," I confirmed with a smile, casting a sideways glance at Tails. "Tails here earned herself quite the promotion."

"Congrats Kat," he said, stunned. "First chick Client Partner. Impressive. You guys have kept that one quiet."

"It'll be officially announced on Monday so no blabbing over the weekend," Tails said sternly.

"My lips are sealed," he said, pretending to zip his mouth shut. "So, who's gonna be CD then?"

"I'm taking back the reins until we leave," said Ash.

"And after that?"

"We've got someone starting in a few weeks. I'll train her up to lead the team on the ground, and then I'll be consulting remotely from Cornwall."

"Ooh another new chick," Christian said, eyes widening with interest.

"Don't even think about it," warned Ash.

"No betting pools on this one huh?" teased Ryza.

"Who's going to be there to stop me?" Christian retorted cheekily.

"I will," Tails said firmly.

"Bah, you guys are no fun."

"Beau said she's come from McCann?" Cody asked Ash.

"Yeah, she's been working on the L'Oreal account there," Ash confirmed. "She seems really switched on and I think she'll be a great fit for Delfontaine Cosmetics."

"Sounds awesome," said Codes with an approving nod. "Bet she can't code like you though."

Ash laughed bashfully. "You never know," she shrugged.

"Cody, we're never going to find another creative type who can code," chimed in Tails.

"That's true," he agreed.

"She's one-of-a-kind I'm afraid," I said, draping my arm over Ashley's shoulder, "and she's all mine."

"Stop," Ash pleaded, with bright red cheeks.

"Nope," I told her with a grin. "You're amazing and I'll keep telling the world."

"Looks like we've also got a new AD lined up," Ash blurted, changing the subject.

"Yeah, it's hard to replace Aims," agreed Tails, "but this girl seems to have the skills. Hopefully we'll have a fully functioning team before the end of the year."

"How come you get all the girls?" sulked Christian.

"Because it's a cosmetics account dumb arse," teased Cody. "If you want more women on your team, you'll have to give up the Milner's Sports Account and harness your feminine side."

"I think you do that enough for the both of us," retorted Christian. The banter continued as we ate, and with only a few scraps of crust littering the empty pizza boxes, we all relaxed, bellies full and muscles aching.

"Anyone up for a drink?" Ritchie asked.

"I'd love to hang for a drink, but I've got to pick up Guillaume from the station," said Cody, getting to his feet.

"Ooh so things are getting pretty serious with you guys then?" asked Tails enthusiastically.

"Meh, I guess," Cody shrugged, attempting to come across casual, but he wasn't fooling anyone. We could all see he was smitten by his Parisian waiter.

"Oh my gosh," breathed Ash, "you're in love with him!"

"I wouldn't say that," denied Codes, with an obvious blush.

"I would!" I teased childishly. "Cody and Guillaume sitting in a tree..."

"Shut up Stoner," Cody said, hitting me across the back of the head. "You're one to talk."

"Hey, at least I put on a ring on it."

"Ooookaaay," interjected Christian, "as much as I love listening to old people talk about their sex lives, I'm off to the pub to drink with people my own age."

"You'd better watch it young whipper-snapper," mocked Ritchie, "or we'll have to wash your mouth out with soap."

"Go ahead and try grandpa," Christian retorted, punching him in the shoulder. "Good luck with the move tomorrow, man."

"Thanks mate," said Ritchie, getting up to shake his hand, "and thanks for your help today. I really appreciate it."

"No stress captain," he nodded, then turned to me. "Thanks for the pizza, Nathan," he added, shaking my hand before waving at everyone else. "See you dudes on Monday."

"See ya Christian."

"I'll walk out with you," said Cody, trotting after Christian. "Bye guys."

"Bye Codes." The boys left and we were back down to five. Our core crew, minus one. We fell into a comfortable silence. I think we were all thinking the same thing. It was hard not to. Our chapter as a group had come to an end.

"So, how's your mum going Nath?" asked Ryza, his arm draped over the back of Kats chair. "Did you get her into the new hospital yet?"

"Not yet," I said with a frustrated sigh. "It's been a nightmare. We're trying to line up an assessment appointment at The Priory, but the Hospital of Horrors is making it as difficult as possible."

"How so?"

"They won't approve her for an offsite visit. Dr Blakely offered to come to her, but they're making us jump through hoops before they'll allow him on-site."

"Can't you just sneak him in there and pretend he's your uncle or something?" asked Tails.

"We thought about it, but he's too well-known in the industry and his licence could be revoked if they put in a complaint. I don't want to cause drama for him, or he might decide not to accept Mum at The Priory."

"Fair enough," agreed Ryan with a nod, before a mischievous look crossed his face. "What if we break her out?"
I laughed so hard I nearly spilt my drink on Ash.

"Wow. One brush with the law and he's a full-fledged criminal," I teased.

"But not a bad idea," said Ritchie. "It could be our one last caper before we part ways."

"You guys watch too many movies," Ash joked, as my brain ticked over the logistics of such a mission. When I didn't laugh, Ashley looked at me sideways. She could see the cogs ticking in my brain. "Nathan, no," she said sternly. "You're not breaking your mum out of prison."

"Prison?" I mocked. "No, we certainly won't be doing that."

"You know what I mean," she said, as the others looked on with interest.

"Yes, I know exactly what you mean, and Prison is a fairly accurate description," I said pointedly, "so why shouldn't we break her out?"

"Because…" she stuttered, letting her words trail off as she failed to come up with one reasonable argument.

"Because?" I prompted.

"Because you can't."

"Solid point Granger," joked Ritchie. "That's definitely a convincing argument, but I say we do it anyway."

"Ritchie!" Ashley scolded him, appalled. "It's illegal. You might be able to vanish off to Australia, but Nathan could get arrested. Do you want to be the one who explains to my child why his father is in prison?"

"It's a 'he' is it?" I teased with a sly smile.

"I don't know," she said defensively, "but that's hardly the point."

"So, what is the actual point, Granger?" asked Ritchie with a grin. He was clearly enjoying winding her up.

"Come on Carlton, give her a break," said Ryan, stepping in to diffuse the bomb he'd detonated. "I wasn't talking about a full abduction. There are ways to get around the rules, we just need to find a loophole and then get Geoff onto it."

"That's actually a really good idea," agreed Tails.

"Yeah, I'm sure my dad would be happy to get involved," said Ash, looking much more enthusiastic about the second plan than she had about the first.

"Given he was willing to commit a murder, I'd say this would be within his remit," Ritchie joked.

"Well, it sounds much less exciting," I said, winking at my hormonal fiancé, "but it just might work. Let's do it."

- RITCHIE CARLTON -

Finding a legal loophole sounded very dull in comparison to a jailbreak, but it was fun to be sharing one last metaphorical adventure with the Artemis crew. I jumped up from my armchair with enthusiasm.

"Time for drinks," I announced, forgetting that 75% of our group couldn't currently drink.

"Wish I could join you," said Ryza wistfully, "but I've still got six months of sobriety before they'll sign me off."

"Oh, sorry man," I said apologetically. "I totally forgot."

"On the plus-side, it's given him more energy for other things," Tails joked with a wink as she playfully squeezed his thigh.

"And that Dad gut is a thing of the past huh?" I teased, backhanding his new six-pack as I walked past. "I'm impressed you've managed to keep it off MacDaddy."

"And I didn't lift one single weight," he retorted, looking sideways at Kat. "Well, at least not in the traditional sense."

"Oi! I'm working on getting rid of my baby weight thanks very much," she said smacking him playfully.

"No, I didn't mean it like that babe," said Ryza, realising his faux pas, "I think you're perfect as you are."

"Just as well."

I grabbed my bottle of bourbon from the kitchen for Nath and myself, along with a few cans of lemonade for the others.

"For you teetotallers," I joked, popping the soft drinks on the coffee table. With Ash pregnant, Kat breastfeeding and Ryan post-rehab, our little crew was certainly a lot tamer than it had ever been before. "Shall I slap a sausage in yours Granger? Extra iron and all that."

"I don't want your sausage anywhere near my mouth Carlton," she quipped back.

"You sure about that?" I teased with a cheeky wink.

"Oi, that's my fiancé you're talking to," Nathan piped up, as I handed him his drink.

"She's the one who started talking about my sausage."

"At least she didn't call it a chipolata," laughed Tails. As I watched the frivolity unfold around me, I felt a heaviness in my chest. I was going to miss these moments more than anything else. Our chill days hanging out together and taking the piss out of each other. This crazy crew was like family to me, and I would be so far away that I wouldn't get to be part of these little, seemingly insignificant moments anymore.

"So have you gone back to visit your friends?" Ash asked Ryan as she handed him a lemonade.

"You mean his famous new besties?" teased Tails.

"Famous?" asked Ash curiously.

"Yeah," said Kat proudly, "and you won't believe who it is."

"Babe, I have a confidentiality agreement remember?" Ryza scolded her. "I'm not allowed to mention names."

"I didn't sign one though," Kat replied cheekily.

"Just wait another few weeks when they're both out," Ryan pleaded, "by then they'll probably be all over the TV as London's hottest new couple anyway."

"Ooh a rehab romance?" said Ash with excitement. "Please can you tell us who it is."

"Nope."

"But Ritchie will be gone soon," Kat piped up.

"And I'm sure he'll be super bummed to miss this riveting news while he's sun-baking on a beach in Perth," Ryan laughed.

"But I don't think they'd mind," argued Tails. "After all, you're the one who got them together."

"No babe," Ryza said sternly, "I'm not breaching my contract."

"Fine" Kat sulked.

"Anyway…" said Ryza, changing the subject. "How's everything with Sandrine? Has she backed-off yet?"

"Nah," I said, gulping a large mouthful of whiskey. "If anything, she's getting worse. It's like she thinks she's gonna change my mind by acting more needy."

"Is it worth getting a restraining order?" Asked Ashley worriedly. "I mean, she's already admitted to drugging you." The topic of controlling relationships was a trigger for her, but my relationship with Sandrine was a far cry from her relationship with her abusive ex.

"It's only a few weeks before I'm on the other side of the world," I said, taking a long sip of my whiskey. "Besides, I don't want to do anything to jeopardise the account."

"The account will be fine Ritch," Tails assured me. "You really don't need to worry about that."

"You know she has the resources to get to Australia though, right?" Ash continued with concern. "Do you really think she's just gonna drop it?"

"I'll be fine Ash. I'm a big boy, I can handle myself."

"So can Nath," argued Ashley, "but look what she did to him."

"Oi," said Nathan defensively, "don't drag me into this."

"Sorry babe," Ash said patting his knee, "but this woman is unstable, predatory and absolutely loaded. She could be more dangerous than you think."

"Chill Ash," said Ryan calmly, always the stabilising voice. "Sandrine isn't Dom," he added, saying the words we were all thinking.

"Wow," Ashley said, recoiling as if she'd been slapped. "Is that really what you think this is about?"

"Isn't it?" asked Tails apologetically. Ashley looked around the room, reading each of our faces in turn.

"You all think this is a trauma response?" she asked with a look of betrayal.

"No babe," said Nath gently, "but it does make you a little more sensitive to things like this."

"No, it just makes me more aware of it."

"Honestly Ash," I intervened, "I appreciate that you're looking out for me, but I'm absolutely fine. There's nothing Sandrine could do that would hurt more than what I've just been through." Silence fell as my truthful words struck a chord with everyone. We all sipped quietly on our drinks for a few minutes.

"On a brighter note," chirped Nathan, breaking the contemplative silence, "it looks like everything is sorted for your leaving party next weekend Ritch."

"Yeah," Ash agreed, visibly forcing herself to be cheery. "Mum and Dad have gone crazy on the event planning."

The rest of us exchanged conspiratorial glances. There was a very big surprise in store for Ash that only a handful of people knew about. Much like her pregnancy, it was getting harder and harder to hide, but we only had to keep it secret for another week.

"That's very generous of them," I said casually, "especially considering they barely know me."

"I think they just wanted to make sure it's special for you," she replied with a smile.

"Yeah, they figured we all probably need to blow off some steam," added Nathan, raising his brows at me in disapproval, from behind Ashley's head. I was tempted to make a 'blowing' pun, but I'd already pissed him off enough by alluding to his secret. "It's the last time we'll all be together for a while."

"Sure," I agreed with a grin, enjoying winding him up. "Until your wedding at least. When's that happening anyway?"

Nath scowled at me. "Right now, we're just focusing on the baby. Right Ash?"

"Yeah," she agreed with a shrug, "it's a little hard to think about planning a wedding with everything that's happened."

"Ah well," I sighed melodramatically, "it gives me a good excuse to come back."

"Exactly," Ash said, as she cuddled up to Nath.

"I can't believe you guys are leaving us," sighed Tails, leaning back against Ryan. "What are we going to do without you all?"

"You'll be so busy with family life you won't even notice we're gone," teased Ash with a sad smile.

"I was hoping we'd be raising our kids together," said Kat disappointedly.

"Yeah," agreed Ash, visibly wracked with guilt.

"Hey, at least you'll have free seaside accommodation," Nath interjected, trying to lift the mood.

"And a good excuse to come to Oz," I added. "Maybe next year you could all come for a hot Christmas so I can meet the future Mac and Stone?"

"Sounds like a plan mate," said Nath.

"That would be wonderful," agreed Tails, "but we'll have to see how crazy life gets with two under two," said Kat, looking at her watch. "Speaking of which, it's time for me to pick up little miss."

"Yeah, Kellie's probably hit her baby quota by now," joked Ryza, helping Kat up from her seat.

"I guess we should probably make a move too," said Nath finishing off his glass of whiskey. "Freddie will be ready for a break from the terrors."

"I still can't believe you kept that fucking cat, let alone all of her kittens," I mumbled, still annoyed that I'd been tricked into cat-sitting a stray cat when Nathan was in hospital.

"We're not keeping them all," said Nath defensively, "Geoff and Mary are taking two."

"Cool so it will just be four cats and a baby then," Ryza teased.

"Or two cats and a baby for us, and two cats and two babies for you?" tried Ash with a cheeky grin.

"Hell no," said Ryan definitively. "There's no fucking way we're getting lumped with any of your stray cats so don't even think about it."

"Mia would love a kitten," joked Nath.

"Nope," said Ryza with a stern smile, "and if you gift her one, I'll make you pay dearly for the rest of your natural life."

"Fine," agreed Nathan, shooting a subtle wink in Ashley's direction. I felt a twinge of sadness at the mischievous look in his eyes. He was so clearly planning on sending at least one kitten into the MacPherson household and it was hard to accept that I wasn't going to be part of these sort of shenanigans anymore.

My guests all said their goodbyes and then the sickeningly happy couples headed off in their respective directions while I stood on my front steps and waved farewell. There was no way I was going to find friends like these again. No matter how many mates I made back in Oz, they were never going to live up to the Artemis crew.

- SOPHIE THOMPSON -

As the make-up lady moved on to my hair, I stared at my reflection in the mirror. She'd done a good job at hiding my puffy eyes and newly formed worry lines. Besides the sad eyes, I almost looked like my old self again. I didn't feel ready to go out in public, but at least I'd look good doing it, particularly in the dress Kane had hired for me. It was absolutely stunning. A strapless, sequined mermaid tail dress in the most striking crimson colour I'd ever seen. If I'd wanted to be noticed, it would have been the perfect choice, but I certainly wouldn't be able to glide under the radar wearing that to the charity ball.

"You look gorgeous," said Frankie, admiring my make-up as she sipped on her martini.

"I really wish you'd come with us."

"Sorry babe, I'm not cancelling hot sex to accompany my brother to a stuffy charity ball."

"Couldn't you do both?"

"Baz isn't exactly Charity Ball material."

"Really? With a name like 'Baz', he sounds so refined," I teased sarcastically.

"I don't care what his name is. The guy is totally ripped and hung like a horse. I'd call him daddy if he asked me to."

"There are so many things wrong with that sentence I don't even know where to start."

"Then don't," she answered with fake sweetness.

"You're all done," announced the make-up lady as she pinned the final curl into place.

"Thank you," I told her with my most convincing smile, "it's perfect."

"Cinderella is ready for the ball," Frankie said over-excitedly, before knocking back the remainder of her drink and plonking the empty glass on my dresser. "And on that note, the fairy godmother is signing off."

"Oh, you think you're the fairy godmother in this story, do you?"

"Of course I am."

"What about Kane? He was the one who organised everything."

"Nah, he's just the goose I turned into an escort," Spanks chuckled as we watched the make-up lady pack up her gear. Frankie caught my eye in the mirror and grinned, "or maybe he's the pumpkin," she added with a shrug. We both laughed and waited for the make-up lady to vacate the room. Frankie strode over to give me a kiss on the cheek. "Now go out there and crush it girl. You've totally got this."

"I can't believe you're abandoning me in my hour of need," I sulked.

"Your guilt trip won't work on me Harris. Besides, you'll have Jughead there to hold your hand."

"It's still not the same."

"I'm going now," she said, rolling her eyes before initiating her escape. "Have fun tonight," she said, stopping at the door. "When people see you looking like that, they're gonna think Brenton is an idiot for letting you go."

"Thanks babe."

"Love you," she waved before slipping out the door.

"Love you too," I called behind her. I rose to my feet and studied my reflection in the full-length mirror. I looked much better than I felt, but I guess it was a matter of 'fake it till you make it'.

"Wow," croaked a familiar voice from behind me. Kane's handsome face appeared in the mirror, and I smiled shyly at his reflection before turning around to face him. "You look breathtaking," he added, striding over to offer me his hand.

"You scrub up pretty well yourself, Mr Thompson," I said, taking in the sight of his broad shoulders, outlined in a perfectly tailored charcoal suit. He was wearing a crimson shirt that matched my dress, with the top few buttons left open to reveal a tantalising hint of his chest. He really was a good-looking man. I could see why so many women in Perth were completely gaga over him.

"Shall we get going?" he asked, catching me in my disturbingly pervy thoughts.

"If we have to," I mumbled with a blush.

"You have to get back out there some time Shorty."

"Yeah, but I was hoping 'sometime' would be a lot further in the future."

Kane let his eyes glide up and down my body for a moment.

"Trust me kid, you're gonna knock their socks off," he said with a wink. A limo was waiting out the front for us, so Kane ushered me into the luxurious vehicle where a bottle of champagne was chilling in the cooler. He poured us a glass of bubbly each and handed me one. "To your debut back into society," he said, clinking his glass against mine. I smiled tightly and sipped nervously on my drink. He took a gulp of his champers and cocked his head, raising an eyebrow in concern. "You okay?"

"Not really," I admitted. My stomach was churning with anxiety so badly that I was struggling to enjoy the Veuve.

"Hey," Kane said, plucking the glass out of my hand and placing it in one of the holders, "I promise you'll be okay. I'll be right there with you the whole time."

"I know," I nodded, wringing my hands together. "It's just so embarrassing that everyone thinks I'm forlorn and heartbroken."

"So, we get out there tonight and show them they're wrong."

"Sure," I said unconvincingly.

"Do you trust me?"

"Of course I trust you."

"Okay then, just relax and let me take the lead." He smiled his sparkly-eyed smile, and I felt a weird flutter in my belly that wasn't the nerves.

"Thanks Jughead."

"I've always got your back Shorty."

We pulled up outside the Crown Casino and there were already photographers and journalists circling the entrance like vultures.

"Shit," I swore under my breath. Kane took my hand and gave it a squeeze.

"We've got this," he said confidently, and gave me a quick peck on the cheek before opening the door. He stepped out of the limo, and the camera flashes went crazy when the paparazzi spotted Perth's most eligible bachelor. Kane took it in his stride, acting as if they weren't even there. He reached in to offer his hand, and then assisted me out of the limo. Kane slid one arm around my waist and pulled me close, closing the door behind me in one sleek move. He held me firmly, guiding me through the fray with grace and ease. He was so comfortable in front of the cameras, whilst I had never gotten used to it.

As we made our way towards the door, the media crews finally realised who I was, and began firing questions about Brenton and the divorce. The butterflies in my stomach kicked to full-throttle, but Kane quickly neutralised the story-hungry journos.

"Tonight is about raising money for a good cause, so let's keep the focus on that huh?" he reprimanded them with a charming smile. Some of them laughed and backed off, but one bitchy reporter stepped onto the red carpet and accosted me.

"Sophie, how do you feel about your husband being seen out with a new girlfriend?"

My jaw dropped and I stuttered in shock. Firstly, because I hadn't been keeping up with Brenton's love life, and secondly, because I couldn't believe she was being so brazen. Kane quickly jumped to my rescue.

"Well, she's here with me tonight so I'd say she's got the better end of the deal, wouldn't you?" he asked her with a suggestive wink.

"Does that mean you're dating your cousin's wife?" the vulture asked with a smug grin as she turned her shrewd gaze on me. "Is that why your husband left you?" she asked vindictively. "Did he find out you were cheating on him?"

"I don't think that's an appropriate question, do you?" Kane said sternly. "The nature of our relationship is a private matter between Soph and myself and no one else," he replied with a friendly smile. "Anyway, if you'll excuse us, we have a ball to get to," said Kane, gallantly ushering me inside.

We escaped into the foyer and I looked back over my shoulder. Most of the paparazzi had moved on to the next arrival, but the bitchy reporter was still watching us with eagle eyes. Kane noticed her looking at us and gently brushed a stray curl off my face in an intimate way that could have been misinterpreted as a romantic gesture. He smiled and leaned in close.

"You okay?" he asked quietly in my ear.

"Yeah," I nodded, looking up at him with admiration. "You're my hero."

"We'll have to wait and see about that," he said with a laugh as he draped his arm over my shoulder. "Hopefully she'll run with the wife-stealer angle, but it's hard to tell."

"You put yourself in the firing line for me?"

"They can say whatever they want about me," he said with a nonchalant shrug. "Now, let's get up there and get this party started."

I held tight to Kane's hand as he schmoozed with the other arrivals, shaking hands and patting backs as if he'd been doing it his whole life. He was so cool and calm being in the spotlight, while I was excruciatingly awkward. Being an introvert, I'd always struggled with this part of footy wife life, but Kane was so naturally enigmatic he seemed to cruise through without even thinking about it.

We stopped to have our photos taken, grabbed a glass of bubbly from the circulating waiters, and then made our way through to the ballroom. I took in the grandeur of the room. I'd been to a lot of charity balls, but this one was taking it to a whole new level.

"You were planning on coming to this alone?" I asked as he led me towards a table.

"No," he said with a grin, "I wasn't planning on coming at all until tonight."

"You bought a couple of $200 tickets just to get me out of the house?"

"Actually, I bought a whole table," he answered with a shrug. "I just never planned on using it."

I choked slightly on my champers.

"You dropped a couple of grand on a table you weren't planning on using?"

"I'm happy to support the cause without having to be here to endure it," he joked. "And lucky I did because now we have an entire table to ourselves," he said gesturing to the eight-person table in front of us. "No need to choose between the chicken and the beef, we can try them both."

I laughed and nudged him playfully. If I had to be out in public, I was glad that I was doing it with Kane by my side.

- KANE THOMPSON -

As the night went on and the champaign flowed, Soph relaxed into the festivities. We ate, we danced, and we laughed a lot. She was almost back to her old self again. In fact, she was actually beginning to seem like a much happier version of her old self, and I was finding it hard to keep my eyes off her.

"What?" she asked as we took another break from the dance floor. "Have I got something on my face?"

"No. Why?"

"You keep looking at me like that."

"Like what?" I asked, my stomach lurching at the knowledge that I'd been caught out.

"Like…" she cocked her head thoughtfully, "…like you're seeing me for the first time."

I raised my brow and shrugged it off, trying to appear casual.

"Maybe I am," I said, taking a long gulp of my drink. "Shall we check out the auction items?"

"Sure, why not." I gave her a hand up and we strolled over to the auction table, drinks in hand. We quietly perused the table of expensive goodies when Soph stopped in her tracks. "Oh my god," she groaned, turning away from the table, so I peered down to see what had caused her response. It was a framed, signed football jersey. Brenton's football jersey.

"Oh geez," I said, not sure what else to say. I looked around the room, and quickly shoved the huge frame underneath the table, making sure it was hidden by the tablecloth. "That's better," I chuckled.

Sophie laughed and glanced around to check if we'd been seen, but no one seemed to have noticed. They were all too busy enjoying the party and too drunk to pay attention to the two of us. We smiled conspiratorially at each other and continued our browsing.

"Oh wow," she breathed, running her hand over a sparkly necklace covered in diamonds, with a large blue stone in the centre. "It's beautiful."

I read the card. "Tanzanite. Isn't that rare?"

"Yep," she confirmed, still gazing longingly at the shiny object.

"What sort of price do you think that would go for?"

"Well, the tanzanite alone is probably worth about six grand, then you add the diamonds and white gold and I'd say this would probably retail at close to fifteen."

"Well, look who's a jewellery expert," I teased, impressed by her knowledge. "Perhaps we just discovered your next career move."
Sophie laughed loudly.

"I do love shiny things, but could you imagine me working in a jewellery store?"

"I could actually," I said honestly. "I think you'd be great."

"Yeah, until someone recognised me and told the media that Brenton's ex-wife was working in retail to make ends meet."

"I don't mean some shitty little generic store Shorty, I mean a high-end, big-ticket jeweller. In fact, a colleague of mine owns a high-end Jewellers in Peppermint Grove. I could ask him if he's hiring."

"Thanks Jughead, but I think I'd rather figure this out for myself. If I do get a job, it needs to be on my own merit."

"Okay fine," I surrendered, hands in air, "but don't disregard it. I think it could be the perfect job for you."

"Maybe," she said, taking one final look at the necklace. "And in the meantime, I'll just fantasise about owning a beautiful piece like that."

I peered at her sideways, sneakily studying her beautiful face. Despite the fact we were thirty years older, I still saw that pretty ten-year-old girl I'd met in suburban Perth. I couldn't believe she was here with me, without Brenton around to ruins things like he usually did. Soph was finally free of my dickhead cousin and for the first time in decades, I had her all to myself. No Brenton, no Spanks, no Taj. Just her and I. Perhaps I would end up with my dream girl after all.

"Shall we dance again?" I asked, realising that I'd been staring at her for way too long.

"Actually, I need to run to the loo," she said with a little jiggle, "I'm busting for a pee."

I laughed in shock. You could put her in make-up and a fancy dress, but she was still the same old Soph.

"Well don't let me stop you. I don't want you making a mess in that dress."

She ran off to the bathroom and I glanced down at the Tanzanite necklace. There weren't any bids on it yet. I checked to make sure Soph was out of sight and quickly scribbled my name on the form. Soph said it would probably retail for around fifteen grand, so I bid twenty in the hope that no one else would want to pay more than that. I plopped the pen back down on the table as I spotted the bidding form for Brenton's jersey still sitting there. I looked around and stealthily slid the piece of paper inside my jacket so no one could bid on the hidden piece. It was a small and immature win, but a win none-the-less. It might take Brenton down a notch or two if no one bid on his memorabilia.

Job done, I quickly moved away from the auction table so that Soph wouldn't return and see my bid on the necklace. I met her at the dance floor and escorted her back to the table for dessert and coffee. The silent auction would be announced at the end of the night, and as it was nearing midnight, we wouldn't have long to wait.

The announcement came as we were sipping on our coffees. "We'll be sealing the bids for the silent auction in five minutes, so if there's anything you'd like to bid on then now is the time to do it."

"It's your last chance to get that necklace," I teased with a wink.

"Yeah, that would look great in the divorce financials," she said with a snort. "I can hear Brenton's lawyer now."

"Do you think they found the jersey?" I asked with a wicked grin.

"I'm sure they would have. They know what's on auction. There's no way they'd let that kind of money slip through their fingers."

"Unless no one was able to bid on it," I said, opening my jacket and showing her the bidding form tucked in my inside pocket.

Sophie laughed loudly. "Oh my god Kane," she said, grasping my arm. "You're terrible… and I love it."

"Anything for you Shorty."

"But you should probably put it back. They're probably wondering what happened to it."

"Really?" I asked with disappointment.

"It's for a good cause," she reminded me with a smile. "But I love that you did that for me."

I smiled, nodded and rose from my seat.

"Fine," I conceded, "but only because it's for charity." I wandered over to the auction table, casting a glance back over my shoulder to see if Sophie was watching. Thankfully she'd been bailed-up by one of the organisers who was probably trying to talk her into donating money. I ran my eye over the necklace form and noticed that some cheeky fucker had bid twenty-one thousand. I looked back to check that Soph was still distracted, then upped my bid to thirty thousand. That should clinch it.

I moved over to the gap in the table where Brenton's jersey had been. I briefly considered not putting the bidding form back, but my conscience got the better of me, so I not only put the jersey and the form back on the table, but also placed a bid of $500. Hopefully someone would out bid me in the next two minutes because I really didn't want one of Brenton's jerseys hanging on my wall.

Sophie was still being bored to death by the uptight woman in the navy-blue satin dress. I'd met her several times before but couldn't for the life of me, remember her name.

"All okay?" I asked, resting my hand on Sophie's shoulder protectively.

"Mr Thompson," the woman said with a wide, fake smile. She reminded me of a crocodile with her beady little eyes and shiny white teeth. "It's so lovely to have you here again," she said reaching out to shake my hand. "However, your table is a little emptier this year," she added with a passive aggressive smile.

"Yes, unfortunately the rest of the party had more pressing engagements to attend," I replied with an equally wide smile. I'd gotten good at playing the game over the years. The key to making insulting comments was to smile afterwards.

"Well, that's a shame," she said, straightening the front of her way too tight dress. "We were rather hoping to see the other Mr Thompson tonight. I wanted to thank him for his donation to the silent auction." Sophie stiffened. I could feel her neck muscles tighten under my hand, so I gave her shoulder a gentle squeeze to let her know I had it under control.

"I'll pass that on to him," I said sternly, my eyes glaring at her while my mouth held the smile, "but I noticed that no one had bid on it." The woman's head retracted into her double chins for a moment.

"Really?" she asked with surprise, "we were expecting that to fetch at least a few thousand."

"Oh, don't worry," I said smugly, "I placed a starting bid of $500 so I'm sure someone will jump on the bandwagon." I let my words hang in the air for a moment. "Perhaps he's not quite the star we all thought he was."

Before the crocodile had time to respond, the MC's voice echoed over the PA system. "Okay Ladies and Gentlemen, the time has come. Bids have now closed and we're ready to announce the winners of the silent auction."

"I guess you should get back to your table," I suggested politely to crocodile lady.

"Yes," she said, unnerved. "Lovely chatting to you both." She quickly dashed away as fast as her tight dress would allow her, and Soph and I exchanged a conspiratorial glance before bursting into fits of childish giggles.

"Oh my god," Soph whispered as I took my seat next to her, "I can't believe you just did that. You're so cruel."

"She deserved it," I said, leaning back in my chair with a smug grin. I rested my arm over the back of Sophies seat as we listened to the MC run through the silent auction items. We remained quiet, until he got to the jersey. Soph and I looked at each other and giggled again as the assistant held up the large frame.

"Well, this one has been bought for a steal," said the MC, "a signed Premiership jersey from Brenton Thompson, valued at over two thousand dollars, goes to our only bidder, Kane Thompson, for just five hundred dollars."

"Oh shit," I laughed as the ballroom full of applauding people turned to look at me.

"You actually won it," Soph whispered with a laugh.

"I'm so excited," I replied sarcastically.

"You'd better go up and get it."

"Right," I agreed, jumping to my feet. I waltzed up to the stage and collected my purchase with a wave to the crowd. I posed for a photo and then lugged the big frame back to our table. This was for sure going to make it into the social pages. I shoved the frame under the vacant side of the table and then leaned over to Soph. "How about we give that one to Taj?"

Soph beamed at me. "I'm sure he'd love that."

"Don't get too comfy Mr Thompson," called the MC from the stage. "It looks like you've also won the bid for our next item."
Soph peered at me with a raised brow.

"What?" I asked with an innocent shrug.

"You didn't?"

"The Tanzanite and diamond necklace, valued at eighteen thousand dollars, has been sold for a whopping thirty thousand dollars to Kane Thompson."

Sophie's jaw dropped. "Thirty thousand?!" she asked, stunned.
I shrugged and made my way back to the stage.

"It's great to see our regular patrons supporting the cause," the MC said, shaking my hand as he presented me with the open box. I once again smiled and posed for the photo, then waved humbly to the watching crowd. "Kane Thompson ladies and gentlemen."
I returned to my seat and handed the box to Soph.

"This is for you."

"Kane."

"Soph."

"I can't accept this."

"Please," I begged, waiting for her to take the box from my hands. "I don't look good in diamonds." My joke broke the tension and she laughed, but still didn't take the box from my grasp. "Can I at least put it on you to see what it looks like?" I pleaded, placing the box on the table, and gently extracting the expensive bling.

"Fine," she relented, undoing the necklace she was wearing so that I could replace it with her new one. I swept her hair gently away from her neck and connected the clasp. I felt an overwhelming urge to kiss her bare neck, but thankfully we were interrupted by the photographer, who wanted to get a shot of Sophie wearing the necklace. Once the photographer was done, Soph turned to me, her hand resting gently on the bright blue stone. "Kane, this is too much."

"No, it's not," I disagreed. "I saw how much you wanted it, so I wanted to make sure you got it."

"That's incredibly sweet, but that's not how life works."

"It's how life works when you're with me," I replied without thinking. Soph looked up at me with questioning eyes. "I mean," I cleared my throat, "you know… that's just how I roll."

"And that concludes tonight's event," declared the MC in the background. "Thank you to everyone who donated and placed bids. We appreciate your ongoing support."
The crowd began to filter out of the ballroom to a cacophony of laughter and rowdy conversations.

"Well, I guess that's that then," I said, clapping my hands together. "Your first public appearance is done and dusted."

"Yes, it is," Soph agreed with a smile. "Thanks Kane."

"Thanks for what?"

"Thanks for everything," she said with a slight blush. "I couldn't have done this without you."

"That's what I'm here for Shorty," I told her with a wink as she hid a yawn. "Yawning already? You used to have way more stamina than this! Remember the night we stayed up until 5am just so we wouldn't miss Maya the Bee?"

"Oh my god, I do."

"Come on Cinderella, it's after midnight," I said reaching under the table to pull out Taj's new West Coast memorabilia. "We'd better get you home from the ball," I said, assisting Sophie out of her chair with my spare hand. "Your chariot awaits, my lady."

- SOPHIE THOMPSON -

We climbed into Kane's waiting limo and I flopped back into the leather seat, exhausted but exhilarated after such a fun evening. My night out with Kane had somehow restored some of my old self, and I was feeling better than I had in months, possibly even years. The gratuitous amounts of champers had probably helped lighten my mood, but still, it was nice to feel like a normal adult for one night.

"Back to Sophie's house please Johnathan," Kane instructed the driver as he closed the door behind us.

"Actually, I don't really feel like going home."

"Okay," Kane agreed chirpily, "where shall we go then? We could jump back out and go into the casino."

"Hmm… I don't think I'm up for the Cass."

"Fair enough. Neither of us are probably drunk enough for that anyway," he joked. The Casino wasn't exactly the height of sophistication. "What about the VIP bar upstairs?"

"Nah I wouldn't mind getting away from here."

"Right… well, that doesn't leave us many options," he teased with a raised brow. "After midnight there's not a lot of choice."

"True," I agreed, "I just can't face my empty house."

"What if we go back to mine for a drink?"

"Perfect."

"Change of plans," Kane said through the front divider window, as Johnathan climbed to the drivers' seat, "we're heading to mine instead."

"Certainly sir," said Johnathan, before winding up the divider to give us some privacy. Kane settled back in his chair and smiled at me curiously.

"So did you enjoy yourself tonight?"

"It's the most fun I've had in a long time," I admitted, eyeing the open bottle of champers that was still sitting in the chiller. "Thanks for getting me out of the house."

"You're welcome," he said, following my gaze to the bottle. "Shall we finish it off?"

"It would be a shame to waste it."

"Absolutely," he said, pouring the remaining bubbles into some fresh glasses. "Cheers to a memorable night," Kane said, handing me one of the glasses.

"Cheers," I said, taking the glass and clinking it against his.

We'd barely finished our drinks when the Limo pulled off Stirling Highway and into the back streets of Peppermint Grove. Brenton and I had lived a fairly luxurious lifestyle in the upper-class suburb of Dalkeith thanks to his AFL salary, but Peppermint Grove was next level. I loved the quiet tree-lined streets and beautiful river views that the area offered. Not that we didn't have either of those things in Dalkeith, but somehow Peppermint Grove just felt different.

We approached the front entrance of Kane's huge house and the gates slid open to grant access to the massive property. It was such a big place for one man. I supposed that was why he'd given us all keys. He probably liked having people around to stop himself getting lonely.

"Thanks mate," Nathan said to Johnathan, as we gathered our things.

"Shall I stay and wait?" the driver asked discretely.

"No, that's fine," Kane said, picking up the framed jersey, "I'll drive her home in the morning. Thanks."

"Not a problem sir."

It suddenly occurred to me that I hadn't thought about getting home. Kane had just assumed that I was staying. Did that mean he thought this was a booty call?

"Is that okay?" he asked, seeing the worry on my face, "I just thought it would be easier if you crashed here."

"Well…" I said, still a little unsure of his intentions, "I guess, it's not a bad idea since my doona is soaked and drying on the line."

"Oh yeah, sorry about that," he laughed, climbing out of the limo.

"Are you though?" I asked, taking his outstretched hand as he assisted me out of the car.

"No, not one bit," he chuckled. The house lit up automatically as we walked silently down the travertine pathway towards the over-sized front door. Kane ushered me inside and, after kicking my shoes off, I followed him into the kitchen. He flicked on the lights and slipped off his jacket, throwing it effortlessly over the back of a chair with one hand, while he untucked his shirt with the other. He turned and looked me up and down as he unbuttoned his shirt. My stomach flipped with either excitement or anxiety, I wasn't sure which. Had

I given Kane the wrong idea by agreeing to stay the night? Had our relationship switched from platonic to sexual over the course of the evening? Perhaps I'd inadvertently tipped the scales of our friendship. If it had been anyone else, there's no way I would have gone back to their place.

"As much as I love that dress on you," he said, letting his shirt fall open to reveal his toned abs, "I think you'd be much more comfortable out of it."

The thoughts whirled through my head at the same speed as my stomach was churning. His six pack was certainly very tempting, but I'd been separated for barely a month. And besides, this was Kane. My best friends' brother.

"Oh, ahh, no, it's fine," I stuttered, stupidly surprised at the direction the night had taken. "I'm fine."

"Don't be silly," he said, waving his hands, "you can't stay in that. I'll go get you a change of clothes."
I breathed a silent sigh of relief that I'd misunderstood him.

"Yeah, okay. That'd be great, thanks," I said, relaxing again as he strutted past me, shirt billowing open, towards the stairs to his bedroom. Of course we were just friends. Why had I assumed his intentions were anything other than that?

I popped my purse on the sideboard and helped myself to some cold water from the fridge. I pulled out a small bottle of Voss and skulled half of it in one go. The champers was starting to hit me. I'd lost count of the number of glasses I'd consumed at the ball, but I'd have to guess at least ten, if not more. That equated to about two and a half bottles. Eek. I polished off the rest of my water and put the empty bottle in the recycling bin.

"Here," he said, descending the stairs, wearing nothing but pyjama shorts, with a t-shirt slung over his shoulder. My jaw dropped as I took in the full impact of his solid chest. I'd seen it a million times before, yet for some reason, tonight it seemed different. He smiled and handed me a neatly folded pile of clothes. "You can get changed in the guest room. It's all yours for tonight."

"Thanks," I squeaked, swallowing hard, as his state of undress elicited all sorts of weird responses form my body.

"No worries," he said, his voice muffled by his T.shirt as he pulled it over his head. "Feel free to have a shower if you like."

"Thanks." I turned in the direction of the guest room realising I'd need help to get out of the dress. "Umm…" I said awkwardly, "would you mind unzipping me?"

"Sure," he said with a shrug, striding over to me while I turned and tucked my hair out of the way. He paused for a moment, but I couldn't see what he was doing. "The necklace really does look good on you," he said quietly. "Are you sure I can't convince you to keep it?"

"I appreciate it Kane, but I really can't."

"Okay," he agreed sadly as he grasped the top of my dress. I felt his warm breath against the back of my neck and my whole body tingled in response. I tried hard to block out the unsettling feeling that flared in my belly. It was probably the champaign putting weird ideas into my head. He slid the zip down and squeezed my shoulders.

"There you go," he said, croakily.

"Thanks," I replied, peering over my shoulder. His head was still lowered when I turned, so our faces were only inches apart, noses so close they were almost touching.

"Yep, cool. No worries," he spluttered, taking a large step away from me. "I'll get some drinks sorted," he added, fleeing to the kitchen. Grasping to the front of my expensive hire dress, I shuffled off to the guest room, perplexed by my unexpected physical reaction to a man I'd known practically my whole life. I closed the door and stared at myself in the full-length mirror.

"What on earth was that?" I asked my reflection, who gave me no helpful response. I let the dress drop to the floor and stared at the sparkling blue stone dangling between my collarbones. Kane was right, the necklace did look good. It was almost as if it had been made just for me, but there was no way I could accept such an extravagant gift. After admiring it one last time, I removed the beautiful piece and placed it gently on the dressing table, letting my finger trail softly over the diamonds for a moment. "No Sophie," I told myself sternly, "you can't keep it."

I stepped away from the dresser and focused on the task at hand, quickly changing into Kane's spare pyjamas. I hung the dress in the wardrobe, then returned to the kitchen feeling much more sensible.

"The essentials," Kane said with a grin as he brandished a bottle of Balvenie and a bag of salt and vinegar Smiths. I laughed as he threw me the bag of potato chips. I opened the bag and threw a couple of chips into my mouth while he poured two large glasses of the whiskey. "Shall we watch a movie or something?"

"Yeah," I said with a smile, "that sounds good."

We took the whiskey and chips into Kane's huge theatre room and made ourselves comfy on the massive sofa. He flicked on his giant plasma screen and scrolled through the streaming sites.

"What do you feel like watching?" he asked, pausing his scrolling to take a gulp of his whiskey.

"I don't mind really," I said, sipping on my own drink. "Oh my gosh," I said, almost jumping to my knees as an idea hit me, "we should do the Princess Bride game."

Kane laughed loudly. "You're on," he said, searching through his library for The Princess Bride. "One sip for every 'Inconceivable', two sips for every 'as you wish' and three sips for the 'Inigo Montya' speech."

"Agreed."

"And double drinks if you miss one."

"Ugh, that rule sucks," I complained. Kane always pushed for that last rule because he knew Frankie and I started to miss things after we'd gone a few rounds.

"Hey, don't complain to me, I don't make the rules," he said with a shrug.

"You're literally the person who made the rules."

"So I am," he agreed with a grin, "I guess we're keeping it then." Kane hit play and thus the chaos began. We'd watched the movie so many times over the years that we could practically recite it word for word, however, the more we drank, the more often we missed the key phrases, and the drunker we became. Drink upon drink and childish giggles escalating with each passing minute, it was like we were teenagers again. All of the weird tension that had accumulated over the evening, had completely vanished.

We drank so much that we barely made it through the movie and by the end of it, things were a blur. At some point, cocaine had appeared, and lines had been inhaled, fuelling our drunken antics further. The alcohol and Class A's were in full control and, by the early hours of the morning, both of us had a lost our grasp on reality.

- NATHAN STONE -

Ash and I had no plans for the rest of the day and since the weather was horrible, we'd decided to treat ourselves to a lazy afternoon. After getting home from Ritchie's, we all snuggled up together while the wind blew a gale outside. Ashley; the growing bump; Fred the cat; her five kittens; and me. My unintended little family, all cozied up on our couch. I peered down at Ash, who was stretched languidly along the over-sized leather sofa, with her head resting on my lap and the cats curled up by her feet. Her belly was starting to round and, now that her morning sickness had subsided, she'd started putting some weight back on her bones again. I ran my hand lovingly over her slightly domed stomach.

"You're finally starting to show," I said delicately, hoping not to ruin the serene mood by offending her. Ash closed her book and looked up at me with a smile, resting her hand lightly on top of mine.

"Yeah," she nodded, plopping her book onto the floor, "I was thinking the same thing."

"We're gonna have to make it public soon," I told her pointedly.

"You mean there's still some people you haven't told?"

"I was wondering if you'd bring that up," I said, guiltily.

"Honestly Nath, you can't go telling everyone."

"Babe… you're in your second trimester. In another month or two, you won't be able to hide it."

Ashley sighed. "I know," she said with resignation. "I was just hoping that we'd be able to tell your mum first."

"Let's just work on getting her out of the hospital of horrors, then we'll tell her."

"You don't think telling her might give her something to look forward to?"

"Maybe," I said, remembering back to Mum's comment about meeting her grandchildren. "You could be right."

"I'm always right," she joked with a wink.

"Let's tell her next weekend then."

"Or…" she said, looking up at me with a hopeful smile, "…we could go tell her now."

"Like now, now?"

"Yeah, why not?"

"Because we just got home."

"So?" she asked with an innocent expression. I stared at her, unable to argue, yet not keen to go back out into the cold again. "Come on babe, while it's still visiting hours."

"You really want to tell her that bad huh?" I asked, touched that she cared so much about including my mum.

"Yeah, I really do."

"Okay then," I said, bending down to kiss her forehead. "Let's go see my mum."

"Yay! Thank you."

"So much for our chilled afternoon."

"Were you hoping for some Netflix and chill time babe," she teased.

"Well, I'd never say no to that."

"How about we lock that in for later?" she said with a wink.

"Deal." We hauled our arses back off the couch and faced the wild winter weather again.

In true hospital of horrors style, our visit wasn't smooth sailing. The moment we walked in, we were interrogated by the Mrs Trunchbull looking registrar behind the reception desk.

"You should know by now, Mr Stone, that we require twenty-four hours' notice for family visitations."

"We've had some exciting news," said Ash, in her sweetest voice, "and we'd really like to share it with her before anyone else does." The registrar peered sceptically over her glasses at us.

"Because of all the other people that come to visit her?" the woman asked with a faintly amused smile. We both looked at each other, unable to argue the truth of her cynical logic. Her eyes darted between the two of us as if we were naughty school kids at the principal's office. "You understand that she may not remember anything you tell her?"

"We do," I confirmed with a nod, "but we'd really like to tell her anyway." The woman stared me down, looking like she could go either way.

"Please?" pleaded Ash, resting her hand on her stomach. Mrs Trunchbull glanced down at Ashley's hand and nodded with understanding.

"Okay," she agreed reluctantly, "but not too long. Visitation hours are nearly over and she's due for her nap soon."

Ash and I exchanged a subtle look of mild concern that my mother was being forced to take naps like a child, but we both smiled and nodded obediently.

"Thank you," I said gratefully.

"Quickly," she ordered with a stern smile, "before I change my mind."

We hastily scampered down the cold, draughty corridor that led to my mum's room.

"No backing out now," I told Ash, as we reached Mum's room.

"It'll be fine," she assured me, before planting a soft kiss on my lips. I nodded and knocked on the semi-open door.

"Come in," Mum called, as I popped my head into her room to gauge the situation.

"Hey Mum," I said quietly, in case she was having a bad day.

"Nathan?" She asked with confusion.

"Yeah Mum."

"But you're so old."

I smiled and edged a little closer. "I'm thirty-six. Do you remember?

I was here a few weeks ago."

A look of clarity crossed her face.

"Oh yes," she nodded, "I do." She reached out for my hand. "It's good to see you again love."

"It's good to see you too Mum."

"Come, sit," she insisted, patting the bed. "Tell me what's been happening. Did you ever call that nurse? What was her name? Ashley? I haven't seen her again so I think they must have moved her to another ward."

I laughed loudly. "The hot nurse is the part you remember?" I teased.

"Of course!" Mum said with a chuckle. "She was perfect for you."

"Yeah, she was," I agreed with a smile. "In fact…" I jumped up and stuck my head out the door to get Ash.

- ASHLEY GRANGER -

I could hear the voices coming from Hellen's room but I couldn't make out what was being said, so I was pleasantly surprised when I saw Nathan's head pop around the door frame with a huge grin on his face.

"Come on in," he said, with a happy wink. I smiled, took his hand and rose inelegantly from the hard chair. My bump might have still been small but the bloating and backpain were well developed. I followed Nathan into the room and waved nervously at Hellen.

"Hi Hellen," I said, standing awkwardly in the doorway.

"Oh Ashley, you're here!" exclaimed Hellen with excitement. "I was starting to worry they'd moved you somewhere else."

"Mum," Nath said, perching next to her on the bed. He took her hand and glanced up at me quickly. "Ash isn't a nurse."

"She's not?"

"No Mum. She's my fiancé."

"You're engaged?!"

"We are."

"That was quick," Hellen said, with surprise. "I told you she was perfect for you."

I swallowed back a chuckle as Nathan laughed.

"No, we were already engaged when you met Ashley," he explained.

"You were?"

"Yeah."

"Well why on earth didn't you say something?" Hellen asked with an embarrassed blush, "I made her fetch me water!" Hellen was clearly mortified as she turned to me with apologetic eyes, "I'm so sorry love."

"It's fine Hellen," I said, patting her outstretched hand, "it was my idea not to tell you. We didn't want to overwhelm you."

"Oh, I see," she said, looking perplexed. "So, when is the wedding?"

"We haven't set a date yet," I explained, subconsciously cupping my belly as I sat on the other end of the bed at Hellen's encouragement. "It's all still very new."

"Okay," she said, looking between the two of us. "That's fabulous news! Congratulations."

"Thanks Mum, but we've got some other news too," Nathan told her. I could visibly see him preparing his speech in his head.

"Don't tell me I'm getting a grandbaby?" Hellen asked before Nathan had a chance to get the words out. Nathan was stunned into silence, so Hellen looked to me for confirmation. I nodded with a smile, and she hooted with excitement. "How wonderful! More tall, blonde, beautiful Stone babies!"

"Just one at this point," Nath said with a nervous laugh.

"For now," Hellen teased with a wink. "Oh Nathan, this really is the best thing I could have heard! Thank you for telling me," she said, wrapping her arms around his neck. "I've always worried you'd end up like Gareth."

"Wow. Harsh but fair," Nath said, taking the unintentional insult in his stride.

Hellen remained lucid and animated as we told her about our lives. Without going into any gory details, we filled her in on how we'd met; Artemis life; our friends; and the cats. All of the good stuff without any of the drama. It seemed as though our news had given her a whole new lease on life, and she listened with great interest. Nathan looked happier than I'd ever seen him before. He was radiating joy as he sat on the bed, gently holding his Mum's hand.

"There's something else we need to tell you Mum," he said, shuffling his body around so he could take both of her hands. "Ashley and I are moving to Cornwall."

"Really?" asked Hellen, looking forlorn. "When?"

"In about a month."

"Oh."

"But we were hoping you might want to come with us," Nathan suggested. Hellen's eyes lit up.

"What do you mean?" she asked with confusion. "You two will have enough on your plate looking after a baby, you don't need to be taking care of me too."

"Actually, there's an amazing facility down there so we'd be able to do both," said Nath, squeezing her hand.

"Really?"

"Yeah. We've been in touch with the head therapist and we're working on a way to get you there."

Tears sprung to Hellen's eyes, and she subtly wiped them away with an elegant, but bony finger.

"Are you okay?" I asked, handing her a tissue.

"Yes," she said, nodding as she wiped her eyes. "I've just been locked up in here so long," she said, patting my hand before turning to Nath. "I've missed your whole life, Nathan. I was worried that I'd miss your kids' lives too."

"I won't let that happen Mum."

- RITCHIE CARLTON -

After wandering aimlessly – or perhaps Amy-lessly - around my box-maze of a house, I couldn't stand it any longer. Part of me wanted to be there for every last second, but the fact was, with everything packed, my house was no longer a home. It was getting closer to dinner time, and I had no pots or pans to cook with, so my options were either order in or eat out. Feeling a little claustrophobic, I decided to take myself out to my local pub for dinner. It would likely be the last time I'd visit the pub that had been my regular for five years.

I rugged up and steeled myself against the cold wind, which assaulted my senses the moment I opened my front door. Winter was coming and, thankfully, I wouldn't be around for the worst of it. I'd be home in sunny Perth, sweating my balls off in forty-degree heat.

I popped the collar on my coat and adjusted my scarf as I felt an icy breeze flow down my neck. Breathing in the crisp air, I took note of everything along the street, taking mental snapshots of my life in London. It wouldn't be long until it would all feel like a distant memory, so I wanted to drink in as much of it as I could while I was still there.

As I neared the pub, I had a weird feeling I was being watched, but there was not a person in sight. I peered over my shoulder, to see if there was someone behind me and almost fell off the curb when I saw the familiar black limo rolling slowly down the road behind me.

"What the actual fuck?" I muttered, pulling my headphones out of my ears. With my ear pods in, I hadn't heard the car pull up. I stopped walking and leaned down to the passenger window. "Wind down the window Sandrine," I instructed, tapping a knuckle on the black tinted glass. I waited as the dark window slowly retracted to reveal the bony features of my sexy stalker.

"Richard," Sandrine purred through her shiny red lips, as if it wasn't unusual for her to rock up in London and stalk me.

"What are you doing here?" I asked bluntly.

"You weren't answering my calls."

"Because there's nothing left to say."

"I disagree," she said, clutching the collar of her posh fur lined coat as the icy breeze blew through her open window. "I think we still have a lot to talk about."

"Like what exactly?" I asked, instantly regretting it. Why was I encouraging her?

"Well Richard," she said, reaching out of the window to run her long, red fingernail along my jaw, "you should know by now that I'm the sort of woman who's used to getting what she wants."

"Right," I grunted, forcefully removing her finger from my face.

"And what I want is for you to come back to Paris with me and be my second in charge," she continued, unphased. I stepped back from the curb to a more appropriate distance.

"I realise that Sandrine," I said, arms folded and stance wide like a security guard, "but it's not gonna happen."

"You keep saying that, but I'm sure there must be something I can offer you to change your mind?"

"No, there's not," I said angrily, "so just drop it."

"You don't mean that."

"Yes, I do. I mean it Sandrine, you need to cut this psycho stalker bullshit and leave me alone," I barked, stomping off down the road.

"Richard, please wait," Sandrine begged. I could see her in my peripherals, scrambling to get out of the limo. I'd never seen Sandrine scramble to do anything. Fighting against the wind, she threw the door open and ran after me, her black fur coat billowing behind her. "Please Richard, I need you."
I stopped and turned to face her, fuelled by rage.

"Exactly," I snapped, "you need me, but you don't give a flying fuck about what I need." She recoiled instantly as the truth of my words hit her like a freight train.

"But, no, mon cheri-"

"I don't want to hear it Sandrine. I'm going home next week, 'coz that's what I need and if you don't like that, it's your problem to deal with, not mine."

"What is it you need at home? I'll make sure you have it in France. I'll do anything for you Richard."

"All I need is for you to let me go."

"But I came to London for you."

"I know, and it's very flattering that you're putting so much effort into this, but it needs to stop. I'm going back to Australia in a week and that's the end of the story. I'm sorry Sandrine, but this is one acquisition you're not going to procure."

- KANE THOMPSON -

"Hi Jughead!" Frankie's voice echoed through my quiet house, bringing me back to the waking world. I squinted to make my tired eyes open and peered down to find Sophie fast asleep on my bare chest.

"Oh shit," I breathed, taking stock of our situation. After a quick inspection I was disappointed to discover that, between the two of us, the only missing item of clothing was my T.shirt, so it was safe to assume that nothing exciting had occurred. Not that a drunken, coke-fuelled shag would have been my top choice for our first time together, but it was nice waking up to the possibility, however brief, that we might finally be more than friends.

"I think we have another Soph issue," Spanks babbled loudly from downstairs, as I heard her making her way through my house, looking for me. What was my intrusive sister doing here so early in the morning? It was hard to get a sense of time in my darkened bedroom, so I craned my neck around to check the clock. It was already midday.

"Shit," I muttered again, wondering how we'd managed to sleep through the entire morning and worse still, what Frankie would think if she found Soph asleep in my bed. My arm was numb from lying in an awkward position, so I gently wriggled my fingers to get the blood moving.

"I just swung past her place, and she wasn't home," Frankie continued, her voice echoing up the stairs to the master bedroom suite. "Have you heard from her? Have you seen the article?" she continued. "What were you thinking, you idiot?"

"Bugger," I whispered, carefully sliding my arm out from underneath Sophie's head to roll inelegantly out of the bed, so as not to wake her.

"Kane? Ka-aane?" Frankie hollered, as I heard her footsteps on the stairs. "Are you here?"

I ran silently to the door to intercept her before she reached my bedroom. I closed the bedroom door soundlessly behind me and jogged down the stairs to meet Frankie at the bottom, rubbing my eyes as the bright sunlight assaulted my senses.

"Hey, what's with all the noise?" I asked, trying to sound casual.

"Don't tell me you were still in bed?" she asked with surprise. Normally I was up at 5am, seizing the day, so a 12pm sleep-in was most out of character for me.

"We had a late one," I said, leading her towards the kitchen and away from the master bedroom wing.

"And a lot to drink by the looks of you."

"Yeah, a bit," I agreed with a shrug.

"Good night then?"

"Yeah, pretty fun," I said, making a B-line for my coffee machine. "Coffee?"

"No thanks, I just had one," she said, studying me with curiosity. "Did you hear what I said about Soph?'

"That she's not home?"

"Yeah," she said, furrowing her brow. "Doesn't that worry you?"

"Nope," I said, focusing on my coffee-making. "I'm sure she's fine."

"Until last night, she hadn't left her house for a month," Spanks said with concern. "What if she's done something stupid after reading the article?"

"What article?" Soph asked emerging, blurry eyed from the stairs that led to my bedroom suite. I literally face palmed at her poorly timed entrance and cringed when I saw the shocked look on Frankie's face. Her wide eyes darted between the two of us, trying to grapple with what she was seeing.

"Looks like she did do something stupid," Frankie said in disbelief. "Or someone stupid more to the point."

"It's not what you think it is," I said, handing Soph the fresh mug of coffee I'd just made for myself.

"And what do I think it is?" Frankie asked with amusement.

"Thanks," Soph said gratefully, sipping on the steaming brew.

"Something that it's not," I answered swiftly.

"We played the Princess Bride game," Soph explained to Frankie, "like the old days."

"Right," Spanks said, eying both of us sceptically.

"Nothing happened," I blurted like an idiot. "At least I don't think it did," I added under my breath.

"So, The Sunday Times is also misinformed?" she teased, pulling a newspaper out of her bag and holding it up so we could see a picture of ourselves, looking very intimate as I affixed the clasp on the tanzanite necklace. Above the photo was the headline, 'Eagle cuckhold controversy.'

"Oh shit," Soph breathed, plonking her mug on the table as she snatched the paper from Frankie's hands.

"You look hot though," Frankie told her supportively. "But you also look like a couple. Anything you two need to tell me?"

We both ignored her question as Soph read the article out loud.

"Perth playboy, Kane Thompson, showed off his latest acquisition last night at the Sunshine Children's Charity ball, and we're not talking about the $30,000 necklace he purchased in the silent auction. The high-profile bachelor arrived at Crown Casino accompanied by the ex-wife of his cousin, West Coast Eagles star Brenton Thompson," Soph paused and looked up at me.

"I guess she took the bait," I said, trying my hardest not to smile. I could see that Soph was concerned, but I was secretly pleased with the article.

"I don't even get a name," Soph muttered, "I'm just 'the ex-wife."

"There's more," said Frankie, "keep reading."

Soph's eyes dropped back down to the paper, and she continued with trepidation.

"When asked about the nature of their relationship," she read, clearing her throat awkwardly, "Thompson said it was a private matter, however failed to deny that the affair was the cause of his cousins marriage breakdown..." Soph stopped reading and lowered the paper. "Now I'm the cheater. Brenton's going to hit the roof," Soph said, handing me the paper.

"He'll be fine," I said, looking at the article for myself. Not only was it a great photo of us, but it was also a bit of a thrill knowing that people would think I'd stolen Sophie from Brenton. "He knows the truth."

"Does he?" she asked, beginning to panic, "because they've made it sound pretty convincing."

"Soph," Frankie interjected, resting her hands on Sophie's shoulders to calm her down, "he was fucking other women for the entirety of your marriage, he's hardly in a position to judge."

"There's nothing to judge," Soph said, her piercing green eyes locked on Frankie. "It sounds like you believe it."

Spanks looked between the two of us. Her gaze ran up and down Sophie who looked very suspicious wearing my PJ's, then over to me, wearing nothing but boxer shorts.

"I mean..." Frankie trailed off.

"Seriously?" Soph asked, devastated. "You've known me my whole life and you think I'd cheat on my husband?"

"No way," Spanks said adamantly, "I don't believe that part for a second, but that doesn't mean you're not..."

"Not what?"

"Well... this," she said, gesturing between the two of us. "It definitely looks like a good time was had by all."

"Frankie, really?" Soph scolded her.

"Why does it matter what I believe anyway?"

"What you believe is what matters to me the most," Sophie said urgently. "You know there's nothing going on between Kane and I right?"

My heart sank at the desperate look on Sophie's face. Was dating me really such an horrific prospect to her? I dopped the newspaper onto the table and returned to the coffee machine to brew myself a cup.

"Soph, chill," said Frankie, "it's none of my business anyway."

"That's not the point though."

"Stop stressing," I said calmly, with my back towards the girls to hide the pained expression that was surely showing on my face. "This was the plan remember?"

"Yeah, but not the affair part. What if Taj sees it?! Or if someone mentions it to him at school. I don't want him thinking I'm some sort of money-grabbing slut."

"Soph!" Exclaimed Frankie in shock. It wasn't that she was offended by Soph's language, it was just that neither of us had ever heard her talk that way before. I stopped watching my coffee pour and turned to face her, finally understanding her concerns.

"Taj will never think that of you," I said reassuringly. "He's a smart kid. He adores you and he knows you better than you realise. There's no way he'd believe any schoolyard gossip about you."

"Do you think so?"

"I know so," I told her assuredly, "but I could do an official interview to set the record straight if you like?" I offered, still feeling a little heartbroken. Sophie sighed and sat down at the table.

"No, it's fine," she said, taking a sip of her coffee.

"Are you sure? Because I'll do that if it will make you feel better."

"That's sweet Kane, thanks, but there's no need. I'm sure it will blow over."

"Okay but let me know if you change your mind."

"Why is it always the women who get torn to shreds while the guys get away with everything?" Soph asked no one in particular.

"Because that's life in a patriarchal society," answered Frankie. "But look on the bright side, this story is much better than people thinking he left you."

"Is it?"

"Yeah," said Spanks confidently. "This puts you in the drivers' seat rather than looking like some sad, forlorn divorcee."

Sophie's head darted up. "Is that what people thought of me?!"

"What?" spluttered Frankie. "No. Not at all," she said, looking to me for assistance.

"Seriously Spanks," I groaned, rolling my eyes, "way to make things worse."

"So, I'm either a pathetic loser, or a cheating slut," sulked Soph. "Great options."

I sighed, grabbed my coffee and took a seat at the table with Sophie, subtly punching Frankie in the arm on my way past. "How about we make a game plan?" I suggested.

"What do you mean?"

"Well… the media are incredibly easy to manipulate, so what if we use this story to our advantage?"

A flash of intrigue crossed her face. "What exactly do you have in mind?"

"We fight fire with fire," I said with a confidence that I didn't feel.

"I'm listening." We sat huddled around the table, both girls staring at me, open mouthed, as I explained my ridiculous idea. "You want to pretend to be a couple?" Soph clarified once I'd finished relaying my plan.

"It would get them off your back for a while," I answered with a shrug.

"But how does that solve the cheating thing?"

"I offer her an exclusive interview and straighten out the facts.

Frankie snorted loudly. "Facts that would actually be fiction you mean?" she teased unhelpfully.

"Most news is fiction anyway," I retorted.

"Fair," she agreed.

"So, what do you think Soph?" I asked, turning back to her. "Shall we beat them at their own game? Once they get bored and move onto other stories, we just let it peter out."

Soph looked to Frankie for guidance. Spanks shrugged.

"I don't think it could do any damage," she said casually, before eyeing me up and down. "As long as you don't mind the embarrassment of people thinking you're dating my idiot brother."

"Funny," I said sarcastically. "Soph?"

Soph pondered for a moment, but her silence was speaking volumes and I wasn't sure how much more my ego could handle.

"What about Taj?" she asked, leaning back in her chair.

"What do you mean?"

"I don't want him getting the wrong idea."

"Fair enough," I nodded, "so what if we tell him the truth? And Brenton too. That way we're all in the loop and no one can get the wrong idea."

"It could work," agreed Spanks. "Brenton's a dick, but he'd play along to protect Taj."

Soph thought for another minute. I could see all the possible scenarios playing over in her mind. Eventually she looked at me and nodded.

"Okay," she said, reaching out her hand. "Let's do it."

"Right then," I smiled and shook her outstretched hand. "I guess we're officially fake dating."

"I guess we are."

"I think that means you have to keep the necklace now," I teased.

Soph laughed. "Sneaky move Jughead."

"Would you expect anything less?" I asked with a wink.

She smiled, shook her head, and rolled her eyes. "I'm going home."

"Turns out my girlfriend is a bad loser," I said to Frankie, unable to stop a huge grin spreading across my face. It's not quite how I'd imagined it over the years, but I finally got to refer to Soph as 'my girlfriend'.

"I can live with that," Soph said, pushing out her chair.

"I'll drop you home," said Spanks. "You can't exactly go out in public wearing Kane's PJ's."

Sophie looked down at her outfit. "Good point," she said with a laugh. "Kane, I left the dress hanging in the wardrobe of the guestroom, along with the necklace."

"You know I'll find a way to smuggle it back into your house."

"You can try," she retorted, as Frankie turned and headed towards the door. Soph looked over her shoulder at Frankie strutting down the hallway, and then back to me. "Thanks for everything Kane. I had a really fun night."

"Me too."

"I guess we might be doing it again," she said with an awkward shrug.

"I hope so," I said with a smile, "even if it is just for show."

Soph looked down at her bare feet for a second. "Do you think this is going to be weird?"

I closed the gap between us and rested my hands firmly on her shoulders.

"Probably. But we've got this. All we can do is fight fire with fire."

"Okay," she nodded, "as long as it doesn't put you out. I can't imagine it's going to be too good for your love life."

"My love life can wait."

"Soph, come on," echoed Frankie's voice from the front door.

"I'd better go."

"Yeah, we all know what happens if we keep princess Spanks waiting," I joked. "I'll call you later to discuss our game plan."

"Sounds good," she said, planting a soft kiss on my cheek. "Thanks Jughead."

"No problem Shorty."

"Soph!" Frankie shouted again.

"Chat later," Soph said with a smile, then turned and ran down the hallway. I heard their chattering begin to fade and then the front door closed with a bang. I was once again alone in my silent house, but this time I didn't care because I was unofficially Sophie Thompson's boyfriend. Pretend or not, I was thrilled about the situation.

- SOPHIE THOMPSON -

We chugged up Stirling Highway in Frankie's crappy old VW Beetle, known as 'Bertie'. Bertie Beetle was a relic of a car, but she'd had it since Uni and refused to let the poor thing die. It was hard to believe Bertie was even running still.

"So now that it's just the two of us," said Frankie loudly, turning down the volume on the radio as if that would help reduce the noise inside the car, "what really happened with you and Jughead last night?"

"Nothing happened," I said defensively. "Honestly Spanks, we got drunk and passed out on Kane's bed."

"So, you were both trashed and somehow managed to get upstairs to the master suite together, but nothing happened?" she teased.

"Yeah," I said uncertainly. I was fairly confident nothing had happened. "I mean… this is Kane we're talking about. Besides, I woke up fully clothed."

"But he didn't."

"No, he didn't," I agreed with a blush, thinking of Kane's sculpted chest.

"If it was anyone other than Kane, I wouldn't believe this bullshit story."

"I know," I sighed with resignation. "I wouldn't believe it either."

"So does that mean you fancy my brother now?"

"Eww… no Spanks, he's practically my brother too."

"A brother that slept half-naked in the same bed as you." Frankie grinned like an evil villain.

"Gross. Stop it."

"Fine," she conceded reluctantly. "You should probably call Brenno before he sees the article."

"He's probably heard about it already. Taj had Surf Club this morning so no doubt one of the Cottesloe parents will have seen it and filled him in."

"Call him anyway," she said, winding up her window. "I think you need to get ahead of it and keep yourself in the driver's seat."

"Fair point," I agreed, fishing my phone out of my purse. I dialled Brenton and strained to hear the ringing amidst the noise inside Bertie's rickety cab, squinting as if that would help somehow.

"Ah it's the talk of the town," said Brenton without even saying hello. "Have a nice night at the ball Cinderella?"

"I take it you've seen it then?"

"We did," he confirmed in a tone that indicated Taj was in hearing distance.

"Taj saw it too?"

"Yep," he said apologetically, "but don't worry, it's taken care of."

I breathed a sigh of relief. "Thanks Brenton."

"All good."

"You know it's bullshit right?"

"Of course I do," he laughed as if Kane and I being a couple was a ridiculous prospect. "Do you want to talk to Taj?"

"Sure. Thanks," I said, before Brenton handed the phone over to my boy.

"Hi Mummy," said Taj happily.

"Hey baby, how was Surf Club?"

"It was good. Daddy took me for breakfast afterwards and we saw you in the paper with Uncle Kane."

"Yeah, we went to a ball together."

"You looked really pretty."

"Aww thanks honey," I said, my heart melting at my sweet boy.

"Was it fun?"

"It was a lot of fun, and Uncle Kane got a present for you," I said, realising I'd left Brenton's jersey at Kane's place.

"Ooh, what is it?"

"I can't tell you, it's a surprise. He'll bring it around when you're back home."

"Okay," he said cheerfully. "Daddy wants to talk to you again. Love you Mummy."

"Love you too gorgeous."

"How about you go have some screen time," Brenton suggested to

Taj in the background, "I'll come and play when I've finished chatting to Mummy."

"Okay!" I heard Taj say excitedly.

"Hey," said Brenton into the phone.

"Hey."

"We should probably chat but – where are you? It's so noisy."

"I'm in Bertie with Spanks."

"Uh-huh," he said knowingly. "I wish she would sell that fucking thing."

"Don't let her hear you say that," I teased, flashing a wink at Frankie.

"Probably hard to hear in that crap heap, but Taj didn't see the article, just the photo so, he's fine."

"Okay, thanks."

"Although headlines like that aren't ideal Soph. What if the kids at school say something to him?"

"I know Brenton, trust me, that was the first thing I thought about. That reporter had it in for me. It was as if she was trying to find a way to make me look bad. That's why Kane stepped in."

"Well, there's nothing we can do about it now, so we'll just have to ride the wave."

"Actually…" I said nervously, "Kane, Spanks and I had a chat this morning and we've got a bit of a plan."

"You, and two people who aren't even involved have come up with a plan, have you?"

"Don't be like that, we were just spit balling solutions."

"Fine," he sighed impatiently, "and what's the plan?"

"Well… we figured it was best to roll with it until they lose interest."

"What does that mean exactly?"

"We just pretend that Kane and I are a couple, but that it only started after we split."

Brenton laughed scornfully. "That's the dumbest idea I've ever heard."

"Why?"

"You want to diffuse a fake story by pretending it's real?"

"Yeah."

"Look, Soph, you're free to do whatever you want, but you need to think about how this will effect Taj."

"All I ever think about is how things effect Taj," I snapped defensively, "can you say the same? How did your cheating effect Taj, Brenton? Have you ever thought about that? Your behaviour destroyed our family and that had a bigger impact on him than any fake news story ever could."

Brenton fell silent. I'd half expected him to kick-off an argument but instead, he sighed loudly. "Fine."

"Fine?"

"Yes, fine. You're right. I'll go along with whatever story you want to spin," he said with resignation. "Even if it's dumb as fuck."

- NATHAN STONE -

The furious pre-winter wind was putting on quite the show. On the other side of our bedroom window, silhouettes of trees thrashed soundlessly against the backdrop of a hazy orange sunrise. Over in Holland Park, the icy breeze whipped the loose leaves into a frenzy of whirlwinds, while the bare trees from whence they had fallen, were ravaged by the savage November wind. With Ashley cuddled into my bare chest, I watched, mesmerised, as Holland Park was brutalised by the Autumn storm.

"What are you thinking?" Ash asked peering up at me through her long eyelashes.

"I'm thinking that we've still got a few hours to kill before I have to get the roast on," I joked sliding my hands under the covers to explore her naked body.

"Hmm…" she mumbled sleepily, "I think I might have an idea how to pass the time."

"Me too," I muttered, letting my fingers trail over her nipples. She moaned and pressed her body against mine. I was primed to go so I didn't need any further encouragement. I rolled on top of her and held myself up to prevent my body weight pressing down on her belly. With her stomach now visibly domed, I was paranoid that I'd squish our unborn child. Most of my effort was focused on holding myself at a safe distance, which proved to be much harder than it sounded. Ash wrapped her legs around my waist, trying to pull me closer.

"What are you doing?" she asked, arching her body towards mine.

"I'm trying not to squash the baby."

She laughed and gently pushed me off her.

"Okay then, if you're going to be weird about it, I'll go on top."

"Yes boss," I agreed eagerly, lying back against the pillow. She knelt over me, and I gripped her hips to steady her as she lowered herself onto me. We both groaned with pleasure, and she began moving steadily. In that position I had a perfect view of her breasts, and they were so round and bouncy I couldn't resist. I grabbed one in each hand and massaged them while she moved. As I did so, a flush crept across her chest and, almost immediately, she was shaking with pleasure.

"Oh my god," she moaned, seemingly taken by surprise by the sudden orgasm.

"Well, that was easy," I said with a laugh, as her hands gripped my chest for stability.

"Whoa," she breathed, looking disoriented. "That was intense. It must be the pregnancy hormones or something."

"How about we really put it to the test?" I teased.

"Absolutely," she said with a husky laugh, leaning down to kiss me. Her long hair encased our faces, and I crushed her mouth to mine as we worked our way into round two.

A few hours later, the roast was on and we were both showered, dressed, and ready for the Granger's arrival. They'd visited the apartment before but was the first time they'd come for a Sunday lunch. Us hosting this particular Sunday lunch also served as good cover to keep Ash away from her folks' place. Their house was full swing with 'party' preparations, and we didn't want Ash getting suspicious.

"Where are my babies?" Mary said, as soon as Ash opened the door to greet them.

"Hi Mum, great to see you too," said Ash sarcastically as Mary looked past her in search of her soon-to-be fur babies.

"Sorry love," she apologised, pecking Ash on the cheek, "I'm just so excited to see them. Hi Nathan love," she said, as I emerged from the kitchen, "lunch smells great."

"Thanks Mary," I said, giving her a kiss on the cheek. "The kittens are in the laundry."

"Great!" Mary made a B-Line to the laundry to see the kittens, while Geoff laughed and wrapped Ash in a fatherly hug.

"Hey Cupcake," he said, planting a firm kiss on her forehead. "How are you feeling?"

"I'm fine Dad, thanks."

"Hi Hotshot," Geoff said, gripping my hand in a firm handshake which somehow turned into a man-hug. "How's things?" he asked, patting my back in his dad-like manner.

"Not bad."

"Everything done at the cabin now?" he asked, in reference to the Cornwall house, which had required some upgrades ahead of our arrival.

"Yeah, pretty much. The nursery is done and that's the most important thing."

"Sure is."

"Hey babe," I said, turning to Ash, "why don't you show your dad the residents lounge and grab a bottle of wine on my tab while you're there?" I needed to get rid of her for a few minutes so I could chat with Mary about the party.

"But we have a whole wine rack here," she said, gesturing towards our incredibly comprehensive wine collection.

"Yeah, but he'll love the wine selection there."

"Will he?" she asked, looking at me like I was mental.

"Yeah, sounds great," said Geoff playing along. "Let's go take a look Cupcake."

"But-"

"Come on, I could do with a walk anyway."

Ashley's brow furrowed with suspicion, and she glanced between me and her father. I shrugged and nodded my encouragement.

"Okaaaay," she agreed, still obviously confused.

"Have fun," I said, with a reassuring smile, "lunch will be ready by the time you get back."

"Great!" said Geoff, taking her hand and pulling her towards the front door. "Let's get going."

"Bye," Ash called as I made my way back to the kitchen.

"Bye babe," I called behind me. Seconds later I heard the front door bang closed and Mary immediately emerged from the laundry, darting into the kitchen to join me.

"Is there anything left to be done for the wedding?" she asked in a whisper.

"I think we're all good," I said at a normal volume, then counted my tasks off on my fingers. "The Celebrant is locked in; the cake will be delivered on the day; the band has confirmed; and the boys and I are going to pick up our suits this week. Did the caterers send through the final menu?"

"They did, and they've also found that champaign you asked for."

"Nicolas Feuillatte? Great!"

"Are you sure you don't want the Bollinger?"

"No, this one is Ashley's favourite," I assured her. "Besides, I think she'd catch on if we served Bollinger at a going away party."

"Good point," she agreed with a nod, before peering towards the door over-cautiously. "Ashley's dress is at my place and Kat will bring the bridesmaid dresses with her on the day."

"Awesome," I said with excitement. "And what about marquee set-up? Is that under control or will Geoff need help with that?"

"We've got a party hire company organising all of that this week, including a dance-floor, a stage, and all the fairy lights."

"Perfect!"

"Oh Nathan, she's going to be so surprised."

"Yeah, she'll definitely be surprised," I said nervously. "I just hope it's a good surprise and not a bad one. I don't want our marriage end before it's even begun."

"Don't be silly. She'll love it."

"Thanks for the tour, Muffin," we heard Geoff say loudly from beyond the front door. "We should go back down there for a drink after lunch."

Mary and I quickly sprung into action. She grabbed the pile of plates and set them on the table while I rattled around in the cutlery draw.

"Why are you shouting?" Ash asked her father, as the door clicked open. "Is it your 20/20 hearing again?" she teased.

"I have perfect hearing," Geoff answered defensively.

"Sure you do Papa Bear."

- ASHLEY GRANGER -

When I walked into the kitchen, Mum and Nathan were busy setting up the table for lunch, however they hadn't gotten very far in the ten minutes we'd been downstairs. They both smiled guiltily and buzzed back and forth from the bench to the table.

"What have you guys been up to?" I asked, noting their distinct lack of progress. "Doesn't look like you've gotten very far."

"Ah, we've just been too busy gasbagging," said my Mum suspiciously.

"About what?" I asked, suddenly curious to know what they'd been doing for the last ten minutes.

"Just chatting about the party," said Nath casually.

"Everything good to go?" I asked, grabbing a bowl of potatoes off the bench to help expedite the table set-up.

"All set," answered Nathan succinctly. "Peas are up."

"I'm on it," I said, popping the potatoes down and returning to the bench to collect the peas. Nath gave me a quick peck on the cheek as he handed them over.

"And what did you think of the resident lounge Geoff?" he asked as Dad joined us in the kitchen. "Pretty good selection huh?"

"Very good indeed," Dad replied, looking genuinely impressed. "They've got some top-quality bottles there. I was thinking we should go down for a quick drink after lunch."

"Sounds like a plan," said Nath as he proudly carried the roast lamb over to the table, "The lamb is ready, so take your seats."

We all got stuck in, piling our plates with much more food than strictly necessary, mine primarily vegetables. I was still finding it hard to get my head around the meat thing.

"Ashley, I thought you were supposed to be eating more meat," said Mum, noticing the plant-heavy contents on my plate.

"I am eating meat."

"That's barely anything," she said, picking up the tongs and scooping up a few extra slices of lamb. "Here," she said, plopping the lamb onto my already full plate.

"Mum!"

"Your baby needs a healthy Mama, so eat up,"

Appalled by my mothers behaviour, I looked over at Nathan for help. Mid gravy pour, he glanced up, smiled and then shrugged as if he agreed with her. Realising it was not the response I was seeking, his attention lingered longer on me than it should have, and he ended up drowning his plate in gravy.

"Bugger," he said, doing his best to salvage his gravy-laden meal.

"You're on their side?" I asked him incredulously. His head snapped up immediately.

"I'm always on your side," he replied quickly, "...but I do think you should eat the meat."

"You lot are infuriating," I sighed with frustration. Why did everyone care so much about my diet?

"And you're stubborn as a mule," Nath teased with a smile, while my parents ate quietly so as not to draw attention to themselves.

"You drive me insane sometimes," I told him grumpily.

"I know, but I think you're adorable when you're grumpy so I can live with that."

I stared daggers at him, trying not to get won over by his cheeky charm. How did he manage to be so sweet and yet so aggravating at the same time?

"So, Nathan," Mum said, breaking the tension, "when will the kittens be ready to leave Fred? We've got their little room all set up."

"How about we bring them over the weekend after the party?"

"Ooh, yes please!" Mum said excitedly, "I can't wait."

"I think Fred will be relieved to have less children to look after."

"Yes, she does look quite exhausted," Mum agreed.

"I know the feeling," I joked, stabbing a piece of broccoli with my fork.

"Don't forget your lamb Ashley," said my mother, as if I was a disobedient eight-year-old.

"No mother," I replied with a sweet smile, "and after that I shall go upstairs and finish my homework."

"No need to be sassy young lady."

"Oh my god Mum," I said with exasperation, dropping my fork with a clatter. "I'm a grown woman, and I'm about to have a baby. I think you can stop treating me like a child now."

"I wasn't meaning to treat you like a child," she said humbly, "I'm just worried about your health. I don't want you going through any more dramas." My heart melted when I realised the motivation behind her nagging. I smiled and rested my hand on top of hers.

"I love you," I said, with tears in my eyes, "and I love that you care so much about me, but you don't need to worry anymore. I've got it under control. And I've also got nurse Nathan who won't let me do anything that would risk myself or the baby."

"Too right," said Nath, sounding oddly like Ritchie.

"I know you do, but that doesn't stop me from worrying. I just want you two to have your happy ending."

"No endings," said Nathan with a mouthful of meat, "this is just the beginning."

"So it is," agreed my dad, while Mum and I shared a moment of womanly understanding.

"We will Mama Bear," I assured her, giving her hand a squeeze, "our happily ever after has already begun."

"It sure has," said Mum.

"We told my mum yesterday," Nathan said to dad, who had been kept abreast of all the dramas with trying to relocate Hellen.

"That's great lad," he said encouragingly. "How did she take it."

"She was really pleased."

"Wonderful."

"Actually Dad…" I interrupted, "we've got a little favour to ask."

"Oh yes?"

"Only if you're comfortable with it," Nathan added quickly.

"We were hoping you might be able to look into Hellen's admission contract and see if you can find a loophole so we can have her assessed by Doctor Blakely at the Priory?"

"Sure can cupcake," said Geoff, before looking over to Nath, "have you got the documents here?"

"Yeah, I do," nodded Nath. "I'll grab them out after lunch."

"Perfect," said Dad with an approving nod. "Don't worry Hotshot, we'll have your mum out of there before you leave for Cornwall."

"Thanks Geoff," said Nath, looking uncharacteristically emotional.

"You're family now," said my dad, patting Nathan on the arm, "and we Granger's take care of our own."

- RITCHIE CARLTON -

Ryan and I watched as the moving truck chugged off down the street carrying all my earthly possessions. I couldn't believe it was nearly all over. Ten years of my life were coming to an end. An entire decade, done and dusted, five of which I'd spent in this house.

"Job done," Ryza said, slapping my back. "Now it's time to celebrate."

"Yeah," I agreed, as we dawdled back into the empty house. I sighed, looking around the lounge room. All that remained was my suitcase and a carry-on, which would come with me to Kat and Ryan's place.

"You right mate?" Ryan asked, grabbing the handle of my suitcase.

"I can't believe it's all over."

"Yeah, but onto a new chapter huh?" he said, patting my shoulder. "No psycho Sandrine and no reminders of Aims."

"True," I agreed half-heartedly. I was excited to be going home, but it was hard to say goodbye to the semi-detached I'd called home for the last five years, let alone the people who'd become more like family than friends.

"I'll put these in the car," said Ryza, wheeling my cases towards the front door. "Take as long as you need."

"Thanks mate." I wandered slowly from room to room. Amy was everywhere. We'd created memories in every single room. Some good memories, some bad, but the house was intrinsically linked to my non-relationship with that woman. Once I closed that front door, I'd never step foot inside the place again and all those moments we'd shared would be gone forever.

"Bye Aims," I said to the empty house. "I hope you've found some peace."

As I strode towards the front door, my footsteps echoed through the empty house. I stopped at the front door, with my fingers resting on the door handle, and turned to take one last glance around my home. My chest tightened with sadness. It was the final farewell. With a deep breath, I flicked off the light and closed the door behind me for the last time. It was time to move forwards. Australia was calling.

- Chapter 2 -

Perth: Chunder Down Under

- KANE THOMPSON -

We were a week into our 'pretend couple' plan, and our little charade was ticking along nicely. My exclusive interview with the bitchy reporter from the Sunday Times seemed to do the trick, and the excitement around our night at the ball began to fade into the background to make way for more scandalous stories. All-in-all, it had been relatively simple and better yet, hadn't required much change in routine for either of us.

The first weekend, however, was a little more awkward. We were both due to attend a mutual friend's fiftieth birthday in Fremantle, and everyone was now expecting us to attend together. Outside of our direct sphere, no one else knew the story was fake, so we had to keep up pretenses for our first public outing as 'a couple'.

The sun was beginning to set over the water and the warehouse brewery looked like it was already pumping. Although the venue was a bit working-class for my taste, I had to admit that the old shipping shed did have a pretty cool vibe. The place was so busy that we couldn't find parking directly outside and had to do a lap around the carparks before we finally found a spot behind the markets. The market building was another re-purposed shipping warehouse known as the B-Shed, but this one was like a ghost town. Considering the amount of cars in the carpark, it was hard to believe the markets were so empty. We wandered down the empty alleyways, passing the quiet stalls and unoccupied shops. It was very different to the bustling hub it had been when I was a kid.

"You okay?" I asked Soph, as she fidgeted nervously. Her big green eyes shimmered with worry.

"Do you think we'll be able to pull this off?"

"We'll be fine," I said, taking her hand as we walked. "Just stick with the story and avoid giving any unnecessary details."

"No unnecessary details? You've met me, right?" she joked flatly.

"I have faith in you," I said with a wink. "We know each other well enough to make it believable."

"True," she agreed, taking a deep breath.

"Just a couple of weeks and it will all blow over," I said, squeezing her hand. "By the time Sean and Isla's wedding rolls around, everyone will have forgotten about us."

"Except that you're the best man and I'm the maid of honour."

"Well, there is that," I laughed, leading her across the road towards the huge brewery. We had a few interested looks from people standing by the entrance, but that was nothing unusual for me. Sophie on the other hand, wasn't a fan of being in the spotlight. I felt her hand tighten around mine, so I gave her a confident smile and ignored the animated whispers emanating from a group of twenty-something's as we passed by.

"Just breathe," I instructed Soph quietly.

"I'm trying," she said with a fake smile.

"At least now it's good gossip," I teased as we walked through the huge entry doors and past the big brass fermenting tanks.

"All hail Kane, the Master of the Perth social universe," she teased sarcastically.

"You know it," I laughed, throwing my arm over her shoulder as I spotted the birthday boy. I directed Soph towards the party, and then greeted Jackson. "Happy Birthday old fella," I teased, slapping him on the back as I handed over his present.

"Hey, watch it. You're only a few years behind me mate," he said, peering inside the gift-bag at the bottle of Grange I'd bought him. "Very nice," he said, impressed.

"Fifty years old, just like you."

"Cheeky fucker," he said, punching my arm. "Thanks Thommo."

"It's from both of us," I said, waving towards Soph.

"Ah yes, the couple of the century," he said with a laugh, pulling Soph in for a hug.

"Happy Birthday Jacko," said Soph awkwardly.

"Thanks love," he said with a wink. "The whole of Perth has been talking about you two," he blathered, sculling the remainder of his beer. "All I can say, is it's about fucking time."

"Huh, yeah," I said much more loudly than I'd intended.

"You landed on your feet miss," Jackson said to Soph with a conspiratorial smile. "From a footy player to the Bachelor of the year. A definite upgrade if you ask me."

"Well, I could do with a drink," I interjected as Sophie's face flared

red. "What can I get you Jacko?"

"Hit me with a tequila slammer, brother."

"Done," I said, taking Soph's hand and dragging her away from Jacko, who swiftly moved on to his next guests like the gracious host he was. We found a spot at the bar, and I took a cursory glance around me to make sure no one we knew was in hearing distance. "So far, so good," I whispered to Soph as the bartender approached.

"What can I get you guys?"

"Ladies first," I said, gesturing at Soph.

"Oh, prosecco please."

"A Single Fin for me, and a tequila slammer thanks mate."

"Sure thing," said the barman as he got to work on our order. A beefy Maori guy barged his way through the heaving crowd and pushed me off-balance. I reached around Soph to steady myself against the bar so I wouldn't squash her, but we were pressed so closely together that I was breathing down her neck.

"Sorry," I said, hearing her breath catch in her throat as she peered over her shoulder at me. In our awkward and overly intimate arrangement, her lips were only a small distance from mine. It would have been easy for me to kiss her, but if I did that, I'd risk ruining everything.

"No worries," she mumbled, her big green eyes boring into my soul, and making it very hard to resist my urges. I straightened myself up again and made the sensible decision to put some distance between our bodies. Soph turned her attention back to the barman as he lined our drinks up on the bar.

"There you go guys," he said, ringing up our total on the till.

"I'll get this round," I told Soph when she attempted to give me some money. "I am your boyfriend after all."

"Apparently so," she answered with a bashful smile.

"Cheers," I said handing the bar guy the cash. We took our drinks out to the beer garden where the rest of the party guests were laughing and chatting jovially. "Jacko," I said, handing over his shot. "Bottoms up mate."

"Thanks Thommo!" He said, before swallowing back the fiery liquid. Jackson punctuated his drink with a loud exhale. "Woo!" he whooped, plonking the empty shot glass onto the nearest table. "I guess I'd better go circulate, but I'll swing back round later."

"Sure thing," I said, slapping him on the back as I spotted Sean and Isla sitting at one of the bench tables further down the patio. "Shall we join them?" I asked Soph, nodding towards our friends.

"God yes," she agreed with relief. I took her hand and led her to the table. The usual greetings and hugs ensued, then when Sophie and I sat down on opposite sides of table, our kneecaps smashed against each other.

"Ow!" she said with pained laugh as she rubbed her injured knee.

"Why is furniture never made with tall people in mind?!" I joked.

"Right?!" Soph agreed, sipping on her bubbly. "Tall person furniture could be a new business venture for you perhaps?"

We shared a chuckle and then eased into the group conversation. As everyone chatted, I wasn't listening to a thing that was being said. My focus was on Sophie. I couldn't take my eyes off her. I knew our whole couple charade was fake, but why did it feel so real? I took a quick glance up the table and noticed that Seany had caught me staring at my pretend girlfriend. I shot him an innocent shrug, but he shook his head and rolled his eyes with a smile.

More friends arrived and the girls trotted off to do their girl gossip circle, so Sean and I took another trip to the bar for our next round.

"Do you think she'll be able to pull this off?" Sean asked, nodding towards Soph as we waited for our drinks. I followed his gaze and studied my fake girlfriend for a moment. She was a notoriously bad liar, but she was also exceptional at keeping up appearances, so the two traits sort of cancelled each other out. We'd been pretty convincing up until that point, but would she be able to keep it up for long enough to fool our wider circle of acquaintances? Most of this crew had known us for years. Would they really believe that after thirty-odd years of knowing each other, the two of us had miraculously realised we were in love?

"Honestly, I don't know," I said, noticing a well-disguised frown cross Soph's brow. "She's doing okay so far, but it's hard to tell."

"Either way, it'll be interesting," joked Sean.

"Ah, the puppy dog stare," said Colin Mendelson, joining Sean and I at the bar. "I remember what it was like in the early days. Enjoy that while it lasts mate," he said, punching my arm.

"Huh?" I asked, confused.

"Sophie," he said, tilting his head in the direction I'd been staring. "You're still in the lovestruck stage I see."

"Oh, yeah. I guess we're still getting used to it," I admitted honestly.

"I'm surprised," Colin mused, sipping on his beer, "I always thought it was inevitable myself."

"What do you mean?" I asked curiously.

"It was obvious that you two had a strong connection. Especially before she and Brenno got hitched. I guess we all figured you'd eventually be the Thompson she'd end up with."

"Really?" I asked, surprised. I turned to Sean, who was grinning like an idiot. "I never knew you all thought that," I said pointedly.

"Oh, come on Thommo," Colin chortled, "there was no hiding the sparks between the two of you."

"Right," I said, wondering why no one had ever said anything before now.

"But at least you finally got your shit together," Colin continued, clearly on a roll and revelling in being the one to break the news to me. "Better late than never huh?"

"Better late than never," repeated Sean with a sage nod.

"I suppose so," I said, gritting my teeth to curb my annoyance at Seany.

"Don't leave it too long this time though," Colin prattled on. "Lock her down as soon as her divorce is final. You don't want to let a girl like that slip through your fingers twice."

"Yeah," I agreed, lost for words. Had my feelings really been that obvious all these years?

"I'm honestly surprised you ever let Brenton beat you to the punch in the first place," Colin babbled cluelessly.

"Well, he is a bit of an idiot," interjected Sean gleefully. "I mean, what sort of dumb arse would wait thirty years to admit how he feels?" Colin laughed heartily and Seany threw me a self-righteous smile, enjoying his little game of torture.

"And on that note," I said, unimpressed with my so-called best friend, "I'm taking my girlfriend another drink. Excuse me boys."

- SOPHIE THOMPSON -

I stood with the girls chatting and catching up on the latest gossip. I always found this part incredibly tedious, but I was well versed in smiling politely and looking sufficiently scandalised when someone dropped a piece of juicy news. These were the people that Isla and I referred to as our 'fake friends'. They were mostly the wives and girlfriends of successful men and didn't tend to have much going on in their own lives. The only thing any of us had in common was the fact that we all lived in the Western Suburbs of Perth.

There was Caitlin, a pointy nosed bottle-blonde, with a frozen forehead and cheek bones so pronounced they were obviously implants. She was married to Henry Rosendorf, a high-flying Investment Banker who was usually too busy to attend events with her. Caitlin had such a sharp personality that it could have cut through steel.

Then there was Adele, a stunning redhead with plump lips and huge boobs that looked like they'd been glued onto her size zero body. She was the nicer of the two, but still someone I wouldn't want to cross. Adele had made her way around the men in the circle and eventually married one of Brenton's teammates, which meant that we'd attended a lot of events together over the years.

Caitlin, Adele and most of the other ladies in our fake friends circle, spent their days brunching and beautifying themselves. They didn't have much to concentrate on outside of their husbands and children so gossip was the only thing that gave them pleasure and purpose. Not that I was one to judge. I had nothing in my life outside of Taj so it was lucky I wasn't as vacuous as them. At least, I hoped I wasn't.

"Not exactly the nicest venue, is it?" said Caitlin in hushed tones.

"Yes, it's got a definite working-class vibe," agreed Adele. "Why on earth didn't he have it at the yacht club?"

"Maybe he wanted to do something different for a change," I said with a shrug, forgetting my Western Suburbs etiquette. The girls looked at me horrified.

"Why would he want a change from the yacht club?" asked Adele, "that's the best venue in Perth."

"I don't know."

"Who knows why men ever do anything," said Isla with her best fake chuckle.

"So true," agreed Caitlin with a posh laugh.

"And speaking of men," said Adele with a raised brow, "what's happening with you and Kane?" she asked, glancing hungrily over at my fake boyfriend who was chatting with a couple of the boys at the bar.

"I don't know," I stuttered awkwardly, nervous from all the attention.

"Yes, you do," Isla piped up, not helping in the least.

"Nothing serious at this stage," I said, shooting Isla a dirty look. "We're just figuring it out as we go."

"You certainly seemed pretty cozy in that newspaper photo," Adele replied with a haughty grin. "It looked like more than a casual fling to me."

"Yes, it did," teased Isla, seizing the opportunity to torture me a little, "do we need to prepare for another wedding?"

"Hardly," I shot back quickly, before remembering myself. "It's still very new."

"And you're worried you're going to jinx it," said Adele, nodding sagely as if she knew what was going on.

"That's right," I agreed, latching onto her viable explanation for my sketchy behaviour.

"Very smart," Caitlin agreed. "Kane has his choice of women, so you don't want to assume anything until you've locked him down."

"Umm…" I muttered, not sure how to respond to her veiled insult.

"Although," said Adele, "I don't think you have anything to worry about there. He may be way out of your league, but he's clearly in love with you."

"Is he?" I asked, taken aback by the non-insulting part of her comment. "What makes you think that?"

"The man has been pining after you for years honey," Adele said with a casual shrug. "None of the rest of us could ever match up to his wonderful Sophie."

"What do you mean?"

Caitlin laughed snidely. "Oh, don't play coy with us," she said, with a sly smile. "You should be proud that you had such a good catch on the backburner. And he's definitely an upgrade on the last one."

"What?"

"A football player is hardly a high-ticket husband," she sneered, insulting both me and Adele simultaneously. "A handsome, self-made millionaire on the other hand… well, that's positively top-of-the-line." My jaw hit the floor as I stared at Caitlin in disbelief.

"There's nothing wrong with marrying a football player," Adele said defensively.

"Sorry ladies am I interrupting?" asked Kane, sliding in next to me with an espresso martini in each hand. "I was hoping to borrow my girlfriend for a moment," he said with his most charming smile as he handed Isla and I a martini each.

"Oh absolutely," twittered Adele, fluttering her long eyelashes at Kane, who raised a subtle eyebrow at the blatant flirting.

"We wouldn't dream of keeping her from you," Caitlin sneered without losing a beat.

"I'll bring her back in one piece, I promise," he said with a wink as he rested his hands on my shoulders to lead me away from the group. "Oh Isla," he called over his shoulder, "Seany was looking for you," he added before guiding me out of the throng, "I'm not sure where he went."

"Thank you," said Isla gratefully, taking the opportunity to escape from the gossip circle.

I followed Kane away from the party area, towards the brewery section of the building. I took a large gulp of my espresso martini and breathed out the rich coffee fumes.

"Yum," I said, before taking another sip. "Where are we going?"

"No idea," he said with a childish grin, "you girls just looked like you needed saving."

"My very own knight in shining armor," I teased.

"At your service my lady," he joked with a sweeping bow. "Is there anything else you need?"

"Actually, you know what would go well with this espresso martini?"

"A woodfired pizza?" he asked, motioning towards the pizza oven in the kitchen area.

"No, a cigarette."

"That bad, is it?"

"Yep," I confirmed with nod.

"Okay, let's get you a pack then."

"Aren't you going to try and talk me out of it?"

"Why?"

"Because normally you're the responsible one."

"Yeah… I guess you've been a bad influence on me lately," he teased, before making his way towards the vending machine tucked away in the back corner of the pub. I pulled out my purse, but Kane had cash ready to go. He brandished his fifty dollar note and leaned over me to feed it into the machine.

"I've got this," he said with a smile, our faces so close I could feel his breath on my cheek.

"Thanks," I squeaked, feeling weird about our overly intimate position. "You know you don't have to pay for everything right?"

"I want to," he said simply, as his change clattered into the tray. Kane bent down to retrieve the coins and when he straightened back up, I could feel the full length of his solid body pressed against mine. Goosebumps erupted all over my skin. Were they because of Kane, or the cold breeze from air-conditioning vent above us?

Kane stood stock still, grasping his change in one hand. There was an indistinguishable look on his face and when I looked up into his blue eyes, his gaze was so penetrating it made my heart jump into my throat.

If it had been any other man, I would have assumed he was about to kiss me. But it was Kane, so there must have been something else on his mind. Either that, or he was keeping up the pretence of us being a couple. Regardless, I was frozen to the spot, waiting to see what was going to happen next.

The cigarette machine clunked as the pack dropped into the dispenser, but neither of us reached for it. Butterflies fluttered madly in my stomach as we stood staring at each other. Why was he suddenly making me feel so nervous? Kane had always been my safe zone, but at that moment, I felt more vulnerable than ever.

The breeze from the aircon blew a wayward piece of hair into my face and before I had a chance to remove it, Kane reached out and brushed it away.

"Thanks," I said in a croaky whisper, choking on my own voice as his hand slid down the nape of my neck. My heart thudded wildly, and my chest was so tight that I'd almost stopped breathing. What the hell was happening? This was all just an act, so why was I flipping out?

"What's going on here then?" Seany asked, breaking the unfamiliar tension. "You know you only have to do the couple thing in public right? Kinda defeats the purpose if you do it in private."
I stepped away from Kane, my face glowing red in humiliation, but he remained where he was, turning to Sean with a cool expression.

"Just grabbing some smokes for Soph," he said with a casual shrug, as if nothing unusual had occurred. Sean looked down at the pack that was still sitting in the machine. He raised one ginger brow, then cast us both a sceptical glance.

"Righto."

"What are you doing out here anyway?" Kane asked Sean, turning the tables. "You taken up smoking?"

"Nah, I was taking a slash," he said, pointing at the toilets right next to us.

"Oh right," Kane said, as we peered at each other awkwardly. "Well," he said, bending down to retrieve my cigarettes, "I believe these are yours."

"Thanks," I said, taking the pack from his outstretched hand. "I'll see you back in there," I added awkwardly, before quickly fleeing out the big doors and onto the harbour promenade. With Summer approaching, the air was warm, and the seagulls were still loitering overhead perched on light poles and railings. I strolled down to the water where the reflection of the moon and harbour lights were twinkling like stars in the softly undulating water.

I leaned against one of the big wooden posts and opened my packet of cigarettes. It wasn't until I'd retrieved one, that it finally occurred to me I didn't have a lighter. One of the traps of being a casual smoker was that I didn't do it often enough to warrant carrying a lighter.

"Bugger," I muttered searching the promenade for a proper smoker. I spotted a couple sitting down near the Leeuwin Ship docked on the jetty, so I headed towards them when a familiar shadow approached from the brightly lit beer garden and intercepted me.

"Thought you might need these," Kane said, walking towards me with a cigarette lighter and another espresso martini. I took the lighter from his hand and looked up at him curiously.

"Where did you get this?" I asked, lighting up my cigarette.

"I bought it off the bar guy," he said with a shrug.

"You just buy anything you want huh?" I asked, breathing out the calming smoke as he held out the martini glass.

"Yep," he shrugged as I took the drink from his hand. "Surely you already knew that about me?"

"I guess I did," I agreed taking a long sip of my drink, followed by another drag of my cigarette. "I don't think I can go back in there."

"Then we'll stay out here," he said, grabbing a couple of empty chairs from the beer garden just as Caitlin and Adele stepped outside. I quickly ditched what was left of my cigarette and took a large gulp of my drink to erase the scent of smoke from my breath.

"Oh, here you are," Caitlin called, setting a direct trajectory towards us. There was no escaping now. Kane groaned under his breath which made me snigger like a child. "We were wondering where you two had gotten to," Caitlin continued, oblivious to our annoyance at her presence. "Sneaking a little private time, were you?"

"Trying to," I answered with a passive aggressive grin, fake enough to match hers.

"We're still in the honeymoon phase," said Kane, wrapping his arm around my waist and pulling my body tight against his. "I just can't keep my hands off her," he joked, shooting me a playful wink.

"We should leave you to it," said Adele apologetically, attempting to usher Caitlin back inside.

"It's so lovely that you've found someone too Soph," Caitlin said with that bitchy tone of hers, ignoring Adele's hint. "I guess it makes things much easier when you've both got new partners."

"What do you mean?" I asked, taking the bait.

"Brenton's new girlfriend," Adele muttered regretfully, stealing Caitlin's thunder before she had a chance to rub it in.

My feelings must have been clear on my face because Caitlin's eyes sparkled with sadistic pleasure. "Oh, you mean you don't know?" she asked with her icy smile.

I felt Kane's grasp tighten around my waist and I knew instantly why Caitlin had been so determined to track me down.

"She knows," Kane intervened sternly, giving Caitlin the same reproachful look he'd given the reporter that night at the charity ball.

"It just isn't really anyone else's business, is it?"

"No, I suppose not," Caitlin agreed, losing some of her blood-thirsty sparkle. "I only mention it because they just arrived," she added flippantly, casting her eyes back to me in the hope that I'd put on some sort of show.

"Great," Kane said calmly, "I'm sure we'll get to chat to them at some point. Now if you'll excuse us, we were kind of in the middle of something."

- KANE THOMPSON -

I turned my back on the princess and the bitch, hoping like hell that Soph wasn't going to lose her shit. She looked panicked, so I took her face in my hands to focus her. I sensed the two evil step-sisters still watching us, but their opinions were of little consequence to me.

"Look at me," I whispered quietly to Soph, and forced her gaze to my eyes. "Just breathe. You've got this."

"I don't know if I can face seeing him with someone else."

"Sure, you can," I said confidently as I saw the two ladies retreat from the corner of my eye. "Just harness your inner Sarah Connor." Soph laughed and her whole body visibly relaxed.

"You want me to kill them all?" she joked.

"Nah, just rough 'em up a bit." I scanned her pretty, but anxious face. "Or we could just stay out here for the rest of the night."

"Now that sounds like a better plan."

"Okay," I said, ushering her to the chair I'd pulled out before her bitchy friends had found us. "Now, you just sit here, and I'll go get you another espresso martini."

"Actually, I think I'm coffee'd out," she said eyeing the cocktail menu. "Could I get a long island iced tea instead?"

"Jesus Shorty, aiming for total oblivion huh?"

"I'll only have one," she said, knowing full well that I knew she was lying.

"Fine, but I'm not cleaning up after you."

"You won't need to."

"Famous last words," I muttered with a knowing smile. "I'm ordering you a pizza just in case."

"Whatever you say boss."

I should have known better. In the thirty-odd years I'd known that women, Long Island Iced Tea's had never ended well. I was enabling her self-destruction by buying them for her, but I felt like she needed it. It was a tough night for her and the least I could do was help make it bearable. Brenton had told me he wasn't going to come to the party, so the fucker had either been lying to my face, or he had changed his mind for some reason.

Thankfully the brewery was big enough that we avoided contact with my dipshit cousin and his new lady, and obviously he had enough sense not to come hunting for us. One salami pizza and two Long Island Iced Teas later, Soph was getting peaky.

"Another one?" she slurred, as she loudly sipped the last of her second Long Island Iced Tea.

"No way. You're smashed," I said, watching as she swayed slightly in her seat.

"You're a party pooper."

"Yeah, and I really should have pooped on your party about two cocktails ago." A frown crossed Soph's face, and I knew exactly what that look was. She was about to hit chucksville. "Right Shorty, it's time for us to bail," I instructed, quickly scooping up her handbag whilst she attempted to get to her feet. I grabbed her by the waist and lifted her out of her seat. "Come on," I said, herding her out of the building as quickly as she could manage, "we don't want anyone seeing you chuck."

I glanced up and down the carpark for a subtle spot for her to vomit, but the only option was on the far side of the harbour behind a dumpster. I could just imagine Brenton and his girlfriend witnessing her in an undignified moment. Or worse yet, the press. With Soph swaying on her feet, looking greener by the second, I was out of options.

"Come on drunkard, let's get you out of sight," I suggested, as I wrapped my arm around her waist and supported the weight of her body.

"I'm not drunk," she slurred in denial as we hobbled at a snail's pace, towards the rubbish bins.

"Well, we both know that's bullshit," I laughed.

"Don't laugh at me Jughead. It's your fault."

"My fault?"

"Yessh," she slurred, "you kept buying me cocktails." Soph paused abruptly and held her stomach then, without further warning, she doubled over, and power hurled all over the ground. "Sorry," she spluttered as I jumped out of the line of fire.

"It's fine Shorty," I reassured her, as I rubbed her back. "You missed my shoes."

"Well, that's a relief," she spluttered sarcastically.

"Probably best not to do this in the middle of the carpark though, let's head for the bin shed over there."

"Fine," she agreed, allowing me to lead her off the road and out of sight. I leaned her up against the shed, so she could balance her weight between the wall and the bin. Seconds after I stepped back, her stomach unleashed again. "Ugh," she grumbled as I patted her back. "I'm regretting that pizza now."
I laughed again, impressed that her sense of humour was still intact.

"To be honest, I think the pizza was your saving grace," I teased. "Just try not to think about it," I advised, looking up to see Isla jogging towards us from the other side of the carpark with Sean trailing behind her.

"Everything alright?" Isla asked, as the pair rushed towards us.

"Soph's not well," I explained, stepping back so they could see what was happening.

"Whoa," Sean exclaimed, jumping over the original pool of vomit.

"Sorry," Soph mumbled again from her position against the wall.

"Oh lordy," Isla chuckled quietly. "You okay babe?"

"Yep," Soph answered, before heaving again.

"Do you need some help getting her home?" Sean asked, while Isla stepped in to hold Soph's hair.

"Nah, I'll be right," I said as Soph retched loudly and emptied her stomach again.

"Hmmm," Isla said dubiously. "Maybe we should come with you."

"It's fine, I promise," I assured them. "This is nothing I haven't done before. I've been cleaning up this girl's vomit since the day she turned sixteen and drank a whole bottle of Passion Pop on her own."

"Fuck you Jughead," she grumbled from her position against the bin.

"Sounds like she's fine," joked Seany.

"I am fine," Soph groaned wearily, wiping her mouth with the back of her hand. She reached out in an attempt to stand upright, so I helped Isla get her to her feet. Once Soph was stable, I rubbed away her panda eyes with my thumbs. "Thanks Mum," Soph sighed, gently pushing my hands away from her face. She looked at the other two. "Just go guys. It's all under control."

"The boss has spoken," I told the pair with an amused shrug, wrapping my arm tightly around Sophie's waist to ensure she didn't fall. "You go back inside and enjoy the party."

"Actually, we were just leaving," Sean said. "That was all the schmoozing we could handle."

"I hear ya," I agreed, hoisting Soph up again as she began to slump in my arms.

"You sure you're going to be okay?"

"We'll be fine," snapped Soph grumpily. I looked down at Soph and hmphed in amusement. It really did feel like we were back in our teenage years at that moment.

"Okay, but call if you need us," instructed Isla.

"Will do."

"I'm fine Isla," slurred Soph impatiently, "please just fuck off and let me die in peace." The three of us exchanged amused glances that our mild-mannered Sophie had suddenly developed a feisty little attitude.

"Well, who are we to argue?" Sean conceded with a shrug, stepping away from us. "Let's leave them to it babe."

"I don't know…" said Isla as Seany pulled her away.

"Go," Soph grumbled at her with annoyance.

"Fine," Isla agreed reluctantly.

"See ya tomorrow Thommo," he called, dragging his concerned wife towards their car.

"See ya guys," I said with a wave.

"Goodluck mate." I watched them leave and then took stock of where we were at. We were still a fair way from my car, but Soph had remained standing and hadn't vomited again, so we were probably past the worst of it.

"Okay Shorty," I said, positioning her for the long-ish walk. "Let's see if we can get you to the car." We trundled across the carpark, Soph attached to my right arm and her handbag dangling off my left. She was moving at a rate of about five millimetres an hour and I was losing patience. "Fuck this," I declared, stopping in the middle of the road to scoop her off her feet.

"Kane!" she squealed in shock as I slung her over my shoulder in a very undignified manner. "You can't carry me around in public with my arse in the air."

I certainly wouldn't have behaved like that with anyone else, but this was Soph, and thirty years of sibling-like behaviour wasn't going to come to an end because she was suddenly single.

"Lucky it's a great arse," I joked, slapping her butt as if she was a prize racehorse.

"You're a great arse," she grumbled with annoyance.

"So I've been told," I laughed. "Now for god's sake, warn me if you're going to spew."

London: Ninja Nuptials

- NATHAN STONE -

"Can I have everyone's attention please?" I called loudly, as I tapped a spoon against my Champaign glass. Our jovial crowd of family and friends slowly fell quiet, and Ash squeezed my hand tenderly as we waited for the silence to fully descend. I looked down at her beautiful face with a grin.

"I just wanted to thank you all for coming today," I said, winking conspiratorially at Geoff who was standing at the back of the crowd, waiting for my signal. "I know it seems weird for us to have a party, given everything that's happened this year, but this is the last time we'll all be together in one place for a while, so we felt like we needed to mark the occasion as well as celebrate a few major events in one go."

Everyone muttered in agreement. I chuckled and gave Ash a nudge to indicate that it was her turn.

"As you all know," she said loudly, to get over the general murmur, "our lovable Aussie Larrikin is moving back home to Oz this week. Ritchie can you come up here please?" Our crowd turned to look at a very bashful Ritchie, who bowed his head and humbly joined us on the little stage. Ash let go of my hand and ducked behind the curtain to grab Ritchie's presents.

"Ritch," I said, slapping him on the back, "you mate, are one of the most down-to-earth, loyal and loud-mouthed people...," I teased, eliciting quiet laughter from the crowd, "...that I've ever had the honour of calling a friend. You've been the heart and soul of our little crew and life won't be the same without you."

"But England's loss will be Australia's gain," Ash said, brandishing the basket full of goodies.

"I was only on loan anyway," joked Ritchie with a sad smile.

"Maybe so, but you're an honorary Brit now whether you like it or not," I joked cheerfully, punching Ritchie on the bicep. "Which is exactly why we couldn't let you leave without giving you a few things to remember us by."

Ash handed him the basket of British memorabilia that we'd

all collected. There was the usual touristy stuff like keyrings, mugs, coasters, a hat, a pencil case, a variety of tea tins, a union jack cushion and some pens and pencils. But in addition to that, we'd also commissioned a personalized map of London that highlighted all of Ritchie's favourite places, as well as compiled a photo album of all our best memories together.

"What?" Ritchie said as he looked through the basket. "You guys, this is ace."

"We wanted you to have something to remember us by," said Tails.

"Yeah, we couldn't let you leave without us," joked Ryan.

"We're going to miss you Ritch," said Ash, giving him a one-armed cuddle around the big basket.

"I'm gonna miss you guys too," he said as a grin crossed his face. He looked at the crowd. "In case any of you haven't heard the news, Tails and Ryza are adding another McPherson to their clan." Cheers reverberated through the room and Ritch let the excitement die down before continuing. "And on top of that, Ashlan here can't handle being in London without me, so they've decided to leave the big smoke and move down to Cornwall."

Laughter ensued and Ritchie took the opportunity to hand his gift basket over to Ryan.

"Summer holidays will be on Nath," Ryan heckled as he popped the basket onto the nearest table, "and we'll expect five-star service."

"There's plenty of beach for you to sleep on Ryza," I teased. Everyone laughed again, and Ritchie continued.

"But seriously, they've all endured more trials and tribulations than anyone should, so I want to wish them the best of luck and raise a glass to their next adventures," Ritch said, holding his glass in the air.

"Here, here," came a chorus of voices as everyone raised their glasses.

"And in other news… I think by now you've all heard that I popped the question," I said loudly, to get over the chatter, "so, whilst we've had a lot to grieve, we also have a lot to celebrate." I looked at each of our group members one by one, "tragic circumstances have a way of showing us what really matters. We've been through several life and death experiences together over the past year, and as well as bringing us closer together, it's also given us a new level of perspective on our lives. The fact that we're missing one very important person at this event is evidence that life is way too short." I glanced down at my fiancé, then looked back at the crowd. "I'd like to propose a toast to Amy Vaughn, who we all miss beyond words," I said raising my glass. "To Amy."

"To Amy," everyone repeated. There was a brief silence.

"Now that we've covered off the serious stuff, we have a couple more surprises," I said, handing over to Ash to make the pregnancy announcement.

"We're having a baby," she blurted with a laugh. "Just in case anyone thought I was getting chubby."
More chatter and cheers emanated from the group.

"That was part of our reason for moving down south," I explained unnecessarily as my nerves kicked up a notch.

"And in an effort to ensure that the next generation of Stones can legitimately terrorize the shores of Cornwall," said Ritchie, nodding conspiratorially, "there's another purpose behind today's event."

Ashley's eyes darted back and forth between us with confusion, but Ritchie continued as a backdrop of curious murmurs echoed around the room.

"Ash doesn't know this," he said loudly, "but we've arranged a little surprise for her."

"What do you mean?" she asked, her face scrunched in bewilderment. Inquisitive faces watched us with interest as Ritchie and I grinned at each other.

"Ashley and I are getting married," I announced more excitedly than I would have liked, "…today."

"What?" Ash asked, her jaw nearly dropping to the floor. "What did you do?" Ashley's question was answered when Geoff swung open the doors to his atrium. The crowd collectively gasped as our lavish set-up was revealed. Rows of elegantly decorated chairs, faced an ornate flower-covered archway, accompanied by a backdrop of fairy lights twinkling from behind it. On the other side of the full-length glass windows, a huge marquee sat regally in the garden, lit up by a sea of more fairy lights.

"The ceremony will be held in the atrium in one hour," Geoff explained, gesturing towards the decked-out room, "followed by a reception in the marquee. In the meantime, please continue to enjoy yourselves."

The room erupted with hoots and hollers of excitement, led largely by Ritchie. Excited chatter bubbled around the room. The whole crowd seemed eager to be part of a surprise wedding, but the only opinion that mattered to me was Ashley's.

"What do you think?" I asked her quietly, ignoring the pandemonium in the room.

"How did you do all of this?" Ash blurted, dumfounded.

"I had a lot of help," I said, nodding towards the crew, who were all revelling in the excitement. "Ritchie didn't want you to miss out because of what happened, and your parents were pretty keen to see us married before the baby came."

"You all planned this together?" she asked in shock. "When?"

"We've been organising it for weeks," I replied with a shrug.

"You have?"

"Yep, and we've got everything covered."

"You do?"

"Of course," I said with a confident grin, "you don't have to worry about a thing. Do you like it?"

"It's beautiful, but…" she trailed off, peering around the room in dismay.

"But?" I asked as my stomach churned with nerves. Perhaps I'd jumped the gun on this whole surprise wedding thing. Ash glanced down at her dress and then back over the sea of animated faces.

"We have a dress for you," Mary said, popping up out of nowhere, "and there's a hair and make-up lady waiting."

"Really?" Ash asked, agape. Her eyes darted between me, her parents, our friends, and the rest of the crowd, who had now ceased talking to watch us with bated breath. My heart stopped as Ash stared at me with complete dismay.

"What do you think Granger?" I asked with a grin. "Are you ready to become a Stone?"

She continued gaping at me for a few seconds before tears welled in her eyes. After a gut-wrenching moment, she finally beamed and threw her arms around my neck.

"Yes!" she exclaimed, kissing me enthusiastically. I laughed with relief and slid my hands around her waist as our onlookers cheered.

"You had me worried for a minute there," I admitted quietly, resting my forehead against hers. "I thought maybe I'd gone too far this time."

"You went way too far," she said with a smile, "but I love it, and I can't wait to be your wife."

- ASHLEY GRANGER -

The noise in the room was sending my senses into overload but Nathan was my lifeline. With his forehead resting against mine, I felt like I was home. I leaned back and cupped his stubbly jaw in my hands, letting my thumb run across his bristly chin.

"I guess I should shave before the ceremony," he joked.

"No don't. I like you with a five o'clock shadow."

"You do huh?" he teased.

"It's incredibly sexy."

"Well in that case I'll keep it."

"Stop canoodling and get a move on you two," tutted my mother, smacking both of us lightly on the back of our heads. "We've only got an hour to get you both dressed and ready. Honestly."

"Yeah, save that for the honeymoon," piped up Ritchie, who had also jumped into action.

I looked at Nathan. "Don't tell me you've organised that too?!"

"Err… no," he said with an apologetic shrug. "I was a little pre-occupied with planning the wedding. Sorry."

"Don't apologise! We don't need a honeymoon. We're moving to Cornwall."

"Come on Ashley, look lively," Mum barked like a drill sergeant. "Off to your room before I make Ritchie carry you there."

"Fine," I sighed, rolling my eyes playfully. "See you soon babe," I said, planting a lingering kiss on Nathans warm lips.

"See you at the alter Mrs Stone," he said, as we reluctantly pulled away from each other.

"She's not Mrs Stone yet," said Kat, grabbing my hand, "and if you two don't hurry up and get yourselves ready she might never be."

She and my mother dragged me away as I gazed over my shoulder at my soon-to-be husband. His blue eyes remained glued to mine as I was herded down the hallway. He tipped his square, slightly stubbled jaw in a supportive nod before we lost sight of each other.

"Quick sticks, Ashley," Mum said as she and Kat hurried me towards my bedroom, "we don't have much time. Katherine, where's Kesha?"

"She's getting the bouquets."

"Good," said my drill-sergeant mother. "Now, let's get you in there Ashley, the ladies are waiting." Mum opened my bedroom door and nudged me inside. "Ashley, this is Amanda and Kylie."

"Hi," I mumbled, distracted by the exquisite wedding gown hanging from the wardrobe door in between two teal coloured bridesmaid dresses. "Oh my," I whispered in awe, drawn towards the stunning gown. "This is beautiful," I breathed, as I ran my hands along the intricate beading.

"You like it?" Mum asked with relief.

"I love it Mum," I said, turning and gripping her in a tight hug. "It's absolutely gorgeous, thank you."

"You can thank Kat for that," Mum said, giving me a squeeze, "she made it."

"You did?" I asked in amazement. Spinning around to hug my wonderful friend. "I can't believe you did that."

"I thought you needed something special and unique, just like you," she said with a smile.

"How come you've been hiding your dress-making talents?"

Kat shrugged. "You code, I sew. We all have our secrets. Now, try it on so I can make any adjustments while you're getting ready."

"Okay!" I carefully removed the dress from the hanger and carried it into the bathroom.

"Quickly though," called my mum, "the ladies need to get started."

I clicked the door shut and took another moment to admire the dress as I laid it out carefully along the bench. It was my dream dress. A halter neck in ivory silk, with a beaded bodice and mermaid-cut skirt with a small train. I'd never spoken to Kat about dresses, so I was flabbergasted that she was so on point with it. Quickly stripping off, I slid myself into the dress. After a few attempts at tying up the bodice myself, I gave up and returned to my bedroom to recruit some help.

"Oh my gosh," Mum gasped as I opened the bathroom door, gripping to the top of the bodice. "You look beautiful love."

"Thanks Mum," I said, taken aback by the tears in her eyes, "but I can't get the bodice done up."

"I've got it," said Kat darting to my aid. She played around at the back, then stepped away. "There, all done. Go have a look."
I walked over to the mirror.

"Oh wow," I breathed in admiration. "Kat, this is perfect."

"I think I might just take it in at the bust a little. I wasn't sure how much room to leave for those growing boobs of yours," she teased.

"I think it's perfect."

"Knock, knock," Kesha called, cracking open the bedroom door. "Can I come in?"

"Yes, quickly," said my mum, "she's got the dress on, come and look."

Kesha ducked into the room carrying a bucket full of pink and cream flowers, punctuated with splashes of teal.

"Oh wow," she said with a huge grin. "You look amazing babe."

"Thanks to Kat," I said, taking another look at myself in the mirror. "I couldn't have chosen a better dress myself."

"You're going to knock Nathan's socks off girl," Kesha joked, popping the bucket onto the sideboard. It was three stunning bouquets of jasmine, rose and snapdragons with some type of dried flowers to match the teal in the girls' dresses. A wave of sadness hit me as I stared at the beautiful arrangements. One big one for me and two smaller ones for the girls. There should have been three smaller ones.

The change of mood must have shown on my face as Kesh stopped talking and cocked her head.

"You okay babe?" she asked, leaning against the sideboard.

"Amy should have been here for this," I muttered quietly, wondering how such sorrow could hit so hard in the midst of my joy.

"Yeah," Kat agreed, wrapping her arms around me, "and I bet she is. She's probably looking down and cheering that Nathan finally got his shit together." A solitary tear rolled down my cheek and she wiped it way. "And you know she'd tell you off for crying right?" Kat teased.

"Probably," I sniffed with a cross between a cry and a laugh.

"Definitely," she said sternly, gripping my shoulders. "Now, let's get this dress off so Amanda and Kylie can get to work."

"Oh," I said, remembering the ladies who were still standing in the corner of the room waiting for me. "Sorry," I apologised with an embarrassed wave.

"Come on Ashley, chop-chop," said Mum, sounding like Mary Poppins. "You don't want to keep your groom waiting."

- RITCHIE CARLTON -

Dressed in his fancy cream coloured suit, Nathan paced the Grangers' upstairs sitting room. His teal shirt was still open at the collar and a pink silk tie hung casually over his neck. I pulled on my trousers, which were thankfully charcoal and not cream like his, as Nath did yet another lap of the floor. I couldn't put up with his pacing any longer, so I zipped up my pants and marched, bare chested, to Geoff's liquor cabinet. After a quick scan, I spotted a bottle of reasonably priced whiskey hidden amongst his ridiculously expensive ones, so I pulled out the bottle and poured Nathan an extra-large serve.

"Here," I said, handing him the tall glass as I intercepted him on his next lap. "Drink that before you wear a hole in the carpet."
Nath took the drink with a grateful nod.

"Thanks man. I don't know why I'm so nervous," he said, knocking back a large mouthful of the whiskey.

"That's weddings mate," I said, slapping him on the back. "If you weren't nervous, I'd be worried about you."

"What if she changes her mind?" Nath asked tapping his finger against the whiskey glass.

"She won't."

"And what about the rings? Where are they?"

"Ryza has them."

"And where the fuck is Ryza?"

"Chill. He's on Mia duty while Tails gets dressed but he's got everything under control," I said calmly, shrugging into my matching teal shirt. Teal was not the most masculine colour, but I was willing to wear it for Ash, it was the pink ties I couldn't get on board with. "Reckon we could go tie-less?" I asked, pulling a face at the pink tie still dangling over the hanger.

"It's a wedding, we have to wear ties."

"Why?"

"Because it's a formal event and a tie is the proper attire," he said slowly and clearly as if he was speaking to a deaf person. "Do you not wear ties in Australia?"

"Of course we wear ties, just not pink ones," I joked, buttoning up my shirt.

"Just 'coz you know you can't pull it off," he teased. "Only a confident man can wear pink."

"No ginger man could," I retorted, checking myself in the mirror as I fastened the final few buttons on my shirt. It looked good without the tie.

"Oh fine," he sighed, taking another giant swig of his whiskey. "I'm wearing mine, but I'll leave it up to you two whether you wear them or not. It's both of you or none though," Nathan said as he looked dubiously at Ryan's tux still hanging on the door. I could see the cogs ticking over in his mind and knew exactly what he was thinking.

"It's fine," I assured him confidently, "we've still got plenty of time. The girls will be ages."

"True," he agreed, taking another sip of his drink, whilst resuming his pacing.

"Dude, stop fucking pacing."

Nath stopped walking abruptly. "Sorry."

It was good practice for Sean's wedding, although I wouldn't be quite as involved in that one. I was closer to Nath than I was to Seany, besides which, Kane seemed to have everything under control for the Carlton wedding. I wasn't needed there in the same way I was here. Not that I loved my brother less than Nathan, or that his wedding wasn't as important to me, but Nathan was the family I'd chosen. There was a certain bond that formed between non-blood family, and it was hard letting that go. I felt like I was sending two brothers off into married life, while I started my life all over again.

"Why don't you go over your vows?" I suggested, pouring myself a glass of whiskey. "It'll give you something to focus on."

"Sure," he said, fishing around in his pocket. He pulled out a pristine piece of paper and carefully unfolded it. "Ashley Jane Granger..." Nath began, just as Ryan reversed through the door, dragging Mia's pram backwards.

"I hope you're both decent; there's a lady present," he declared loudly, banging and cluttering through the door with all his baby paraphernalia. Nathan strode over, whiskey in hand, and held the door open for him.

"Jesus mate, did you bring the entire nursery with you?"

"You'd better get used to it Stoner because this is what it takes to look after a baby," Ryza told him, handing Nath the nappy bag that was slung over his shoulder. "Now make yourself useful and grab that."
Stoner let go of the door and took the bag instead. The door began to swing closed and bumped Ryan, sending him off balance.

"You couldn't have put the drink down?" Ryza asked indignantly, bent over the pram in a most undignified pose.

"Nope," Nath replied with a smile, as he walked away and placed the nappy bag on the table, leaving Ryza to battle the door. It was painful to watch, so I stepped up and helped him into the room.

"Whiskey?" I asked him, as he faffed around with Mia's pram.

"Still in rehab," he reminded me with annoyance.

"Oh yeah," I said apologetically. "I keep forgetting that."

"Yet you're the one who talked me into it," he said pointedly.

"Whoa there MacDaddy, I saved your butt," I said defensively.

"Sorry. You're right, I'm just a little highly strung today," he apologised. "Nath, the rings are in the nappy bag."

"Why would you put them in the nappy bag?"

"Because I knew I wouldn't forget it," Ryan said with a shrug. "You'll understand soon enough."

"Five months," said Nath, sipping his whiskey. "Only five months to go before I'm responsible for a small human."

"And only a few months until Ryza is responsible for two of them," I joked. "Looking forward to being a house-husband mate?"

"Now there's a thought," muttered Ryan stripping down to his jocks. "I'm not sure how I feel about my wife being the breadwinner."

"You'll get over it," Nath said flippantly. "It's about being a team, right?"

"Sure," Ryza agreed half-heartedly. Nathan foraged around in the nappy bag while Ryza stepped into his trousers.

"What do you think of the pink tie Ryza?" I asked, taking a seat in one of the big leather armchairs.

"It goes well with the teal," he replied with a shrug,

"But do you really want to wear pink?"

"I look great in pink," he said with a smile, zipping up his fly. "Why is that?"

"He doesn't want to wear it," Stoner answered for me, "and I told him he'd have to wear it if you did."

"Oh, in that case," Ryan said with a grin, "I'm definitely wearing it."

"That's how you're gonna play it?" I asked, squaring my jaw in annoyance.

"Sure is," he chuckled, threading his arms into the teal shirt.

"Even though I'm moving across the globe next week?"

"Absolutely."

"You're uninvited to Australia."

Ryan laughed and buttoned up his shirt. "You're just pissed because I'm going to look better than you."

"Fuck off cunt," I retorted in true Aussie style, "you'll never look better than me."

"Right," said Stoner, brandishing the little blue box that contained the wedding rings. "Enough of this bullshit. Let's get these pink ties on and get down there. There's no point in hiding up here when we've got guests downstairs." A loud knock echoed through the room, and we all looked at the big wooden door. "Come in," called Nathan, rings still in hand.

"Sorry to interrupt," said Gaz as he stuck his head in the door, "but I was hoping to get a moment with the groom."

"No worries," I said, downing the remainder of my drink.

"I've gotta get Mia down to the babysitter anyway," Ryan added, gathering all the baby stuff, along with the baby. "Nath, do you want me to take the rings?"

"Looks like you've already got your hands full," Nath said, looking down at the ring box in his hands.

"I've got it," said Gaz, holding out his hand towards Stoner.

"Thanks Gaz," Nath said, plopping the box into Gareth's palm.

"Right," I said with a nod, grabbing the nappy bag for Ryan. "We'll see you down there then."

"See you down there," confirmed Nath, returning my nod. I turned to follow Ryan out the door when Stoner called me back. "Ritch," he said with a grin, "you forgot your tie."

- NATHAN STONE -

Gaz waited for the boys to vacate the room, then turned to me with an expression I couldn't decipher.

"Big day," he said simply.

"Yeah," I agreed with a nervous chuckle.

"How you feeling?"

"Nervous."

"That's understandable," he agreed with a nod. He put his hands in his pockets and looked me in the eye. "I'm really proud of you Nath. You've become a good man, and I know your dad would be proud of you too."

"Thanks Gaz," I said, shuffling my feet.

"You're going to be a great husband and a wonderful father. Better than I ever was."

"You were great."

"Hmph, we both know that's not true," he said gruffly. "But I did my best." He paused and looked over his shoulder. "I've got something for you."

"Oh really? You didn't have to get me a wedding gift."

"Oh, I think you'll change your mind when you see it," he said with a sly smile. "Just a minute." He ducked out of the room, and I waited curiously to see what his gift was. A moment later, he pushed the door open, and my mother's face came into view behind him.

"Mum?" I asked, tears springing to my eyes.

"Hi love," she said as Gaz helped her into the room. "Look at you," she breathed, resting her hand on her heart for a moment. "You look so handsome."

"What are you doing here?" I asked, striding over to wrap her up in a bearhug. "I can't believe you're here."

"Did you really think we'd let you get married without your mum?" Gaz asked with a grin.

"But how did you even know?" I asked Gaz. He hadn't been part of the inner circle of our wedding surprise.

"Geoff reached out. He was so touched by what you were doing for Ash that he wanted to give you a surprise of your own."

"But-"

"He worked some magic with the hospital, and we got Cinderella out for a few hours," he said, winking at my mum. "But I have to get her back there by 10pm or we'll be in trouble."

"Okay," I said, peering down at my mum with a chest full of emotion. "I'll take whatever time I can get."
She looked up and grasped both ends of my tie.

"Now, let's see…" Mum muttered. "It's been a while, but I think I remember how to do this," she said, threading the tie as if she'd done it all her life. I smiled and looked over at Gaz, who quickly wiped a tear from the corner of his eye. "I'm so proud of you love," my mother said as she finished tying the tie. She straightened my collar and then patted my chest. "You've turned into a wonderful young man Nathan. Dad would be so proud if he could see you now."

"Thanks Mum. I'm so glad you're here," I said, grasping her shoulders.

"Me too," she said, patting my cheek.

"Shall we head downstairs?" Asked Gaz. "We need to get you to the alter ahead of your bride."

"Sure," I said, stepping back and offering Mum my arm. "Shall we?"

"We shall," she agreed with a proud smile. Gaz and I escorted my mum downstairs to join the waiting crowd. The other two boys had obviously handed off Mia successfully as they were both loitering around the alter, ready to perform their groomsmen duties. I settled Mum into the front row, next to Mary and left her in Gareth's capable hands.

I joined the boys under the archway as people filed into the room to take their seats in anticipation of the ceremony. My nerves escalated the longer we waited, but finally, we were given the word that the girls were ready. The music began to play and Kesha led the way down the aisle, followed by Kat. They both looked beautiful, but my attention was stolen by the bride when she stepped into the atrium on Geoff's arm. My heart stopped. She looked like a princess.

The crowd turned to watch her walk down the aisle and I noticed her grip tighten around the bouquet as all eyes fell on her. She smiled nervously at me, and my chest pounded. I was floored. It was exactly the same feeling I'd had at Bordello that night she'd walked in wearing the little white dress. The only difference was that tonight it was a wedding dress, and I knew for sure that I'd be taking her home with me. I took a deep breath and kept my eyes locked on her.

"You okay mate?" Ritchie whispered into my ear.

"Yep," I croaked, choking back some unexpected tears. Ritch patted my shoulder supportively, but I kept my gaze firmly on Ash. I couldn't tear my eyes away from hers. She was the only thing I could see in that moment and her green eyes had me tethered. After everything we'd been through that year, we were finally moving on. She was finally going to be Mrs Stone for real.

All the moments we'd shared since the fateful night we'd met at the nightclub half a decade ago, began running through my mind. Our flirtatious little drug drop; the day outside the taxi; the yoga class; our non-date; the night at Brick Lane; our days in the hospital together; our fight; the night we fell asleep on the phone; my return to Artemis and our kiss against the glass wall with the entire office watching. Then there was the night at Bordello; Dominic finding us; Ash moving in with me; Fred the cat; the day Mia was born; meeting Geoff and Mary; and then the moment when I thought I'd lost Ash forever. Next was Paris and the Eiffel Tower; our trip to Cornwall; her pregnancy news; the ultrasound; and the day she found Amy. All of it played through my mind as if I was watching a movie of our life. Who would have imagined, through all of that, we'd still be together.

Geoff delivered my fiancé to the flower-covered alter and gave me a nod. He let go of her arm, hugged her quickly, and then turned to me.

"Hotshot," he said with a smile, before gripping my hand and pulling me in for a firm man-hug. "I know you'll take care of our girl."

"I will," I assured him. He smiled and took his seat in the front row next to my soon-to-be Mother-in-Law. I turned back to Ashley with a joyful smile. "Hey," I whispered to her, grasping her elegant hands in mine.

"Hey," she said, with twinkling eyes.

"You look breathtaking."

"You look pretty good yourself Mr Stone," she answered with a wink. "You okay?"

"I'm better than okay."

"I can't believe your mum's here."

"Me either," I whispered, casting a quick glance towards Mum. "Your dad did that."

"He did?"

"He's a good man."

"Takes one to know one," Ash said with a smile, squeezing my hands as the celebrant began the service.

- ASHLEY GRANGER -

My heart pounded uncontrollably as I walked towards the atrium door, gripping my dad's arm like my life depended on it. In hindsight, it was probably for the best that I hadn't had time to think about it or I would have been a total wreck. Kesha and Kat both glided elegantly through the doors ahead of me… and then it was my turn.

"It's time," my dad said quietly. I looked up at him for reassurance and he patted my arm. "This is the start of the rest of your life cupcake."

I was too nervous to respond, so I gave him a quick peck on the cheek and then we were off, walking slowly, step-by-step towards the room where my future was waiting.

As we cleared the doors, all eyes were on me and my heart took off again, beating a rhythm so wild it could have lit up the dance-floors in Ibiza. What if I tripped and fell? What if my dress got caught on something? 'What if…' My anxious thoughts ceased immediately when my eyes caught Nathan's. His bright baby blues felt like pools of calm amidst my emotional storm, and all my worries dissipated instantly. I was home. Nathan was my man and I'd have him by my side until the end of our days.

The panic in my chest eased, and I let out a long but subtle exhalation, letting go of all my neurotic concerns. It was fine. Everything was under control and this wedding was already perfect. All I needed was Nathan.

Dad guided me right up to my waiting fiancé and then, once I'd officially been 'handed over', the ceremony began. I wasn't particularly conscious of what was going on, but I knew that I was about to be Nathan's wife and that was all that mattered.

The celebrant launched into the opening sermon while Nathan and I stared at each other, communicating without speaking. Neither of us were listening to her words, we were merely holding onto each other and biding our time until we could call ourselves husband and wife.

After she was done, the celebrant invited Cody to give a reading. Nathan and I finally broke eye contact and watched Cody as he made his way up to the little podium.

"When Nathan asked me to do a reading today, I was panicked about what I could come up with in less than an hour," he joked, eliciting quiet chuckles from the crowd, "but then I remembered an excerpt from a book called 'The Alchemist' by Paulo Coelho. It was one of my favourite books as a young man and there's a paragraph in there that I think sums up love perfectly."

Cody pulled his phone from his pocket and looked down at the screen, then, with a deep breath, read the excerpt. "When he looked into her eyes, he learned the most important part of the language that all the world spoke — the language that everyone on earth was capable of understanding in their heart. It was love. Something older than humanity, more ancient than the desert. What the boy felt at that moment was that he was in the presence of the only woman in his life, and that, with no need for words, she recognized the same thing. Because when you know the language, it's easy to understand that someone in the world awaits you, whether it's in the middle of the desert or in some great city. And when two such people encounter each other, the past and the future become unimportant. There is only that moment, and the incredible certainty that everything under the sun has been written by one hand only. It is the hand that evokes love, and creates a twin soul for every person in the world. Without such love, one's dreams would have no meaning."
He put his phone down and smiled at the two of us.

"When I look at you two, that's the sort of love I see," he said, casting his eyes over the rest of the silent room. He'd done such a beautiful job that there was barely a dry eye in the place. "Umm… amen?" he concluded with a brief curtsey, before returning to his seat.

"Thank you, Cody," said the celebrant, breaking the emotional silence. "That was beautiful."

Our vows were next, and not having had much time to prepare mine, I chose to keep it as brief as possible.

"Nathan, life has been crazy since we met, but you've been my rock. You've taken care of me without question - even though sometimes it was totally misguided," I teased with an emotional smile. "but you've kept me strong. Your steadfast loyalty and your big, beautiful heart have been unwavering in situations that would have tested the toughest of men. You've held me together, even when you were on the verge of breaking and I promise to spend the rest of my life doing the same for you. I never would have imagined all those years ago in that dodgy nightclub in East London that one day I would end up going home with you… forever."

Nathan's eyes shimmered with tears, as he grabbed my face and kissed me hard, causing everyone to laugh.

"Slow down there chief," teased the celebrant, "it's not time for that yet."

"Sorry," said Nathan, pulling away from me and surreptitiously wiping a tear from his cheek.

"Your vows first, then you can kiss her all you like." Another round of laughter. "No rush, whenever you're ready," she added comfortingly, as Nathan extracted a piece of paper from his trouser pocket with shaking hands. He read over his vows for a moment, then took a deep breath and looked up at me with the most intense expression I'd ever seen on his face.

"Ashley Jane Granger, you are the love of my life. You are the first, and last, woman I'll ever fall in love with. It's true, you brought untold chaos into my well-ordered existence, and you completely blew apart my life plans but… I wouldn't change any of it. Not one little bit. Not even getting hit by the car," he joked. I laughed in shock and so did a few others. Nath peered quickly down at his paper and then continued. "You won my heart five years ago in that nightclub. I don't know how, but I knew with every fibre of my being that we belonged together, I just didn't realise I'd have to wait five years for you." He smiled and took my hand in his, ignoring his written vows. "You're my life, Ashley Granger. You and our baby. And I promise you that I will spend the rest of our lives making sure things are as normal and unexciting as possible." I laughed and cried simultaneously. Nathan wiped a tear off my cheek as his Colgate smile sparkled brightly. "You're the most amazing, determined, authentic, loving, caring person that I've ever met, and I feel so unbelievably honoured that you want to be my wife. I love you now and forever Ash, and I will do everything in my power to make sure the rest of our story is nothing but happy."

"I love you too," I breathed, feeling like my heart was about to burst out of my chest.

"It's time to exchange rings," announced the celebrant, and beyond that, everything was a blur. My body was going through the motions, while my brain was floating above us in fluffy clouds of love. We exchanged our rings and signed some paperwork and eventually I heard the celebrant say, "you may now kiss the bride."

And that was that. We were officially married. The rest of the evening passed in whirlwind of laughter and merriment. We ate, we drank, and we danced. It couldn't have been more perfect if I'd planned it myself.

"Before we bring out the cake," Nathan announced after we'd finished dinner, "I want to say an extra big thank you to my in-laws, for hosting. Mary, Geoff, thanks for organising everything. It was better than we ever could have imagined."

"Our pleasure hotshot," called Dad with a wink, "we just wanted to make sure that you made an honest woman out of her."

"Oh my god Dad," I groaned in embarrassment while Nathan, who shared my fathers' cheesy sense of humour, laughed loudly.

"And thanks for everything you've done for me and my Mum. I really couldn't ask for better in-laws."

"We're glad to have you in the family love," Mum said proudly. Nathan smiled and then looked over at his own Mum, who was sitting arm-in-arm with Gaz.

"And for anyone who doesn't know my Mum, this is her," he said, gesturing in Hellen's direction. "It means so much to have you here with us today and I hope this is the first of many Stone family dinners."

"Thanks love," Hellen replied bashfully as Gareth patted her arm supportively. Nath walked over and planted a kiss on her forehead. I could see tears glistening in Nathan's eyes and, although he was a softy in front of me, the last thing he would have wanted was for other people to think he had feelings, so I took over the speeches.

"We couldn't be happier to have you here Hellen," I said. "And Gaz... thank you for all the support you've given of us this year, I know we've been business kryptonite for you, but we really appreciate you giving us the space and time to work through all of the dramas." Gaz laughed.

"You Stones are a pain in my arse," he joked with a wink.

"I'll drink to that," joked Nathan. "Drink up everyone! Let's make this a party to remember."

- RITCHIE CARLTON -

I was incredibly pleased to see my friends finally get their fairytale ending. In a weird way, it made it easier for me to leave knowing that they were all going to be okay. More than okay in fact. I watched as the two couples danced and laughed without a care in the world. Life seemed perfect for them all, but amidst their revelry, my heart was breaking. In stark contrast to the joy surrounding me, my pain felt more intense than ever.

Feeling the tears welling, I plucked a drink off the tray of a passing waiter, and skulled the entire thing on my way out to the garden. When I broke out into the cold, crisp air I felt like I could finally breathe. I watched my warm breath turn into puffs of steam as I looked around the extravagant property. The whole garden was covered in fairy lights, which twinkled in the darkness, and lit my way down to the gazebo.

The comparative silence was sweet relief. I leaned my elbows on the railing and looked out over the pond, as the reflection of the fairy lights danced on the water. A lone crow cawed from a tree somewhere above me, and I chuckled sadly.

"One for sorrow," I mumbled, recalling the nursery rhyme from my childhood.

"There you are," called a voice from behind me. I craned my head to see Ashley's silhouette as she made her way down to the gazebo with something glowing in her hand.

"G'day Mrs Stone," I said with a smile, as she joined me at the railing.

She grinned happily. "I'll never get tired of hearing that," she said, leaning her back against the wooden balustrade. "Ritch… there's something I think you should have," Ashley said, holding up the thing that was in her hand. I immediately recognised the florescent orange phone case.

"Where did you get Amy's phone?" I asked, standing upright.

"I took it from her flat."

"You did what?" I asked with horror. "Ashley you can't tamper with a crime scene."

"I-I didn't mean to," she stuttered, "I wasn't really thinking. I just saw it sitting there and thought you might want it."

"Oh."

"I kinda forgot I had it until the other day."

"Well… thanks," I said, reaching out to take it.

"I charged it up," she said, placing it firmly into my palm and my stomach lurched at the solemn look on her face.

"What is it?" I asked with trepidation.

Ash sighed and tapped the phone screen as it laid in my hand, "Ritch… there's a message from Sandrine on there."

"Huh?" I looked down at the glowing screen to see a creepy message from an eerily familiar number.

"You know he deserves better than you can give him," Ash said gravely, as I read those exact words on the screen.

I peered up at her with disbelief. "How do you know that's Sandrine's number?"

"Because I have her number for work." She took a breath and looked me dead in the eyes. "Ritchie… I think this is what made Amy kill herself."

"Ash," I said sternly, not willing to entertain her irrational theory, "this is the grief talking. Amy had issues and she said as much in her letters. She knew what she was doing."

"But what if she didn't," Ash argued almost desperately. "What if Sandrine was the one doing the pushing? I mean, she certainly had plenty of motive to get-"

"Ash, stop it," I growled, cutting off the end of her sentence more tersely than I had intended. "Please let this go. I can't move on if you're trying to pull Amy back from the fucking grave."

"But just think about it Ritch," Ash pleaded, frantically pointing at the phone in my hand, "it doesn't make any sense."

"This…" I hissed, waving my hands at her to indicate her absurdity, "is what doesn't make any sense Granger. It's your wedding day, you should be in that tent having fun, not out here talking about fucking conspiracy theories. I don't know why you're instigating this wild goose chase, but it's insanity."

"But-"

"Just stop. I know you think you're helping but you're not. This crazy notion of yours will make everything worse. I need to leave London and get my life in Perth started with a clean slate." I sighed and rubbed my face, "Yes, Sandrine is mental, but Amy killed herself Ash, and nothing is going to bring her back, especially not blaming Sandrine for her death."

"I know," she said quietly. It seemed like she'd finally seen sense, until she opened her mouth again. "It's just that I can feel it in my bones. This woman is dangerous Ritchie."

"Ugh," I groaned, losing my patience. "I get why you're suspicious okay? After everything you've been through, you have every right not to trust people, but sometimes shitty things just happen and there's no one to blame."

"But…"

"No," I said, raising my hand in front of her face. "I love you mate but, I really need you to drop this." I paused and took a deep breath.

"I'm sorry," she whispered, as her eyes dropped to her feet. I could see that she was holding back tears.

"Apology accepted, but right now I just need you to leave me alone, okay?"

Ash looked up, complete devastation on her face.

"Okay," she nodded, backing away. I watched Ash turn and begin walking, barefoot, across the lawn towards the marquee with the train of her white dress trailing along the dewy grass. When she reached the paved courtyard, she stopped and turned. I gritted my teeth in preparation for whatever crazy shit was about to come out of her mouth. "Just know I love you Ritch, and if you ever need to talk…" she let her words trail off, then turned and ran full pace back to the house.

"I love you too Granger," I muttered under my breath as I wiped a tear from the corner of my eye. I looked down at Sandrine's ominous message. How had Sandrine got hold of Amy's number? Was it possible that she really did push Amy over the edge?

- ASHLEY GRANGER -

Before returning to the reception, I took a detour past the bathroom to collect myself. Ritchie was still grieving so I couldn't take his words personally, but they'd stung none-the-less. Perhaps there was some truth in what he'd said. Maybe I'd always bear the scars of my abusive relationship, but still… I couldn't shake the feeling that somehow Sandrine was at the epicenter of all of this.

I tidied up my makeup and leaned against the sink, staring at my reflection. I barely recognised the mature, elegant woman looking back at me. She seemed so content and collected it was hard to believe it was me. As my gaze lingered, a vision of the old me appeared in the mirror. The battered face of the scared young woman I'd been all those years ago. Gaunt and pale, with wisps of died black hair glued to her bruised face by thick red blood. Bright green eyes, wild with fear and dilated from drugs, stared back at me, pleading for help. That girl, that night, that memory… it felt like a lifetime ago, yet the pain and trauma were still lingering beneath the polished façade of this new Ashley. My name might have changed now, but scared little Ashley Granger was still hiding inside me.

Ritchie was right. I was letting my history taint the present and it was time for me to stop. It was time for me to let it go. I splashed some water on my face, and then fixed my make-up again. I closed my eyes and took a deep breath, in… and out. Letting go of my past; releasing the old Ashley; and purging myself of Dominic's control once and for all.

By the time I returned to the marquee, I was centered and calm. The music was cranking, and everyone but Ritchie was on the dance-floor. People drank, laughed and joked, congratulating and hugging me as I moved through the room. Happy noise buzzed all around me, but all I could see was Nathan, my husband and the father of my unborn child.

Nath looked up from his conversation with Gaz and caught me staring at him. He shot me a wink, along with one of his award-winning smiles, and our baby gave an almost imperceptible flutter, as if to be included. I chuckled quietly to myself and rested my hand on my stomach. We were a family, and the people in this room were part of it. This was 'us' now. The three of us together with an army of supportive people around us.

I saw Nathan look over at Ryan, who quickly jumped up onto the stage and grabbed the microphone.

"Sorry to interrupt the festivities folks, but I've got one last surprise for the bride," he said, grinning in my direction, before looking over his shoulder to the curtain behind the little stage. "I'd like to welcome Sloane Sutton to the stage."

My jaw dropped as Sloane Sutton stepped out and gave Ryan a kiss and a hug. Gasps, cheers and sounds of shocked joy emanated from my family and friends.

"Thanks Ryan," Sloane said, squeezing his arm affectionately, before he left the stage. "And I'd just like to say a big congratulations to the happy couple, Ashley and Nathan. I'm so honoured to be part of this special occasion. Ryan has told us so much about you two that I feel like I already know you." Sloane looked at me and smiled. I couldn't believe that an international popstar was at my wedding, let alone knew who I was. "Before I get started, I just want to introduce a special someone who wouldn't be in my life if it wasn't for Ryan. Rod, could you come out and join me?"

At that point, I nearly passed out, because soap star Rodney Barker stepped out onto the stage.

"What?" I muttered in shock as Nathan sidled up next to me and slid his arm around my waist. "Did you know about this?"

"Nope," he said, shaking his head with a smile. "This was all Ryza."

"I can't believe it."

"Congrats Nathan and Ashley," said Rodney, shooting us a wink, "Like Sloane said, Ryan has told us a lot about you both, so we were flattered that he asked us to be part of your wedding. If anyone deserves a happy ending, it's you two."

"So anyway," Sloane said, nudging Rodney with a joyful grin, "from the bottom of our hearts, we wish you the absolute best for your marriage and your new life in Cornwall." She paused and looked around the room. "Now... who wants to hear some music?"

The small crowd cheered, and Rodney moved away to the side of the stage as Sloane began her set. It was surreal. I felt elated as I danced with Nathan, watching the world-famous Sloane Sutton performing in my parents' atrium. Maybe my Mum was right, and I'd finally gotten my fairytale ending after all... or maybe our fairytale was only just beginning.

– Chapter 3 –

Return to Oz

- RITCHIE CARLTON -

"Flight QF10 is now boarding," echoed a voice over the PA.

"That's me," I said, turning to the small band of misfits who'd come to Heathrow to see me off. I was disappointed that Cody hadn't made it but he'd been in Paris all week for Delfontaine, so he'd probably decided to stay on and spend the weekend with Guillaume. I looked over the faces of my friends, who had become more like family in the last few years, and my heart wrenched in my chest. I'd expected this moment to be hard, but this was excruciating.

Kat was the first to move. "Oh Ritch," she sobbed, wrapping her arms around my waist as she buried her face into my chest. Her curly hair bounced as she cried into my T-shirt. "I'm going to miss you."

"I'm gonna miss you too Tails," I said, swallowing a lump in my own throat as I patted her back comfortingly.

"Come on babe," said Ryza, gently peeling his wife off me, "Ritchie has a lot of goodbyes to say." He seamlessly transferred Tails from my chest to his and gave me a quick one-armed hug. "See ya man," he said, slapping my shoulder, "give us a buzz when you land yeah?"

"Will do mate," I said with a nod. "Thanks for having me the last couple of weeks."

"Our pleasure brother." We exchanged a fist bump before he guided Tails back to Mia, who was sleeping in her pram. Damn, I was going to miss that little munchkin.

"Carlton," said Nath, swinging a hard punch into my bicep.

"Stoner," I said, punching him back. We both chuckled sadly and pulled each other in for a hug and a mutual back slapping.

"It's not going to be the same here without you," he said, stepping back. "Who's gonna spot me now?" he teased with a wink.

"Time for Ryza, to get his lazy arse into the gym," I joked.

Ryan flipped me the bird. "Not happening man," he said, shaking his head with a smile.

I laughed and turned back to Nathan. "You'll come and visit right?"

"We'll lock it in as soon as the baby's old enough," he said with a nod, eyeing me up and down dubiously. "You gonna be okay?"

"Yeah," I said with a nod. "Fresh start will be good." I glanced over his shoulder at Ash, who was hanging back. She'd been actively avoiding me since our argument at their wedding. "Get over here Granger," I said, holding out my arms. Ash hesitated for a moment then ran over and threw her arms around me.

"That's Mrs Stone to you," she joked through her tears.

"Nope. Tails will always be Tails, and you'll always be Granger," I teased squeezing her tightly.

"I'm really story I overstepped Rich," she muttered into my chest. I paused and took a breath.

"Actually, I think you could be right," I admitted hesitantly. Her head flew up and her bright green eyes pierced into me. "But don't go getting any ideas," I added quickly, "regardless of the circumstances, Aims made her decision, so promise me you'll let this go."

"But-"

"No," I said sternly. "I need you to let this go." Her eyes held mine, flaring with defiance. I tilted my head and set my jaw, daring her to argue with me. "Please just do it for me? I can't move on if you open this can of worms. It's better left as it is."
Eventually she sighed and nodded.

"Fine."

"Thank you," I said, squeezing her shoulders as she stepped away from me. "I want you to focus on this kid," I said, gently poking her stomach, "and that husband of yours."

"I will," she said with a tearful nod.

"Love you, Granger."

"Love you too, Ritch." I stepped back and she returned to Stoners side. There they were: the two happy little families. I took one final look over their faces before grabbing my carry-on.

"Later fuckers," I joked to break the sombre mood. "If you can't be good, be good at it." I waved at them all and then and turned to leave when a frantic voice shouted from somewhere behind me.

"Wait!" called Cody, sprinting through the airport towards me, wheeling a suitcase behind him. I dropped my bag and grinned at the crazy poof.

"Wow I've never seen him run before," I mocked, as we watched my unfit friend approaching. "I'm surprised he even knows how to do it."

"Ritch," Cody puffed, drawing closer to our little crew.

"You here to tell me you love me and you're coming with me to Australia?" I teased, opening my arms for a hug as he let go of his suitcase and jogged towards me, panting.

"Of course," he joked, wrapping his arms around me with breathless laugh, "why else would I run?" We hugged, chuckling. "I came straight from the Eurostar but there were delays on the tube."

"Well, I appreciate you making the effort. I'm really glad you made it man."

"Ritchie, I wouldn't let you go without saying goodbye."

"Just as well."

"I'm going to miss you, big man. Life won't be the same without you around."

"I'm gonna miss you too little poof," I teased, punching his arm.

"Ritchie!" exclaimed Ash with horror, "you can't say things like that."

"I can say whatever I want," I told her, winking at Cody, "I'm leaving remember?" We all fell silent, and another boarding call echoed over the PA. "Well, I guess I'd better get on that plane, or they'll leave without me." I turned to Cody and gave him one last slap on the back. "Thanks for getting here Codes."

"No probs man."

"Take care of yourself and keep me posted on any Guillaume news. It seems to be the time for weddings and babies, so I want to be the first to know if something exciting happens."

"Sure thing," he said with a teary smile. "Although I think we're safe on the accidental pregnancy part."

I laughed and looked around, taking one last look at them before picking up my bag again. "Love you guys."

"We love you too Ritch."

"See you on the flipside," I said with a casual wave, as if I was heading off for a quick weekender, before quickly striding through the departure gates so I couldn't change my mind about going home.

I felt like I was like leaving a part of myself behind. Every moment we'd had together over the last few years, flashed through my mind like a movie montage. Once I was safely through the gates, I took one last glance out to the departures area and waved sadly at my crew. How would I ever find friends like that again? They all waved back as I was ushered away from my past by the moving crowd. It was time.

I focused on the journey ahead of me and strode quickly to my gate. As I boarded the Dreamliner, I couldn't help but feel a sense of emptiness inside me. I had just walked away from my entire life and everything I'd known for ten whole years. My friends, my home, my job, and most importantly, Amy. The thought of her still lingered in my mind. Would Ash really let it go? Was I doing the right thing by ignoring it, or would Sandrine get worse if she thought she got away with it? Hopefully she'd just give up and move on once I was on the other side of the world.

I found my seat and settled in. When the plane took off, I gazed out the window, watching as the city of London slowly disappeared from sight. The dreariness of the city sky reflected my emotions. I felt lost and alone, with no idea of what the future would hold. All I knew was that it was the end of an era and the beginning of a whole new life.

- NATHAN STONE -

As Ritchie's bald head slowly disappeared from sight, I felt a lump growing in my throat. I couldn't believe he wouldn't be around for this next chapter of my life. Our little crew was now done to four, plus kids. Ash squeezed my hand as if sensing the sorrow hiding under my stoic expression. I peered down at her and wrapped my arm around her shoulder.

"I can't believe he's gone," I mumbled to no one in particular.

"Yeah, me either," said Kat, checking on Mia who had begun to stir.

"Shall we grab lunch while we're here?" suggested Ryan.

"Yeah, I'm starving." It was after midday and my stomach was rumbling. The four of us began to move but Cody stood still, hand resting on his suitcase handle. "You coming?" I asked, nodding my head to indicate he should follow.

He looked surprised but grateful. "Yeah, thanks. I could do with a feed."

We all strolled silently through Terminal 3 towards the pub we'd passed on the way in. Besides Mia's groggy cooing, not a sound was uttered between us. Life would never be the same again and we all knew it. Ash and I would be heading down to Cornwall; the McPhersons would be venturing into their new family dynamic.; and Cody was facing the prospect of working with an almost entirely new team. Life as we'd known it, was no longer.

"So how are things going in Paris?" I asked Cody. "Sandrine behaving herself?"

"Yeah, she's been kinda scary to be honest," he said quietly. "I don't know how they're going to find someone to replace Didier because he's the only person in the world who could take that much crap and still have a smile on his face."

"Is there anything I can do to support our team over there?"

"Actually, Beau's handling her well. It hasn't been easy but he's starting to build a good rapport with her so hopefully, once she's over this Ritchie thing, she'll settle down."

"Well, that's good to hear," I said, surprised that Beau was the one seemingly keeping a sinking ship afloat. "And what about your French bloke? How's that going?" I asked once we'd all sat down.

"Really good," he said with a smile, "in fact, Gaz was looking to relocate some of the team to Paris full-time so I thought I'd volunteer."

"Wow, that's great Cody," said Ash.

"Yeah," agreed Tails, partly distracted with feeding Mia, "I think you and Beau will make a good team over there."

"Yeah, thanks," Cody said with a shy shrug. "It would be an amazing opportunity." We all ate in silence for a little while until Cody spoke up again. "I can't believe you guys had Sloane Sutton sing at your wedding," he said to Ash and I. "That was next level."

"That was all Ryza," I said with a mouthful of fries, "I can't take any credit for that one."

"Yeah," Cody said, eyes wide as he turned to Ryan, "and Rodney Baker. How the heck did that come about?"

"That's a long story," Ryza laughed.

"Ryan got them together, so they owed him one," said Tails proudly.

"We were all in rehab together," explained Ryan.

"Well, that's pretty awesome."

"Yeah, to be honest... rehab wasn't all bad."

"But I'm very glad to have you home," Tails said, staring at Ryan lovingly.

"And I'm very glad to be home," Ryan said. "Imagine if you'd had to manage two kids and two cats on your own."

I laughed with great amusement.

"Holy shit," said Codes, looking between Ryan and myself, "did he actually end up convincing you to take the kittens?"

"No," Ryan grumbled, "he targeted my wife on that one."

"Come on Ryza," I said with a chuckle, "you love them."

"No, Kat loves them. I just tolerate them."

"He says that," Tails said with a wink, "but I see him secretly cuddling them when he thinks I'm not watching."

"Fuck you all," Ryza retorted with a grin.

- ASHLEY STONE -

"And how are you feeling Ash?" Kat asked, as she tucked away her boob and rested Mia over her shoulder. "I know we see each other every day, but work's been so busy I feel like I've hardly spoken to you."

"Yeah same," I agreed. "I'm feeling much better now that the morning sickness has gone," I said thankfully. "And how are you with everything that's going on? Not long before Kellie's due."

"Yeah, it's been a whirlwind. I don't really know how we're going to make it all work. Or how I'll cope when you two are gone too."

"You'll be fine. You've got it completely under control."

"Thanks. Everything is changing so much."

"Sure is," I agreed, "but it will be good. It's the next level for all of us. I mean, look at you. You're running a multi-million-pound account."

"Honestly, I'm trying not to think about that."

"But why? You're so good at it and you clearly love it."

"Yeah, exactly. My career is finally where I want it to be and I'm only just keeping things together. With me working reduced hours and Ryan only part time, we have it under control, but another baby is going to tip the scales and I just don't know whether I'm going to be able to keep all the balls in the air."

"Kat," I said, thinking carefully about my next words, "it's totally normal to be worried, but you said yourself that you've wanted a family for years. Well, now you're getting it. It might not be quite how you'd planned it, but this is your dream coming true. You'll find a way to make it work."

"You think so?"

"I know so."

"I guess just having a taste of my career again has reminded me who I am. I love working. What if I have to give that up again?"

"You won't." And let me just remind you that there's no way Ryan would let you walk away from something that makes you so happy. Between the two of you, you'll figure it out."

- RITCHIE CARLTON -

When the plane began its descent into Perth, my heart was racing with anticipation. The city looked so small and compact compared to London. The CBD was just a small group of buildings clustered on the edges of the Swan River, surrounded by suburbs which were bordered by the ocean. That turquoise shoreline was something to behold. After visiting countless oceans in various locations across the globe, Perth beaches were officially unbeatable. In my decade of travels, I'd not found one that had matched up.

I knew my family would be waiting for me at the airport, but I wasn't sure if I was ready to face them yet. I'd only told them the top-line details of my recent experiences and the thought of having to explain everything to them felt overwhelming. I just wanted to get back to Mum and Dads and curl up in bed. I didn't want to see anyone. I didn't want to have to pretend to be happy, or convince them that I was okay, I just wanted to burrito myself in a blanket for a while. It was going to be hard enough to re-acclimatise to my small hometown where everyone knew everyone's business.

At that moment, I was between two lives; two worlds; two versions of me, but my London life would be officially over, the second that I stepped off that plane.

The plane touched down as the warm Australian sunshine shone down around us. I'd forgotten how bright the Aussie sun could be. As I waited for the doors to open, I fished around in my carry-on for my sunnies. I retrieved the shades, slid them onto my bald head, then pulled my phone out of my pocket to text Ryza and let him know I'd landed safe.

"Thank you for flying QANTAS," announced the pilot over the intercom, "we hope you enjoyed your flight on the Dreamliner, and we look forward to hosting you again. For those of you here holidaying, we hope you enjoy your stay in Perth, and for those returning home, welcome back."

The hostesses took their positions at the door and began ushering a slow-moving crowd down the aisles to where we were farewelled by a tall brunette with a glaringly white smile.

"See you next time," she said, with well-rehearsed friendliness.

I nodded my appreciation and stepped into the tunnel. That was it. I was off the plane and back in Perth. I swallowed back a deep breath and rolled my carry-on up the long tunnel. I followed the crowds as my mind pondered possibilities of my future. I had a job waiting and a family that was eager to see me. I'd lost touch with all my friends over that decade so really… the job and my family was all I'd be starting with.

I mindlessly wandered towards the baggage claim, completely lost in my own thoughts until I heard someone calling my name.

"Ritchie Carlton?" I heard from the direction of one of the carousels. I looked up to see the vaguely familiar face of a guy I couldn't quite place. "Holy shit, it is you!" The guy exclaimed, striding towards me. "Besides the bald head, you haven't changed a bit," he laughed, reaching out to shake my hand.

"Yeah the ginger dreadies fell off," I chuckled amicably, rolling with the conversation in the hopes that I'd remember who he was.

"Great to see you mate, it's been too long," he said, concluding our handshake with a friendly slap to my shoulder. "You been on a holiday?"

"Nah man, I just moved back from London," I said, waving towards the carousel board that said 'London Heathrow – Perth'.

"Oh nice. Were you over there for long?"

"Ten years."

"Well that explains why no one's seen you around then."

"Heh, yeah," I chuckled awkwardly, wondering who 'no one' was. "How about you? Been away?"

"Yeah, just took the family over to Bali to beat the school holiday rush."

"Sounds great," I said, starting to reacquaint myself with Perth life. Bali felt like such a foreign concept after living in Europe for so long. The Indonesian island was Perth's favourite holiday destination and a large percentage of Perth-lings considered it their quota of 'international' travel. All the tourists sporting Bintang singlets and weird tan lines, believing they were the height of sophistication.

"That's my wife and kids over there," he added, gesturing towards an average looking brunette wearing a tie-died dress, and organising three kids of various ages with Bali-braided heads.

"Lovely family," I said, not sure what else to say. He was a stereotypical Aussie male and for some reason that was grating on me. I'd always considered myself a typical Aussie bloke, but I'd obviously changed more than I'd realised.

"You got your own place or you staying with your folks?"

"Just staying with the folks until I find a place."

"Oh sweet. Say hi to them for me."

"Will do," I agreed with a nod, still no clearer on who he was or how he knew my parents. Thankfully, my luggage carousel began moving, and bags began appearing through the little plastic flaps. "Looks like my bag is on its way," I said, pointing towards the slow-moving carousel. "It was great to see you though."

"Likewise," he agreed with a nod, "hit me up when you get settled and we'll catch up for a drink."

"Sounds great," I lied.

"Catch you around."

"Absolutely." I held my smile for an appropriate amount of time and ducked through the loitering crowd to the furthest conveyor belt.

I hadn't been mentally prepared to speak to anyone besides my family. I'd been saving all my peopling energy to get through that particular emotional whirlwind, and the unexpected human interaction had drained most of what I'd set aside. I felt exhausted already and I hadn't even seen my mum yet. I already knew she'd end up in tears of joy, so I'd have to put on a happy face.

I collected my bag and wheeled it towards customs, deliberately avoiding the same queue as my new BFF. He clocked me walking past, so I smiled and waved, giving him a friendly nod as I trundled through the cordoned lines.

The long customs line was a blessing as it gave me time to collect myself. Thankfully there wasn't anyone else I knew so I was able to stand and wait in silence and re-gather my energy enough to face my family. But the line flowed smoothly and, sooner than I'd hoped, I'd found myself walking out into the arrival's hall.

My family was there, all gathered together eagerly awaiting my arrival. Mum and Dad; Sean and Isla; Jasmine and her husband Ben, with their two kids: their new baby Lily, who I'd never met, and my four-year-old niece Ivey. As I emerged from the doors, my mother rushed over to hug me, tears streaming down her face, and I couldn't help but feel a sense of comfort in her embrace. Despite the pain and confusion I was feeling, seeing my family again made me realize that I wasn't completely alone in the world. I knew that there would be many challenges ahead, but with their love and support, I was ready to face them head-on.

"You're looking good shitbag," said Sean punching me in the shoulder before wrapping his arms around me.

"Thanks, Seany," I said, patting his back to extricate myself from his hug.

"Yeah, you are," agreed Isla with a cheeky wink, "I'm starting to think I picked the wrong brother."

I laughed and gave her a hug.

"Well I'm here any time you come to your senses," I teased.

"Oi," warned Sean with a smile. Jaz and Ben hung back with the pram and waited for the rest of the gaggle to finish fussing. Dad grabbed my suitcase, and Sean took my carry-on so I could hug everyone unimpeded. "Hey Spaz," I teased, smiling at Jaz.

"Hey Snitch," she retorted, stepping up to give me a hug. "I missed you big brother."

"Missed you too."

"You doing okay?" she asked, scrutinising my face.

"Yeah."

"Liar," she teased with a knowing smile.

"Ritch," said Ben grabbing my hand for a firm handshake. "How was your flight mate?"

"Pretty good actually. Much better than the old stop-over flights."

"I can imagine."

"And who's this young lady? That can't be Ivey, She looks way too grown up."

"It's me Uncle Ritchie."

"Are you sure?"

Ivey giggled. "Yes."

"Well then, you must be in high school by now huh?"

"No," she laughed. "I'm only four."

"No way."

"Yes way."

"I can't believe it."

"Right," announced my dad with a clap of his hands, "shall we get this show on the road?"

- KANE THOMPSON -

Only a week to go before Sean's Bucks night and nearly everything was in place. It was the first time I'd ever been a best man and I was taking my duties way too seriously, but I didn't care. I was determined to make it memorable for my best mate, and I would go to any lengths to make that happen. I'd organised an entire weekend on Rottnest Island, complete with an itinerary of activities that ranged from nerdy to dangerous.

"Kane, you've been working all day," called Soph from my swimming pool. "It's 35 degrees on a Saturday evening, get off the phone and into this pool."

"Yeah, Uncle Kane," agreed Taj, climbing out of the pool to grab a giant inflatable unicorn.

"I'm not working, I'm organising the buck's night."

"You had it organised months ago," she said, splashing playfully in my direction. "How much more can you possibly plan by next weekend?"

"I just want Sean's bucks to be epic."

"It will be epic," she said, patiently. "Now put the phone down or it'll take a swim."

"You wouldn't dare."

"Try me."

"Fine," I sighed with a smile as she stared me down. I stashed my phone out of the sun, stripped off my T-shirt, then ran at the pool in full bombie mode.

"Kane, no!" Soph squealed as I jumped into the air, legs tucked tight for maximum impact. I hit the surface with a huge splash, which sent a gush of water out onto the travertine pavers. When I came back up, Taj was giggling uncontrollably and Soph was absolutely drenched. Her hair was plastered to her cheeks, and streams of water ran down the front her face. I grinned proudly at Taj, and then turned to Soph who was still spitting the chlorinated water from her mouth.

"What?" I teased with a grin. "You were the one who told me to get in."

"You're going to regret that," she warned, an evil smile crossing her face as she dove straight at me with the speed and agility of a dolphin.

I grabbed her around the waist seconds before her hands landed on my shoulders to push me under the water. I wrapped my arms tight around her middle and we both went down, bodies pressed together. The feel of her wet skin sliding against mine was too much for my body to handle and I felt an uncontrollable shift in my boardshorts. Panicked that Soph would feel it too, I quickly released my grip on her bare skin and attempted to dart back up to the surface. Unfortunately, she clutched tightly to me, and we came up together, re-surfacing face-to-face in a way that would barely pass as PG rated.

"G'day," Sean called pointedly from the side of the pool, where he and Isla stood watching us with stunned amusement. Sophie and I broke apart. "Didn't realise it was dinner and a show," he teased.

"I try to make my events entertaining," I retorted, risking a quick glance at Taj, to see what he'd made of our little spectacle. He seemed completely unphased.

"Did Ritchie get in okay? How was the family reunion? I bet your mum was stoked." I asked in quick succession, deflecting the attention back towards Sean.

"Yeah, it was good," he said blankly, "obviously not as much fun as whatever was happening here though."

"We were having a water fight," chimed in Taj with impeccable timing.

"Fun," said Sean with an intrigued look on his face.

"I brought margherita mix," declared Isla, who was either ready to party or keen to diffuse the awkwardness.

"Ooh, let's go make a jug!" Soph said enthusiastically, jumping out of the pool at a rate of knots. The water droplets rolled down her tanned skin and made her curvy body shimmer in the sunlight. For a moment, the world shifted into slow motion and, as she towel-dried her long blonde hair, I felt like I was watching a movie. It was so surreal I almost expected to hear Dream Weaver drifting out of the speakers, Wayne's World style. She peered over her shoulder at me, snapping me out of my trance.

Feeling embarrassed that I'd been caught perving, I grabbed a stray pool noodle and launched a foam attack on Taj. I bopped the child gently over the head with the blue Styrofoam tube and he reached for the mega super-soaker.

"Stick 'em up Uncle Kane," he said innocently oblivious to the fact that I was already well and truly 'up'.

"You got me kiddo," I joked. "I surrender."

"Dad will be here soon Tajy, so it's time to get out," Soph called, wrapping a towel around her bare waist.

"Aww mum, do I have to go to Dads?" Taj whined. "Can't I stay at

Uncle Kane's with you?"

Sean darted a curious look in my direction at the fact that Soph was staying over. I shrugged as subtly as possible, to indicate that it wasn't what he was thinking.

"You haven't seen your dad in a week," Soph said, seemingly unaware of the unspoken discussion happening around her, "and he misses you babe. He'd be sad if you didn't go."

"Fine," Taj agreed with an over-exaggerated sigh.

"Thank you," Soph said, before following Isla inside. Sean stashed the beers in the bar fridge, leaving two out on the bench, presumably for us to drink immediately.

"Hey Uncle Sean," Taj called over to him, "check out what Uncle Kane taught me." Taj then proceeded to recreate my bombie, running towards the pool and tucking his legs tight.

"No, Taj, wait," I said as he jumped right over my head and hit the water with a splash. The wave got me hard the face and I spat out the water with a splutter. The boy came up giggling hysterically, and Sean joined in the laughter as I wiped the water off my face.

"That was awesome mate," Sean laughed, picking up the two beers from the counter, "perfect aim."

"Thanks!" Taj said, making his way to the steps. "I reckon that was better than Uncle Kane's one."

"Probably," I chuckled.

"I bet I could go higher," he said, climbing out of the pool.

"Maybe next time mate," I said with my serious Uncle Kane voice, "your mum just asked you to wind it up remember?"

"Fine," he grumbled, "I guess I'll go have a shower then."

"Good man," I told him proudly, as he grabbed his towel and trudged inside. Once the coast was clear, Sean sat on the edge of the pool and gave me his most serious look.

"What are you doing man?" he asked, handing me one of the beers before swinging his legs into the water.

"What do you mean?" I asked innocently.

"You know exactly what I mean," he said, unamused. "You and Soph and this happy little pretend family you've got going on here. You guys have barely been apart since the charity ball."

"Yeah, we're just putting on a show."

"In your own home?" he asked judgmentally. "I don't see any journos here, do you?"

"Are you saying we can't hang out unless we're in public?"

"You're twisting my words," he said with a sigh. "All I'm saying is the only people you guys are fooling are yourselves."

"Meaning what exactly?"

"Meaning that you're so busy trying to convince people you're a couple that you've fooled yourselves into believing it too."

"You're being ridiculous mate."

"You're in a fake relationship for the benefit of public opinion, and I'm the one being ridiculous?"

"A hundred percent," I said, ignoring his dig.

"You want to hear it straight mate?" he asked, holding no punches.

"Not really," I muttered, taking a swig of the ice-cold beer.

Sean continued regardless. "She's clinging to you because she doesn't know how to be alone, and you're clinging to the fantasy that you're together, because you're in love with her."

"Wow," I said, feeling both insulted and seen in equal measures.

"How long has it been you got laid?"

"What's that got to do with anything?"I asked, gruffly.

"It's got everything to do with everything," he said, exhaustedly. "You're quite clearly thinking with your dick right now, so you need to get your end away before you do something you'll regret."

"And by 'something I regret' you mean shagging Soph?"

"Bingo," he said like a gameshow host. "I know you want this Thommo, but you need to give her time to grieve for her marriage."

"She had a whole month of grieving before I coaxed her out."

"One month for a twenty-year relationship? You really think she's over it that quickly?"

"No, but-"

"But nothing Kane. She's not ready. If you keep living in this la-la land of make-believe, you're gonna get your heart broken."

"How could I get my heart broken when I have no expectations?"

"All I'm saying is just take a breather. Put some space between you for a little while."

"I'm not gonna do that Sean. I promised her we'd see this thing through until it faded away."

"Fine," Sean shrugged, "but don't say I didn't warn you."

"Warning heeded," I said snidely, before changing the subject. "What are you doing here anyway? Shouldn't you be spending time with Ritchie?"

"The guy just spent 24hours on a plane. He was shattered," Sean said, taking a long swig of his cold beer. "I'll have plenty of time to hang out with him once he's acclimatised again."

"Fair point," I agreed with a nod. "Is he happy to be home?"

"I think he's got mixed feelings," Sean said, chugging his beer. "He's smiling on the outside, but he seems completely broken. He's not the same man he was when he left. He's had a rough year, and it shows."

"His old boss said something similar. What happened to him in London?"

"His girlfriend killed herself."

"Fuuuck," I breathed in shock, not expecting something so heavy.

"Yeah. And he was there when they found the body," Seany said with a nod, "I think it messed him up a lot."

"That's good to know. At least I can be mindful of where he's at and keep an eye on him."

"Thanks man," Sean said with an appreciative nod. "Anyway, onto funner topics… what's happening for your birthday weekend? We doing the usual?"

"We haven't even gotten to your Bucks' night! How are you already thinking about my birthday?"

"I haven't had to think about my Bucks because you've had it under control," he joked. "So… we gonna go down to the beach house for the birthday bash?"

"I guess so," I said with a shrug. "I haven't really thought about it."

"Well, I reckon it would be good to have one last getaway together before the wedding."

"How would that even work with Soph and Brenton in the same house though?"

"Just don't invite Brenno."

"He might be a dick, but I can't exclude him. Taj would be expecting him there."

"Just set some ground rules," he said, with a shrug. "It's your house, and your birthday, you get to make the rules."

"Do I though?" I asked sceptically, knowing full well that our annual trip down to my beach house was now based on expectation rather than an invitation.

"It would be good for Taj to keep some normality don't you think?" he said casually, knowing that Taj was my weakness.

"Yeah, I guess," I agreed noncommittally, unwilling to let him know he'd won that round.

"You reckon you're up for a weekender then? Isla and I want to head down to scope out the venue again one last time, so we thought we'd combine it." And there it was. That constant expectation. It wasn't about my birthday at all. It was about their wedding prep.

"Well as long as it's convenient for you," I muttered snidely, rolling my eyes.

"You know what I mean," he said with an apologetic shrug. "She's in full planning mode so she wants to get it locked in."

"Fine," I sighed, "let's do it then."

"Sweet, want me to tell the troops?"

"Nah, I'll do it. I wanna chat to Soph first to make sure she's okay with Brenton being there."

"And if she's not?"

"Then I'll cross that bridge when I come to it."

- SOPHIE THOMPSON -

I followed Isla and her margherita mix, into the kitchen, drying myself as I walked.

"Oh my god," she said as soon as we were out of earshot, "what the hell was that?"

"What was what?"

"That thing with you and Kane. It looked like you two were getting sexy under the water."

"What?! No," I said, appalled. "It wasn't like that, we were just mucking around. Kane's practically my brother."

"A brother that you're pretending to be dating."

"That's out of necessity," I said defensively.

"Sure it is," Isla agreed with a raised brow. "But for the record, I've never seen him do anything like that with Frankie, which is just as well because I'd be traumatised if I had."

"Seriously, what's wrong with you? My son was right there with us."

"Yeah, he was," she agreed with a teasing grin, "and you two were giving him quite the education."

"Oh, for God's sake," I said, rolling my eyes and grabbing the cocktail mix off her, "nothing happened."

"Fine," she laughed, "be in denial."

At that moment, Taj burst in the back door. "I'm having a shower," he called, heading straight through the kitchen and down the hall towards the guest room.

"Alright babe," I called after him. "Just hang your bathers in the bathroom. I've packed a dry pair for you to take to Dads."

"Okay." We waited to hear the bathroom door close, and then Isla looked at me with a raised brow.

"You need to get laid."

"I'm fine."

"No, you're not," she teased, pulling a massive bottle of tequila out of her bag, "How long's it been since you split? A couple of months?"

"Actually," I said, tipping the mix into the blender, "Brenton and I hadn't been together for a long time before we split."

"Like how long exactly?"

I paused and thought back over my sex life, while Isla swigged straight from the tequila bottle, awaiting my answer.

"I think Taj was a baby the last time we had sex."

"Holy shit," she said, nearly choking on the tequila. "You haven't had sex for like, a whole decade?"

"Give or take," I answered with embarrassment. "Brenton stopped wanting it, so I stopped trying. I just figured that was parenthood and I focused on looking after Taj. I was so busy with him that I never really thought about it." I grabbed the bottle of tequila out of her hand. "I guess it makes more sense now I know he was getting it from elsewhere," I added, taking a huge gulp of the burning liquid.

"We need to find you a rebound fling asap," she said, while I breathed out the tequila fumes, "Sean's brother is pretty hot. If I wasn't with Sean, I'd definitely hit that."

"There are so many things wrong with that sentence I can't even respond," I said dryly.

"Ritchie is single and hot, why not?" she asked, genuinely dumbfounded as to why I wouldn't jump at the chance. "Besides, you have to shag someone before you malfunction and bonk Kane."

"It's not like that. We're just pretending to be together to keep the media off my case."

"Soph, cut the bullshit and be honest with me," she said, rolling her eyes. "Have you got the hots for Kane?" I stepped back from her, almost as if her words had thrown me off balance.

"I mean…" I said, drawing the word out to give my brain time to compute the question. "I can see why other women think he's hot," I concluded with a shrug. Why would she even ask me that?

"But do *you* think he's hot?"

"He did look pretty good in his tux at the charity ball."

"So that's a yes then?" she asked, dumping a tray full of ice into the blender.

"I guess," I said with a shrug, "but we're family so it's all theoretical."

"You're not blood related."

"No, but that doesn't make him any less family," I told her firmly. "I could never sleep with him."

"Technically you already have."

"You know what I mean."

"You mean you wouldn't bonk him."

"No. I mean, yeah. I mean… no, I wouldn't bonk him."

"Are you sure about that?" she asked, before blitzing the cocktail ingredients. The noise of the blender was overwhelming and made any further conversation impossible. Isla winked at me, knowing she'd given me some food for thought. Would I ever consider Kane seriously? He knew me well, he was smart, and funny, and kind, and rich, and really good-looking, and best of all, he loved my son to bits. On paper, he was the perfect man. Isla turned off the blender, and we could hear Brenton calling from the front door.

"Hellooo," his voice echoed through the house.

"Oh, hey!" I called overly chirpily, running to meet him at the door. "Sorry, we were making margaritas."

"Big night on the cards then?" he asked, giving me a peck on the cheek as he stepped into the entrance foyer.

"Isla's keen to party."

"Getting the partying out of her system before she's weighed down by the old ball and chain huh?"

"Some people actually enjoy marriage Brenton," I said icily as he made his way towards the kitchen.

"Speaking of which," he said with a mocking wink, "any wedding bells in sight for you? What's it been now? Three weeks?"

"Very funny," I said, unimpressed. "You know what the media's like. Once they get set on a story, they're like a dog with a bone."

"Hopefully that's the only bone happening," he said snidely.

"You lost the right to talk about my bones the moment you started sharing yours around town."

"Chill," he surrendered, raising his hands in the air, "I was just kidding. No need to be so touchy."

"The Eagle is in the nest," teased Isla from her position at the blender.

"G'day love," Brenton said, giving her a hug and dipping his finger into the margarita mix to taste test it. "Planning a messy night are ya?"

"You know it," she said, smacking his hand away from the drink. "The boys are out the back if you want to say hi," she said, trying to get rid of him on my behalf.

"Nah, I've gotta get going. I've booked us movie tickets," replied Brenton, turning his attention back to me. "Taj ready?"

"He's just in the shower."

"Okay, I'll go get his A into G." Brenton disappeared down the hall and Isla shot me her 'that was close' look. I could only imagine what Brenton would have said if he'd overheard our conversation.

- NATHAN STONE -

After a month-long battle to get my mother assessed by Doctor Blakely, the day had finally arrived for him to get into the hospital of horrors for Mums assessment. To keep things as subtle as possible, we had agreed that it would only be he and I making the visit, so as not to draw attention to the situation. The hospital was concerned about appearances and, after fighting so hard to get even that far, I was willing to do whatever it took to get the assessment completed.

I introduced Mum to Doctor Blakely and them left them to it, while I wandered down the road to get a coffee. I found a cozy little café on the high street, the perfect place to shelter from the icy breeze. Winter had taken hold now and the Autumn chill had turned into a sharp wintery bite. I ordered my coffee and glanced at my watch. It was 11am here, which meant in Perth it would be around 4pm. Ritchie should have landed a few hours ago, so I found a table in a quiet corner and pulled out my phone to Facetime him.

"Now there's a face that's perfect for radio," Ritchie chuckled when he accepted the call.

"You looking in a mirror Carlton?" I retorted as he moved locations. "How was your flight?"

"The flight was good. Dreamliner is the only way to go, so remember that when you bring the Stone clan out here," he teased jovially, stepping out into bright sunlight that reflected off his bald head.

"Yeah, might have to book a flight tomorrow. It looks like you're in paradise with that sunshine."

"Yeah, it's, like 35degrees. I'm half expecting my body to go into shock."

"It's about 5 degrees here today so I know where I'd rather be," I joked. "Besides the great weather, how is it being home?"

"Weird," he said, looking around and then walking a little further into what I assumed to be the backyard. "It's good to see everyone, but it all feels so surreal. Like I'm dreaming or something."

"I can't even imagine."

"Everything is exactly the same but also completely different. I feel like I'm a visitor in my hometown. Sean and Jaz are both so happy and settled that it's hard not to feel jealous. It just seems like their lives are perfect, while mine is in tatters."

"It's not in tatters man. You're just starting a new chapter."

"Yeah, back from the exact same place I was when I left."

"Not really. You've got money and a great career behind you, plus a good job lined up. That's no small achievement."

"Yeah, good point," he agreed with a sigh. "I'm sure once I get my own place things will feel different."

"Exactly. It's only been a few hours, it's bound to feel strange."

"I don't know if it's that or if I've changed too much you know? I feel like I'm on a totally different wavelength. I went through hell with you guys, and they've been here living this happy little family life. It feels so far removed from me, like I'm watching a game from the sidelines."

"I know that feeling. Why do you think we decided to move down to Cornwall?"

"How do I even begin to explain any of it to them? They'd have no comprehension."

"Mate, I don't think anyone outside of the five of us will ever be able to comprehend what we went through. We lived through a bunch of shit that most people only see in movies. Life and death situations change a person and it's impossible for someone to fathom if they've never been through something that extreme."

"Yeah, I guess."

"Just look at it as if you're a soldier coming back from war. People will intellectually recognise what's happened to you, but they'll never understand how and why it's changed you. Your family will always be your family, but don't expect them to get you. You'll find your people soon enough. Once you start getting into the swing of your new life, the right people will cross your path."

"Thanks man."

"Give yourself a few weeks to settle in and I'm sure you'll find your footing. For now, enjoy having meals cooked for you," I joked. Ritchie threw his head back and laughed.

"I might even try to slip in some laundry too," he chuckled. "My mum's gone straight back into mum-mode so I'd better milk it before the novelty wears off and she realises I'm pretty much a middle-aged man." We both laughed.

"Absolutely."

"Speaking of mums, shouldn't you be at your mum's assessment?"

"I am. Doctor Blakely is in with her now."

"Nice. So when will you know if she can be admitted?"

"Hopefully today."

"That's great mate. I hope it all goes well."

"Me too."

"Anyway, I guess I should get back to the ginger brigade."

"Yeah, I'll let you go. Just wanted to check in on you."

"Cheers man," he said with an appreciative nod. "Seriously, it's been good to see your face. It's given me a bit of normality in amongst this craziness."

"No problem buddy. I'm always at the other end of the line whenever you need me."

"Likewise," he said, looking over his shoulder. "Better go. Send my love to Ash and the others."

"Will do. Later Ritch."

"Later Stoner."

I ended the call and focused on my coffee. I was a little worried about Ritchie, but he'd find his feet eventually. There was nothing I could do for him from here. It was his journey now and he had to navigate it for himself. My mother's happiness, on the other hand, was somewhat within my control.

I finished my coffee as slowly as possible, then made my way back to the hospital, stopping to grab mum a box of chocolates from Waitrose on the way past. When I returned to her room, Doctor Blakely ushered me out into the hallway.

"Nathan," he said solemnly, "I'd like to do some further tests on your mother."

"Okay," I agreed with a nod, "when? Now?"

"No, I'd like to get her transferred to The Priory ASAP."

"Really?" I asked, elated. "She's passed the assessment?"

"Well, it's not a matter of passing or failing," he said with a hearty chuckle, "but I do think your mother meets the criteria, and I do believe we have the facilities to treat her effectively."

"Great!"

"I'm going to have my receptionist process these forms this afternoon so we can get things moving," Dr Blakely said, tapping the folder under his arm with a reassuring smile, "I'd like to get her out of here sooner rather than later."

"Let me know what you need me to do."

"Will do," he said, looking over his shoulder to ensure there was no one lurking. "Nathan, I'm not a hundred percent certain at this stage, but I suspect that your mother might not actually be schizophrenic at all."

"What?" I asked in shock, wondering whether perhaps I had misunderstood him.

"Well… if they're using the meds to keep her confused, then it's possible the original prognosis was incorrect too. I won't have an accurate picture until she's off those meds, but from what I've seen of her, I'd say she was probably just suffering from PTSD."

"PTSD? Don't soldiers get that from war?" I asked in shock, "is that something normal people get?"

"Yes and no," he said obscurely. "It's very common in war vets, but it can occur in civilians after any event that the brain processes as being traumatic… like the death of your father."

"Wow, okay," I said as my head swirled, "so what does that mean exactly?"

"Well, the good news is that if that's the case then, once your mother has detoxed from the meds, all we'll need to do is address the PTSD, which is primarily just psychological treatments."

"Great… but why do I get the feeling that there's also bad news?" I asked dubiously.

"It's a possibility that the Antipsychotics may have caused some permanent damage."

"I don't understand."

"Those drugs alter the neurotransmitters in the brain," he said unhelpfully.

"Okay," I said trying to act as if I understood what he was saying.

"If a person has mental illness, they have abnormal levels of neurotransmitters and this kind of medication helps to restore the balance of hormones in the brain," Doctor Blakely explained.

"Right," I nodded.

"So, the problem is that in a healthy brain, where there is no neurotransmitter imbalance, these drugs can cause permanent brain damage because they're altering hormones that were previously functioning at normal levels."

My heart sank. "Oh."

"After being on the meds for so long I'll be very surprised if Hellen hasn't suffered some amount of brain damage, but it will take some time to determine to what extent that may be," he paused. "Look Nathan don't be disheartened, it's still quite possible that your mum will recover from this with minimal damage. Her current lucidity is a very positive sign, but I do need to make you aware of the worst-case scenario."

"Okay Thanks Doctor Blakely." I nodded, feeling completely devastated.

"You did the right thing by coming to me Nathan. We're going to do everything we can to get your mother back to some semblance of a normal life. If all goes well, there's no reason why she couldn't have her own apartment in our low care residential village."

"Wow."

"Now go home and wait for a call from my admissions team. Until then, there's nothing else you can do. I'll be in touch once I have all the test results back."

"Great. Okay. Thanks," I said shaking his hand mindlessly. He strode off down the eerie hallway, and I leaned against the wall with a sigh. It was a lot of information to take in. Was my mum going to be okay or had the decades of drugs damaged her brain permanently? Either way, I couldn't get her into The Priory quick enough.

- RITCHIE CARLTON -

I hung up from Stoner and looked around the garden I grew up in. This dinky little backyard in Joondana was a far cry from my London life. I took a deep breath and soaked up the sun. Maybe one day this life would feel more normal again. I opened my eyes to see Jaz stepping out onto the deck with baby Lilly propped on her hip.

"Was that the hot blonde one?" my sister asked.

"He thinks he hot," I joked, shoving my phone into my back pocket. "Did Ben win the Uno cup?"

"Nope, Dad still has holds the title."

"One day the king will fall." We both chuckled, and the baby gurgled in response. I smiled and gently bopped her tiny little nose. Everyone but me seemed to have one of those things either in their arms or on the way. Would I ever get the chance to be a dad?

"You okay big brother?" Jaz asked, eyeing me intently.

"Yeah, I'm good," I said with a dismissive shrug. "Can't complain with weather like this."

"Cut the bullshit Ritch," she said with a raised brow. "You might've been away for a while, but I know you remember?"
I signed and dropped the fake smile.

"I just can't believe I've missed so much. You guys all have your lives sorted and I'm nearly forty and starting all over again. I just feel like such a fuck up."

"You're kidding me right?" she asked with a laugh. "Ritch, you've been off seeing the world. You've travelled, you've built a career and you've saved a nest egg… you're far from being a fuck up."

"Doesn't feel that way."

"Hey… no one's expecting you to put on a brave face you know?" She said, rubbing my arm supportively. "You lost your girlfriend. That's huge babe. You're allowed to be sad."

"Oh, I am fucking sad," I said a little defensively. "But I've done my grieving. Now I just want to get on with my life."

"Okay," she placated, squeezing my arm, "but you know I'm always here for you right? If you ever need to talk about it, I'll be there to listen."

"Thanks Jaz."

"Just give yourself some time huh? You don't have to have it all figured out straight away. Just take a few months to re-acclimatise before you start making any big decisions."

"No time. I start my new job in two weeks, and I want to have a place sorted before then."

"Ritch, listen… I know you want get back to a normal life, but why not just enjoy being doted on for a while? Mum is so stoked to have you home, just let her spoil you for a month or two."

"Yeah, maybe."

"No maybe. Just do it. Once you find your feet with your job, then you can go all-guns blazing, but until then, just tackle one thing at a time."

"Okay fine," I agreed reluctantly. "I'll stay here for a while, but only until I settle in at work."

"Perfect."

I narrowed my eyes. "When did you get so wise?"

"When I popped out a couple of small humans," she joked.

"Gross."

"Anyway, I just came out to say bye," she said, kissing me on the cheek. "We've got to get the kids home to bed."

"Yeah, I think I need to go to bed myself."

"Try and push through for as long as you can. It'll help with the jetlag."

"Well thanks miss jet-setter. I didn't realise you were such an expert in travel," I teased.

"I watch a lot of reality TV."

"Ah well then it must be true."

"Mum wants us all to come around for brunch tomorrow, then she's promised to let you have some chill time."

"Thanks Jaz."

"I love you," she said, giving me a sideways hug."

"Love you too," I said, giving Lilly's head a gentle rub, "and you too little dude. It was good to finally meet you."

"See you tomorrow, Ritch."

"See ya." I watched Jaz vanish behind the flywire door and felt a sense of peace knowing that she could see through my bullshit. Maybe she didn't understand what I'd been through, but she did understand me.

"Ritch hurry up," called Ben, sticking his head out of the door Jaz had just gone into. "Your mum has made a Pav and Jaz is trying to make me leave before she serves it."
I laughed and wandered back towards the house.

"Well, I wouldn't want you missing out on any pav," I teased, back-handing his squishy gut.

"Oi, this is my cuddle cushion," he joked, tapping his belly as I followed him inside. "It makes me cuddlier."

"Whatever you say chubster."

"Stop picking on my husband," scolded Jaz. "I like him cuddly," she said, sliding her arm around his waist as she snuggled into him. Why was everyone around me so sickeningly in love? When would it be my turn?

– Chapter 4 –

One Month Later...

A Stone's Throw: Life in Cornwall

- ASHLEY STONE -

We rounded the final bend to our new home as the sun set over the Cornish hills behind us. In the rear-view mirror, the rocky green countryside framed an orange ball of light, while ahead of us, the ocean reflected the warm pastel colours of the coastal skyline. Thankfully the rain had held out for moving day and the skies had remained cloudy but dry. Not that we'd had much to load up. The purpose of our move was to get a fresh start, so it was mostly clothes, cat related paraphernalia and personal items that had relocated with us. We'd sold and given away all the furniture from my flat before the lease had ended, and we'd kept Nathan's apartment fully furnished to be our London base. Besides the cats, there hadn't been much else to bring.

As our brand new, fully loaded Range Rover rolled quietly into our new driveway, a sense of peace and calm washed over me. This was our home now. I rested my hand on my round belly. This beautiful place was where we'd be raising our child. Children hopefully.

Had I not needed to pee so badly, I would have stopped and soaked it in. This was the beginning of the rest of our lives, and I didn't want to rush that moment, but my bladder was demanding to be emptied. Peeing had pretty much become a hobby since I'd hit my third trimester.

"Home sweet home," said Nath as he switched off the ignition and looked at me with a proud smile. "Welcome home Mrs Stone."

"Thanks babe," I said, quickly undoing my seatbelt, "but I'm busting for a pee."

"Nothing unusual there then," he teased with a laugh as I scrambled inelegantly out of the car with the grace of a turtle that had been flipped upside down. My middle was no longer bendy, so movement was now ten times more awkward. I was eternally thankful that Nathan had bought me the Range Rover because the little two door Tesla, parked securely in our new garage Nathan had built onto the cottage, was no longer a viable mode of transportation for the fat pregnant lady.

"Just wait!" Nathan called, jumping out of the car, and running around to intercept me before I reached the front door.

"Nath, I'm serious. I'm busting."

"Just give me a sec," he said, holding his hand out to stop me as he unlocked the door.

"Hurry," I pleaded, jiggling on my feet.

He turned back to me with a cheeky smile, and I wondered for a moment if he was going to deliberately procrastinate to try and make me pee my pants.

"Okay my queen," he said with a little bow, before scooping me off my feet, "let's get you to the throne room." I laughed and grabbed his shoulders as he carried me over the threshold, which was quite an impressive feat given my sizable new proportions.

"I think I can walk now," I chuckled as he carried me all the way into the laundry toilet.

"Door to door service for my lady," he said, depositing me gently onto the floor. "I shall leave her majesty to pee in private and then I'll give her the royal tour." Nathan had spent the past few months project managing renovations on the beach house, to make sure it was ready ahead of our arrival.

"Why thank you my lord," I laughed and, without bothering to close the toilet door, I quickly unbuttoned my jeans and plonked my butt on the seat. Nath left me to it and ducked back out to the car to continue unloading. I sighed with relief as I felt the pressure in my bladder ease. I'd forgotten all the weird and wonderful side effects of pregnancy.

I washed my hands as Nathan brought the cat cage into the laundry.

"Feeling better?" he asked, letting Freddie and Shadow out of their cage.

"Much," I said, bending down sideways to give shadow a pat.

"Ready for your tour?"

"Absolutely," I agreed, following him out into the living area, finally able to concentrate on the cottage upgrades.

"Oh Nathan, it's beautiful," I gasped with surprise, as I looked around our new home. It was almost as if I was looking at a totally different house.

"I'm glad you like it."

I looked up at him, my heart close to exploding, and kissed him softly.

"You're amazing Mr Stone," I said, arms slung around his neck.

"So are you," he said, leaning in for another kiss, before pulling away abruptly. "But that's just the start of the tour," he said with an excited grin. "Let me show you the rest."

"Sure," I agreed, chuckling at his child-like enthusiasm.

"Come on then, let's start with the nursery." Nathan wrapped his fingers through mine and pulled me towards what used to be the guest room. He grinned at me with anticipation, then swung open the door.

Tears sprung to my eyes at the sight of the beautifully styled room. He'd chosen a coastal décor theme with beautiful ash-coloured oak furniture and white and turquoise tones throughout.

"Oh my god," I said, as warm, salty streams exploded from my eyes.

"You don't like it?" Nath asked with concern. "We can change it. I thought the turquoise would work either way, but you can choose whatever you want."

"No," I whimpered between the tears, "I love it."

"You do?"

"Yes. It's beautiful babe."

"Then why are you crying?" He asked, worriedly rubbing my shoulders.

"Because you're so amazing," I sobbed.

"Oh, okay," he laughed, wrapping me up in a hug. Nathan had been so loving and supportive that it was hard to believe any of it was real. This pregnancy was so different to the last one and this time it was exactly how I'd always dreamed it should be, which made it hard not to compare the two. My happiness this time around made me feel inconceivably guilty about Mia's brief existence.

"I keep thinking about last time," I sniffled between sobs, "with Mia."

"Ah, I see," he said kissing the top of my head as he squeezed me a little tighter.

"This has all been so perfect," I said, peering up at him. "You've been so supportive, and I love how excited you are."

"Do you need me to tone it down?"

"No, please don't. I need you to keep being you."

"That, I can do," he said with a smile as he brushed the tears from my eyes. "But I've gotta be honest babe, I'm not entirely sure what's happening in your head right now."

"When I found out I was pregnant this time, I knew straight away that I wanted this baby. It didn't even matter if I'd had to do it on my own, I just knew that I wanted it."

"Did you really think I'd walk away from you and our baby?" He asked, appalled.

"We were still so new Nath, and with everything that had happened I didn't want to put any pressure on you."

"Wow," he said, stepping back as he rubbed his face.

"Babe, you know what I went through. It was never about my faith in you. It was my trauma making me assume the worst."

"Okay," he said running his hands up my arms.

"And besides, that's not even the point right now."

"I'm sorry," he said, sheepishly. "Are you trying to say that you weren't so sure the last time?"

I nodded silently, remembering back to the day I'd found out I was pregnant. "I wasn't just unsure about it. I was completely devastated when I found out Nath," I said, tears welling in my eyes again. "I didn't want her in the beginning." The warm tears continued to fall, as I thought back to that heart wrenching day...

"I take it this wasn't planned?" The doctor asked, watching me with sympathetic eyes. All I could do was shake my head in response. She put her hand over mine and said seriously, "you do have options Ashley. It's still early days."

Before I realised what was happening, I found myself in tears. I was pregnant with Dom's child. A child that would be the nail in my coffin. If I had this kid, I'd be officially trapped in my sad excuse of an existence forever. It hadn't occurred to me before that moment that I'd planned to leave Dom again one day. I suppose I had never been sober enough to consider it seriously, but in the back of my mind, I guess I had always left room for another escape plan. With a baby there would be no getting out.

I left the doctor's office in a daze. I had no clue what I was doing or where I was going, all I knew was that I needed to think. I had to clear my head. Rain bucketed down around me, but I didn't care. It felt appropriate considering the circumstances and, weirdly, the storm somehow felt soothing as if it might have been able to wash away my pain.

The promenade was deserted, because no one else was stupid enough to be out in that weather. Wandering mindlessly alongside the racing Thames, I waded through shin-high puddles of dirty footpath water, bracing myself against the heavy rain. I was soaked through.

I felt the tears start to break again and they mixed seamlessly with the rain drops that were already rolling down my face. How could I have possibly let my life get so out of control?

"What am I going to do?" I shouted at the empty street as my entire body shuddered underneath me. The sobs took control of me, and I couldn't summon enough energy to support my own weight, so I collapsed to the ground, weeping fiercely as the rain drenched me to the core. By the time my tears had subsided, I was freezing and sore. My hair was glued to the side of my face and my clothes were plastered like bindings against my skin. "I can't have this baby," I muttered to any gods that would listen. "Please find me a way out of this."

I wiped a tear from my cheek and stared up at Nathan.

"Maybe it was my fault Mia didn't make it," I said guiltily, "Maybe I wished her away."

"That's not true babe," Nathan said, holding me tight. "You were in an extreme situation, and you did the best you could."

"But what if that was God's way of granting my wish?"

"I don't think you can look at it that way," he said, concern in his blue eyes. "I think it was more that he was saving you both from a lifetime of violence." He paused and cupped my face in his hands. "What can I do to make this better?"

"You've already done it," I told him with a smile. "I love you so much."

"And I love you, Mrs Stone," he said, planting a soft, sensuous kiss on my lips that made me melt like putty in his hands. Heat quickly flared in the pit of my swollen belly as I pressed my body against his. My bladder hadn't been the only body part to take things up a notch during my pregnancy. My libido had decided it would not be outdone, so for the last few weeks, all Nathan need do was smile at me and I'd be ready to go. I'd heard other women talk about an increased sex drive, in fact, Kat had told me in way too much detail about her pregnancy sex experience. I hadn't been able to relate because I'd never felt it during my last pregnancy. I guess the constant threat of danger had cancelled out my raging hormones, but this time, my body was making up for it.

It didn't help that Nathan had been extra amazing since the wedding, and I was completely blown away by what an impeccable job he'd done on the house. I really shouldn't have been surprised that my perfectionist husband had created a perfect home for us, but I still found it hard to process the fact that he'd gone to so much trouble for me. I really had hit the jackpot with him.

"In fact, maybe I should show you exactly how much I love you," I teased, pressing my body against his a little more firmly.

- NATHAN STONE -

"Hmmm...." I muttered, enjoying our intimate moment a little too much as Ash squeezed her round body against mine. I loosened my grip around her waist and let my hands drop to her hips, removing my mouth from hers despite the vehement protests from my body. "Let's hold that thought," I suggested, pulling my body away from hers. "I want to show you the rest of the house."

"Really?" she asked, running her hand up my zipper seductively, "you sure you don't want to do this first?"

"Umm..." I faltered for a moment, enjoying her attention. She grinned wickedly and started to unbutton my jeans. "Nope," I said, grasping her hands so she couldn't continue her mission. "Tour first, then sex."

"Spoil sport," she teased withdrawing her hands.

"Or maybe I'm just prolonging your pleasure," I joked with a wink, running my thumb over her bottom lip. My wife's eyes flashed with desire, and I laughed at her level of enthusiasm. "Or perhaps I should put you out of your misery now?"

"That would be the humane thing to do," Ash agreed with a mischievous smile that put an end to my self control. I grabbed her by the hips and lifted her up, grasping her bottom with both hands while she wrapped her arms and legs around me as best she could with the bump between us. Our mouths melded together with frantic need as we mauled each other.

"I fucking love you," I said between kisses.

"That's lucky," she said breathlessly, "because I fucking love you too."

"Let's not do this in the nursey," I said as I walked us, slowly and awkwardly, down the hallway to our new stairs. With her back towards the extension and her mouth pressed firmly against mine, Ash didn't notice the stairs until I started to climb them. I gripped tight to the railing with one hand and began our ascent one careful step at a time.

"What...?" she said, ceasing her kissing as she looked over her shoulder to see the new addition. "What?" she repeated, stunned.

"This is our new master suite," I said proudly, boosting her bottom up to a higher position so I could climb the rest of the stairs with more ease. Ash gripped tight to my shoulders and looked at me with wide eyes.

"You added a floor?"

"Yeah, I figured we'd need our own space eventually. You know, as the Stone clan grows." We reached the landing, and she wriggled down out of my arms. I gestured towards some doors on the right, "that's an extra toilet, and the linen closest. And this…" I said, reaching for the bedroom door, "is our room."

I pushed open the door to reveal the huge room with floor to ceiling windows that overlooked the ocean.

"Oh my god Nath, this is breathtaking," she muttered, walking around our new bedroom in wonderment. Our new super-king bed sat in the center of the wall, facing the windows so we could have sea views from bed. Ash brushed her hand over the soft, sandy coloured quilt as she headed towards the walk-in wardrobe. "You didn't?" she asked with an excited grin.

"I did," I said, following her in. "I know you love the one at the apartment, so I doubled it and gave us one side each."

"Holy shit," she squealed, seeing the sheer size of the wardrobe. "This is more like a dressing room than a wardrobe."

"Only the best for my wife," I said with a smile. Even after a month of being married, I still hadn't gotten bored of calling her my wife. Her eyes locked on mine from the other end of the wardrobe, and I knew exactly what she was thinking. "Time to christen your dressing room my lady?"

Ash grinned and perched her bottom on top of the built-in dresser, leaning back on her hands to allow room for her domed stomach.

"I guess we'll find out how sturdy this is," she joked, tapping her fingers against the dresser top.

"I made them reinforce it," I said with a grin, striding over to her, "so it should be strong enough to withstand an earthquake."

"Get a lot of earthquakes in Cornwall, do they?" she teased, as I wedged my body between her thighs.

"They will now that we've moved in," I joked, leaning in to kiss her. Ash wrapped her legs around my waist, and I pulled her in gently, making sure I didn't squish her tummy. She ran her finger along my jaw and all talking ceased as we picked up exactly where we'd left off.

I kissed my way down her neck and felt her hands slide underneath my sweater. Shivers shot through my body as her nails trailed up my back. I snogged her hard, letting my tongue roam her mouth while her hands explored my bare skin. Ash returned my kiss eagerly and I heard her stifle a tiny little moan when I twisted my fingers through her hair. Breathing heavily, she tugged at my jumper and I obediently lifted my arms so she could pull it over my head. Ash dropped the jumper onto the floor, and did the same again with my shirt, before I repeated the process with her top layers. Jumper, T.shirt, bra. All discarded onto the floor in an untidy pile on top of mine.

With my flesh pressed against hers, I couldn't wait any longer, so I stripped Ash of her jeans and then quickly disposed of mine. I ran my hands up her bare thighs and pulled her towards me. Her green eyes flared with desire, so I wasted no time. I slid straight into her, and she moaned with relief, wrapping her legs tightly around me.

We had a good stint on the dresser, but it was getting too awkward, so I lifted her by the bottom and relocated us to the floor to finish off. Sex had definitely become more difficult with the bump, but not impossible. I did my job and made sure I left my woman satisfied, then rolled off her and flopped next to her on the plush carpet. We laid, entangled on the floor of the closet, puffing and panting.

"So… now that we're here," I asked breathlessly, "how are you feeling about the move?"

"I'm really happy babe. Zero regrets," she said, looking over at me with a smile.

"You sure?"

"Absolutely! This is the start of the rest of our lives. I'll miss yoga for sure," she said, peering down at her rounded belly, where we'd both subconsciously rested our hands, "but I can pick up a teaching class once the baby is old enough. I was thinking I might even start a mums and bubs class down here."

"That's a great idea," I agreed hesitantly.

"But?" she asked with a raised brow, leaning up on one elbow to better assess my facial expression.

"But… could we perhaps just enjoy family life for a while? I'm looking forward to having a six-month sabbatical. We've earned it."

"We certainly have." Ash cleared her throat quietly and wriggled her growing body up to a seated position. I sat up and offered her a hand in support. "Thanks," she said with a blush. "Can I be honest about something?"

"Please do."

"I feel a bit guilty," she said, entwining her fingers with mine.

"For what?" I asked, an icky feeling creeping through my belly.

"I'm so excited about what's happening for us, but…" she paused, tears sparkling in her green eyes, "…I really miss Aims."

"Me too," I agreed, with a sigh of relief that it wasn't something worse.

"I thought she was going to be around for the baby," she said, pausing for a moment. "I think she would have been proud of us for moving down here."

"Yeah, she would have."

"I've been thinking about baby names," Ash said, changing the subject.

"Have you now?" I said with a grin, pleased we were moving onto a happier topic. "And what have you come up with?"

"I was wondering what you think of Amy if it's a girl, and Vaughn if it's a boy?"

I took her face in my hands as my chest heaved with a weird mixture of grief and joy.

"I think they'd both be perfect," I said, clenching my jaw to swallow back unwelcome tears. "Red would love that." I leaned in and pressed my lips to hers. "I love it."

"Vaughn Stone," Ash said with a smile as moved herself into a less awkward position. "He sounds like a rock star."

"You really think it's going to be a boy huh?"

"I don't know, I just have a feeling," she said with a smile as I pulled her onto my lap, "but we should plan for either."

"Okay, so Vaughn or Amy Stone. What about middle names? I think we need something from your side," I said, sliding my hands around her waist as she draped her arms over my shoulders. "Geoff and Mary?"

Ash grimaced, "I love the sentiment but Vaughn Geoff Stone and Amy Mary Stone? Do you really want to be shouting either of those names for the rest of our lives?"

"Yeah, I guess they're both a bit clunky."

"Dad's middle name is Noah," she muttered, thoughtfully, "he was named after his grandfather."

"Vaughn Noah Stone," I said with a smile, "that sounds pretty good. I think that's the one."

Ash grinned. "Me too," she said, trailing her fingers through the back of my hair. Her touch sent goosebumps across my skin. I held her green gaze and saw desire sparkling in her eyes, so I took her face in my hands and crushed her mouth to mine. Our passionate kiss quickly began to heat up again.

"Let's move this to the bed," I suggested, lifting Ash to her feet. She laughed and allowed me to pick her up and carry her to the bed. I plopped her gently on top of the huge mattress and let my eyes wander over her beautiful pregnant body.

"What's that look?" she asked, leaning back on her elbows.

"I'm appreciating how beautiful you are and how lucky I am to have you as my wife," I said, climbing onto the bed and crawling carefully on top of her, like a lion stalking its prey. "Now, where were we?" I ran my hands up her smooth thighs.

"You were about to show me your skills," Ash said breathlessly as I kissed her neck.

"Yes, I was. And I'll keep demonstrating them for the rest of our lives."

"Is that a promise?"

"It sure is."

"Then I'll hold you to that Mr Stone."

And thus we've come to the end of Ashlan for this book.

This, however, is just the beginning of their story as they venture into their happily-ever-after as 'The Stones'.

Nath, Ash and Baby Stone will be back in other books, so you can rest assured you haven't heard the last of them.

In the meantime... let's focus on me!

It's time to return to oz and see what's happening in the land down under.

x Ritchie.

- The Final Chapter -

Coastal Chaos

- RITCHIE CARLTON -

"Holy shit," I breathed, turning into the long gravel driveway to see what looked more like a resort than a beach house. "This guy is Stoner tripled," I muttered to myself.

I pulled the car into a flat spot under the trees. There was only one other car in the driveway, which meant that Sean and Isla still hadn't arrived. I felt a bit weird having a weekend away with my new boss, but he was Seany's best mate, and he seemed like a good bloke, so I was rolling with it. Either way, it was nice of Kane to invite me to his birthday weekender. I jumped out of my Prado as Kane stepped onto the front deck.

"Welcome to mi casa," he called with a proud grin. "What do you think?"

"I think you could give my mate Stoner a run for his money," I joked, knowing that he'd have no idea what I meant by that. "This place is huge."

"Got to accommodate the fam," he said, descending the stairs. "You can park in the carport if you like. First in, best dressed around here."

"Nah, she'll be 'right," I said, meeting him halfway to shake his hand. "Happy birthday boss. Thanks for inviting me."

"No worries," he said, slapping me on the back and following me to my car. "More the merrier, I say."

"This is for you," I said, handing him the bottle of Nathan Stone's 105 proof I'd brought back from London. "Best whiskey ever made according to my mate Nath."

"Nice," he said accepting the bottle, "Thanks mate. I've heard about this stuff, it's bloody hard to find."

"Not when you know Nathan Stone."

"Seriously?!"

"Well… not the same Nathan Stone, but he's got connections."

"Sandrine Delfontaine, Gareth Hemsworth and an international whiskey guru. Sounds like you're the one with connections mate," he joked.

"Hardly," I snorted, looking around the property. "So, what's the surf like around here?"

"Brilliant," he said, pointing down a gravel path that led through the trees, "In fact, it's looking pretty good out there now if you want to fit in a quick one before everyone arrives."

"I like the way you think," I said, slinging my backpack over my shoulder, and hauling my esky out of the boot.

"Leave your stuff here. I'll show you the rec room so you can get changed and get out there."

"Great!"

"Just down here," he said, leading me towards what looked from the outside, to be a garage. "I get the feeling you'll like this room," Kane said with a grin, as he bypassed the roller door and opened a hidden side door to reveal what could only be described as the ultimate toy room.

"Holy shit," I muttered in awe as I took in the sight before me. The outdoor room housed an array of snorkelling gear; five different types of surfboards; a SUP; two kayaks; several push bikes; a jet ski; and a dinghy. I'd never seen such a well-equipped beach house. "I take it you're pretty into water sports then?

"Not really, I prefer to be on dry land."

"What's all this then?" I asked, confused.

"This is for everyone else," he said casually. I glanced at him sideways. Kane wasn't at all what I'd expected. At work he was decisive and driven, but on his home turf, he seemed to be lost and maybe a little lonely. I knew both of those feelings well. Perhaps that's why I could see them in him. "You do a lot for your family huh?"

"Yeah," he nodded. "Somehow I ended up becoming responsible for everyone."

"Huh," I chuckled, "meanwhile… I've somehow found myself with zero responsibilities."

"Wanna Trade?"

"I'm not sure I'm even taking care of myself right now," I admitted way too honestly. Kane was my boss after all.
We shared a comfortable silence for a moment.

"You'll be right mate," he said eventually with a knowing look, which I assumed meant Seany had told him about Amy. "It'll just take time."

"Yeah," I agreed with a nod.

"How about I leave you to it so you can get down to the beach? I'll take your bags inside."

"You sure?"

"Yeah man," he said patting me on the back, "better to get out there before the sun goes down."

"Thanks." I'd been hanging out all day to get on the waves and although it had been decades since I'd been down to Margaret River, I was sure I'd be able to handle the surf.

"I'll see you upstairs when you're done."

"Cheers Kane," I said, following him back outside.

"No probs," he said as he grabbed my bags. "My sister is mad on surfing so I know how itchy you surfers get for the waves," he joked before heading inside.

I quickly changed into my wetsuit and pulled out my board, then headed down the bush path towards the ocean. The beach in front of Kane's place was a little slice of heaven. White sand and crashing turquoise waves… pure freedom. I took a deep breath of the salty fresh air and smiled as it filled my lungs. The smoggy London air felt like a whole lifetime ago.

- SOPHIE THOMPSON -

We were only one hour into our three-hour road trip when Taj's Switch battery had run out, and he'd been complaining relentlessly since then. As we pulled into Kane's driveway, the whining was still going strong.

"Seriously mate," I snapped over my shoulder, "you've done nothing but whinge the entire way."

"Not the whole way."

"Most of the way."

"Well, it's not my fault my stupid Switch ran out of battery," he muttered as I parked the car.

"Technically it is your fault," I said tactlessly. "I did suggest that you charge it this morning."

"How was I supposed to know it wouldn't last the whole trip?"

"Because your mother told you it wouldn't," I said, climbing out of the car to stretch my back. "Now, can you please hop out and take your bag up to your room?"

"Ugh," he grumbled loudly, not moving a muscle.

"Watch out Soph, I think I hear a grizzle monster in that car," called Kane, walking down the front steps to greet us. "Quick, lock it in the car. I don't want that thing in the house."

Taj groaned moodily from inside the car. "Ugh, you know it's just me Uncle Kane."

My heart sank a little that he was getting too old for Uncle Kane antics. My baby boy wasn't a baby anymore and it was hard to accept that he was moving into the phase where he thought we adults were boring, uncool and most definitely not funny.

"Are you sure?" Kane asked, as he shot me a playful wink, "because I've met a Grizzle Monster before, and it sounded exactly like that."

"You're not funny Uncle Kane," Taj retorted, sounding more like a teenager than a ten-year-old.

"Oh Really?" Kane asked loudly, before descending upon him with a tickle attack. Despite my son's best efforts, he couldn't hold back his laughter, which spurred Kane on. "Look mummy, the Grizzle Monster has been defeated," said Kane, still tickling the boy, "but, oh no, he's now turned into... the Giggle Monster," he added in a theatrical voice.

"You're... still... not... funny," spluttered Taj, between giggles.

"How very dare you," Kane teased with mock offense, "I'll have you know, I'm the funniest man in the world," he retorted with the same silly voice. "Just ask your mum."

"Mummy?" Taj asked, still laughing.

"I don't think so," I teased, shooting Kane a cheeky wink.

"Oh, come on. I used to do funny stuff all the time when we were kids."

"If you consider holding someone down and farting on their face, funny," I said, opening the boot. Taj laughed harder.

"Yeah okay, that's pretty funny," he told Kane approvingly.

"Oh, my word," I muttered, bemused by how much joy boys found in toilet humour.

"Right Giggle Monster, time to get out of this car and take your stuff inside," said Kane, switching into serious uncle mode.

"Do I have to?"

"Pretty sure I heard your mum ask you to do that a few times, so... yes, you do."

"Fine," Taj pouted, but didn't argue. I looked at Kane over the roof of the car and mouthed 'thank you'. He nodded and herded Taj along.

"Your room is all set up for you champ. How about you grab your bag and go unpack."

"Ugh, okay," Taj grumbled.

"Enough of the attitude please. How about wishing Uncle Kane a

Happy Birthday?"

"Happy Birthday Uncle Kane," Taj called unenthusiastically as he headed towards the house, rolling his Ninja Turtles luggage behind him. "Congratulations on being old," he added cheekily over his shoulder. Kane laughed.

"Thanks buddy," he called, turning back to me with a smile.

"Sorry," I apologised, giving him a quick peck on the cheek before he helped me unload my very full boot. "Happy birthday."

"Thanks."

"Your present is in here somewhere," I said, noticing the unfamiliar Prado parked in the driveway as I riffled through the boot. "Bring a new friend along, did you?" I teased, as we both loaded ourselves up with bags and boxes.

"Sean's brother," grunted Kane under the weight of my full esky.

"You invited one of your staff members on a personal holiday?" I asked, surprised that Kane was mixing business with pleasure. A concept he was normally very much against.

"He's not just a staff member," Kane said defensively, "he's my best mate's brother. Besides, I feel for the guy," he added, shrugging as best he could under the weight of his load. "According to Sean, he barely leaves the house."

"I know that feeling," I said, remembering my month of self-imposed isolation. "That's very considerate of you," I added, impressed by Kane's empathy, but still slightly confused. It wasn't like him to go out of his way for a stranger.

"His girlfriend killed herself just before he left London," he explained, sensing my confusion.

"Oh shit," I gasped, "poor guy."

"Yeah, he's working through some pretty heavy stuff. Sean said he used to be quite outgoing. 'Life of the party', was the phrase he used if I recall correctly."

I looked around to make sure the guy wasn't in hearing distance. "Am I supposed to know that, or do I need to keep it to myself?" I whispered.

"It's okay, he's gone for a surf," Kane said with a smile, "but it's probably best to keep it to yourself unless he says something. I'm not even sure he knows that I know."

"Gotcha. Play dumb," I said with a cheeky grin, "like… I can totally do that." I flicked my hair like a bimbo.

"You've got it in the bag," he teased, hauling the esky up the front steps.

I followed Kane inside, laden with our things. It was amazing how much extra 'stuff' a child could generate. Before Taj, I'd do these weekends with nothing more than a small suitcase, but now I had to bring our entire house along. Kane dumped the esky in the kitchen while I went to put my stuff in our room.

I paused in the hallway. "Shit," I muttered, suddenly realising that 'our room', wasn't 'our room' anymore.

"You right?" Kane asked, peering down the hall to check on me.

"Which room should I take?"

"Whichever one you like," he said, coming over to take the suitcase out of my hand. "I've set them all up so you can go with your usual or start afresh."

I looked up at him with a grateful smile. "I think I'll start afresh."

"Good choice," he said with a wink. "Why don't you take the one next to mine."

"But that's your parents' room."

"No, it's the guest room which my parents usually take, and this weekend it's yours."

"Are you sure?"

"Of course. It's the best room, plus you'll be further away from 'he who shall not be named'."

"I think a weekend with Voldemort would more preferable at this point," I joked as Kane opened the bedroom door. Orange light spilled out into the hallway as the setting sun shone in through the large window. Kane stood back with a smile and waved me in ahead of him. I'd peeked into that room before, but never actually been in there. "Wow," I breathed, taking in the spectacular view of the sunset above the trees.

"Looks like we might be in for a summer storm," Kane said, peering out the window at some dark clouds looming on the horizon."
I plopped my pillow onto the bed and noticed a vase of fresh orchids placed elegantly on the bedside table. Orchids were my favourite flower, and Kane knew that.

"You knew I'd want to change rooms, didn't you?" I asked, turning to face him.

"Of course I did," he shrugged, setting down my suitcase on the dresser. "I'll leave you to unpack." He smiled, turned and strode towards the door.

"Kane," I said, stopping him in his tracks.

"Yeah?' he asked, looking over his shoulder.

"Thanks."

"No probs Shorty," he said, then vanished down the hall.

- KANE THOMPSON -

I was out grabbing some firewood from the wood box, when Frankie arrived in her dusty old Beetle. I hated that crappy car, but she loved it and refused to let me buy her a decent one. I dropped my handful of wood and waved as she pulled into the long driveway.

"G'day Jughead," she said, opening the creaky door as I strolled over to help her unload.

"How was the drive? I'm amazed you made it here in that thing."

"Ha-ha," she said sarcastically, giving me a quick hug before grabbing her wetsuit off the back seat. "Bertie Beetle will still be running long after your fancy Rover is dead."

"Honestly Spanks, I wouldn't be surprised."

She banged the back door closed and the whole car shook. I was half expecting it to fall apart like in the cartoons, but Bertie remained, albeit dubiously, in once piece. Frankie grinned and dashed past me towards the rec room.

"Oi! Aren't you even going to unload?"

"Nope," she called, "I've gotta get a quick surf in before the sun goes down. I'll unpack later." She dashed through the hidden door, and I sighed, returning to the wood box to resume wood collecting. My free-spirited sister was a lost cause.

Within minutes, Frankie emerged from the rec room in her wetsuit. She pulled her board down off Bertie's rickety roof rack and headed down towards the beach track.

"Spanks, if you're not back by dark I'm coming out to find ya," I yelled after her. I loved my little sister, but even at the age of thirty-eight, responsibility still wasn't a life skill she possessed. She was so gung-ho that she never stopped to think things through, which meant that I usually ended up having to bail her out.

"No worries," she called back at me with a cheeky salute before disappearing into the trees. I already knew that she wouldn't. The was one certainty with Frankie was that she was predictable in her unreliability. I shrugged with resignation. Ritchie was still down there, so at least she wouldn't be out there alone.

I took the pile of wood inside and watched quietly from the doorway as Soph attempted, unsuccessfully, to light a fire in the fireplace. I couldn't help but grin. She was way too cute for her own good, biting her lip in concentration as she flicked another match onto the messy pile of twigs and paper. One piece of paper caught alight but then quickly fizzled out.

"Need a hand Shorty?" I asked with a smile.

"Umm... yeah," she said with a blush, as I dropped the wood into the wood basket. "I don't think fire-starting is my strong suit." She wiped her forehead and unknowingly smeared charcoal all over herself. I laughed, pointing politely at her forehead.

"Can I just...?" I asked, before wiping the smudge off her face with the sleeve of my jumper.

"Oh. Thanks." I smiled nervously and put some distance between our bodies, turning my attention towards the sad looking pile of sticks she'd set up.

"Stand back and let the master show you how it's done," I joked, re-organising the pile of kindling and newspaper. Sophie knelt next to me, watching intently as I balanced a couple of bigger logs in a triangle formation above the pile. "The trick is to get a good base of twigs and paper," I explained as professionally as possible, "that way they'll burn long enough to light the bigger bits of wood on top."

"That makes sense," she nodded.

"Of course it does," I said with a cheeky wink as I lit one of the balls of newspaper. The flame sparked a twig and the fire started to take off. "Voila!"

"Very impressive yoda," Sophie teased, with a smile that made me feel strangely proud of myself.

"I'm a man of many talents," I joked nervously.

"One of which includes the ability to hold a girl down and fart on her face," Soph quipped with a teasing smile.

I burst into laughter at her quick retort.

"Hey, your son thought it was funny," I said with a blush. "Don't tell me you're gonna hold it against me forever?!"

"Hmmm..." Soph pretended to think on it for a moment. "Yep," she confirmed categorically. Her green eyes sparkling with mischief. She'd always had a quick wit, but it had progressively diminished in the years she'd been married to Brenton. I was dreading his arrival, and secretly wished I hadn't invited him, but this trip had been an annual tradition since I first built the place, and I wasn't going to be the one to ruin it for Taj.

"Fine then," I replied smugly, "I guess I'll have to keep reminding you of the time I saved you from drowning in our pool."

"Kane, you were the one who threw me in there in the first place!"

"Oh yeah I forgot that bit," I conceded as we shared a conspiratorial chuckle. We looked at each other for a short moment, until a blonde-headed munchkin tore down the hallway towards us.

"I've unpacked my bag, had a shower and put on my pyjamas so can I please, please, please watch TV now?"

"Okay, you can have thirty minutes while I cook your dinner," Sophie agreed, "but no arguments when it's time to turn it off or there won't be any screens at all for the rest of the weekend."

"Aww but-"

"I wouldn't argue if I was you champ," I advised. "Just take the win before you lose it all."

"Fine," he agreed with defeat, before turning and retreating to the TV room, mumbling under his breath.

"You're great with him," Soph said appreciatively.

"Meh, he's a good kid. He's just testing boundaries," I replied with a shrug.

"That's amazing insight for someone who's never around kids."

"No, but I've been around that kid his whole life, so I know how to read him."

Soph stared at me with an unidentifiable expression. She opened her mouth, as if to say something, then closed it again and stood up abruptly. "I'd better get his dinner on," she said, heading for the kitchen.

- RITCHIE CARLTON -

The sun was starting to set, so I figured it was time for my last wave of the day. As I paddled out to the break, I saw a chick stride out of the bushes with a shortboard wedged under her arm. Even from a distance I could see that she was chock-full of attitude. In fact, there was something about her demeanour that reminded me of Amy.

I watched as she dumped her towel on the sand and sussed out the break for a brief moment before slapping on her leg rope and throwing her board into the water. Sunset wasn't the time to be heading out there, but I got the feeling she wasn't the sort of woman who'd listen to reason.

"Looks like there's a storm brewing," I called as she paddled past me.

"Nah, it's December. It'll blow over," she said with a shrug, giving me a look that dared me to disagree with her.

"Maybe," I nodded, eying the strange, grey clouds on the horizon. I was used to seeing clouds like that in the UK, but it was summer in Australia and tropical storms were not commonplace on the West Coast. Feeling obliged to keep an eye on the crazy surfer girl, I sat on my board and keep watch in case she got herself into trouble. I didn't want another death on my conscience.

I let my legs dangle on either side of my board, while Little Miss Surfer Girl zoomed over the reef break. The sky was getting dark, but her wild mop of spiky blonde hair, stood out against the inky blue backdrop. I didn't know what she was trying to prove, but she was absolutely ripping it up out there.

She glided into the middle of a hefty peak, then rode it to the shoulder where she did a crazy cutback across the wave. I was in awe. I'd never seen a girl that gutsy on a board and she was pulling off manoeuvres that even some guys wouldn't have tried. The chick definitely had talent, but she was also reckless. She surfed like she wasn't afraid of dying. That level of fearlessness could take someone far, but it could also get them killed.

The sun had almost completely disappeared, and it was starting to get quite dark, so I was relieved when she headed towards the shore. I rode a small wave back to the sand, satisfied that she hadn't killed herself on my watch. I stripped down the top of my wetsuit and wrapped my towel around my shoulders as the crazy surfer chick waded out of the surf.

I nodded at her again and, as she drew closer, I was able to get a better look at her face. She had bright blue eyes and big pouty lips. Lips which were to beginning to turn blue from the cold.

"Have you got a death wish or something?" I called as she ripped off her leg rope and sunk the tail of her board into the sand.

"Pardon?" She asked, looking up at me with fiery eyes.

"What were you doing out there? You could've killed yourself."

"Thanks for your concern, Mum, but I'm still alive," she said narkily, peeling off the top of her wetty. I tried not to perve, but she had a banging bod. When she scooped up her towel, I snuck a quick peek at her rack.

"That's not the point," I argued.

"Look mate, what do you care if I kill myself?"

"I don't."

"Great. End of discussion then," she said with a shrug.

"Wow, you're a feisty one, aren't ya?" I said, picking up my board.

As much as I'd enjoyed the show, it was time for me to get back up to the house.

"I like to think so," she retorted.

"You're pretty fearless on that board," I said nodding at her Thruster.

"You say that like it's a bad thing."

"Nope. It's just an observation," I paused and watched her for a second. "You surf good for a chick."

"Thanks. You talk good for a cave man."

"No need to be bitchy, I was trying to give you a compliment."

"No. A compliment would have been to tell me that I'm a good surfer. The chick part is irrelevant."

I laughed loudly at her response. She was like Amy, Ash and Kat all rolled into one super-feisty little pocket-rocket. "What?" she demanded angrily.

"Nothing," I said, shaking my head. "You just remind me of someone. Several someone's actually," I added as I turned towards Kane's beach track. "Anyway, now that I know you're not going to kill yourself, it's time for a shower. Catch ya later crazy chick," I said, waving back over my shoulder.

"Kill myself? I'd kick your arse in a comp any day," she snapped, marching after me.

"No doubt," I agreed, puffing a little as I trudged through the soft sand. I glanced back over my shoulder and took a good look at her bikini-clad top half. I raised a brow to make my point obvious, "and you'd look better doing it too," I said with a wink.

"Eww, perve much?" she said, wrapping her arms protectively around her chest.

"Again… it was intended as a compliment."

"A pervy compliment. Do you often follow half-naked women home?"

I looked over my shoulder again, amused by her need to argue. "Far as I can tell, you're the one following me sweetheart."

"Ugh, you know what I mean," she said, stomping her foot like an angry two-year old.

"Do I?" I laughed, as she stormed irately behind me.

"Yes,"she snapped, "and why are you going this way?"

"My mate's house is just up here," I said without turning around.

"Who's your mate?"

"See you around crazy girl," I called back to her with a salute. "Don't stay out too long."

"You can plainly see I'm going home."

"I doubt it," I said with a grin, not bothering to look back.

"Why?"

"Because you left your board on the beach."

"Shit," she said, realising that she'd been in such a hurry to harass me, she'd forgotten to grab her board.

"Later," I called with a chuckle, stepping up the pace while she ran back down to the beach. I felt slightly disappointed to part ways with crazy surfer chick, but I suspected I'd see her out on the waves again before the end of the weekend.

When I emerged through the bushes at Kane's place, I noticed two extra cars in the driveway. It looked like the troops had arrived, but none of the cars were Sean's. I hosed down my board and stripped off my wetty, then hung it over the rack. I wrapped my towel around my waist and let myself into the house through the adjoining door. I navigated my way up the stairs and through a hallway, following the sound of the voices. I eventually found myself in the living area to see Kane standing in the kitchen pouring drinks.

"Ah, here he is," Kane announced to a tall blonde woman, who was busy cutting up a chunk of steak for a floppy-fringed blonde kid, presumably her son. "Soph, this Seany's big brother, Ritchie."

The woman looked up from her chopping to scrutinise me. There was an unnerving air of Ashley Granger about the woman. I couldn't tell if it was the height, the blonde hair, the green cat-like eyes, or the whole package put together, but there was definitely a likeness. The Ashley doppelgänger, placed down her cutlery with a gentle clink, and came over to introduce herself. Tilting her head sideways, she smiled.

"Put a red wig on him and I could certainly see the resemblance."

I laughed and rubbed my bald head. "Yeah, Sean had more luck in the hair department."

"But not as much in the muscle department," she teased, amusement shimmering in her green eyes as she scoped out my bare chest. It wasn't in a pervy way, it was more like curiosity, but the attention made me blush none-the-less. Not a situation I'd ever found myself in with Ashley. "I'm Sophie," she said offering her hand.

"Nice to meet you," I said, shaking it.

"And this is Taj," she added, gesturing towards the boy, who was in the process of squirting a litre of tomato sauce onto his steak. "Taj, no," she scolded him, as the tomato sauce bottle made a loud farting sound. The boy erupted into joyful laughter and we adults sniggered quietly, trying not to encourage the lad. Sophie grabbed the bottle and twisted the lid back on.

"Hi Taj," I said with a wave, "quite the masterpiece you're constructing there."

"Sauce is the best bit," he said, happily swirling the red sauce all over his steak cubes.

"Yeah, but you're supposed to have sauce with your steak mate," chuckled Kane, "not steak with your sauce." They seemed to be a little family unit, but I knew for a fact that Kane was single, so I wondered whether maybe Sophie was his sister.

"Welcome back to Perth," said Sophie, ignoring the growing mess on Taj's plate. "You enjoying being home or do you miss London?"

"A little of both," I said, not ready to discuss London. "So, are you Kane's sister?" I asked as a loud popping sound echoed through the kitchen, followed by a splat, and a clatter of cutlery. The three of us turned to see the lid shoot off the tomato sauce bottle and land smack, bang, in the middle of the already large puddle of sauce.

"Oh honey," moaned Sophie, darting over to clean up the mess.

"Oh, geez buddy," said Kane, throwing Sophie a roll of paper towel. "I might have to take you outside and hose you down."

"No, Uncle Kane!" said Taj, who was splattered in sauce. "It's cold outside."

"Them's the breaks kid," Kane joked, extracting him from the chair and holding him up like a ragdoll.

"No please!" giggled the boy.

"Too late," Kane teased, swinging Taj towards the back door, "you're getting hosed."

"No, stop Uncle Kane!" he squealed with laughter, "I don't want to get hosed."

Sophie chuckled at their antics. "Kane, don't wind him up so close to bedtime," she scolded with a smile that was not the kind of look you'd share with a sibling. Kane put the boy down gently on the floor and pretended to kick him on the butt, which made the kiddo laugh again. "Looks like you're having another shower, child," he said, nudging Taj towards his mother.

"Come on sauce monster, let's get you cleaned up," Sophie said, herding her giggling son to the bathroom. Kane watched them go, with a longing in his eyes that indicated Sophie was most definitely not his sister. After a moment, he snapped out of it and returned to his position at the bench.

"How was your surf?" he asked, pouring me a glass of whiskey.

"Pretty great," I said, taking the glass from his outstretched hand. "It was good to get back on the water again. Plus, I met this crazy hot chick down there," I said taking a big gulp of the amber liquid in an attempt to warm myself from the inside out. "And I don't mean 'crazy-hot'," I said with air quotes, "I mean literally insane as well as hot. I think she had a death wish or something," I concluded, taking another long sip of my whiskey, just as the afore mentioned crazy hot chick walked through Kane's front door. I choked on my drink, coughing to prevent it coming out of my nose.

Surfer chick stopped dead in her tracks, and Kane glanced between us with knowing amusement.

"What are you doing here?" Crazy chick asked with disdain. She was much hotter up close and in the light. In fact, she kind of reminded me of Keanu's girl in Point Break.

"Ritchie, this is my sister Frankie," Kane said calmly. "I think maybe you've already met her. Spanks, this is Sean's brother Ritchie."
Frankie's jaw dropped and I felt smug that I'd managed to shut her up.

"You're Sean's brother?" she asked, running her hands through her wet hair.

"Guilty as charged," I said with a nod. "And you're Kane's sister," I added with an ironic smile. Of course the first girl I'd been even remotely attracted to since Amy was my Boss' little sister. "Hey, I think we got off on the wrong foot," I said, sticking my spare hand out towards her.

"Clearly," she answered coldly.

"Aww come on, let's start over," I said, wiggling my hand so she would take it. "I'm Ritchie."

She paused for a moment but then rolled her eyes and shook my hand with a resigned smile. "Hi Ritchie, I'm Frankie."

"Nice to meet you, Frankie. Can I just say you're a brilliant surfer?"

"Yes, you can," she smiled, grabbing the glass out of my other hand, and knocking back the remaining whiskey in one gulp. I raised a brow as she handed me back the empty glass. "So Ritchie, do you usually stalk women while they're surfing?" she asked with a cheeky grin.

"Only the really crazy ones," I retorted.

"You're pushing it baldy," Frankie replied with an arched brow.
I chuckled and popped the empty glass down onto the bench.

"Well, I was going to grab a shower, but I think Sophie might be busy scrubbing tomato sauce off Taj for a while."

"You can use the ensuite in my room Ritch," Kane offered pouring Frankie a glass of her own, "it's the one at the end of the hall. There are towels in the cupboard."

"Cheers mate," I said, as I caught Frankie eying my bare torso hungrily. When our eyes met, she realised she'd been busted perving but instead of being embarrassed, she shrugged like it was no big deal. I raised one ginger brow at her and swaggered off down the hall. I got the distinct feeling that girl was going to be trouble.

- KANE THOMPSON -

Ritchie strutted off for a shower leaving Spanks and I alone in the silent kitchen. Somehow, we'd found ourselves in the midst of tension and I had no idea if it was me who was pissed at her, or vice versa. I slid a glass of whiskey towards her as a peace offering.

"Here," I said, not sure how else to break the tension. She looked over, edged towards me, and then took the glass from the bench.

"Thanks," she said simply, as I pushed a stool out for her to sit on. She looked at it but didn't sit.

"Are we cool?" I asked, cracking a bottle of sparkling water. Normally I'd have partaken in the whiskey, but I wasn't in the mood for drinking.

"I don't know. Are we?" Spanks asked snidely.

"It's hard to tell," I said honestly as I poured myself an entire pint of San Pellegrino.

"I'm sure you'll find something to be angry about," she quipped, taking a big swig of her drink.

I sighed and sipped my bubbly water. "Why would I be angry at you?"

"I don't know Kane. Why would you?"

I raised my brows and looked around the empty room for some semblance of sanity, but no one was there to intervene. "I'm not angry at you Frankie," I told her, to make sure that we were both clear on the situation.

"You're not?"

"No."

"Oh."

"So... we're good?" I asked, feeling exhausted by the interaction. Our relationship had been like this our entire lives. No matter what I said, Frankie was always defensive, and I had no idea how to break through that prickly exterior of hers. If we weren't family, I wouldn't have bothered trying. We were such different people. She was a reckless, free-spirited, surfer girl and I was... well... I was me. If it hadn't been for Sophie coming into our lives, we probably would have never hung out together.

"Yeah, I guess," Frankie said, with a shrug as she finally took the seat, still wrapped in her beach towel. "I just assumed you were pissed at me."

"Am I really that bad?" I asked, wondering how and when we'd gone so far astray.

"Yeah," she said with a nod, "usually I do something that shits you."

"I don't mean to be like that."

"Meh, I love you anyway Jughead."

I poured her another glass and sat down at the bench opposite her. "I'm sorry if I'm hard on you. I guess I forget that you do things your own way."

"Dad was the same with you, so that's all you know."

I looked at her with a whole new level of respect. She was way more switched on than I'd ever given her credit for.

"Yeah, you might be right," I agreed. I eyed the bottle of 14-year, barrel aged whiskey, tempted to pour myself a glass. We heard a faint rumble in the distance and looked at each other. "Thunder?" I asked hopefully.

"Nope. Brenton," she said cheerfully.

"Fantastic," I mumbled, swiping her glass, and downing the remainder.

"Well… I'm gonna get changed," she said rising from the stool. "Happy Birthday Jughead."

"Thanks Spanks."

As Frankie took her leave, the rumble of Brenton's motorbike grew louder. Soph herded Taj out of the bathroom while he jumped around in excitement, still damp and wrapped in a towel.

"Daddy's here," he repeated over and over again.

Soph cast me a nervous glance over her shoulder. "Yes, so you'd better get into your room and get dressed young man," she said, smacking him gently on the butt. Taj ran down the hall to his bedroom and Sophie turned with a sigh before joining me in the kitchen. "I don't know if I can do this Kane. A few minutes to do a handover is one thing, but a whole weekend?" She flopped down on the stool that Frankie had vacated, so I topped up the glass and pushed it in her direction. After a lifetime of friendship, sharing glasses was nothing out of the ordinary for us.

"You've got this Shorty," I said, as the roar of the Ducati grew loud enough to announce that it was right outside.

"Sure," she said, and skulled the whiskey in one very long gulp.

The bike engine stopped, and we waited. A few minutes later, we heard footsteps on the porch and the door swung open to reveal Brenton and some random girl as they unzipped their leather jackets. My gaze darted to Soph. Her eyes were fixed intently to the girl, who took Brenton's hand as they walked through the door.

"Hey dudes," Brenton said cheerfully as he led the girl inside. "Bloody windy out there."

"Yeah," I agreed, as the two of us stared at him in shock.

"Happy Birthday Thommo. This is Jess," he added, waving towards the girl as if it was nothing unusual.

"Hey," I said, jumping up to shake her hand so Soph didn't have to respond, "I'm Kane."

"Happy Birthday Kane," Jess said with a shy smile, "thanks for inviting me."

Soph shot me a dirty look and I tried to ESP her that I hadn't, in fact, invited the girl.

"No worries," I said awkwardly.

"Daddy!" Called Taj, running into the kitchen wearing a pair of fleecy Harry Potter pyjamas. He jumped into Brenton's arms.

"Hey buddy," Brenton said, wrapping him up and planting a kiss on his forehead. As much of a selfish prick as he was when it came to Soph, Brenton had always been great with Taj, and it made me feel weirdly jealous. "Hazza Potter night is it?" he asked, tickling the boy.

"Yep!" said Taj proudly. "Mummy said we can even watch the movies this weekend."

"Well, aren't you lucky?"

"Brenton, why don't you show Jess to your room so she can get settled in?" I suggested, aching for the tense moment to end.

"Yeah sure," he answered, placing Taj down gently on the floor. "Back in a sec mate," he told the boy, then turned to his date and said, "follow me."

Taj looked confused and his blue eyes darted between Brenton, Jess and Sophie. "Why is Daddy sharing a room with that lady?" he asked me curiously.

"Err… Umm…" I stuttered, looking at Sophie for help.

"Because she's Daddy's new girlfriend," Soph explained flatly.

"Oh," said the boy with a furrowed brow. "A pretend one like you and Uncle Kane?"

"No, a real one," Soph said through gritted teeth.

"Oh," repeated Taj, frowning again.

"Should we get Philosopher's Stone set up in the cinema room?" I asked, changing the subject.

"Yay!"

"But first…" I said, rummaging around in the pantry to pull out a bag of Taj's favourite salted caramel popcorn, "I got you this." I threw him the bag and he caught it excitedly.

"Thanks Uncle Kane! It's my favourite!"

"My pleasure buddy." I shot Soph a quick glance to make sure she was okay, and then left her with the bottle of whiskey while Taj and I got our Harry Potter on.

- SOPHIE THOMPSON -

I took a swig of whiskey straight out of the bottle and then filled up my glass. Normally I would've started with something a little softer, like bubbles or white wine, but the whiskey was there, and I needed a hard drink to get me through this new level of hell that Brenton had inflicted upon us.

After another of glass of the warming liquid, I felt a little happier... or more specifically, numb to emotions. Which was just as well, because the happy couple emerged from their room before anyone else had returned. Where the hell was everyone?

I took a deep breath and relocated to the fireplace, grasping the half empty bottle of whiskey in one hand and my half full glass in the other.

"Whiskey?" Brenton teased as he grabbed a beer out of the fridge.

"Yep," I replied with a fake, slightly drunk smile.

"Mind if we join you?" He asked, gesturing towards himself and the girl who's name I hadn't registered.

"It's a free country," I said with a shrug, taking a large sip of my drink. There was no doubt that it was an uncomfortable moment, but after a few glasses of Kane's expensive Whiskey I was beyond caring. The girlfriend was clearly uneasy with my childish behaviour, but I couldn't help it. Brenton handed her a Bacardi Breezer and she took a big gulp of the bright pink drink. "I didn't realise they still made Breezers," I said snidely, "I don't think I've had one of those since I was eighteen."

"Yeah, they're great right?" she said, oblivious to my veiled insult. Brenton glared at me with annoyance and guided her over to the sofa in a very gallant way that he'd never done for me once in the history of our entire relationship.

"My taste has matured a bit since then," I said, knowing full-well that I was being a bitch, "but I did love them in my teens. I guess you're probably not far off that are you?" I asked her in my sweetest voice. Brenton almost choked on his drink while the girl stared at me with wide eyes, like a deer in headlights.

"Where's Taj?" Brenton asked loudly, quickly changing the subject.

"In the cinema room with Kane," I said, with my glass up to my mouth, ready to knock back another large swig of whiskey.

"Don't tell me he started Hazza Potter without me?" my cheating ex-husband joked cheerfully. "Shall we go check it out Jess?"
Ah… Jess. That was her name.

"Yeah sure," she agreed meekly, her eyes fearfully darting towards me.

"Have fun," I said obnoxiously, raising my glass at them with a big, fake smile. "It's just Philosopher's Stone so it isn't too scary, but Taj has read all the books, so he'll be able guide you through it if you get frightened."

"Soph!" Brenton hissed, shooting me a furious scowl before leading Jess out of the lounge area and down the hall towards the TV room.

"Happy weekend to me," I mumbled, swallowing my fourth glass of whiskey, before flopping back on the couch. Where the fuck was Isla in my hour of need?

- RITCHIE CARLTON -

As I hauled open the heavy double doors to Kane's master bedroom, my jaw nearly hit the floor. It looked like something straight out of the Nathan Stone playbook. Solid, double-glazed floor to ceiling windows created two of the walls, providing 180-degree views of the dense bushland that surrounded the block, with a spectacular backdrop of the ocean beyond the trees.

"Whoa," I muttered as I walked over to admire the view. Even in the dim light, it was magical. The big, white moon was reflecting on the choppy waves, creating a natural light show as the sea swirled with the wind. The unseasonable storm was brewing, and the trees were blowing about. I took a moment to appreciate the Australian landscape until a shiver of cold wracked my body. "Shower time," I announced to the empty room.

I made my way into Kane's elaborate, space-aged looking bathroom. The shower was so fancy it looked like I'd require an engineering degree just to make it work. It turned out not to be as complicated as it looked, and I jumped under the waterfall of hot water. I felt my body slowly warming as I rubbed myself down with the expensive body wash mounted on the wall, as if it was a hotel.

When I turned around again, I nearly slipped over with surprise when I saw Frankie standing in middle of the bathroom.

"Holy shit!" I said, as my hands immediately dropped to cover my cock. "Frankie, what are you doing in here? I'm naked."

"I know," she said appraising my bare flesh with a wicked smile.

"You need to get out of here," I said, grabbing a flannel off the rail to provide better peen coverage. "This is your brothers' room."

She smiled patronisingly. "Don't tell me a big burly guy like you is scared of Kane?"

"I'm not scared of him," I babbled, "it's a respect thing."

"But it's really cold out here and I'm all wet and sandy," she said pouting, as she dropped her beach towel on the floor and started to untie her bikini top.

"Jesus, fuck," I blurted like an idiot. I hadn't seen a naked woman since the last time I'd been with Amy, and I had no intention of breaking my drought with my new boss's sister. "Don't you dare take those off," I warned her nervously. "In fact, put your towel back on."

"Oops," she said, holding the string on her tiny little bikini.

"Frankie, I'm warning you."

"Aww you're too cute," she said, letting go of the string. Her bikini top fell to the floor, revealing her incredibly perky tits. I bit my spare knuckle and tried to look anywhere but there.

"Put it back on," I said, backing up against the cold, tiled wall as she stepped closer to the shower.

"Don't be a prude," Frankie teased, opening the shower door.

"What are you doing?"

"I'm getting warm," she said with mock innocence as she glanced down at my growing package. It was getting increasingly harder to hide the fact that I wanted her. "You don't seem like the shy type."

"I'm not," I said, looking up at the roof and pressing my back hard against the wall in an attempt not to touch her. "But you're my boss's sister, and really like my job."

"More than me?"

"I don't even know you Frankie," I spluttered, still peering at the roof as if it was the most interesting thing I'd seen in years.

"You really mean it don't you?"

"I do."

"Huh," she said simply. She was silent for a moment, so it felt safe to look down. Frankie was studying me with interest, "you're different to other guys, aren't you?"

"I guess so."

"What's your deal Ritchie?"

"No deal, just trying to carve out a life here."

"Hmm…" she muttered, stepping back and letting herself out of the shower. "I hope we can do this for real some time."

"Yeah, that'd… be… good," I stuttered ineloquently, as I exhaled the breath I'd held in for our entire interlude. She picked up her bikini top, eyes still on me, and wrapped the towel around her body.

"I get the feeling it would be better than good," she teased with a wink before exiting the bathroom, bikini top in-hand.
I breathed a sigh of relief and looked down at my over-excited cock.

"Down boy," I told it, as I resumed showering. "I know it's been a while, but this isn't the time to get back on the bike."

- KANE THOMPSON -

Taj and I were kicking back in our recliners, half watching Harry Potter. I could see his little brain ticking over as he munched on his popcorn, but I figured he needed time to process Brenton's new relationship status, so I let him be. Once again, Brenton's selfishness was impacting the people I loved. I turned back to the screen and tried to look enthusiastic about the movie.

"So, Daddy has a girlfriend now?" Taj asked quietly, still staring at the screen.

"Yeah buddy."

"Does that mean he won't be coming back home?"

"It looks that way."

"Oh." He threw some more popcorn in his mouth and watched the movie for a little while. "I think this is going to make Mummy sadder."

"What do you mean bud?"

"She doesn't think I know, but she cries a lot since he's gone."

"Oh." It was my turn to go quiet. The kid was way too perceptive for his own good.

"You can't tell her I told you, but I hear her all the time. It's mostly when she's in the shower, but sometimes when I've gone to bed too. I think she misses Daddy."

"I'm sure she probably does, but she'll be okay. Your mum is one of the toughest people I know."

"She is pretty tough, but I think she's lonely," he said, sounding like a fifty-year-old man rather than a ten-year-old boy. I studied him as he chomped down another handful of popcorn, then turned to me meaningfully. "Uncle Kane?"

"Yeah Bud?"

"Can you look after Mummy and make sure she doesn't feel lonely?" He asked, his big blue eyes drilling into mine. My chest seized momentarily as I tried to interpret the innocent words of a ten-year-old boy, without putting my own spin on it.

"Sure kiddo," I said casually. "You know I'll always be here for your mum. And for you too. You guys are like family to me."

"I know, but I was thinking maybe you could be Mummy's boyfriend? For real I mean. Not pretend."

"Oh, well, err… I'm not-"

"I can't believe you started without me," announced Brenton as he burst through the TV room door.

"You don't even like Harry Potter Daddy."

"But I do like spending time with you little man," Brenno said, perching on the arm of Taj's recliner. "Mind if Jess and I watch it with you?"

"Sure," Taj shrugged. I felt a small sting of betrayal. Harry Potter had always been the thing that Taj and I had nerded-out on together. We'd read the books, played all the games, even done the quizzes to discover that we were indeed, both Gryffindor's. No doubt Brenton would be a Slytherin.

I stood up from my recliner and offered my seat to Jess. "Here," I said, motioning for her to sit down.

"Oh, thanks," she said shyly.

"Brenno, can I borrow you for a sec?" I asked, pulling him by the arm towards the door before he had a chance to answer.

"Whoa, gentle with the money makers Amigo," he joked, straightening himself up. "What's up?"

"What are you thinking mate?" I hissed quietly so that Taj and Jess wouldn't overhear.

"What do mean? Aren't I allowed to watch a movie with my son?"

"I'm not talking about the movie, I'm talking about Jess," I whispered irately. "There's so many things wrong with this situation I don't even know where to start."

"How so?"

"You mean besides the fact that she's about twenty years old and you've brought her along to hang-out with your son and your ex-wife who you only broke up with a few months ago?"

"For a start, Jess is twenty-five," Brenton replied defensively.

"I'm not sure that's much better mate."

"And secondly... Soph doesn't care. You guys pretending to be together anyway, how's this any different?"

"Wow Brenno, you truly astonish me sometimes."

"Look Thommo, it'll be fine. Trust me."

"Just at least try to keep it low-key in front of Soph huh?"

"Fine," he agreed with a nod. "As long as you guys keep your play-acting to a minimum."

"There aren't any journos here, so there's no need for play acting."

"You're right, which means there's also no need for you to keep fawning over my wife."

"Ex-wife, and I'm not fawning over her."

"If that's what you have to tell yourself mate," he sneered, rolling his eyes. "Now, can I go watch the Philosophy Stone with my kid?"

"It's Philosopher's Stone," I mumbled, with another pang of jealousy that he was stealing my Taj-time.

"That's what I said," he answered with a shrug, and left me standing at the door as he lifted Taj up and shuffled into the recliner with him.

I felt a sharp stab of something unpleasant in my chest, which only grew stronger as I watched Taj snuggle up on Brenton's lap. I wanted that to be me. I wanted to be his dad. I wanted to be the only man Taj looked up to and the one he watched with admiration glimmering in his eyes. But I wasn't, and there was nothing that could change that. I'd never be able to compete with his footy star dad. I was just silly, nerdy Uncle Kane. I sighed and backed out of the cinema room feeling like a loser.

- SOPHIE THOMPSON -

I was still lying on the couch when Kane came out to start dinner.

"Oh no," he chuckled, jumping over the couch to torture me, "look at the state of you woman."

"I'm fine," I said, forcing a smile to my face, while he stared at me dubiously.

"No you're not," he said with a stern shake of his head. I stared at him sulkily and although a flicker of empathy crossed his face momentarily, he opted for being annoying instead, and began to bounce me around on the cushy sofa.

"Stop it, Jughead," I groaned, smacking his arm as he ruffled my hair playfully, like he used to when we were kids.

"Nope, if you're drunk, you're fair game," he teased, before sitting still and giving me his serious look. He patted his thigh with encouragement, so I rested my head on his leg. "Joking aside," he said as I got comfortable, "are you going to be okay?"

"Just have to find the will to live through this weekend," I sighed, self-piteously.

"Yeah," he agreed, stroking my hair reassuringly, "I honestly dunno what to say that will make it any better."

"There's nothing you can say."

"I'm sorry."

"Why are you sorry? It's not your fault."

"I should have specified that it wasn't a 'plus one' situation."

"Kane," I said, struggling to sit up in my whiskey-fuelled state, "you shouldn't have had to specify that. He's just being a selfish prick as usual," I blurted, before remembering that I was insulting Kane's family. "Oh sorry, I shouldn't say things like that."

"Why not? It's true," Kane said, staring into my eyes. His intense gaze made my stomach flip. Or perhaps that was the whiskey? "Look Shorty," he said earnestly, "I know he's my cousin, but I also know he's a narcissistic arsehole, so if you want to vent its fine." He locked me in his penetrating gaze and, for some reason, our closeness suddenly felt overwhelming.

I broke eye contact and wriggled up the couch a little. "Thanks, but I'll be fine," I assured him. "Honestly." I knew he could tell I was lying but I didn't want to ruin his birthday weekend.

"Okay, but if you want me to kick his arse I will," he offered with a grin.

"I'll let you know."

"The offer will stand from now until the end of time," he said with a wink. "Anyway, I'd better get dinner on, or we'll be eating at midnight, and I don't think you're going to last that long."

"Ha-ha, smart arse."

Kane chuckled and jumped off the couch, shooting me a cheeky smile over his shoulder as he headed to the kitchen.

"Hopefully Sean and Isla get here soon, or they'll miss dinner."

"Yeah," I agreed, "what time did they leave Perth?"

"I don't know."

"I'll text Isla."

Kane got cooking while I texted my rogue friends to find out where they were. I needed my bestie there to run interference between me and the replacement me. And hopefully keep Brenton as far from me as possible.

Frankie must have smelt the onions cooking, because she appeared from her bedroom, looking particularly well-groomed. Her hair was blow-dried and she was wearing eyeliner.

"Smells awesome Jughead," she said plonking down next to me on the couch as if it was normal for her to be wearing make-up.

"I could do with some help," Kane called over the sound of the rangehood.

"No thanks," she said cheekily, grabbing the whiskey bottle from the floor. "Soph and I have some catching up to do," Frankie added, taking a long swig straight out of the bottle before handing it to me.

"Starting with why you're so made-up on a family holiday," I teased, looking her up and down.

"I'm not made-up," she said defensively, "I just blow-dried my hair and put on a bit of eyeliner."

"Yeah," I agreed, "and you only ever do that when you're going out on the pull."

"Shut up and drink your whiskey," she ordered, guiding my hand, and the bottle, towards my mouth. I conceded to the peer pressure and took a chug of the whiskey as Brenton and Jess emerged from the cinema room, hand-in-hand. I wondered how long would take Spanks to notice.

"G'day Spanks," Brenton said, proudly showing off his new girlfriend.

"What the fuck?" Frankie blurted, unable to help herself. Frankie and Brenton were close, but she and I were closer, and she always took my side without question.

"This is Jess," explained Brenton, "Jess, this is my cousin Frankie."

"Right," Frankie replied, before looking at me with bewilderment. Brenton took the hint and dragged Jess over to join Kane in the kitchen. "I mean… what the actual fuck?" Frankie asked me, astounded.

"It's fine," I lied. I was trying to sound convincing but there was very little point. She knew me too well.

"No, it's fucking not," she said defensively, "what the hell is he thinking?"

"I honestly don't think he was," I said, trying to diffuse the situation.

"Clearly not," she agreed, as Brenton and Jess giggled from the kitchen. We looked over to see him trying to throw M&M's into her mouth. "This is gag-worthy," Spanks said, rolling her eyes. "Are you honestly okay with this?"

"Not really no."

"He's a dick."

"He's your cousin Frankie."

"Doesn't mean he's not a dick."

"True." She had a point there, but still...I didn't want to be the one to come between her and Brenton. I needed Isla so I could bitch and vent without guilt.

"I can't believe he brought a chick with him," she said, shaking her head at their playful antics as Ritchie emerged from his room looking clean, fresh and quite huggable in tracksuit pants and a hoodie. He was definitely my type, so I could see why Isla was keen to get us together, but there hadn't been any chemistry between us. He and Frankie on the other hand... had so much chemistry that it was bubbling over.

I followed Ritchie's eyeline as he blushed at the sight of Frankie. I peered at her, and she blushed in return. Another thing I'd never seen her do before.

"Ah Ritchie," called Kane from the kitchen, "this is my cousin Brenton and his... err.." Kane's eyes darted to me, "Um, Jess. Guys, this is Ritchie, he's Seany's brother." Ritchie walked past us with a furtive glance back at Frankie, before joining the others at the bench.

"Hey," he said shaking Brenton's hand first, then Jess'.

"Nice to meet you man," said Brenton, "So you're the one who just got back from London?"

"Yeah."

"Must be a bit of a shock to the system being back in sleepy little Perth huh?"

"Honestly... after the year I've had, I'm okay with sleepy."

"It must have been one hell of an exciting year if you're happy to settle in boring-as-batshit Perth." Brenton laughed.

Frankie's eyes were riveted on Ritchie. I handed her the whiskey bottle while she watched the conversation unfold.

"Are you going to spill?" I whispered quietly as the rest of them chatted at the bench.

"There's nothing to spill," she said way too casually. She was lying. I knew it, she knew it.

"That look on your face says otherwise," I said quietly.

"Fine," she answered with a weird little smile that I'd never seen before, "I really like this one."

My jaw dropped. "Uh-oh, unchartered territory," I blurted.

"I know right?" Unlike me, Frankie wasn't the commitment type. I'd never heard her utter the words 'I really like this one' in the entire thirty-odd years we'd been friends. It was normally more like 'he's an awesome kisser' or 'he's so hot I wanna bite his arms'...but never 'I really like him".

"Just be careful Spanks. Please don't go getting attached. I don't think he's very available."

"What do you mean?"

At that moment, the front door flew open, and Sean burst in waving a half empty bottle of Limeburner's Whiskey.

"Hello party people," he declared with a flourish.

"Oh boy," laughed Ritchie, darting over to support his brother as Isla appeared in the doorway.

"Sorry," she apologised on his behalf, as Ritchie ushered Sean into the house. "We stopped at Limeburner's to choose a couple of bottles for the wedding and he ended up getting drunk with the owner."

"That's okay," called Frankie, "Soph drank half a bottle of Balvenie so we can lock them in the cinema room together." Isla cast me a worried glance and with our best friend ESP, I told her I was not okay, before nodding towards Jess.

"Yeah, fine," slurred Sean with a grin, while Isla's jaw dropped at the sight of Brenton sitting with his arm slung casually over Jess' shoulder. Sean was too drunk to notice. "Soph and I will go have fun while you boring party poopers just sit and talk about the stock market," he declared, waving his bottle with a laugh.

"Jesus," chuckled Ritchie, rolling his eyes, "how much did you drink?"

"A little bit," said Sean squinting to assess what was left in his bottle while, behind his back, Isla indicated that he'd drunk a lot.

"How about we get you in the shower before dinner?" Ritchie suggested, as Frankie practically drooled over him. He was definitely a cool customer, I'd give him that, but what was it about the guy that had turned my hard-arse Frankie into a pile of mush?

"Fine," agreed Sean like a reluctant teenager, "I'll have a shower, but after that we're getting this party started."

"Sure mate," Kane placated him.

"Love you Thommo," he called as Ritchie assisted him towards the bathroom. "Happy Birthday buddy."

"Thanks Seany."

Ritchie and Sean disappeared down the hall and Isla did a quick round of hugs, starting with Kane.

"Happy Birthday babe, sorry I couldn't stop that idiot from trashing himself," she apologised handing him a gift bag.

"It wouldn't be my birthday weekend if there wasn't at least one drunk idiot on the premises," he joked, peering over at me with a grin, "and this year I got two of them."

"Oi," I replied pathetically. I couldn't deny that I was drunk, and unfortunately it was for that exact reason my brain had no witty retorts to provide.

Isla greeted Brenton with a quick peck on the cheek and then turned her attention to Jess.

"And who's this you've brought with you?" Isla asked with a smile. How did she always manage to be so perfect and amenable? No wonder everyone loved her.

"This is Jess," said Brenton, without further explanation. I could sense what Isla was thinking but she remained gracious and welcoming.

"Well… lovely to meet you Jess," she said, shaking Jess' hand before turning to Frankie and I. "Looks like I've got a bit of catching up to do," she teased, plucking the whiskey from my hand. She gave me a quick hug before taking a swig straight from the bottle.

"I haven't drunk that much. I was out surfing," said Frankie in defense of her sobriety.

"Surfing with Ritchie," I teased with a drunk giggle. Isla's eye widened with a mixture of amusement and disappointment. I could tell she had mixed feelings about Frankie throwing a spanner in her plan to hook me up with Ritchie.

"Right," she said with a smile, "we need a debrief in the morning," she whispered quietly into my ear. "Speaking of Ritchie, I'd better go help him tend to my drunk fiancé," Isla announced, then grabbed their luggage and dragged it down the hall towards their room.

"At least you're in good company Shorty," Kane called over, shooting me a wink that made my stomach flip. What was going on with me tonight?

"Definitely an improvement on current company," I said without thinking. Jess visibly shrunk in her seat. I felt slightly bad, but not bad enough that I'd lose sleep over it.

"I'll try not to take that personally," teased Kane, successfully deflecting the insult away from my ex-husband's new girlfriend. He smiled with his lips, but his eyes shot me a warning look.

"Yeah, me too," added Frankie, throwing a cushion at me just as I turned in her direction. The cushion thwacked me in the face, and I flopped backwards on the big, plush sofa. I laughed and, not having the energy to sit up again, I snuggled into the couch and closed my eyes. "You okay?" Spanks asked. I could feel her hovering above me.

"I'm great," I mumbled sarcastically. "All I have to do is get drunk enough that this becomes bearable."

- RITCHIE CARLTON -

Seany was so drunk, it was like a trying to undress a human-sized ragdoll. I'd managed to strip him down to his undies but, by that point, he'd lost the ability to hold himself up so I'd lugged him into the shower as he was. Sean was almost the same size as me, so it had been no easy feat. To be honest, I was pretty okay with not having to see my brothers dick up close, so I hadn't tried too hard to get him completely naked.

Sean was now slumped on the shower floor in soaking wet jocks, while I stood and watched him to make sure he didn't slip or drown in the small puddle of water that was pooling beneath him.

"I think it might be better if I just to get him to bed," said Isla, hopelessly as she joined us in the bathroom.

"Yeah, probably," I agreed, studying my drunk brother with amusement. "He used to be a much better drinker than this."

"Dinner's up!" called Kane from the kitchen.

"Right, let's get this drunken idiot to bed," sighed Isla, grabbing a towel out of the cupboard. I switched off the water.

"I'll lift him while you dry," I suggested, positioning myself so I could get a good grasp under his armpits.

"Thanks Ritchie," she said as I hauled the drunkard off the shower floor. Sean mumbled something, but neither of us understood what he was saying. We managed to get him dry enough not to drip all over Kane's nice floors, so Isla wrapped the towel around him and stripped off his jocks. With the towel securely fastened, I gripped my idiot brother tightly around the waist and lugged him down the hallway behind Isla.

"We're in here," she said, opening the door of the room next to mine. "Just put him on the bed and I'll deal with the rest."
I plopped Sean ungracefully onto the bed and the towel unravelled around him.

"So much for not seeing his dick," I joked as Isla quickly threw the covers over him.

"Sorry Ritch."

"Meh, nothing I haven't seen before," I shrugged. "You gonna be okay with him?"

"Yeah, it's not my first rodeo," she joked.

"Okay," I nodded. "You want me to bring you some food?"

"Nah, I'll be fine thanks Ritch. I'll pop out later."

"Righto." I left Isla to deal with her drunk fiancé and joined everyone else in the kitchen.

Dinner was like a slow-motion car crash. The Thompson clan were just as mental as the Artemis Crew, if not more. The drama that had already begun to unfold over the evening, hit full throttle during our meal. We sat around the table quietly, the tension rife as if we were all waiting for something to happen but none of us knew what or when.

"What do you do for work Jess?" I asked, seeing how uncomfortable she was to be there.

"I'm one of the Physio's for the team," she answered with a thankful smile.

"Wow," said Frankie, reluctantly impressed. Clearly she didn't want to like the girl.

"That's great," I said encouragingly, "how did you manage that?"

"I was working for the senior physio before she won the contract, and she brought me over with her."

"And when was that exactly?" Sophie asked snidely.

"About a year ago," the girl answered innocently.

"So, you've been massaging Brenton's thighs for quite some time then?" Sophie said with amazingly quick, but nasty, wit.

"Sophie!" hissed Frankie, nudging her well intoxicated friend in the ribs.

"What?" asked Sophie loudly, "I'm just making conversation."

"Well stop," Frankie muttered through her fake smile.

"I'm not allowed to make conversation?"

"Not right now, no."

I had no idea what was going on, but it was clear that Sophie hated Jess, which was surprising given she and Kane seemed to have a thing going on. The dynamics of this family were way too confusing for me.

"So, Kane," I said loudly, attempting to help Frankie change the subject. "I noticed you have a jet ski down in the rec room. Reckon we'll get a chance to crack it out this weekend?"

"Depends on this weather," he said, nodding gratefully for the change of topic. "It was supposed to be warm, but those storm clouds would indicate otherwise."

"Yeah, a bit out of season huh?"

"Maybe you brought the shitty weather back from England," he joked.

"Wouldn't surprise me," I chuckled.

"So, Jess," said Sophie, taking the opportunity to hijack the conversation again, "how long have you and Brenton been dating?"

All eyes darted to Jess, and I could almost hear a collective intake of breath. Brenton's face grew pale, and he opened his mouth to speak, but Jess beat him to it.

"About six months now," she said with a smile. She and I were both clearly unaware of something that the rest of the group was privy to, because all four Thompsons fell silent. Frankie's jaw was nearly on the floor whilst Kane's was clenched tight, and Sophie looked as if she was about to vomit.

"Is that right?" Sophie said through gritted teeth, "and did you know that he was married at the time?"

Holy shit. My jaw dropped at the same time as Jess'. It was apparently our turn to look flabbergasted. I wanted to intervene to put the poor girl out of her misery, but I was too stunned to say anything, so I sat and watched the carnage unfold.

"Uhh, I don't think we need to talk about this right now," Brenton said, desperately trying to avoid a scene.

"Oh, you don't think we do, do you?" Sophie hissed. I was shocked that the woman who had seemed so sweet and gentle, was full of so much rage and hatred, but honestly, I couldn't blame her. "Well pardon me your majesty, I forgot that the whole world revolves around you and what you want."

"Hey, so I reckon it's time for dessert huh?" said Frankie loudly as Isla emerged from her room.

"So what did I mess?" she asked chirpily as we all looked in her direction. Her eyes widened as she took in the vibe of the room. "Oh wow, I really did miss something."

"I could defo go some sweets," I declared enthusiastically.

"Yeah," grunted Brenton.

"Okay," said Kane, standing up abruptly, causing his chair to squeal against the floor. "Dessert coming right up." He cleared a few dishes and them came back for Sophie. "Soph," he barked, prising her out of her seat, "you're helping me."

- KANE THOMPSON -

Sophie was totally smashed, and Jess' last little truth-bomb had shattered her ability to cope. I encouraged her up from her seat, as she sat there looking almost catatonic.

"Sure," she said unenthusiastically, letting me assist her to her feet. I guided her into the kitchen and leaned her against the bench. "I think we need to get you to bed, before you say anything else you're going to regret," I said, holding her shoulders to keep her from sliding sideways.

"I'm fine," she said, resisting my efforts.

"No, you're not," I disagreed. "You're the exact opposite of fine. In more ways than one."

She tried to push my hands from her arms but I held tight. "Kane I can stand up on my own."

"Can you?" I asked, letting her go. The second I released my hands, she began tilting sideways, so I quickly replaced them. "Soph, you know the drunk-tank drill," I teased, "it's either bed or a cold shower. What'll it be?"

"Neither," she argued. "You don't get to boss me around Mr bossy pants."

"Solid burn," I mocked, "but I've been bossing you around for thirty years so I'm not giving that up now." She slurred a response that I didn't quite catch, so I rolled my eyes and laughed as Isla joined us in the kitchen.

"Everything okay in here?" She looked from me to Sophie and back again. "Oh dear."

"Yeah," I agreed, "she's refusing to go to bed. Do you think you can talk some sense into her?"

"Not any more than you could,"

"Stop talking about me like I'm a child," Sophie grumbled, sounding eerily like Taj. "You guys are being melody-meldadom-melodramatic."

"Oh Jesus," I said, facepalming. "you leave me no choice woman," I told her, lifting her up and throwing her over my shoulder. "Cold shower it is."

"Are you sure that's the best idea?" asked Isla with a concerned raise of her brow. I could only assume she and Seany had been discussing my inappropriate feelings for Soph. This moment certainly wouldn't help alleviate any of her concerns.

"Yeah," I said, giving her a nod. "It's fine," I assured her, before carting Soph out of the kitchen.

"Kane!" Sophie squealed, hitting my back as I carried her towards the bathroom. "Put me down."

"Sorry, no can do," I laughed as the rest of the group watched with amusement. "Say goodnight to everyone."

"Goodnight to everyone," she muttered grumpily as we retreated down the hall. Once we reached the bathroom, I flicked on the shower but placed her gently on the bathroom floor. Normally I would have thrown her straight in, but the look on her face made me want to take pity on her.

"You going to be okay?" I asked as she flopped against the sink.

"I don't know," she said, shaking her head in a drunken fashion. "How many more bottles of Balvenie have you got?"

I laughed and gave her a hug. She let her head rest against my chest for a moment, before peering up at me with sad eyes.

"Why is this so easy for him?"

"It probably isn't."

"You really believe that?"

"Not really," I admitted. "The guy is an emotionless arsehole."

She smiled sadly and peered up at me with tearful eyes. "Why didn't he love me? What made Jess worthy of his attention when I wasn't? Why didn't my own husband want to have sex with me? What's wrong with me Kane?"

"Nothing's wrong with you," I said, pushing some wayward hair out of her face. "It's him who's the problem. He's an arrogant dick."

"Yeah, but a dick who's getting laid," she slurred, making me laugh.

"You're gonna be fine Shorty," I chuckled, letting go of her and backing away before I did something stupid. "Now get in the shower by choice or I'll throw you in there."

Soph smiled sadly. "Thanks Jughead. For everything."

"That's what I'm here for."

"You are, aren't you? You're always here for me... And Taj," she muttered thoughtfully. "It doesn't go unnoticed you know?"

"I know." I let myself out and closed the door behind me, leaning against it for a moment to gather myself. That woman knew exactly how to floor me, but that wasn't a conversation I wanted us to have while she was blind drunk.

When I returned to the table, Ritchie and Frankie were the only two left. "Where is everyone?" I asked, looking around the empty dining room.

"The general consensus was that an early night would be best for everyone," Ritchie said tactfully.

"Probably best," I agreed with a nod.

"Sophie okay?" Ritchie asked, clearing up the last of the dishes.

"Yeah, but she might not be so great in the morning," I joked with a grimace, taking a seat at the table with an exhausted sigh. "What a night."

"It's certainly had the drama factor of a night with my London crew," Ritchie joked from the kitchen.

"Poor Soph," Frankie said sculling the rest of her beer and going to the fridge for another. She returned with three bottles, and handed one to each of us. "Brenton is such a dick sometimes. I can't believe he brought the girl he was cheating on her with."

"Yeah, that's an all-time low even for Brenton."

"Ouch," cringed Ritchie. "I take it Sophie didn't know Jess was coming then?"

"No one did," I said, leaning back in my chair and taking a sip of my beer.

"On your Birthday weekend?"

"Yeah," I nodded, "welcome to life with Brenton." We all fell silent as we sipped on our beers. We heard the bathroom door open and I could envision Soph creeping sheepishly down the hallway to her bedroom.

"Are you ever gonna tell her?" Frankie asked breaking the silence.

"Tell who what?" I asked, pretending not to know what she was talking about, even though I knew exactly what she meant. There was no way I was gonna admit it, especially not in front of Ritchie.

"Tell Soph that you're in love with her," Spanks clarified bluntly.

"I'm not in love with her," I protested.

"Yes, you are."

I sighed, risking a glance at Ritchie, who hadn't battered an eyelid. Obviously, he'd noticed it too, which made it one of the more excruciating moments of my life. I couldn't believe my little sister was initiating this conversation in front of an employee, or that she'd figured out I was in love with her best friend, but there seemed no point in denying it.

"Okay, I am," I admitted reluctantly.

"So, are you going to tell her?" Ritchie asked curiously.

"No way!"

"Why not?" Asked Frankie.

"What am I supposed to say? I've loved you my whole life, but I've been too gutless to tell you?"

"Exactly."

"Be serious Spanks."

"I am being serious. She would never admit it, but that woman has had a thing for you since we were ten."

"No way," I disagreed, "she was always more interested in Brenno."

"Was she?" Frankie asked with a raised brow, "or was it just that he was the first one to make a move?" I shook my head, but Spanks nodded. "She wasn't into Brenton in the same way she was into you, but he had the balls to step up and you didn't."

"You're full of shit."

"I swear to God Jughead," she said earnestly, "if you'd asked her out before Brenton, things would have worked out very differently."

"For what it's worth," interjected Ritchie, "I got the impression she's into you."

"Seriously big brother, you have to say something," said Frankie. "If you love Soph you need to tell her. She's damaged now and she's not gonna put her heart on the line easily after what Brenton did. You'll have to make it happen. You need to show her that you care about her. If you want her, it's time to step up."

"And you'd be fine with that?" I asked in surprise.

"Why wouldn't I be?" she said with confusion. "You guys make each other happy, why would I want to get in the way of that? Besides, you'd treat her much better than Brenton ever did."

"Hmm…" I mumbled as I swilled my beer around in my mouth.

"Well, I think I'm gonna hit the hay," said Ritchie, rising from the table.

"Really?" said Frankie, "but it's so early."

"It's been an eventful day," chuckled Ritchie. "Thanks for inviting me along Kane. I haven't socialised since I left London so it's been nice to get out again."

"Any time mate."

"Night," Ritchie said, heading off to his room.

"Night," Frankie and I echoed simultaneously.

"And then there were two."

- RITCHIE CARLTON -

By morning, the storm had well and truly set in. I peered out the window of my plush bedroom and watched the wind whip the trees around outside. Whilst my view was not quite as impressive as the one from Kane's bedroom, I still had a good outlook over the bushland. I rubbed my aching temples. My head felt heavy and foggy after last night's drinking session, so I really wanted to go for a run to shake it off. It looked like there was a decent gap in the rain, so it was now or never. I hadn't let bad weather stop me running in London, so I wasn't going to let it stop me in Australia.

I pulled on my running gear, and grabbed the well-worn, light-weight rain vest that I'd bought for these exact occasions when I'd first moved to London. I reached for my sneakers (aka: trainers, for the Poms in the audience), but then changed my mind and slipped on my thongs (or flip-flops as my Pommy mates called them) and snuck quietly out of my room, so as not to wake anyone. The house was still quiet and dark with all the ridiculously expensive block-out screens still closed shut. It wasn't until I reached the kitchen that I found signs of life.

Taj sat at the table eating a massive bowl of Nutri-Grain, with big headphones clamped over his ears. His legs swung happily just above the floor, and he giggled quietly at whatever he was watching on the iPad. I smiled, remembering back to a time when life's pleasures were that simple. Cereal and Saturday morning cartoons.

Kane emerged from the pantry with a bag of coffee beans in one hand and a tin of Milo in the other.

"Oh, morning Ritch," Kane said cheerily, as he plonked his bounty onto the bench, "I didn't hear you come in."

"I was trying not to wake anyone but looks like you guys are early risers too."

"Yeah, unfortunately my body doesn't know the difference between weekdays and weekends."

"I don't think mine has even realised I'm not in London anymore," I joked. "Everyone else still asleep?"

"I think so, and I reckon Soph will be nursing a killer hangover this morning, so I figured I'd get this kid sorted," he said, nodding at Taj with a fatherly smile. "He can't hear a thing with those headphones on," he joked as we both watched Taj, happily oblivious to the fact that I'd even entered the room. "Fancy a coffee?" Kane asked, indicating a very fancy looking coffee machine sitting in the corner of the bench.

"No thanks, I'm about to go for a run."

"Wow, you're dedicated."

"Nah, it just helps clear the hangover," I said with a chuckle, "plus the novelty of the beach still hasn't worn off."

"Pretty stormy out there."

"I've jogged through worse," I said with a shrug. "Anyway, I'd best get to it before you talk me out of it."

"See you on the flipside," Kane said, with a salute, as he got to work making the coffee.

I let myself out the front door and flipped up my hood. The wind was hectic, but it didn't feel cold compared to a wintery day in London. I breathed in the fresh air and headed off down the beach track. Black rain clouds were looming ever closer, so I'd have to make it a quick one.

As I drew closer to the beach entrance, I noticed a silhouette out in the frothy waves, and judging from the frenetic way they were navigating the surf, they were in trouble. I spotted a towel sitting on the beach and recognised it instantly.

"Fucking Frankie," I muttered, stepping up my pace, when I saw a massive foam-covered wave drawing up behind her. The stupid woman was right out on the reef break and still hadn't noticed it on her tail. "Frankie!" I yelled, waving my hands to try and get her attention as I pointed towards the wave. It was no use. The wind and crashing waves were so loud they drowned me out. I stripped off my jacket and ran straight into the water.

"Frankie!" I yelled again. This time she saw me and looked over her shoulder seconds before the huge waved crashed over her. My heart pounded in my chest as she fell backwards and her board flew into the air. After careening upwards like a rocket, the aptly named Thruster, flipped and then hurtled back down clocking Frankie hard in the head. Her body went limp, and she vanished under the water. "Shit." Without even thinking about it, I swam furiously towards her. "Frankie!" I yelled, swallowing mouthfuls of salt water, as the rough ocean threw me about like a sock in a washing machine. A loud clap of thunder rang out over the beach and the heavens opened, unleashing an ungodly amount of rain, adding to the frothy chaos.

"Fuck," I spluttered, kicking harder and faster towards Frankie, as her lifeless body floated back up to the surface, still tethered to her board by the leg rope.

By sheer dumb luck, the two of them were pushed towards me by the tide. Regardless, I didn't stop for a breath until I reached her. She wasn't breathing, so I hauled her onto the board, breathed a few breaths into her mouth and then jumped on behind her, paddling with all my strength to get us safely back to the shore so I could administer proper CPR. My heart was pounding in my chest and the blood was rushing in my ears. It felt like Amy all over again.

The moment the board hit sand, I dropped to my knees and started chest compressions on her cold, limp body.

"Come on Frankie," I pleaded, having traumatic flashbacks of holding Amy's dead body, "I won't let you die on me too. Come on," I said, going for a second round. My heart was pounding so fast that I could barely breathe. I hadn't realised how traumatised I had been by Amy's death until I was faced with this horrific do-over. I wouldn't let Frankie die. I couldn't.

I pumped her chest as rain pelted down on us. "Please Frankie, I can't do this again," I begged, breathing one more big breath into her lungs. Finally, her chest heaved, and she coughed up a shitload of water. "Oh my god," I said, only just realising that, along with the rain, tears were streaming down my face. "Are you still with me?" I asked, as she opened her eyes and tried to get her bearings. The rain pelted down around us, and the wind was so frantic, it almost seemed to be alive.

"Ritchie?" she asked, squinting her eyes against the rain.

"Yeah. Are you okay?"

"I don't know," she croaked, spitting out some leftover water as she tried to sit up.

"Don't move," I told her, gently pushing her back down to the board, "you could have broken bones, or concussion or something."

"I'm fine," she said, taking stock of her body. "Nothing hurts, besides my head and my pride."

"What the fuck were you thinking?" I asked, as my fear was replaced by rage. "Why would you go out there in this weather, especially by yourself?"

"Storms make the best waves," she said flippantly, waving her hand at me. "Come on, help me up."

"Are you serious?" I asked, helping her to a seated position. "You could have killed yourself."

"But I didn't."

"What would have happened if I hadn't come out here?"

"Then I guess it would have been my time to go."

"How can you be so fucking blasé about this?" I growled loudly, trying to make sure I could be heard over the thundering rain. "If you've got a death wish, fine, but I won't let you kill yourself on my watch."

"On your watch?" she shouted back, the wind whipping her wet hair around. "What is that supposed to mean? Is that why Kane invited you on this holiday? To keep an eye on me?"

"What? No, that's not it at all," I yelled, pointlessly wiping the streams of rain off my face, as they were quickly replaced by more.

"Really? Because that's literally what you just said."

"No, it isn't," I argued, leaning closer so I wouldn't have to shout as loud. "Don't put words into my mouth. And do me a favour… look up the definition of 'literally'."

"I know what literally means."

"No, I don't think you do," I argued, "because I literally didn't say that."

"Then why did you say, 'on your watch'?"

"It's hard to explain."

"Try using small words, it might be easier."

"Ugh," I growled with frustration. "You're infuriating, you know that?"

"I could say the same for you."

Without knowing how or why, I found myself grabbing her face and kissing her hard as the rain belted us sideways. I don't know which of us moved first, but we were quickly entangled, sandy, soaked through and totally oblivious to the storm raging around us. Frankie wrapped her arms around my neck and pressed her body tight against mine, returning my kiss with vigour. It was passionate and filled with lust, rage, and something else I couldn't put my finger on. Whatever it was, it was driving me forward against my better judgement and I wasn't sure I'd ever be able to make it stop. Or if I wanted to.

- SOPHIE THOMPSON -

I was mortified by my undignified behaviour at last night's dinner. I'd known that I was being a total bitch, but I hadn't been able to stop myself. It definitely hadn't been my finest moment ever, and then topping it off with the stomach explosion to end all others only added to my embarrassment. Not that anyone else knew – unless they'd heard me – but I'd been up all night, purging the whiskey from my system, which primarily entailed me sitting on the toilet with my head in a bucket. Well… technically it was a rubbish bin that I'd upended in desperation, unsure from which end the whiskey was going to make a reappearance. Turns out, it came out both ends, and overnight I had completely emptied my body of all its contents, so the dehydration was now exacerbating my hangover.

I groaned in both shame and pain, rolling onto my side. I could hear movement in the quiet the house and I knew Taj would be hiding somewhere with his eyes fixed to that damn Nintendo screen. It was unlikely that Brenton would get up and sort him out so I'd have to haul my arse out of bed if I wanted him off it.

"Come on body," I muttered quietly to myself, "you can do this." After several failed attempts to sit upright, I settled for rolling out of the cushy bed instead, kneeling on the floor for a moment to find my balance. I'd really done a number on myself. I seemed to be making a habit of writing myself off since my split. It was probably time I reigned that in and sorted my shit out. I climbed gingerly to my feet and shuffled slowly out to the living area.

"Eek, watch out bud, the zombie apocalypse has started," Kane teased, when he saw me emerge from the darkness.

"Funny," I replied flatly, unable to manage more than that.

"Morning mummy," Taj said, way too loudly, running over to give me a hug. His Switch was tucked away neatly on the bench with his headphones.

"Morning baby," I said, planting a kiss on the top of his blonde head. "I'm surprised you're not on that thing," I said nodding imperceptibly at the aforementioned device.

"Uncle Kane made me turn it off."

"Did he?" I asked, feeling pleasantly surprised. I looked at Kane with a grateful smile. "Thanks."

"That's what I'm here for. Now sit," Kane ordered, pointing to a seat at the bench. I did as ordered, and he placed a super-strong black coffee in front of me. "Triple shot," he explained. "Drink."

"Thanks." I once again followed orders without argument and sipped cautiously on my coffee. Kane plonked a glass of fizzing cloudy orange liquid in front of me. I squinted up at him sceptically.

"Its Berocca and aspro clear," he explained. "It'll help your head and rehydrate you."

"Can I have one?" Asked Taj eagerly.

"Sorry Bud, that's for grown-ups only."

"Aww… no fair," whinged Taj, "grown-ups get all the good stuff."

"It's medicine mate."

"Why? Are you sick mummy?"

"I'm fine buddy," I said, as Kane slid a plate of vegemite toast in front me. My stomach churned at the yeasty whiff. Normally I loved the smell of vegemite, but that morning my stomach wasn't in agreement.

"You don't look fine," said Taj, eyeing me sceptically.

"Right kiddo," interjected Kane, "we're going on a bush walk."

"What? But it's raining outside," Taj argued.

"No such thing as bad weather, just the wrong clothes. Isn't that right Mummy?" Kane said cheerfully.

"Mm-hmm," I agreed, leaning my aching head on one hand as I attempted to nibble on the vegemite toast.

"Okay Tajinator," Kane said chirpily, "let's go get you kitted out." He herded my unexcited child off to get weather-proofed while I slurped on the big mug of triple-strength black coffee. I must have dozed off because before I knew it, Taj came bounding back into the kitchen.

"Look at me Mummy, I look like an army man."
I peered up from my coffee to see him dressed in super expensive survival gear.

"Wow," I said, concerned about Kane's hiking plan, given the way he'd kitted out my child. "Are you guys going to Antarctica?"

"Maybe," Taj replied with a grin as he explored all of the pockets in his new jacket.

"Just wanted to make sure he was appropriately dressed," said Kane, appearing from the hallway in an almost identical jacket. I couldn't help but laugh, despite my painful head. It was so sweet that Kane always went to such an effort for Taj.

"Well don't you two make a handsome pair. Are you planning to traverse the three peaks?" I teased half-heartedly. My head throbbed angrily with the effort.

"Ignore her Taj, she's just annoyed because I didn't get her one,"

Kane joked, shooting me a wink. "Anyway Zombie overlord, we're going to leave you in peace now. Why don't you finish that and go back to bed?"

"Yeah I might do that."

"Bye Mummy," Taj called as Kane led him outside. I remained slumped at the kitchen bench, sipping my triple-strength coffee, with my head resting in my hands. I wasn't sure I'd even be able to finish any of it.

"You look as bad as Sean does," Isla teased as she quietly snuck up behind me.

"I probably feel worse than I look," I admitted.

"Where's Taj?" she asked, taking a bite of my toast.

"Kane took him out for a bush walk."

"Did he now?" she said with a raised brow. "And I suppose he made you this hangover breakfast too?"

"Yeah, so?" I asked, wondering what she was getting at.

"What happened to the Ritchie plan?"

"There was no Ritchie plan."

"He was supposed to be your rebound bonk," she said, extracting the mug from my limp hand and taking a sip. "He was meant to distract you from Thommo, but you guys seem cosier than ever."

"We're fine Isla. You're the only one who's worried about it." I swallowed a few mouthfuls of the Berocca cocktail and cringed as my stomach lurched ever-so-slightly. "Besides, Frankie is really into Ritchie. I've never seen her so keen on a guy."

"Yeah, they were looking pretty comfortable with each other last night," she agreed, finishing off my toast. "How do you think Kane feels about that?"

"Why would Kane care?"

"Err… his promiscuous little sister hooking up with his new MD. It's a recipe for disaster don't you think?"

"I thought they looked kinda cute together."

"Hmm… we'll see," she said, chewing on the toast. "I just hope she doesn't break his heart. The poor guy doesn't need any more dramas. You would have been much better for him."

"Clearly he doesn't think so," I said, beginning to feel annoyed by her badgering.

"Okay grumpy," Isla said, finally dropping the matter. "Hey, Sean and I were supposed do a final viewing of the venue today and I was going to suggest you come along, but from the look of you I'm guessing you're not up for it?"

"Sorry babe, you know I normally would."

"No worries. I'm not even sure if Sean will make it to be honest."

"Sorry," I apologised again.

"All good. It's not like it would have changed much since we first saw it, but I thought it would be nice to stay on for a wine tour."

"Bleaugh," I muttered as my stomach reacted unfavourably to the idea of wine. "I think I'll go back to bed," I said, sliding off the stool.

"Okay babe," Isla said, "I'll see you when we get back. Sean ordered a cake for Kane for tonight, so we'll pick that up on the way back."

"Awesome, he'll love that. Have fun."

"Will do. Sleep well."

"Pass out more like," I joked before shuffling back down the hall to my room.

- RITCHIE CARLTON -

Frankie and I were practically dry humping on top of her surfboard, on the sand, in the middle of a storm. The only reason I couldn't technically categorise it as dry humping, was that we were both wet through. I was being driven by forces beyond my control and although my better judgement was telling me to stop, my body was in the driver's seat. It wasn't until a huge wave crashed over us that we both finally came to our senses. I pulled back from her, breathless and horny as hell.

"Whoa," I said, forcing myself to cease and desist.

"What was that?" she asked, equally as breathless.

"I don't know. Sorry."

"Don't be. I liked it."

"Me too," I agreed unashamedly, "but right now we need to get you back up to the house or you'll end up with hypothermia."

"Yeah." I gave her a hand up and we tried to brush the wet sand off ourselves, to no avail. I retrieved my now damp jacket from the sand and threw it over her shoulders. She slid her arms through the rain-soaked sleeves, while I picked up her board and threw it under my arm. I offered her my spare hand. Frankie smiled and slid her fingers through mine. "You can't tell Kane what happened."

"I assume you mean the part where I mauled you in public?" I joked nervously, as we wandered slowly towards the bush track.

"No, I mean the accident."

I stopped walking. "Frankie, you nearly died."

"Exactly," she said adamantly. "I'd never hear the end of it. I'd never be able to ever go surfing without a two-hour lecture."

"You're a grown woman," I said resuming our snail-paced mission. "And Kane is Kane."

"I still think you should tell him."

"Okay, I'll tell him about the accident if you tell him we made-out."

"No fucking way."

"But you're a grown man."

"Touché," I laughed. "Okay… so we tell him nothing."

"Correct." We stared at each other for a moment, her bright blue eyes burning into mine. That same hot, flash of desire came over me and I could see it on her face too.

"But I would like to resume that second nothing, once you're dry and warm," I admitted.

"Or you could help me warm up," she said with a grin, just as we caught a glimpse of Kane and Taj through the trees. We instantly dropped hands and split apart. Thankfully, Kane's view was obstructed by branches, so he hadn't noticed us yet. The odd pair strolled down the path, chatting intently, as if the weather wasn't storming around them. "Where are you two GI Joes off to?" called Frankie, instigating question time ahead of Kane.

"Aunty Spanks!" Called Taj excitedly waving. I peered at her sideways, amused by her unusual nickname.

"Aunty Spanks?" I teased, under my breath.

"Shut up," said Frankie with a smile.

"We're having a bush adventure!" said Taj, running towards us with a hand full of twigs, rocks and gumnuts.

"That sounds awesome buddy," Frankie said as we met the pair at the fork in the path where the white sand turned into red gravel, and the beach track veered off into the trees. "Great weather for it," she teased Kane.

"No such thing as bad weather…" Kane began.

"Only wrong clothing," finished Taj.

"Oh my god," sighed Frankie, rolling her eyes at Kane, "you're turning him into a mini-Kane."

"Nothing wrong with that," he said with an amused grunt.

"Uncle Kane's going to show me how to make a shelter."

"That sounds fun," said Frankie, raising a brow at her brother. "Trying to earn brownie points?" she teased.

"Where have you been?" Kane asked, ignoring her dig. "I thought you were still in bed."

Frankie glanced at me quickly, realising she looked pretty suspicious wearing my jacket.

"Went for a surf," she said with a shrug as Kane eyed me suspiciously, taking note of Frankie's board tucked under my arm. "Water was a bit rough, so Ritchie made me get out," Frankie said, when she saw Kane's eyes narrow, "he's almost as bossy as you," she joked convincingly.

"She looked like she was about to pass out from hypothermia," I said, my chest thudding a little at having to deceive my new boss. "We should probably get back up to the house."

"Good idea," Kane nodded. "Thanks for looking out for her Ritch."

Frankie and I exchanged another subtle glance.

"No problem, man," I said with a stiff nod, "see you back at the house."

"Enjoy your walk," called Frankie to Thommo and mini-Thommo as we set off in the opposite direction. "That was close," she said quietly, casting a quick glance over her shoulder.

"Ten minutes earlier and I would have been either dead or unemployed. Or both."

"Nah, but you might have ended up with a black eye," she said, nudging me playfully.

"Does he punch people often?"

"He has a few anger issues, but it's usually reserved for people who deserve it."

"And would I have deserved it?"

"Absolutely," Frankie replied with a grin, "especially if he'd known all the dirty things I was thinking about doing to you."

I laughed loudly and threw my spare arm around her shoulder now that the coast was clear. "Lucky you're an impeccable liar then," I teased.

"I've learnt how to work Kane," Frankie explained, threading her arm around my waist. "If you bury a lie amongst the truth, he never suspects a thing."

"I'm not sure whether to be concerned or impressed."

"Don't worry, I don't make a habit of lying to anyone besides my brother," she said as we arrived back at the house.

"Whatever you say Aunty Spanks." Frankie laughed and pulled the zipper cord on her wetty.

"In that case," she said cheekily, "Aunty Spanks says you should come to the rec room and help me get out of my wetsuit."

"I think I could handle that," I replied with a wink, but our flirting was put on hold when Brenton and Jess ran out of the house, sheltering from the rain as they darted towards Kane's car.

"Oh, hey guys," said Brenton, as surprised to see us as we were to see them. "Isn't it a little stormy for a surf?"

"Yep, but you know me," said Frankie with a shrug, as I leaned her surfboard against the wall.

"True," he agreed, thinking nothing more of it. He unlocked the Rover so Jess could jump in. "We're doing a wine tour with Sean and Isla if you want to join?"

"I'm about to grab a shower," said Frankie with a shrug, "but thanks."

"Cool," said Brenton, turning to me, "Ritchie?"
Frankie looked at me, silently willing me not to accept the offer.

"No thanks mate, I need to grab a shower and some breaky before I start drinking, but I appreciate the invite. I'm surprised Sean's even up for that after his efforts last night."

"I don't think he is. Isla's still trying to get him out of bed."

"That sounds accurate," I joked.

"Have fun guys," Frankie said as Brenton climbed into Kane's Rover. We patiently waited for them to drive away, and the second the four-wheel drive was out of sight, we ran into the rec room like over-eager teenagers. Frankie dragged me inside and locked the door behind us, her hands all over me as soon as the lock clicked.

Frankie threw my jacket off her shoulders and I did my best to peel off her cold, damp wetty. It was proving difficult, so she finished the job for me while I admired her bikini clad body. She caught me perving and smiled, then peeled my sodden T-shirt off me and dropped it on the floor. I wrapped my arms around her, and pulled her close, trying to warm her with my body heat.

"You're freezing Frankie," I said with concern as I felt her cold flesh press against mine. "You really should get in the shower to warm up."

"What about a sauna?"

"Well, I guess that would work too," I laughed.

"Follow me," she said, wiggling her eyebrows as she pulled me around the corner to a full-sized sauna room.

"Holy shit," I said, stunned. "Kane thinks of everything."

"I don't think he was envisaging this particular scenario when he had it installed," she laughed, flicking on the sauna and pulling me inside. "It doesn't take long to heat up," she said, pushing me down onto the bench seat, "but I think we can probably help it along."

She straddled my lap and wrapped her arms around my neck as her mouth closed on mine. Any thoughts of getting my face pounded by Thommo quickly disappeared and I lost myself in the moment. I pulled Frankie tight against me and ravaged her hungrily. She untied her bikini top and let it plop onto the bench behind me, while I kissed her neck. When she ran her hands down my chest, she shattered the last of my self-control. That was it. I was done. I couldn't fight it any longer. Rational thought was no longer an option.

I yanked off my shorts while she knelt above me, and the moment they hit the floor, she shifted the crutch of her bikini to the side and lowered herself on top of me. I groaned at the feel of being inside a woman again and Frankie matched my enthusiasm with a moan of her own. Our hands roamed each other, exploring the unfamiliar naked flesh, as she moved rhythmically on top of me. It had been so long since I'd had sex that I'd almost forgotten what it felt like.

The sauna was beginning to heat up and the sweat beaded on our bodies, but neither of us were ready to stop. I grasped her bottom hard and clutched her tight against me, feeling the pressure mounting. I was getting close, but I'd never left a job unfinished before. Frankie was certainly not the woman I intended to break that tradition with so I was determined to hold off until she was done.

"Ritchie," she panted, squeezing her body hard against mine. I could feel her body contracting around me and then she threw her head back with a loud moan. I gripped her tight and moved her hips on top of me to make sure she was completely done before I pulled out. Once I was sure she was finished, I attempted to lever her off me. "What are you doing?" she asked with confusion.

"We don't have protection," I grunted, concentrating on holding my load.

"It's fine, I'm on the pill," she said, pressing her body more firmly against my lap so I couldn't lift her off. "Just do what you have to do."

"I can't."

"Why not?"

"It's not right." I was right on the edge, and she knew it. Frankie squeezed her thighs tight around me. "Ogh," I groaned, doing everything I could to hold off.

"Let go Ritchie," she whispered in my ear, grinding her pelvis hard against mine. "I want you to."

I couldn't hold back with Frankie sliding back and forth on top of me. My body took the lead and I exploded with a loud moan, gripping her bum cheeks tightly.

"Ohhh," I groaned, unable to stop it.

"Good boy," she said, wrapping her arms around my neck so that her breasts pressed tightly against my chest. "Now doesn't that feel better?"

"Uh-huh," I nodded, unable to speak.

- KANE THOMPSON -

As Taj and I piled dry branches, onto our shelter frame, he chatted happily about school and his friends. He was such a great kid and the fact that he'd already given me his blessing to date his mum, only compounded the obvious fact that I needed to tell Soph how I felt about her. The irony being that Sophie seemed to be the only person who didn't already realise I was in love with her.

"… and that's why Daniel thinks Ella likes me," Taj concluded, as he balanced a leafy branch on the roof of the shelter.

"Okay. And do you like her?"

"I dunno," he said with a shrug, "she's really nice, and she's fun, plus she knows how to play basketball, which is cool."

"Yeah, she sounds pretty cool."

"But how do I know if she's a girlfriend or just a friend that's a girl?"

"Do you like her the same way as you like Daniel?"

"I think I like her better than Daniel."

I laughed and patted him on the back.

"Maybe, just hang out with her a bit and see if you have anything to talk about."

"That's a good idea."

"Either way, you'll either make a new friend or end up with a girlfriend."

"Would I have to kiss her?"

"Only if you both wanted to do that. But you could just hold hands too."

"I could do that," he said after thinking about it for a moment. "I guess having a girlfriend wouldn't be so bad."

"It's pretty great if you find the right girl."

"Then why don't you have one?" he asked curiously. "A real one I mean, not just a pretend one."

"Can I tell you a secret?"

"Mummy says I'm not allowed to have secrets with other grownups."

"Hmm… well she is right about that."

"You can tell me anyway."

"I don't think we should break your mum's rules."

"Okay, well what if it wasn't a secret?"

"I suppose it's not really," I said with a sigh, as I thought back to my conversations with the rest of my friends and family who all seemed to know that I was in love with this kids mum. I sat down on a nearby log and Taj watched me with interest. "The truth is kiddo… I've never really found a girl who matches up to your mum."

"Does that mean you want to make her your girlfriend?" he asked eagerly, eyes bright and full of excitement.

"Well… I've been thinking about what you said," I told him honestly, "and I'd like to talk to mummy to see how she'd feel about it. As long as you're still on board with that plan?"

"Yeah!" He said, pumping his fist in the air. "That's awesome uncle Kane."

"Don't get too excited. Nothing is decided yet. You mum might not want to be my girlfriend."

"Of course she will! You're the best Uncle Kane."

"Aww, thanks buddy."

"Plus, you're already pretend girlfriend and boyfriend, so you've had good practice."

I laughed at his adorable innocence. If only we'd had some practice at the fun parts too.

- SOPHIE THOMPSON -

When I eventually woke up, it was close to midday and the house was silent. I shuffled out to the living room, letting out a huge yawn as I straightened up my messy hair. I'd assumed everyone was out so I jumped when I heard a weird noise as I passed the games room door. The balls were clinking around the pool table, but it didn't sound like an actual game.

"Hey," I said, swinging the door open. "Oh my god," I blurted, as I was confronted with the sight of Ritchie's bare bottom, and Frankie's legs wrapped around it. "Shit! Sorry!" I apologised frantically, backing quickly out of the room.

"Fuck," I heard them whispering and scrambling for their clothes.

"As you were," I called awkwardly, "I thought you were playing pool."

I ran into the kitchen, buried my face in my hands and burst into shocked hysterics. That was an image I'd never be able to get out of my head. I mean, Ritchie did have a spectacular arse but I didn't need to witness it in quite that fashion! Frankie and I had shared many personal moments over the years, but that was the first time I'd seen her naked with her legs in the air.

I flicked on the coffee machine, but I couldn't see the buttons clearly because I was laughing so hard there were tears were pouring out of my eyes. My lungs hurt and I had to gasp for breath, while I attempted to calm myself down.

It wasn't that it was funny as such… it was just… oh who was I kidding? It was, bloody hilarious.

"That wasn't what it looked like," declared Spanks as she burst into the kitchen, barely decent.

"There wasn't much room for misinterpretation there," I said, unable to old back another round of laughter as the visuals of Ritchie's bare arse burned fresh in my brain.

"You're not going to tell Kane, are you?"

"No way!" I said adamantly, "I don't want anything to do with this. In fact, I don't even know what you're talking about."

"Soph, be serious."

"I'm trying."

"No, you're not."

"Look Spanks, you're consenting adults, what you do in your own time is entirely up to you. I will have a hard time scraping that image from my retinas, but besides that… it's none of my business."

"Thank you." She let out a sigh of relief and then shot me a mischievous grin. "He's huge," she divulged, unable to help herself.

"Oh my god, please don't talk to me about it while you're halfway through the job."

"But seriously Soph-"

"Nope. Don't want to hear it. Just go finish the poor guy off - but take it to your bedroom. And hurry up, Kane and Taj will be back soon."

"Yes ma'am," she saluted, strutting out of the kitchen. "I'll happily take on for the team."

"Oh my god," I repeated, literally face palming at my uninhibited bestie. It was hard to imagine being that open about sex. I'd completely disconnected from that side of myself over the past ten years and seeing their little display on the pool table just reminded me how long it had been since I'd had a man's hands on me.

The thought of being that intimate with someone again was nerve-wracking. How would I ever feel comfortable enough with anyone to get naked with them?

A memory of Kane's bare chest during our coke-fuelled night after the charity ball flickered ever-so-briefly through my mind. I shook my head and disregarded the uninvited thought.

The bigger concern, if I did get to that stage with someone, would be whether I'd even remember what to do. And bigger still was the possibility that I never knew how to do it properly to begin with. Brenton was the only man I'd ever slept with, so I had no idea if I'd even been doing it right in the first place. My cheating ex clearly hadn't been satisfied with me, so perhaps I was crap in bed. What if I'd been the problem in our relationship and I just never realised it?

- RITCHIE CARLTON -

"That was so close Frankie," I said laying flopping down onto her bed after we'd fled the scene of the crime. "What if that had been Kane?"

"Then we would have dealt with it," she said straddling me with a mischievous grin. "Now shut up and finish the job," she teased, wrapping her arms around my shoulders.

"I kinda feel like the mood is gone."

"Oh come on. The adrenaline rush will make it even better."

"I'm too busy thinking about your brother."

"Well that's definitely a mood killer," she said, sliding off me.

"How exactly would I have explained that?" I asked, rubbing my temples. "Sorry boss, I fell and landed on your sisters vagina?"

Frankie laughed loudly. "You stress too much."

"Maybe. But I really like this job Frankie and I don't want to fuck it up by putting my dick in places it doesn't belong."

"Is that how you see it?" she asked with an indistinguishable expression.

"Well... Yeah. I don't see how else it could be interpreted."

"That's where I disagree," she said, pushing me backwards. I let her win, and let myself flop down against the mattress. "Because I think you're dick very much belongs here."

"Frankie," I said, holding her back as she tried to straddle me again. "Frankie, stop."

"Why?"

"Your brother will be home any minute and I'd rather not ruin his birthday by getting him thrown in jail for murdering me."

"You're cute when you're petrified."

"Stop," I told her firmly. "I'm gonna get showered and dressed, then we'll go out there for lunch like nothing has happened."

"Are you forgetting that Soph knows?"

"I don't think I'll ever forget that moment for the rest of my life."

"Well your plan kind of hinges on her being able to keep her shit together."

"What's likelihood of that?"

"Slim to none."

"Bloody hell," I swore, rubbing my face.

"The cat will be out of the bag whichever way you look at it, so we might as well enjoy it while we can." She grinned and leaned down to kiss me. This time, I didn't fight it. Kane was probably going to kill me anyway; I might as well die a happy man.

- KANE THOMPSON -

With the rain growing heavier, it was time to head back to the house. I shoved our empty protein bar wrappers into one of my million jacket pockets and stood up with a groan, dusting the leaves and dirt off my butt.

"Well, I think it's time to head back to the house, Tajinator."

"But we haven't finished the shelter."

"We can come and finish it off tomorrow."

"Promise?"

"Absolutely."

"Okay then," he agreed with a shrug.

"Plus, we should really check on your mum."

"Yeah, I hope she's feeling better."

We set off on the path through the bushland towards the house, climbing over rocks and ducking under branches. It had been really fun just hanging with the kiddo. It was weird to realise that after Sean, Taj was probably my next best mate. I really was a loser.

"I think I've decided that I want Ella to be my girlfriend," Taj declared as we wandered.

"That's great but remember, she needs to agree to that as well mate. You can't just decide without asking her."

"Yeah, I know."

"Good," I said with a proud nod. "As men, we've got a responsibility to the women in our lives to make sure they're okay. We have to look out for them and take care of them."

"Like you do for Mummy and Aunty Spanks."

"That's right."

"How come Daddy doesn't?"

"Doesn't what?"

"Look after any of them."

"Well… umm… I don't really have an answer for that mate. We all have to make the choice as to what sort of man we want to become. I think footy was Daddy's choice."

"I'm really glad Mummy has you Uncle Kane," he said, reaching up to hold my hand. "I hope she says yes to being your real girlfriend." My heart melted and I nearly had to wipe a tear from my eye.

"Me too Buddy. Me too."

- SOPHIE THOMPSON -

I'd showered, changed and had lunch together by the time Taj and Kane returned to the house, yet there was still no sign of the happy new couple. I silently hoped that they were smart enough to lie low for a little while. I wasn't sure I'd be able to keep a straight face in their presence.

"Smells good in here," said Kane, helping Taj out of his wet jacket.

"Lunch is ready whenever you are," I said, unable to hide a smile at how sweet the pair of them looked. They were wet and famished but surprisingly chipper for having spent four hours out in the rain. "How was it?" I asked Taj, as I served up their ham and cheese toasties.

"It was great!" he said excitedly, sharing a mischievous look with Kane. "We collected gumnuts and made a shelter and ate protein bars."

"Sounds like you had quite the adventure."

"We sure did," Kane said, shooting Taj a conspiratorial wink.

"What's going on with you two?" I asked suspiciously.

"Just man stuff," answered Taj with a grin, sounding like an eighty-year-old man. I looked to Kane for an answer, but he just shrugged with a proud smile.

"Like he said, 'just man stuff'."

I studied them both for a minute, but they looked so pleased with themselves that I didn't want to burst the bubble with an interrogation.

Even without the matching jackets, they looked like two peas in a pod. It was as if I was looking at current Kane and child Kane simultaneously. Why had I never noticed how alike they were? In fact, Taj was looked more similar to Kane than he did Brenton. It was weird.

"Did Frankie and Ritchie go with the others?" Kane asked, looking around the empty house.

I choked on my sandwich. "Umm… no," I said clearing the food from my throat, "they're around somewhere." I threw a pointed glance around the otherwise empty living area. "They were playing pool earlier so they might still be in the games room."

"I'm surprised they haven't come out for lunch. Frankie never misses a feed."

"To be fair, I didn't let them know I was making it," I joked, hoping that would make him drop the subject. Kane was the one person in the world it was impossible for me to lie to. He could always see through my bullshit, and I didn't want to be the one to ruin his birthday with a family drama.

We finished our lunch in relative silence, the two boys occasionally exchanging knowing glances.

"I'm done," declared Taj, pushing out his chair with a scrape of the legs. "Can I go to my room and have some Taj time?" Taj time was what we said when he needed some down-time. It was his time to unwind and recharge, but I was surprised to hear him ask for that over screen time when he'd been out in nature all morning.

"Sure buddy," I agreed casually, trying not to sound too pleased in case he changed his mind.

"I want to save my screen time for later. Uncle Kane and I are going to watch as many Harry Potter movies as we can."

"Ah, okay," I said casting a sideways glance at Kane. "Well, that makes more sense."

"Okay bye, I love you," Taj said, giving me a kiss. "I'm glad you're feeling better."

"Thanks baby," I said, touched at his behaviour. I watched him happily trot off to his room and then turned to Kane. "What did you say to him out there?" I asked, stunned at the change in my child. "He's like a different kid. You didn't swap him for another one while you were out, did you?"

Kane laughed loudly and stood up to take the dirty dishes to the sink.

"We just had a little man-to-man chat," he said cryptically. "I'd tell you, but then I'd be breaking the bro-code."

"Well, whatever you said… thank you."

Kane looked over at his guitar leaning against the fireplace. "Sing-along time?" He asked with a grin.

"Yeah, I could do a sing-along," I agreed with a content smile. He was so safe and familiar that I almost felt more like myself when he was around. "Besides there's not much else to do in this weather."

"I could think of a few things," he joked as we re-located to lounge area.

"Trust you to think of that," I teased and snuggled down onto the couch. "I don't think I'd even remember how to anymore," I added, leaning back into the soft cushion.

"I'm pretty sure you'd figure it out quick enough," he said awkwardly. "Wonderwall?" He asked, abruptly changing the subject as he propped the guitar on his knee.

"Sure," I agreed.

Kane began to strum and we sang along together, lost in the tune and our own thoughts. I peered over at him and my stomach did the weird flippy thing again as I watched him play his guitar. His sparkly blue eyes, his square jaw, his broad shoulders, and his sexy five o'clock shadow... Kane was an incredibly handsome man, and a proper man at that. Not a boy, like Brenton.

I pulled myself up on that strange thought just as Kane peered up from his guitar. I felt embarrassed that he'd caught me staring at him, but he just smiled and held his gaze on me. The look on his face made my stomach flutter again, so I blushed and looked away.

When the song finished, silence fell and there was nothing but the peaceful sound of the rain falling outside. I had no idea where Frankie and Ritchie had gotten to, but I hoped like hell that they wouldn't reappear together.

Kane cleared his throat and rested the guitar against the coffee table. His eyes held mine intensely, causing my smile to falter as my chest tightened with anticipation. Something was brewing in his head. I could see it on his face. Something had changed since his outing with Taj, and I couldn't get a clear read on what was happening behind those blue eyes of his.

"Soph," he said seriously.

"Yeah?" I asked quietly, my stomach in knots.

"We need to talk."

"We do?"

"Yeah," he said, wriggling closer. There was a weird electrical current running between the two of us that had never been there before. "Look, I know this might not be the best timing, but there's something I need to tell you." Kane stared straight into my eyes and goosebumps erupted all over my skin. I wasn't cold, so it must have been him that was causing them. "I know you're having a hard time with this Brenton stuff," he said, clearing his throat for a second time, "but the thing is Soph..." he paused and cleared his throat again. He only ever did that when he was nervous. "The thing is..." he tried again. I waited silently, holding my breath with anticipation of him telling me what 'the thing' was.

"What's the thing Kane?" I asked, when he still failed to continue

He took a deep breath and then spoke. "The thing is Soph... I'm in love with you."

My heart stopped beating for a moment. Had I heard him right? Did he just say he was in love with me? Perth's most eligible bachelor, the man who could have any woman he wanted, was in love with me? Kane Thompson, my best friend's big brother; my protector; my safe man; the goofy guy who used to throw me in the pool fully clothed, and fart on my face when we went to the drive-ins… the man who had always been just out of reach, hiding in the background of my life, was in love with me?

I looked up at him in shock, wondering if he was pranking me.

"I always have been," he said, answering my unasked question. I stared into his sparkly eyes, with no idea how to respond. For some reason, the information wasn't sinking in. I had so many emotions bubbling around inside me that I couldn't make sense of them. I was definitely attracted to him, that much was true, and I'd always loved him as a brother, but...was I in love with him? "I'm sorry, I shouldn't have said anything," he retracted quickly.

"No, I... umm... it's... I..." I stuttered, unable to form a complete sentence. I'd never had the slightest inkling that Kane was interested in me.

"I should go," he said, rising to his feet.

"No, Kane... stop," I said, finally getting some coherent words out. "Please, sit," I pleaded, reaching for his hand. He allowed my fingers to entwine his, but he didn't move. "Please?" I asked again, tugging on his hand to encourage him to sit back down.

He eventually softened, and sank down onto the couch next to me, sitting so close that our legs were touching. I kept hold of his hand, too scared to let it go in case he made a run for it.

Kane searched my eyes for a moment looking for a sign that I felt the same way. Before he could say anything more I leaned into him so close that my lips were almost brushing his. His hand slipped out of my grasp and ran softly up my arm, landing gently at the nape of my neck, causing the butterflies in my stomach to take flight.

My breath caught in my throat as I waited for the moment to unfold. It felt like everything was moving in slow motion. Kane cupped my face in his hands and, after an excruciating pause, he kissed me gently. His lips were so warm that I melted into him. It was weird but amazing. Strange yet familiar at the same time.

I wrapped my arms around his neck and let myself get lost in the moment. We were locked together, our tongues exploring each other's mouths, all thoughts of the outside world gone, when Brenton and Jess walked through the door in a gust of wind. Kane and I flew apart guiltily.

"Oops," said Brenton, "didn't realise you guys were busy."

"Umm..." Kane spluttered awkwardly.

"Good to see you're keeping it in the family Sophster," said Brenton obnoxiously. "Where's our son while you're sucking face with my cousin?"

"Are you serious?" Kane snarled at Brenton. I'd never seen him so angry before.

"I'm sorry to be concerned about the welfare of my son," Brenton replied snarkily.

"Our son is perfectly fine," I interjected. "He's in his room having some Taj time because he's been out adventuring with Kane all morning."

"So, you're trying to cut in on my kid as well as my wife?" Brenton challenged Kane. Jess looked heart broken.

"Ex-wife," I clarified sternly, feeling sorry for the poor girl, "and maybe you should be asking yourself why your cousin is busy looking after your son while you're out drinking with the woman you cheated on his mother with." I snapped, once again feeling awful for Jess. I looked at her apologetically. "Sorry Jess, none of this is your fault."

"You're right Soph," retorted Brenton, "maybe I should be asking myself why a grown man spends so much time with a ten-year-old boy."

"Don't be disgusting," I shot back, shocked that he'd even suggest such a thing.

"Do you honestly think I would ever do anything to hurt that kid?" Kane asked, clearly devastated.

"Come on man," said Brenton with an arrogant shrug, "you've gotta realise it's weird."

Kane fell silent. He looked like he'd been stabbed in the chest. I could almost see his heart shattering right in front of my eyes.

"Enough Brenton," I said firmly, worried about Kane, who seemed to have shrunk several feet in an instant.

"Of course, you'd take his side," Brenton snorted.

"There are no sides here," I said with exhaustion. "And to be honest, I'm not even sure what you're getting upset about. You're the one who cheated on me," I gestured to Jess, "with her apparently. Did you really think you could just bring her here and it would all be fine and dandy? Sorry Jess." I added before turning my attention back to Brenton. "You've put everyone in a horrible position Brenton. You created this awful situation. This whole thing is on you."

"Whatever," he muttered, knowing he didn't have a leg to stand on. "Come on Jess, let's go play some pool.

"Good idea," I agreed, once again offering an apologetic look to Jess as she walked past.

"Oh," said Brenton, turning back to Kane, "just a warning mate, she's not super experienced so go easy on her huh?"
Kane's whole body turned rigid, and I could see his fist clenching.

"Let it go Kane, he's not worth it." I said calmly.

"No, but Soph is," Brenton taunted, knowing full well that he was poking the bear. "She didn't know anything before I broke her in, but I think I've trained her fairly well for you."

That was all it took to make Kane snap. With the speed of a cheetah, he jumped over the back of the couch, and lunged at Brenton with the full force of his weight. I could see it happening, but Kane had moved too fast for me stop him.

"No Kane!" I shouted as he swung hard at my drunk ex-husband. In the blink of an eye, Brenton was flat on the concrete floor, with blood dripping from his nose. Like a fish out of water, he gasped for air, as the wind was completely knocked out of him.

Kane jumped backwards as if he was shocked by his own strength, while Brenton scowled up at him, the alcohol fuelling his rage. He wasn't down for long. Brenton roared and climbed unsteadily to his feet, taking a wild swing at Kane.

"Brenton, stop it!" I shouted, feeling totally helpless as he dove at Kane, flailing his arms wildly. Both men fell to the floor trying to rip each other to shreds but all I could do was watch. Jess stood frozen in shock, like a deer caught in headlights.

Footsteps pounded against the floor as Ritchie ran out of the hallway, bare-chested. "Oi! Break it up you two!" he growled, pulling Brenton off Kane.

I darted over to check on Kane while Ritchie restrained my psychotic ex-husband. "Are you okay?" I asked Kane, inspecting his bruised face.

"I'm fine," he muttered, wiping a tiny drop of blood off his lip as he glared at Brenton.

Ritchie turned to Kane. "What's going on mate?" he asked, as Brenton struggled against him like a wounded bull.

"Oh my god!" Frankie exclaimed, emerging from the direction of the bedrooms, wearing nothing but Ritchie's jumper. Kane's eyes flicked between Ritchie, who was naked from the waist up, and Spanks, who was obviously naked from the waist down.

"I could ask you the same thing mate," he snapped angrily.

"Look Thommo..." Ritchie began, raising one hand in surrender as Frankie stepped in front of him.

"Knock it off Kane," she said sternly. "There's no problem here."

"I think we've had enough agro for one day huh?" I interjected, planting my hand firmly on Kane's chest. He continued to glower at Ritchie, like a Lion defending his pride. "Kane," I warned, "this doesn't involve Ritchie. Let it go." He looked down at me and his gaze softened. "You knew?"

"Mummy?" a little voice asked from the hallway, "what's going on?"

My heart skipped a beat as I saw my son staring wide-eyed at the scene before him. I stepped away from Kane and rushed over to embrace Taj. With all the drama I'd almost forgotten he'd been close enough to hear it all.

"Nothing baby," I said, brushing his floppy fringe away from his face. "Daddy and Uncle Kane were just play fighting and got a bit carried away, that's all."

Taj peered over my shoulder at Kane with his bloodied nose, and then to Brenton, who was still trapped in Ritchie's tight grasp. He looked up at me with confusion. "Why is Ritchie hugging Daddy?"

We all laughed at his innocent interpretation of the situation, and Ritchie released Brenton.

"He was just making sure Daddy was okay."

Taj looked to Brenton for confirmation. Brenton nodded and knelt on the floor next to me.

"That's right buddy," he said, patting his arms reassuringly. "We got a bit rough, and I fell over, but I'm fine now."

Taj nodded and then peered over at Kane. "Are you okay Uncle Kane?" he asked, noticing the blood dripping from Kane's lip and eyebrow.

"I'm fine mate," he said with a nod, "but I made a stupid decision. This was my fault, and I'm sorry for setting a bad example."

Taj walked over and patted Kane's bloodied hand. "It's okay Uncle Kane, we all make mistakes sometimes, but you're still a good man."

Tears sprung into Kane's eyes, and he looked like he wanted to give

Taj a hug, but didn't. Taj must have picked up on the vibe because he reached up and wrapped his arms around Kane's waist. Kane looked awkward, like he didn't know what to do, until Taj peered up and beckoned him down. Kane leant down to his level and Taj whispered something in his ear. Kane laughed and nodded.

"Yep," he said, casting a glance in my direction.

"Yes!" cheered Taj in a very Leighton Hewitt sort of way. Brenton looked pissed at the interaction and intervened.

"Hey Taj, you want to go watch the next Harry Potter? Jess and I brought back some chocolate coated pretzels from the Chocolate Factory." He smiled smugly at Kane, who straightened up and stepped back from Taj with his head slightly bowed as if relinquishing his dominance. I'd never seen Kane submissive. He was usually the Alpha in any given situation. Brenton's dumb accusation must have hit him hard.

"I was going to watch Chamber of Secrets with Uncle Kane," Taj told his father factually.

"Okay, well maybe we could watch something else?"

"I guess," agreed Taj, weighing up his screen time options.

"You can watch it without me buddy," offered Kane, "then we can all watch Prisoner of Azkaban together tomorrow."

"Okay," Taj agreed reluctantly, looking a little betrayed.

"Come on kiddo," Brenton said lifting up Taj and playfully throwing him over his shoulder, "let's go find out what's so secret about Harry's chamber. You coming Jess?" he called over his shoulder.

"Yeah, I'll be there in a sec," she said unconvincingly. I felt bad for her, but my focus was on Kane and his injuries.

"How about we get you patched up?" I suggested. He looked down at his hand as if only just noticing the damage.

"Yeah, okay," he nodded like a lost puppy dog. It was clear that Brenton's words had broken something in Kane's soul. My ex-husband had a way of doing that to people. He knew exactly which buttons to push for maximum impact. It made me wonder how I ever married him in the first place.

- RITCHIE CARLTON -

Sophie led Kane away to tend to his wounds while I stood, shirtless, in the loungeroom, looking between Frankie and Jess, who had both been stunned into silence.

"Well, that was dramatic," I said, not sure what else there was to say after an event like that. "Are you okay Jess?" The girl looked shell-shocked.

"I think…" she said nervously, "I think I need to go home. I shouldn't be here."

My sympathy went out to the poor girl. She was caught in the middle of an epic shitstorm and there was nothing she could do about it.

"Why don't you sleep on it?" I suggested. "It will probably all have blown over by tomorrow.

"No, I think I just need to get out of here. This whole weekend has been a disaster."

"How about you sit and have a cuppa with us first?"

She sighed, and looked around, as if searching for a viable exit.

"Okay," she agreed with a defeated nod.

"I'm gonna put some clothes on," said Frankie, disappearing to the bedroom to make herself decent.

I guided Jess to the bench and sat her down on a bar stool, before putting the kettle on. I searched through a million cupboards trying to find mugs. Frankie returned, fully clothed, and grabbed some cups from a drawer under the bench, right below where the kettle was sitting.

"Thanks," I said with a sheepish shrug. "I'm still not used to big kitchens after living in London so long."

"What was London like?" asked Jess with interest, as Frankie handed me my crumpled T.shirt with a cheeky wink.

"Very different from Perth," I said, pulling on my shirt as Frankie took over the tea making.

"How long were you there for?"

"Ten years," I said, pulling up the stool next to her.

"Wow," she said, as if a whole new world had opened up to her. "What made you move over there?"

"Honestly… I just wanted to get out of Perth," I joked.

"I get that," Jess laughed. It wasn't a proper laugh, but at least there was a smile on her face.

"Nah, I love Perth, but I was young and driven." I said, as Frankie slid me a hot cup of tea, listening to me talk with intense interest. "I was working for this little marketing agency in Subi. Going to the same bars every week, hanging out with the same crew and I guess I felt like there was more to life. I had a bit of cash saved up, so I took a year off and went back-packing through Europe and when I got to London, I met a chick who was the Account Director for Universal Pictures. It turned out that they were looking for a Project Manager, and I somehow got the job. That was my first experience managing a big client and it spurred me on. I stayed there for a while, and eventually ended up at Artemis Advertising."

"And that's where you were when you left?"

"Yeah."

"What clients were you working on there?"

"Well actually, I was running the Delfontaine Cosmetics account before I left."

"Oh my god! I love Delfontaine. Did you ever get to meet Sandrine Delfontaine?"

I choked on my tea, unsure how best to answer that question. I wiped my face and put my mug down on the bench. "Uh… yeah. I worked quite closely with her actually."

"Wow, that sounds amazing."

"It was pretty cool," I agreed, noticing Frankie's amused look of curiosity. I got the feeling we'd be circling back to that subject later.

"So why did you come back?"

I fell quiet for a moment, and picked up my mug again, sipping slowly to buy myself some time. "My girlfriend died," I muttered quietly into my cup.

"Oh," the two girls said, shocked. They both fell silent, and I could feel them staring at me with pity, so I avoided eye contact with either of them by studying a sparkly fleck in the granite bench top.

"I couldn't stay there when everything reminded me of her," I explained unnecessarily. Frankie rested her hand on top of mine. I peered up at her nervously, expecting to see pity in her eyes, but instead, they were full of comprehension and compassion. It was clear that she'd just made sense of my reaction that morning.

"I'm sorry," she said breathlessly, looking as if she was fighting back tears.

"It's okay. You weren't to know." I was so wrapped up in Frankie that I'd momentarily forgotten Jess was still sitting next to me until she spoke.

"That's so sad," Jess said, causing me to jump. "What happened?"

"She killed herself."

Both girls' jaws had dropped, until my raucous brother burst in the door, breaking the pityful silence. I was oddly pleased to see him in that moment.

"Honey, we're home," announced Sean loudly, as he and Isla came into the kitchen, ladened with packages.

"Where is everyone?" Isla asked, carefully placing a huge cake box down on the table.

"Don't ask," warned Frankie.

"Oh dear," said Sean. "How bad was it?"

"Black eye and split lip bad," I told him. They both looked shocked.

"Soph hit Brenton?! "Sean asked dumbfounded.

"No. What?!" I asked laughing with dismay at my idiot brother.

"Kane punched Brenton, then Brenton went psycho on Kane," Jess clarified. "But to be honest, Brenton deserved to be punched."

"Why? What happened?"

Jess shrank back awkwardly in her seat as we all looked to her, waiting eagerly to hear the full story.

"It's not really my place to say. I shouldn't even be here. It would be better to ask Sophie."

Isla looked around again. "Where is Soph anyway?"

"Patching Kane up," I said, gesturing over my shoulder. Isla and Sean exchanged a dubious glance. It didn't take a genius to guess what they were thinking. Frankie shot me a similar look and comprehension seemed to wash over everyone. Isla turned back to Jess.

"They were fighting over Soph?" she asked, stunned. Jess nodded. "So, I take it Kane and Soph..." she said, letting her sentence trail off. Jess nodded again. "And then Brenton got jealous."

"Yep."

"I'm really sorry you had to see that," Isla apologised to Jess. "Are you okay?"

"Not really," she admitted. "I'm pretty keen to get home to be honest. It's not appropriate for me to be here, but I came with Brenton on his bike, so I'm not even sure how I'd get home."

"Do you want us to drop you somewhere?" Sean offered.

"Is there a train station or anything?" Jess asked.

"Don't be silly," said Isla kindly, "you can't catch a train back at this time." She rested her hand on Sean's shoulder, "why don't we take her back to Perth?"

"Today?"

"Yeah."

"But what about Kane's birthday?"

"It sounds like the party is pretty much over anyway," said Isla.

"What if I take her back?" I suggested. "I'm an extra here too, and I'm not exactly in Kane's good books right now."

"Why?" Asked Sean with concern. "What did you do?"

"Me," joked Frankie. I cringed and shook my head in resignation for whatever was about to come.

"Huh?" asked Sean, like an idiot.

"He did me," she added for unnecessary clarification. Isla and Sean stared, open-mouthed, at the two of us, finally noticing our disheveled state.

"Holy shit," said Seany. "We go out for a few hours, and it turns into Lord of the Flies here."

"Not really. No one killed anyone," said Frankie unhelpfully.

"Right," said Isla in full problem-solving mode, "Ritchie and Jess, go back to Perth and then we just need to figure out what to do with Brenton."

"He's pretty drunk after the wine tour, so there's no way he could ride anywhere, let alone all the way back to Perth," said Jess.

"Okay, so we just have to keep him and Kane apart then," Sean said, cracking one of the bottles they'd just brought back from their tour.

"What are you doing?" Isla asked, eyeing him and the opened bottle with disbelief.

"What? It feels like a drinking moment," he answered with a shrug. Isla sighed and rolled her eyes.

"Go pack your stuff Jess," I said, ignoring my idiot brother. "I'll take you home."

- KANE THOMPSON -

"That's your hand done," Soph said, chucking the soiled alcohol wipes into the bin. "Now for that eye," she turned back and examined my bloodied eyebrow for a moment. "It might actually need stitches, you know?"

"I doubt it," I grunted, "he didn't hit me that hard."

"A punch doesn't have to be hard if you swing at the right angle," she said, as if she was some sort of boxing guru. I stared at her with amusement accidentally raising my split brow.

"Ouch," I winced at the involuntary movement.

"Serves you right."

"What? I can't tease you for pretending to be a punching expert."

"Kane, I've been doing self-defence classes since I was eighteen."

"Really?"

"How could you not know that?! You were the one who put me onto it after that guy attacked me remember?"

"You've been going to Morrie's all these years?"

"Yeah. I felt like it was important to keep it up."

"It is. That's great. I can't believe you actually stuck with it that long."

"Believe it or not, I actually listen to you Jughead. I'm not Frankie."

"And thank god for that," I joked, thinking about how wrong my feelings for her would have been otherwise.

"I'm not an expert, but I do know a thing or two and I'm telling you, that looks like it might need stitches."

"I'm not going to the hospital for a split eyebrow. I've got liquid stitches in the First Aid kit. Just put some of that on it."

"Why yes my lord, is there anything else you require?" she retorted, in her best English accent, .

"I didn't mean it like that."

"Well, that's how it came out," she said in her normal voice, unimpressed. She tipped Betadine onto a cotton ball to disinfect the wound and I winced again as she dabbed hard with the brown soaked cotton ball to emphasise her point.

"I'm sorry," I said, getting the message loud and clear. "I guess I'm used to bossing people around. I'll try not to do it again."

"Thank you." She finished her dabbing and threw away the cotton ball, digging back through the First Aid kit to find the liquid stitches.

Pulling out the little bottle, she tried to get a good view of my eyebrow, but the sideways angle was making it difficult, so she climbed onto the bed and straddled my lap. My whole body reacted favourably to the intimate position, so I did my best to concentrate on anything else.

I peered out the window at the growing storm and then my eyes unintentionally wandered back to Soph. She bit her lip in concentration as she started her little surgery on my eye and her face was so close to mine that I had to drop my gaze and focus on her shoulder mole instead. Despite the fact that my eye stung like a motherfucker, my excitement at having Sophie on top of me, far outweighed the pain. I'd spent decades imaging what it would be like to have that woman on my lap, and there she was. My eyes drifted from her mole to her face.

"I'm glad you didn't get that removed," I said, running my finger over her elegant shoulder.

"Why?"

"Because I think it's hot," I admitted honestly, admiring her gorgeous face as she dutifully tended my wound. Soph paused her procedure as she caught the expression on my face and, probably, felt the movement in my jeans. I swallowed the lump in my throat as her green eyes locked on mine.

"Are you okay?" she asked, as she studied my face intently. "You know Brenton was just being a prick, right? He didn't actually mean any of those things he said."

I felt a blush creep over my face. "But he wasn't entirely wrong, was he? I'm a forty-year-old man with no wife and no family, who's second best friend is a ten-year-old kid. I'm a loser."
Soph laughed in shock.

"Kane, you're many things, but a loser is not one of them," she told me earnestly. "You don't really believe Brenton's bullshit, do you?"

"It's hard not to when he's just voicing what I already think."

Soph rested her arm over my shoulder, still holding the little bottle of liquid stitches. "Listen to me Jughead," she said, unintentionally readjusting her hips in a way that instantly took my mind off our conversation. "That voice in your head isn't real, it's your dad, and we both know he loves you but he's always put you down, so you can't listen to it. You're one of the most-"

"You're beautiful," I interrupted with croaky voice. Soph fell silent and her words faded off as she stared into my eyes. I swallowed back the growing lump in my throat, but the growing lump in my pants, however, was a little harder to hide. With Soph in that thin summer dress, there was no way she wouldn't have felt it and, by that point, she seemed to have forgotten what she'd been saying.

"You're all done," she muttered eventually, still holding my gaze.

"I'm sorry I was out of control tonight. I hope I didn't scare you."

"You could never scare me Kane. I've seen you in every possible state remember?"

"Not every possible state," I said, running my hands up her legs. I heard the breath catch in her throat and she swallowed hard. "Are you okay?" I asked with concern, giving her thighs a reassuring squeeze.

"What if I'm no good at this?" she asked in a whisper.

"Then I'll teach you," I whispered back, unsure why we were even whispering. Soph dropped the bottle of liquid stitches and wrapped her arms around my neck, kissing me hard. We kissed and groped and squeezed each other tight, getting more desperate in our need as we moved together. "You're doing pretty well so far," I joked breathlessly as I flopped backwards onto the bed with Sophie still on top of me. My need for her was so great I thought I might explode.

Our bodies were pressed together and her leg was wedged between my thighs, rubbing against my already excited cock. I ran my hands over her breasts and teased her nipples through the soft fabric of her dress.

Soph let out a little whimper of pleasure and pressed her hips firmly against mine. Without breaking our kiss, I let my fingers roam down her body and underneath her dress to fulfill her unspoken need. I slid my finger inside her undies, and she moaned with relief, kneeling to unbutton my jeans while I continued my enticing exploration.

She wriggled away from me as she tried to pull my jeans down, but I pinned her in place with my spare hand, and gripped her hip firmly so she couldn't move. Soph's eyes moved from my jeans to my face.

"Slow it down," I told her with a smile. "Just take a breath and enjoy this. There's no rush."

She nodded nervously, but her body visibly relaxed, and she let go of my waistband. When I continued, she closed her eyes and let her head tilt backwards. I wanted to make sure she was ready for me, so I took my time and gave her the full royal treatment.

Once I felt like she was good to go, I finally let her strip me of my pants. Her eyes widened as my cock jumped out at her. I wasn't sure whether it was fear or excitement on her face.

"We don't have to do this," I told her, worried that she might actually want to stop.

"I'm good," she said breathlessly. "Just nervous."

"Because we can stop if you want to."

"No, I definitely don't want to stop."

"What if I take the drivers seat?" I offered, silently pleased that

I wouldn't have to reign myself back in. "Will that make you less nervous?"

She nodded with a relieved smile, and I needed no further encouragement. I immediately rolled us over so that she was lying on the bed underneath me. Her eyes flickered with desire as I took control. I kicked off my jeans from where they hung lifelessly around my ankles, then ran my hands up her thighs, sliding up the hem of her dress as I went. Soph arched her hips in response to my touch and I pulled her dress right up and over her head. I didn't want to wait any longer.

I hooked my fingers around the sides of her G-string and pulled it off in one seamless move, pausing to admire her naked body. I briefly tested the waters with my fingers again, but she was raring to go. I leant over to kiss her, then slid into her slowly and carefully, enjoying every second of it. A loud moan escaped her throat, and her hand flew to her mouth to silence herself.

"Oops," she said with embarrassment.

"It's okay," I chuckled, "Make as much noise as you want. I didn't skimp on the soundproofing in this room."

"But Taj is out there."

"Okay, if it makes you feel better..." I trailed off, leaning down to plant my mouth over hers, kissing her hard as I moved on top of her.

Her muffled moans grew quickly, and she wrapped her thighs tight around my waist, moving in time with me. She certainly hadn't had any cause for concern in the sex department, because she'd already taken the top spot on my 'best lays' list. Brenton was a fucking idiot to let this woman go.

Desperation was building in both of us as we moved harder and faster. Her fingers gripped my shoulders tight, and I could feel every movement in her body.

"Oh my god," she breathed, getting close to the edge. I kissed her again and balanced on one arm so I could pinch each of her nipples in turn. She gasped both times and ground her hips harder against mine.

I was getting close, and feeling her warm breath against my cheek, and her moans echoing in my ear, wasn't doing anything to slow that down. I shifted my hip position to get better movement and I felt her body respond.

"Kane," she gasped, digging her nails into my back as her whole body began to shake. She gripped me tightly and threw her head back. I stopped holding back and let myself go with her, groaning loudly with pleasure and relief.

"Oh my god," she laughed, as our orgasms eventually subsided. She squeezed me tight and then looked up with a smile. "We should have done that years ago."

"You were a little pre-occupied with my cousin," I teased, rolling carefully off her.

"I always had a crush on you though."

"I wish you'd made that more obvious."

"Maybe the timing wasn't right back then."

"Maybe not," I agreed leaning on my elbow to get a good look at her. "So, what happens now?" I asked, wondering how to proceed from here. Sex was one thing, but telling everyone would be another.

"I don't know," she said, trailing her fingers up and down my arm. "Can we just lock ourselves in here for the rest of the weekend?"

"I'd love to, but they'd all wonder where we were. Actually, they're probably wondering where we are right now. Isla and Seany should be back by now."

"Oh god, they're going to be unbearable," she groaned, rolling her eyes with a smile.

"They've been on at you too huh?"

"Constantly," she nodded, "Isla was even trying to hook me up with Ritchie to take my mind off you."

"Your mind was on me?" I teased with a raised brow. She blushed and looked down at her hands.

"Maybe a little bit," she admitted with an embarrassed smile. "I might've been enjoying our pretend relationship a little too much."

"Me too," I told her, running the back of my finger down her cheek and under her chin. "Like I said Soph, I'm in love with you." I used my finger to tilt her face upwards so she was forced to look me in the eye. "I've loved you since the day you pulled up on Meharry Road in that in crappy old Commadore."

Her green eyes searched mine, until a loud banging made us both jump out of our skin.

"Kane, sorry to disturb you man," Ritchie called from the other side of the door, "but I was packing my car and I saw Brenton load Taj into your Rover."

"What?!" Soph asked breathlessly, quickly climbing off the bed to find her dress.

"He's pretty smashed," said Ritchie through the closed door, while I scrambled for my jeans and Soph threw her dress over her head. "He shouldn't be driving anywhere, especially not in this weather."

"On my way," I called, awkwardly pulling my jeans on as I followed Soph to the door. She threw it open, nearly clocking Ritchie in the head, and all three of us rushed down the hall.

"What's he thinking?" Sophie asked rhetorically, with a tinge of fear in her voice.

"He's a fucking idiot," I growled, sprinting towards the kitchen to get Brenton's bike keys. Sean and Isla were pottering in the kitchen and they both looked up with surprise as I ran in, shirtless.

"What's going on?" Sean asked, as Ritchie and Soph both ran out the front door.

"Brenton left with Taj," I barked, before following the other two outside. I parkoured over the railing and landed next to the steps in time to see Ritchie and Sophie chasing my Range Rover up the driveway. Soph stopped running and stood barefoot in the storm, watching helplessly as the car drove away.

Isla, Frankie and Sean all burst out of the kitchen door, with expressions of both horror and confusion as they witnessed the dramatic scene unfolding. Ritchie and I followed my Rover to the end of the driveway on instinct, but it was no use.

"Fuck," I swore into the pelting rain, before I came to my senses and turned for the Ducati.

"Here," said Ritchie, stripping off his wet shirt and throwing it at me as I ran past him. "You'll need that."

"Thanks," I grunted, pulling the sopping tee over my head inside out, as I ran towards the bike.

"Kane!" Soph called, the rain dripping from her hair and rolling down her beautiful face. I stopped running and turned back, expecting her to say something more, but she stood silently, her rain-soaked dress clinging to her skin. No further words left her lips, but her pleading eyes said everything I needed to know.
I nodded, holding her gaze.

"I'll find him," I promised.

Soph gave a small nod and then ran towards me. With a few long strides, I closed the gap between us, and she threw her arms around my neck, kissing me hard. Her hands gripped the shoulders of the inside-out, wet t-shirt as she pulled away from me.

"I'm in love with you too," she said in a revelatory tone, as if she'd only just realised it.

"I've waited for a long time to hear you say those words," I croaked, resting my hands on her hips as the rain pelted down on us, "but right now, I've got to stop Brenton." I slid my arm around her waist, pulled her close and kissed her firmly. "We'll finish this later," I said, letting her go as I threw my leg over the leather saddle of Brenton's Ducati. "I'll bring your boy home safe," I said, kicking the bike into life. "I promise."

- SOPHIE THOMPSON -

It was the sexiest kiss I'd ever experienced. Actually it was probably the single sexiest moment of my entire vanilla life.

As Kane let me go, my whole body felt the loss. Now that we'd discovered each other, it was hard to tear myself away from him. We'd wasted so much time not being together that I didn't want to waste any more, but he was right, Taj needed him and I could hardly jump on the back of the bike.

Looking super sexy in Ritchie's rain-soaked, skin-tight tee, Kane started the Ducati. The engine roared as I stood, breathless, and watched him ride away from me. I had to remind myself why he was leaving. My stomach churned at the thought of Taj being in a car with his drunken father in the middle of a freak storm.

I took a deep breath and looked up at the rain as it pelted my body, cleansing me of all my sins. If I hadn't been in Kane's bedroom, Brenton wouldn't have been able to walk out of that house with my son. I didn't regret what had happened with Kane, I just felt like I'd let my child down in doing so. I'd put my own needs first.

I opened my eyes and Ritchie was standing next to me, shirtless. He rested his hand on my shoulder. "Kane will find them."

"Thanks," I patted his hand, then we both turned back towards the house, where Frankie, Isla and Sean were all watching with intrigue. There was no sign of Jess. Had she gone with Brenton?

Ritchie led me back down the long driveway while the curious threesome stood on the front patio, eyeing me with curiosity. I could see a million questions running through Isla's mind, but I wasn't in a state to answer any of them.

I straightened my shoulders and walked up the steps with as much dignity as I could muster. Frankie smiled supportively but Isla's eyes followed me the whole way. As I opened the front door she finally detonated.

"Are we going to talk about that kiss?" she asked with shock. I paused, with my hand on the door handle.

"Nope," I said with my back to her, then let myself into the house. I wasn't ready to talk to anyone other than Kane about what we'd done.

I didn't look back. I just let the door slam behind me, and headed directly to my bedroom. I needed to hide out for a little while. I didn't want to ruin the magic of what had happened between Kane and I, with their concerned looks or disapproving words.

As I stripped off my wet dress I could still feel the warmth of Kane's flesh burning on my skin. Being with Kane had felt more right than anything in my life ever had. I didn't care what Brenton thought. I didn't even care what Sean and Isla would say, because I knew, with every fiber of my being, that Kane and I were meant to be together.

I slipped into my tracksuit and curled up in my bed with my phone. All I wanted was Taj home, safe and sound in his bed, so that I could get back into Kane's.

- RITCHIE CARLTON -

Frankie glanced at me with a mischievous smile and slid her arms around my bare, wet waist, while Isla stared at the front door as it closed in her face.

"Oh, she's gonna talk about it," Isla declared adamantly, pushing the door open again and striding after Soph. Sean obediently followed her inside, and I looked down at Frankie to see a lustful look in her eyes.

"Shall we go get you warmed up?" she asked with a wink.

"Actually," I said, taking her hand as she ran it up my chest, "I'm gonna follow Kane." I pulled my car keys out of my back pocket, where they'd been tucked ever since I saw Brenton loading Taj into the Rover.

"Why?"

"I just have a bad feeling," I told her quietly.

"Okay," she nodded and squeezed my hand, "but I'm coming with you."

"Doesn't Soph need you here?"

Frankie shook her head. "She'll be fine. She's got Isla and Sean."

"Okay," I nodded. "Let's go then."

We ran, hand-in-hand, down the steps and jumped into my Prado. Kane had gotten a good head start on us and the country roads were winding and littered with tree branches.

Hot Summer streets didn't mix well with unexpected rain as it made the bitumen road extra slippery. I was paranoid about aquaplaning into a tree, so I flicked the headlights on and drove as cautiously as possible whilst still speeding.

"Would you mind grabbing a shirt out of my bag for me?" I

asked Frankie as I concentrated on the road. "It's sitting on the back seat."

"Sure," she said, leaning into the back to fish around my bag. "So, you were really gonna drive back to Perth huh?"

"It seemed like the best solution," I answered with a shrug.

"Here," she said, sitting back down in her seat as she handed me a dry button-up shirt.

"A little dressy for a road trip," I joked, threading one arm through the first sleeve, then switching hands to do the other.

"What if I didn't want you to leave?" she mumbled quietly. I took my eyes off the road for a second, as she studied my face intently.

"Are you saying you want me to stay?" I asked, shifting my focus back to the road.

"I mean... yeah," she said nervously. "I know I talk a big game but..." she paused, so I glanced over at her again.

"But what?"

"I really like you Ritchie."

"I really like you too."

"Okay," she said quietly. "So, do you think we could catch up when we're back in Perth?"

"I was hoping so," I said honestly.

"Does that mean you don't regret putting your dick where it doesn't belong by fucking your boss sister?"

"Oh," I said, suddenly understanding her concerns. I felt like an absolute prick. "Hey, I'm sorry I said that. I was stressed and I honestly didn't mean it to come out like that." I took a quick glance at her. "I don't regret this at all."

"You sure?"

"A hundred percent."

"So you're not worried about losing your job?"

"Well... no. I'm still worried about that but... Frankie... you're the first person I've been attracted to since..." I let my words trail off.

"Since your girlfriend?"

"Yeah," I nodded. "And whatever happens, I get the feeling you're worth it."

"Wow," she said breathlessly, before getting distracted with something up ahead. "What's that?" Frankie asked, as we saw a bright light shining through the trees. It was hard to make out in the rain, but it looked like headlights.

"They don't seem to be moving," I said as that bad feeling stirred in the pit of my stomach again.

"There's the Ducati," Frankie said, pointing to the side of the road where the bike was parked sideways.

"Where are the lights coming from then?"

"Oh my god," Frankie said in a panic, "stop the car."

The lights were coming from down the steep hill where a mangled, overturned car was wedged precariously in the trees. I pulled onto the gravel shoulder behind the bike.

"Have you got your phone?" I asked, realising that I'd left mine at the house.

"No, have you?"

"Nope." I said, pulling on the handbrake. "Stay here and see if you can flag someone down," I told Frankie, before jumping out of the car at lightning speed. I ran down the slope towards the bright lights, grasping tree branches to avoid slipping on the loose gravel.

"Kane? Brenton?" I called unable to see much through all the bushes and that blinding light.

I could see movement around the area, but it wasn't until I cleared the scrub that I could see the full scope of the situation. Kane's Rover was crumpled and smashed, tipped sideways and wedged between two trees that looked like they weren't going to hold it's weight for much longer.

"Holy shit," I swore running as best I could on the sloped, uneven ground. "Kane?" I called again, ducking around the side of the vehicle.

"Over here," he called, emerging from behind the Four-Wheel Drive with Taj grasped to his chest, sobbing.

"Shit, is he okay?"

"He's fine, he was still strapped in. A few bumps, scrapes and bruises but mostly scared out of his wits."

"Where's Brenton?" I asked, peering into the crushed shell of a car. The driver's seat was empty and the front window had blown out.

"Haven't found him yet."

If Brenton had been thrown out on the way down, he could have been anywhere, but hopefully the trees and bushes had broken his fall.

"I'll look for him, you get Taj up to Frankie," I said, springing into action.

"Right," Kane nodded, beginning his difficult ascent back up the hill, without the use of his hands.

I ran around the other side of the wrecked vehicle and crawled around in the sharp-leaved bushes, searching for any signs of life. Where the fuck was Brenton?

After some amateur detective work and a good amount of crawling around in prickly bushes, I spotted Brenton lying on his back in a bottlebrush bush.

"Brenton?" I called, but there was no response. I shuffled in a little closer and my heart thumped in my chest when I saw the extent of the damage. "Ah shit," I swore quietly. It was bad. His face was bloodied, and his arm was at a weird angle which made me think he'd either dislocated his shoulder or broken his collar bone. The one thing Rugby had taught me was how to identify certain injuries.

"Brenton, I need you to wake up mate," I said, moving some leaves off his face. I tried lightly patting him, but he didn't stir. "Come on mate. Open your eyes for me."

I lowered my cheek to his mouth, and I could feel a very faint, warm breath against my skin.

"Ritchie?" Called Kane from halfway up the hill.

"I found him," I shouted over my shoulder. Brenton groaned and gripped his chest with his good arm. I wondered if maybe he had a few cracked ribs too. If that was the case, there was no way we'd get him out of there without a stretcher.

"Brenton I'm gonna need you to stay awake mate. You think you can do that for me?" I asked loudly. He groaned again and flicked his eyes open. "Good work mate. Just hold on a little longer, okay?"

"Taj?" he croaked with extreme effort.

"He's okay," I assured him. He nodded and his eyes fluttered closed again. "Keep those eyes open buddy," I instructed him sternly. "I'll be back in a second."

I backed out of the bush and peered up to where Kane was grasping to Taj with one hand and gripping a tree trunk with the other.

"Have you got your phone with you?" I called up to him.

"No," he called back, shaking his head solemnly. "Is Brenno okay?"

"We're gonna need an ambulance," I told him meaningfully, not wanting to upset Taj any further.

"There's a satellite phone in the glove-box of my car," he nodded, letting go of the tree momentarily to stroke Taj's hair.

"Right," I said, looking back at the car that was hovering precariously on its side.

"Be careful Ritch," called Kane.

"Roger that," I called back with a thumbs up. I took a deep breath and searched for a way to climb up there without risking it toppling over or snapping the trees.

I scaled an adjacent tree to reach the bumper bar, then carefully crawled up and along the side of the bonnet until I reached the passenger door. The whole car groaned under my weight, and I heard the tree trunks cracking with every move I made.

"Fuck," I swore under my breath, heart pounding. How did I always find myself in these crazy situations?

I laid flat on my stomach to distribute my weight and then, carefully and slowly, reached through the broken window. I pushed aside the airbag to access the glove-box and after a bit of effort, I managed to locate the phone. I slowly swung my legs over the side, then jumped and quickly darted out of the way in case the car came down on me.

As I cleared the danger zone, there was an almighty crack, and the trees that had been holding the car, collapsed, sending the car rolling further down the hill as if the trees were playing catch with it.

"Ritchie!" Screamed Frankie from the top of the hill.

"I'm fine," I yelled up to her, poking my head out from the solid old gumtree I'd been grasping to. "I got the phone," I called to Kane, who had finally reached the road. I took a second to catch my breath and calm my nerves before heading back to where I'd left Brenton.

"Brenton?" This time he was unresponsive so I dialled 000 and did my best to wake him up. "Yeah, hi," I said when the operator answered, "I'm out at Prevelly and I've got a guy in a bad way. I think it's either a broken collarbone or dislocated shoulder and I suspect cracked ribs and possibly some internal bleeding. He's drifting in and out of consciousness. I can't tell the extent of his injuries, so I don't wanna move him."

"Okay," said the emergency services operator, "sounds like you're doing all the right things. Don't move him and try to keep him awake. I'll send a team out now."

"Thanks." I hung up and ducked out to fill Kane in. He'd handed Taj over to Frankie and was already making his way back down the hill. "Ambulance is on the way," I called up to him as he scrambled down the rocky slope.

"How long will they be?"

"No idea."

"Okay," he said, shuffling carefully down to where I was standing, "why don't you wait up there with Frankie and I'll stay with him."

"You sure?"

"Yeah. He's my cousin, my responsibility."

"Alright then."

"Just get Taj back to Soph and tell the others what's happened."

"Will do," I nodded. "I'll be back soon." I handed him the Satellite phone and climbed back up the hill.

It wasn't until I reached the top that I realised my shirt was still unbuttoned and billowing in the wind.

"Are you okay?" Frankie asked as she gave me a hand over the last rock.

"I think so," I said, as she inspected my body for damage.

"I thought you'd gone down with it," she said, throwing her arms around me with tears in her eyes.

"I'm fine," I said, rubbing her back reassuringly as I caught sight of Taj, red-eyed and panicked in the backseat of my car. "We can do this later. Right now we'd better get Taj back to his mum."

"Yeah," she said with a nod. We climbed silently into the car and shared a moment as we clicked our seatbelts in simultaneously.

"Is Daddy going to be okay?" sobbed Taj.

"Uncle Kane is gonna do his best to make sure your dad is fine," I told the boy. "Right now, we need to get you back to your mum. She's really worried about you."

"Okay," he agreed.

"There's a towel back there," I said, pointing to my beach towel flung carelessly over the backseat, "wrap that around yourself. It'll keep you warm."

I took a deep breath and turned the car around on the tight road, starting to wonder if I was cursed. First Nathan's accident, then Ryan's breakdown; Ashley's attack; Amy's suicide; Frankie's surfing accident; and now this. I was the common denominator. It seemed like all the people I loved ended up either hurt or dead. Maybe the best thing I could do for Frankie would be to disappear.

- SOPHIE THOMPSON -

I hadn't long been in my bed, mindlessly scrolling on my phone, when someone banged on the door.

"You decent?" Called Isla, seconds before letting herself in.

"Too bad if I wasn't huh?" I said with a raised brow.

"I gave you plenty of time," she shrugged, unrepentant. I watched silently as she made herself comfortable on the foot of my bed.

"Shouldn't you be spending time with you fiance?"

"He's taking Jess down to the B&B around the corner."

"Probably for the best," I nodded, feeling genuinely bad for the girl. She'd been a victim in all of this too. Probably more so in fact.

"Poor girl was over it. Apparently Brenton cracked it when she told him she was leaving."

"She was leaving?" I asked with confusion.

"Yeah. You missed a few things while you were busy in Kane's room," she teased, fixing her expectant gaze on me. "Well?"

"Well, what?" I asked, giving nothing away.

"Start talking lady," she said, cutting right to the chase. "What happened with you two? That was quite a kiss."

"I already said we're not gonna talk about it."

"You can't pull a stunt like that and then not talk about it."

"Watch me."

"Soph, that snog was movie level steamy."

"Yeah," I agreed, biting my lip at the vivid memory of that intense kiss. It had definitely had tinge of Hollywood about it.

"So how did you go from 'he's like a brother', to sexy rain-storm motorbike pash?" I felt my heart race at her accurate description of our moment, but I didn't want to tell her about the epic event that had led to that point.

"I don't know," I said with an awkward shrug.

"Yes, you do."

"Yeah, I do," I admitted, "but I'm not going to talk about it."

"Seriously?" she asked, looking equal parts appalled and offended. "You're really not gonna tell me?"

"I can't," I said apologetically. "I haven't had time to process it myself, and I need to talk to Kane before I say anything."

"Oh my god. You're in love with him," she said accusingly, as if I'd borrowed her best shoes without asking. When I failed to respond, my lack of denial made her eyes bulge out of her head. "You actually are. You're in love with Kane." Again, I remained silent. She stared at me wide-eyed and wriggled further up the bed. "You know he's in love with you too, right?"

"Yeah, he told me."

"He did?!"

"Uh-huh."

"Holy fuck Soph, this is huge," she breathed. I could see her brain ticking over at a million miles an hour. "So, then I assume it wasn't just his wounds that you were busy tending to in his bedroom earlier?" she asked with raised brows.

"It was," I said defensively.

"Until it wasn't?" she teased knowingly.

"Maybe."

"Holy Shit babe. This is gonna change everything," Isla said, visibly trying to piece together the situation. "Is that why he and Brenton were fighting?"

"No, they were fighting because Brenton was being a dick."

"Sounds accurate," she nodded, then sat quietly for a moment, pondering this new status quo. "I'm really happy for you babe."

"Really?" I asked cautiously, wondering what the catch was.

"Yeah," she said, rubbing my leg. "You deserve to be happy and so does Kane and if you've both found that in each other then I'm all for it."

"Thanks chick. That's definitely not what I was expecting you to say," I admitted, still wondering whether it was a trap. "So… you don't think this is a big mistake then?"

"How could I after witnessing that sizzling little scene out there. You two are fucking hot together. I mean… honestly… I was half expecting you to catch fire." We both laughed and I could feel the tension dissipate. She did seem to be genuinely okay with it. "So does that mean you're officially a couple now?"

"I have no idea," I sighed, chewing on my bottom lip again. "We didn't exactly get a chance to talk about it before Brenton ran off."

"Right," she said, as if only just remembering that my child had been semi-abducted by his father. "They've been gone a while. Do you think we should go find them?"

- KANE THOMPSON -

I looked down at Brenton, lying crookedly in the bushes. He was conscious but only barely. His face was all messed up and his arm was stuck out at an unnatural angle. It wasn't looking good.

"Come on Brenno, open your eyes," I begged him, patting his face. "I'm not letting you go out like this man."

He groaned quietly, so I patted him again.

"Wake up mate, Taj needs you."

"Taj?" he answered, scarcely above a whisper.

"That's right. Taj. He's safe and he's waiting for you to come home."

"Kane," he croaked, trying to open his eyes.

"Yeah?"

"Look…" he groaned with a wince. I looked behind me, expecting to see the paramedics, but there was nothing but rain, trees and bushes.

"Look at what mate?"

"No," he muttered, rapidly losing energy. "Look after." His eyes fluttered closed again and I could see his energy waning.

"Come on buddy don't fall asleep again. Keep those eyes open huh?"

"Look after them," he mumbled in a raspy whisper.

"Taj and Soph you mean?" I asked. Was he really preparing for the worst? With his eyes still closed, he gave the faintest of nods. "You're not done here so open your damn eyes and stay with me, okay?"

"She loves you," Brenton mumbled almost incomprehensibly, as he attempted to open his eyes again. "She always has."

"It sounds like you're giving up mate, and I'm not willing to let you do that."

"It was never me," he said, finally opening his eyes, squinting as he tried to focus on me. "It was always you Thommo."

"Save your energy mate. We'll talk about this later."

"No," he spluttered with a cough as he forced out the word. "Now."

"Okay," I agreed with a nod. "You know I'll always look after them."

He tilted his head slightly in an attempt to nod. "Thank you."

"Hello?" we heard a voice call out in the rain. I peered over my shoulder and saw a Search & Rescue crew standing at the top of the hill.

"Hey!" I called, waving. "Down here!"

"We're on our way down," the guy shouted over the wind and rain as the team began strapping up harnesses and setting up pulley systems.

"You're gonna be fine mate," I said with relief, as I turned back to Brenton. "Brenno?" I asked, patting his face again. He was unresponsive and his breathing was so faint I could barely feel it on the back of my hand. "Hurry," I called up to the team who were all in action mode. "He's unconscious again and barely breathing."

I wasn't a religious guy but at that moment...I was praying like hell that Brenton pulled through.

- RITCHIE CARLTON -

When we pulled up to the house, Taj looked like he was starting to go into shock. He was pale, and quiet and staring off into space with a glazed look in his eyes.

"You right buddy?" I asked, killing the ignition.

"Uh-huh," he said in a daze.

"We need to get him inside," I told Frankie.

"Yeah," she agreed. We jumped out of the car and, while Frankie unbuckled Taj, I ran around to their side so I could carry him in. There was no way Frankie would be able to get a kid half her size up those front stairs. I lifted Taj carefully out of the car, still wrapped in my beach towel, and Frankie ran ahead of us to open the door. "We're back," she called into the house, as I carried Taj through the kitchen and into the living room.

"Mummy?" Taj wailed when he saw Sophie sitting on the couch.

"Taj!" Soph jumped off the sofa and ran over to us. I put him down gently on the floor and Soph knelt down and wrapped him up in her arms. "Oh my God!" she said, taking in the sight of his damaged face. "What happened?"

"We had a car crash, "Taj said through a barrage of sobs as Sophie gripped him tightly in her arms.

"What do you mean?" she asked, looking to Frankie and I for an explanation. "Where are the others?" Frankie shook her head silently and Sophie's eyes widened with fear. "What's going on?"

"Kane's fine," I answered quickly, seeing her brain jump to the worst-case scenario, "he stayed with Brenton."

"Why?"

"Brenton got thrown from the car. He's not in a great way but there's and ambulance on the way to him," I told her as calmly as possible.

"Oh my God!" she said in a panic. "I need to go! I have to make sure he's okay."

"I think it would be best if you stayed here with Taj," I said, taking charge of the situation so it didn't barrel into an emotional shit-storm. "Kane has everything under control."

"Don't worry Mummy," said Taj, still clinging her, "Uncle Kane will look after Daddy."

"I'll go back out there to help," I told her before turning to Sean. "Can you come with me and ride the bike back?"

"Sure," he nodded, "what about Kane's car? Should Isla come too?"

"There isn't much of Kane's car left," I answered awkwardly, trying not to stress Sophie or upset Taj.

"We went upside down," said Taj, quickly coming back to life now that he was safe in his mother's arms, "and then we landed in a tree."

"Oh baby, I'm so glad you're okay," Soph said tearfully as she examined his damaged face. "How about we get you patched up?"

"Okay."

"Spanks, would you mind grabbing the First Aid Kit from Kane's room?" she asked with a slight cringe, followed by a furious blush as all the adults realised why she didn't want to take Taj in there.

Frankie understood immediately. "On it," she said, jogging down the hall to the master suite.

"Where's Jess?" I asked, wondering why the commotion hadn't brought her out of her room.

"Sean dropped her at the B&B," said Isla with a grimace. "She didn't want to be here when Brenton got back."

"Do you think we should get a message to her?" I asked.

"She was pretty done," Isla said sympathetically. "His disappearing act was the final straw, so I don't know that she'd be interested in seeing him again anyway."

"Well, she might not have a choice," I told her meaningfully, trying not to make it too obvious in front of Taj.

"Here," said Frankie, rushing back into the room with the First Aid Kit. Soph got to work on fixing up Taj, so while he was distracted, I muttered quietly to Isla, "I think you should probably call her and give her the option."

"Oh my god," she whispered, looking over at Seany with concern in her eyes.

He nodded and squeezed her arm. "Everything will be fine babe."

"I hope so," she said quietly, peering over at Taj.

"Right Seany," I said calmly, patting his back as a sign to get moving. "I think we should get back there." I turned to head back out the door.

"Don't you want to change into dry clothes first?" Isla asked, eyeing my damp shirt as it hung open and lifeless against my wet skin.

"No point," I said with a shrug, "it'll just get wet again. Come on Sean." I strode straight out the door, not looking to see if Sean had followed. I got the feeling we didn't have a lot of time.

"I'm coming with you," said Frankie, running out the door behind me. I nodded and silently offered her my hand. "Do you think he'll be okay?" she asked worriedly.

"I honestly don't know, Frankie."

- KANE THOMPSON -

It was starting to get dark, and I'd been sitting at Margaret River District hospital, in soaking wet clothes, since they'd loaded Brenton into the chopper. I could have gone with him, but I'd promised him I'd look after Taj and Soph so that's what I intended to do.

The hospital staff had rung Aunty Joan when we'd first arrived, so she and Uncle Mike would be at Royal Perth Hospital waiting for him by the time he got there. I had no idea how long I'd been there, it could have been twenty minutes or two hours for all I knew. Time had lost all meaning. Brenton had seemed resigned to death, but I wasn't willing to let him off that easy. He needed to be here to straighten out his mess.

All I could think about was Taj and Soph. How would they cope if something happened to Brenton? How could I possibly fill his shoes? I'd always be there for Taj, but the fact was that a boy needed his father, not just an uncle or even, perhaps, a step-dad. Not that having my father around ever did me much good. All he'd ever done was criticise me. But for all his faults, Brenton was still a better man than my father, and he was a good dad to Taj.

I leaned back in the plastic seat and stared vacantly at the TV screen mounted on the wall in the corner of the room. I just wanted to get home. Frankie and Ritchie were on the way to pick me up and Taj was safe at my place with Sophie. Apparently, she'd handled the news well but if I knew Soph, and I did, she'd want to be on the next plane back to Perth.

"And in breaking news," said the anchor-woman on the TV, "West Coast Eagles star, Brenton Thompson has been airlifted to Royal Perth Hospital in critical condition after being thrown from a car in the Margaret River region. The extent of his injuries is not known at this time. No one else was injured in the crash, but it's reported that his son was in the car with him at the time. The football star had a blood alcohol reading of 1.5 so a full investigation will be launched to ascertain the cause of the accident. Our condolences go out to his family at this very difficult time, and we'll have more updates on his condition as we receive them."

"Yeah right," I huffed as I stared at the TV screen with disgust. How had they found out already? Who'd given them all that info? Brenton was fighting for his life, and someone was out there, serving him up to the vultures.

"Kane!" Frankie called, running into the waiting area.

"Spanks," I said standing and opening my arms as she ran over and buried herself in my chest.

"Is he okay? What's happening?"

"He was still unconscious, but they'll be taking him straight into surgery. Aunty Joan and Uncle Mike are meeting him at the hospital."

"Okay good," she said with a nod. "Are you okay? You look terrible."

"It's been a long day."

"Yeah," she agreed, "but also a somewhat momentous one from what I've heard. You finally got your girl huh?"

I nodded and sank bank down to my seat. "That's exactly what caused this mess in the first place. This is all my fault," I said with a sigh. "If I hadn't kissed Soph, then none of this would have happened."

"Oh Kane, that's a tenuous causation link at best," she said, resting her hand on my shoulder as she perched on the seat next to me. "Do you regret what happened with Soph?"

"No way," I said, shaking my head adamantly, "that's the one thing in my life that I can honestly say I'll never regret. But I do regret starting that fight."

"Firstly," she said sternly, "from all reports, it sounds like it was Brenton who started the fight by being a prick. And secondly, you couldn't have known that he'd do this. No one could have."

"Yeah, I could have. He's Brenton. And Brenton does dumb shit. I shouldn't have punched him. I should have just ignored him like I normally do."

"You have to let it go Jughead. You made a mistake. You're human," said Frankie, rubbing my back, "and what Brenton did was beyond your control."

"I should've known better Spanks. I'm the older one, I'm supposed to be responsible. I'm supposed to look after you guys not put you in hospital."

"Hitting him wasn't the best thing you've ever done but you didn't do this. Brenton did this to himself," she said reassuringly. "Besides which, you're not responsible for any of us. We're all adults now, it's not up to you to save us. And you definitely can't blame yourself for his dumb-arse decision to get in a car drunk."

"But it is up to me, isn't it? I'm the one responsible for cleaning up everyone's messes. You guys all get to fuck-up, because you know I'll have your back. But not me. I can't make mistakes Spanks...I've never been able to make mistakes. If I fuck-up, who's going to clean up my mess?" Frankie's jaw dropped and she fell silent, staring at me as if the reality of my life had only just occurred to her.

"Hey," Ritchie called as he strode purposefully through the door, "you guys, okay?"

"Yeah," said Spanks with a nod.

"As okay as I can be under the circumstances."

"Shall we get you out of here?" he asked, looking me up and down with a grimace. "I don't want to have to bring you back here with pneumonia."

"Sure," I agreed with a shrug as he offered me a hand up. Once I was on my feet, Ritchie stepped back and studied Frankie. The look of concern on his face told me how much he cared about her.

"You doing alright?" he asked, edging towards her with a quick glance in my direction.

"Yeah," Spanks said, smiling shyly as she looked up at my big, bald Managing Director. It was an expression I'd never seen on her face before. She looked like she'd found home.

"Liar," Ritchie teased with one raised brow.

"Just processing."

"It's gotta hit some time," he said sagely, reaching out his hands for her. In that moment, I finally understood the depth of his loss. He'd been so calm and collected throughout this whole ordeal because he'd already faced similar demons.

Frankie took Ritchie's hands, her bright blue eyes were full of so much love and trust that it was almost disconcerting. My tough, commitment-phobic little sister was actually in love. Ritchie pulled her onto her feet then wrapped her in a hug, casting me a furtive look as she cuddled into his chest. I gave him a stiff nod of approval and walked towards the door to leave them to their private moment.

I stood outside the hospital door, listening to the sound of the rain on the tin roof. I shivered as a gust of wind blew. It was quite a mild breeze but it felt cold through my damp clothes. Despite my initial reaction, I was glad that Frankie had Ritchie. I didn't love the idea of her dating a work colleague, but it was about time my sister found someone decent. Maybe Ritchie would even be the guy to settle her down.

The thought of settling down made my mind jump to Soph and I automatically searched my pocket for my phone, until I realised I didn't have it. I peered over my shoulder into the waiting area where Ritchie and Frankie were still locked in a tight embrace.

I needed to get back to Soph. I needed to see her beautiful face and wrap her up in my arms and tell her that I wanted to spend the rest of my life with her.

- Epilogue -

Two days later...

- BRENTON THOMPSON -

As the dark fog in my brain started to lift, the outside world had started to become a little clearer. All the pain in my body was gone. In fact, I couldn't really feel my body at all…I kinda felt more like I was floating on a white fluffy cloud. It was nice.

I could hear hushed voices talking from somewhere below my white cloud of happiness. For a while there, I had no idea where I was, but I definitely wasn't at home. What had happened? Where was I? The last thing I could remember was driving back to Perth.

My cloud began to float back down to earth, which was a shame because I was enjoying the floating. I could now hear a machine beeping. What was that? Regardless, it was pretty annoying and I wished someone would make the fucking thing stop.

As I surfaced closer to reality, the memory of my accident came flooding back. I began to recall the everything from the weekend from hell. My slimy, backstabbing cousin seducing my wife; my fight with Jess; the accident. Shame flared through me as I remembered the crash. I'd put Taj in danger and I'd never forgive myself for that.

I recognised the voices as they continued whispering in hushed tones. It was my mum and… hang on… that sounded like Kane. Was I still at his beach house? I tried to open my eyes, but my body wasn't having a bar of it.

"I'm so sorry Aunty Jean, this is all my fault," he said, sounding like a broken man. Which, honestly, pleased me a little.

"Oh sweetheart," my mum said sympathetically, as if he was her child. Perfect Kane as always. I often wondered whether my parents would have preferred him to me. "None of this is your fault love," she assured him. "Brenton does what Brenton does regardless. I don't know what happened between you two but I imagine he wouldn't have listened to you even if you'd tried to stop him."

And there it was. The Golden Child versus The Black Sheep. Ever since I could remember, Kane has been the favourite of our family. In our entire lifetime, no matter what achievements I made, how famous I was or how much money I earned, I had never been able to match up to Kane. My parents, Frankie, Sophie, even our grandparents... they all thought the sun shone out of Kane's arse... and they may have been right because the entire world had always revolved around him.

"But it *was* my fault," Kane argued. "I kissed Soph, Aunty Joan, and Brenton saw us."

I was expecting my mum to get angry, or at least berate him for snogging his cousins wife, but instead, she let out an amused chuckle.

"Well I can't say I'm surprised," she said understandingly. "You two have always had such a strong connection. To tell you the truth, I was a little surprised when she started dating Brenton. I was sure you two had a thing going on."

"Thanks Mum," I croaked in a weird raspy voice that didn't sound like my own. I heard them both gasp, as I peeled my eyes open to see them both looking over at me with relief.

"You're awake!" Mum exclaimed, as she ran over to the bed to take my hand. "We've been so worried about you love."

"Yeah, sounds like it," I muttered sarcastically. Thommo continued hovering by the door as if planning a quick escape. He looked ashamed of himself and I almost felt a bit sorry for him. Almost. The fucker stole my wife. He deserved to suffer a bit. Kane had always looked down at me and he'd never thought I was good enough for Soph. In fact he'd never thought I was good enough for anything.

"How you feeling mate?" He asked sheepishly as my mum ran to get the nurse.

"Feeling pretty bloody good right now," I joked wearily. "I dunno what drugs they've got me on but they're brilliant."

He chuckled and shifted on his feet. I'd never in my life seen Thommo look so uncomfortable. Mr Perfect seemed to have broken. For the first time ever, the guy actually appeared human.

"Look mate-" he began to say.

"It was my fault Thommo," I interrupted. I'd deliberately stirred him up, so I had to take responsibility for that. I was angry and I'd been trying to piss him off. It was selfish and childish and even I had to admit that. "You were right to defend Soph. I was being a dick."

"Okay," he agreed dubiously.

"I mean it," I told him earnestly. "I was trying to get a rise out of you and you took the bait so I take full responsibility for what happened."

"Well…" he said, looking lost for words. "Thanks for acknowledging that." He edged a little closer to the bed. "But why did you take Taj?"

"Honestly?"

"No, I want you to lie to me," he teased with a half smile.

"I wanted Soph to hurt as much as I did. It killed me to see you two together."

"But she was already hurting Brenno. You cheated on her. You broke her heart, and then you brought the girl you cheated with to my birthday weekend. How did you think that was gonna go down?"

"Well I didn't think it would push her into hooking up with you, that's for sure," I said with an attempt at humour. Kane remained silent as he stood, stoically, in the middle of the room with his arms crossed over his chest. "Look Thommo, people make mistakes and I'll admit, I made a huge one."

"Yeah."

"For the record, I never meant to hurt Soph with the cheating. The first one just sort of happened and then it was way too easy after that," I admitted with a sigh, unable to believe that I was about to open up to the guy who had always been my biggest competition. "Despite what you think, I always loved Soph - I still do love her actually. She knows me better than anyone else and that's exactly what scared me about her. She's the only woman who's ever seen through my bullshit and I couldn't handle it. It was like she could read my mind. Meanwhile, there were all these young girls throwing themselves at me and they all thought I was a total hero. They saw the football star and not the broken guy underneath it. It was easier and funner and it seemed like a good idea… until I saw Soph with you." I 'hmphed' sadly before looking back up at Mr. Perfect. "She's in love with you Thommo. She always has been. I just got to her before she had a chance to realise it."

"I don't know what to say."

"There's not much *to* say. Just promise me you'll treat her better than I did."

"Well that's not much of a challenge," he teased dryly.

"Fair," I agreed, without argument. We sat in silence for a moment, neither of us sure what to say. "I blew it with Jess too," I said, breaking the silence.

"Yeah, you did."

"Did she head back to Perth?"

"Yeah, the next day."

"What do you mean?" I asked with confusion. How many days had it been? "How long have I been in here? And where exactly am I?"

"Two days. And Royal Perth."

"Right," I said, trying to wrap my head around everything that had happened. "I'm sorry about your car, man," I apologised as the memory of rolling down the hill in Kane's Rover flashed into my mind.

"Cars are replaceable. I've already bought a new one. I'm just glad Taj was okay and you're alive."

"Yeah, what's the damage on that by way?" I asked, peering over my immobile body, wrapped in bandages.

Thommo looked at the floor. "You'll have to ask your doctor about that," he said gravely.

"Why?" I asked, starting to feel panic rising in my chest. I couldn't actually feel any of my limbs, let alone control them. I'd assumed that was the drugs, but what if was worse than that? "Thommo?" I asked, trying to disguise my growing anxiety.

"I'm not - I can't-" he stuttered as my mum walked back into the room with a doctor. We both turned to look at the doctor. Thommo was visibly relieved to be out of the hot-seat.

"What's going on Doc?" I asked quickly, before the guy even had a chance to introduce himself. "What's the damage? Will I still be able to play footy?"

The Beginning

This might be the end of the book but it's only the beginning of my story.

After all the dramatic events in that year, I never expected my life to fall into place quite so easily, yet the pieces just slotted together without me even trying. I didn't realise it at the time, but meeting Kane changed everything.

When I first got back from London, I thought my life had gone backwards, but I couldn't have been more wrong. Moving home, taking that job, and saying yes to Kane's birthday weekender, it all led me to exactly where I was supposed to be…

…with Frankie.

She was the woman I'd been waiting my whole life for. She was my fate and all of the other women before her, Amy included, felt like they'd been nothing more than a dress-rehearsal for Frankie Thompson.

When I'd set off to Kane's birthday, I hadn't expected to fall in love but that weekend turned out to be the beginning of the rest of my life.

Unfortunately, this is where I sign-off so you'll have to read Stories from the Sun to find out all the juicy deets of my new relationship.

See you on the flip-side.

x Ritchie

A note from Nikki

I can't believe the original series is now complete!

Thanks for sharing this journey with me, it's been amazing. Rest assured, there's more to come for all of our characters but the initial story, as it began a decade ago, has now come full circle.

Nathan and Ash have been such a big part of my story for so many years, it's hard to fathom life without them. I know them inside out and back to front, particularly Ashley, whom I have shared and processed many of my own life experiences through. Needless to say, it was very hard to say goodbye with this book and I expect that's why Stories from the Sea was such a long time coming!

But it's now time to let them go. I have to set them free into the world to continue their next chapter, while I move onto mine. I do have several more 'Stories from' books in the works, where we'll get to know some other the other characters in a little more depth:

Stories from the Sun will probably be the next one released as it's a direct follow-on from this one. The story picks up where we've just left off and Brenton joins the ranks as our fourth story-teller. We'll find out about the extent of his injuries, and we'll watch the two new relationships grow as Ritchie and the Thompson clan navigate this new chapter of their lives. It won't be smooth sailing, but it will be fun!

Stories from the Suburbs, will likely be book five. This one circles back to Kat and Ryan as they settle into family life, facing a few unexpected turns along the way! They'll be joined by Kat's sister Rosie, as well as her ex-boyfriend Xavier, as they step into the limelight and become

our two newest protagonists.
Beau will also be getting his own book.

Stories from the Siene (a little bit of a giveaway in the title), will bring him out of the background, and we'll get to know him a lot better. He'll also be bringing Cody along for the ride, but that story is yet to unfold so you'll just have to wait and see what life has in store for the Delfontaine boys!

After that... who knows?

The '*Stories from*' series may come to an end, and I might even write a book under my real name. But your guess is as good as mine! Thanks for reading the books and supporting this labour of love.

STORIES
from the
CITY
N.J. EWING

Between
CITY
&
Sea
N.J. EWING

BRANDARTISANS.COM.AU